Praise for Candice Fox

"A fantastic standalone psychological thriller with compelling characters and an edge-of-seat ending."
—Adrian McKinty,
New York Times bestselling author of
The Chain, on *Gathering Dark*

"If you haven't read Candice Fox yet, you're missing out! I can't wait to read what this talented writer does next!" —Chevy Stevens

"A prolific storyteller with a great touch for offbeat, memorable crime fiction characters . . . Fox delivers a strong sense of humanity as the at times helter-skelter action unfolds. *Gathering Dark* is an alluring read." —*Mystery Scene*

"A new novel from Candice Fox is a must-read event. . . . Reads like a modern-day Raymond Chandler novel. Candice Fox, who clearly is not out of her element writing about the dark side of L.A., has more than a few tricks up her sleeve to keep the plot pumping along right through to the staggering finale."
—*Bookreporter* on *Gathering Dark*

"Fox has created the most seductive setting for this powerhouse crime series to commence. . . . A perfect mystery cocktail!"
—Wendy Walker on *Crimson Lake*

"Compelling . . . Boasts full-bodied characters, suspense with a quirky edge, and a strong sense of place."
—*Booklist* (starred review) on *Crimson Lake*

GATHERING DARK

CANDICE FOX

A TOM DOHERTY ASSOCIATES BOOK NEW YORK

This is a work of fiction. All of the characters, organizations, and events portrayed in this novel are either products of the author's imagination or are used fictitiously.

GATHERING DARK

A Forge Book
Published by Tom Doherty Associates
120 Broadway
New York, NY 10271

www.tor-forge.com

Forge® is a registered trademark of Macmillan Publishing Group, LLC.

ISBN 978-1-250-31762-9

Our books may be purchased in bulk for promotional, educational, or business use. Please contact your local bookseller or the Macmillan Corporate and Premium Sales Department at 1-800-221-7945, extension 5442, or by email at MacmillanSpecialMarkets@macmillan.com.

First U.S. Edition: March 2021
First U.S. Mass Market Edition: February 2022

Printed in the United States of America

0 9 8 7 6 5 4 3 2 1

For Violet

BLAIR

I looked up into the eye of a gun. She'd been that quiet. That fast. At the edge of my vision I'd half seen a figure pass the front window of the Pump'n'Jump gas station, a shadow-walker blur against the red sunset and silhouetted palm trees. That was it. She stuck the gun in my face before the buzzer had finished the one-note song that announced her, made her real. The gun was shaking, a bad thing made somehow worse. I put down the pen I'd been using to fill out the crossword.

Deep regret: *Remorse*. Maybe the last word I would ever write. One I was familiar with.

I spread my fingers flat on the counter, between the bowl of spotted bananas at a dollar apiece and the two-for-one Clark Bars.

"Don't scream," the girl said.

As I let my eyes move from the gun to her, all I could see was trouble. There was sweat and blood on her hand, on the finger that was sliding down the trigger, trying to find traction. The safety switch was off. The arm that held the weapon was thin and reedy, would soon get tired from holding a gun that clearly wasn't hers, was too heavy. The face beyond the arm was the sickly purple-gray of a fresh corpse. She had a nasty gash in her forehead that was so deep I could see bone. Fingerprints in blood on her neck, also too big to be her own.

Screaming would have been a terrible idea. If I startled her, that slippery finger was going to jerk on the trigger and blow my brains all over the cigarette cabinet behind me. I didn't want to be wasted in my stupid uniform, my hat emblazoned with a big pink kangaroo and the badge on my chest that truthfully read *"Blair"* but lied *"I love to serve!"* I had a flash of distracted thought, wondering what my young son, Jamie, would wear to my funeral. I knew he had a suit. He'd worn it to my parole hearing.

"Whoa," I said, both an expression of surprise and a request.

"Empty the register." The girl put out her hand and glanced through the window. The parking lot was empty. "And give me the keys to the car."

"My car?" I touched my chest, making her reel backward, grip the gun tighter. I counseled myself not to move so fast or ask stupid questions. My bashed-up Honda was the only car visible, at the edge of the lot, parked under a billboard. Idris Elba with a watch that cost two college funds.

"Car, cash," the girl said. Her teeth were locked. "Now, bitch."

"Listen," I said slowly. For a moment I commanded the room. The burrito freezer hummed gently. The lights behind the plastic face of the slushie machine made tinkling noises. "I can help you."

Even as I said the words, I felt like an idiot. Once, I'd been able to help people. Sick children and their terrified parents. I'd worn surgical scrubs and suits; no kangaroos, no bullshit badges. But between then and now I'd worn a prison uniform, and my ability to help anyone had been sucked away.

The girl shuffled on her feet, waved the gun to get me moving. "Fuck you and your help. I don't need it. I need to get out of here."

"If you just—"

My words were cut off by a blast of light. The sound came after, a pop in my eardrums, a whump of pressure in my head as the bullet ripped past me, too close. She'd blown a hole in the Marlboro dispenser, just over my right shoulder. Burned tobacco and melted plastic in the air. My ears ringing. The gun came back to me.

"Okay," I said. "Okay."

I went to the register, snuck a sideways look at her. Gold curls. A small, almost button nose. There was something vaguely familiar about her, but during my time in prison I'd probably cast my eye over a thousand troubled, edgy, angry kids who knew their way around a handgun. I took the keys from the cup beside the machine.

"This is a cartel-owned gas station," I said. I realized my hands were shaking. Soon I'd be sweating, panting, teeth chattering. My terror came on slowly. I'd trained it that way. "You should know that. You hit a place like this and they'll come for you and your family. You can take the car, but—"

"Shut up."

"They'll come after you," I said. I unlocked the register. She laughed. I glanced sideways at her as I scooped out stacks of cash. The laugh wasn't humor, it was ironic scorn. Something sliced through me, icy and sharp. I looked at the windows before me, at our reflections. She was looking out there, too, into the gathering dark. No one else was visible. We seemed suddenly, achingly alone together and yet terrifyingly not alone. I handed her the cash.

"Someone's already after you," I surmised. She gave a single, stiff nod. I slowly took my car keys from my pocket and dropped them into her hand. When the barrel of the gun swept away from me, it was like a clamp loosening from around my windpipe.

I watched her turn and run out of the shop, get in the car, and drive away.

Through the windows, Koreatown at night seemed to breathe a sigh of relief, to become unpaused. Long-haired youths knocked each other around on the corner. A man returning home from work let the newspaper box slap closed, his paper tucked under his arm. The malignant presence I'd felt out there when the girl had been in the store was gone.

I could have called the police. If not to report the robbery, to report a girl running from something or someone with the furious desperation of a hunted animal, a girl out there in the dark, pursued, surviving for who knew how long. But Los Angeles was full of people like that; always had been. A jungle, prey fleeing predators. I'd give the girl a little head start with my car before I reported it missing. I lifted my shirt and wiped the sweat from my face on the hem, trying to regulate my breathing.

My addiction pulsed, a short, sharp desire that made me pick up my phone beside the register, my finger hovering, ready to dial. I forced myself to put the phone down. The clock on the wall said I had an hour left of my shift. I thought about calling Jamie but knew he'd be asleep.

Instead I went to the ATM in the corner of the store. I slipped my card into the machine and extracted four hundred dollars, about the amount I knew the girl had taken. I went back and put the notes in the register.

Though I'd never met the gas station's true owners, I'd known cartel women in the can, and had picked up enough Spanish over the years to eavesdrop on their stories. The girl, whoever she was, didn't need the San Marino 13s on her tail. Neither did I.

I hardly looked at the ATM receipt before I crumpled it and let it fall into the bin. It was going to be a long walk home.

JESSICA

"Here's what I don't understand," Wallert said. He'd been saying it all day. Listing things he didn't get. Waiting for people to explain them to him. Jessica guessed they were probably into the triple digits now of things Wallert couldn't comprehend. "What the hell did you do on the Silver Lake case that I didn't do?"

She didn't answer, just looked at Detective Wallert's bloodshot eyes in the rearview mirror. Jessica hated the back seat of the police cruiser, didn't belong there. She was used to the side of Wallert's ugly head, not the back. A biohazard company gave the back seat a proper clean out every month or so, but everybody knew that it never really got clean. The texture of the leather wasn't right. Gritty in places. But Wallert was looking at her more than he was driving. Combined with the frequent sips of bourbon-spiked coffee from his paper coffee cup, he was eyeing the road about once every fifteen seconds. In this case, she was in the dirtiest but likely the safest place in the car. Detective Vizchen, who they were babysitting for the night, sniffed in the front passenger seat when Jessica didn't answer Wallert, as if her silence was insolence.

"I was there," Wallert continued. They cruised by

a bunch of kids standing outside a house pumping music into the night. "I was *in* the case. I was available to the guy whenever he needed me. Day or night. He knew that. It was me who came up with the lead about the trucker."

"A lead that went nowhere," Jessica finally said. "A lead I *told* you would go nowhere before you began half-heartedly pursuing it. You weren't of much assistance to Stan Beauvoir the few times he called on you."

"This. Is. Bull. Shit," Wallert snarled. He slammed the steering wheel with his palm to the beat of his words. Jessica said nothing. To say that Wallert wasn't of much assistance on the Silver Lake case was an understatement. The nearly decade-old case had been handed to her and Wallert as a "hobby" job, a spare-time filler, something Wallert hadn't taken seriously from the beginning. The series of abductions and murders of young women taken from parking lots in the Silver Lake area had ended as suddenly and mysteriously as it had begun, four women dead within the space of three months in 2007. Wallert was sure that the killer had been a long-haul trucker, someone who probably carried on their killing spree in another state, making it someone else's problem. He'd looked at the photographs of the four young women who'd gone missing when Jessica first handed them to him and yawned, then remarked on Bernice Beauvoir's full, pouty lips. "You don't get lips like that from suckin' jawbreakers," he'd said. The picture was of Bernice's head sitting like a trophy on a tree stump in the wooded area where she had been found.

"House like that," Vizchen broke the silence. "Gotta be—what? Five million dollars?"

"You don't just give a five-million-dollar house to someone who worked on a case for you." Wallert's eyes seared into Jessica in the rearview mirror. "Just say you sucked his dick, Jess. It would make me feel better."

Jessica felt her teeth lock together.

"I'd suck a dick for five million dollars," Vizchen mused.

"Vizchen, you shut your mouth or I'll stick my gun in it. See how you like the taste of that," she snapped.

They pulled in to Lonscote Place. Blackened houses, perfect stillness. Wallert kept the emergency lights off but gunned it to number 4652, where the sighting had occurred, and slammed the car into park. He wanted to get this over with so he could go back to his pity party.

Jessica got out of the car, checked her weapon, called in the 459—possible burglary—and told the operator they were responding as the nearest unit to the scene. She looked at the moonlight reflecting off the stucco walls of the houses around her, dancing through diamond wire onto bare yards. No dogs barking. Wallert's hand on her shoulder was like a hammer swinging down.

"You're going to take the house, aren't you?" He turned her too roughly. "Is it just like that? They just give you the keys?"

"Get your fucking hands off me, Wally." Jessica shoved him in the chest. "I've had one phone call about this mess. *One.* I know as much as you do. I've got to meet with the executor of the guy's will and see what it's all about. This could all be a stupid goddamn mistake, you know that? You're treating me like I've taken the inheritance and moved to Brentwood already, and all I've got so far is—"

"Every house in Brentwood has a pool," Vizchen

said. He was leaning against the car, his arms folded. "Place has got a pool, right?"

"If there was any justice"—Wallert poked her in the chest—"you'd split the house with me. It's only fair. I was on that case, too."

"You didn't work it! You—"

"I don't see any goddamn prowler." Wallert stormed back toward the car and flung a hand at the surrounding neighborhood. "It's a false alarm. Let's get out of here. I need a proper drink." He leaned on the car rather than getting in, big hands spread on the roof, his round belly pressed against the window. He looked at Vizchen. "Even if she gave me a quarter of what it's worth, I'd be set for life."

"Set for life," Vizchen agreed, nodding, smiling at Jessica in the dark like an asshole.

Jessica heard the whimper.

She thought it was Wallert crying and was about to blast him for a day's covert drinking ending in a mewling, slobbering, pitiful mess. But some instinct told her it was a sound carried on the wind, something distant, half-heard. Sound bounces around the poorer neighborhoods. All the concrete. She looked right, toward the silhouette of the mountains.

"Doesn't Harrison Ford live over there?" Vizchen wondered aloud. "I know Arnie does."

"Did you guys hear that?"

"She got on pretty damn well with the guy. The father. Beauvoir," Wallert grumbled to Vizchen. "I mean, if you'd seen them together. She spent hours at his place. Just 'talking about the case,' about the dead daughter. Yeah, right. Now we know the truth."

"Shut the fuck up, both of you." Jessica flipped her flashlight on. "I heard something. That way. We gotta go. We gotta check this out."

"You check it out." Vizchen jutted his chin at her. "You're the hero cop."

The sound returned, faintly this time, no more than a whisper on the breeze. Vizchen smirked at her as Wallert fished in the car for his cup.

Jessica headed east along the curve of the road, waiting for the sound to come again. Between the houses she caught a slice of gold light. Movement. Rather than continuing to follow the road around, she walked down the side of a quiet house, brushed past wet palm fronds as she found the gate leading into the yard. She vaulted it, jogged across the earth in case of dogs, vaulted the next fence. The house in Brentwood and Wallert's rage were forgotten now. She could feel the heat. The danger. Like electricity in the air. She hit the ground and grabbed her radio as she headed for the garage of a large brick home.

A body. She knew the instant her boot made contact with it in the driveway, the sag of weight forward with the impact and then back against the front of her foot. It was still warm. Damp. She bent down and felt around in the shadows of a sprawling aloe vera bush that was growing over the low front fence. Belly, chest. Ragged, wet throat. No pulse. Jessica's heart was hammering as she grabbed her radio.

"Wally, I've got a code two here," she said. "Repeat. Code two at 4699 Lonscote Place."

A sound in the garage ahead of her, up the driveway. The roller door was raised a foot or so, and from its blindingly bright interior she heard the whimper come again. A thump. A growl.

"Wallert, are you there? Vizchen?" she whispered into her radio.

Nothing.

"Wallert, Vizchen, respond!" She squeezed the receiver so that the plastic squeaked and crackled in her hand. Static. "Fuck. Fuck. Fuck."

Jessica pulled her gun and headed for the garage. Stopped at the corner of the building to radio command.

"Detective Jessica Sanchez, badge 260719. I've got a 10–54 and code three at 4699 Lonscote Place, Baldwin Village. Repeat, code three."

There was a flash in her mind of Wallert and Vizchen laughing. Another officer might have wondered about the two of them, why they weren't responding. If they were in danger. But not Jessica, not today. She'd heard Vizchen's words, knew she would hear them again in the coming weeks, from her brethren at the station. *You're the hero cop.* No one was coming to help her. She'd betrayed them all with the Brentwood inheritance. She'd marked herself as a traitor.

She sank to the ground, flattened, and rolled under the garage door, rose and held the gun on him. He was a big man, even crouching as he was, a heaving lump of flesh, bent back straining. At first she thought the old woman and the young man were kissing on the ground. Intimate. Mouth to throat. But then she saw the blood on his hands, all over his face, her neck. Jessica thought of vampires and zombies, of magical, impossible things, and had to steady herself against a pool table. Her mind split as the full force of terror hit it, half of it wailing and screaming at her to flee. The other half assessing what this was. A vicious assault in progress. Assailant likely under the influence of drugs. Bath salts—they'd been hitting the streets hard in the past few weeks, making kids do crazy things: gouge their own eyes out, kill animals, ride their bikes off cliffs. She was watching a man eat a woman alive.

"Drop her!" she shouted. An absurd part of her brain noted she was talking as if to a dog. A wolf. A werewolf. "Drop her! Stand back!"

The man raised his bloody face. The old woman in his hands bucked, tried to shift away. Too weak. Almost dead. Every vein in the man's body was sticking out like a slick blue rope on his sweat-soaked skin. He wasn't seeing Jessica. He was trapped in his fantasy.

"Back up now or I'll shoot!"

The man lifted the woman to his lips. Jessica fired over his head, hit a dart board hanging on the wall, sending it clanging to the ground. He got up, staggered away from the noise. She fired again and hit him in the left shoulder. The bullet flecked his shirt with blood, embedded itself in the muscle. He didn't flinch. The man came for her, gathering speed in three long strides. She fired again, a double tap in the chest. A kill shot. He kept coming. A big hand seized her face and shoved her into the wall, then dragged her toward him with the strength of an inhuman thing.

She thought of Wallert as the man's teeth bit down into the flesh of her bicep. Her partner out there, somewhere in the dark, laughing at her.

Jessica grabbed at the man's rock-hard shoulders and landed a knee in his crotch. They went to the ground, rolled on the floor together. He pinned her on her front, his belt buckle jutting into her hip. Another bite on her left shoulder blade, the *pop* sound of the fabric as his teeth cut clean through her shirt. Jessica pushed off the ground the few inches she could manage and smacked her elbow into the man's face. The crunch of his nasal bone. He bit her left shoulder. Clamping down, trying to tear the flesh away, a good mouthful. She looked into the eyes of the now-dead old woman only feet away from her and thought again about how no one was coming.

He tried to get on top of her, accidentally nudging her dropped gun within reach. Jessica grabbed the weapon and twisted under him, put the gun to his forehead as the teeth came down again toward her.

She fired.

BLAIR

I started missing kids the morning after I was arrested. Nine years as a surgeon, four of those as a pediatric specialist, had brought me into contact with tens of thousands of children: mopey, sick teenagers and mewling newborns and wide-eyed, excited eight-year-olds whooping as they were wheeled down the hospital corridors on stretchers, their white-knuckled parents following. In an instant, my world was full of angry adults. For nine years the only kids I saw were behind scratched, faded glass in the prison visiting room or in the pictures fellow inmates stuck to the walls beside their bunks.

When I found my apartment in Crenshaw, there was plenty I didn't like about it. Dangerous-looking men in long white T-shirts rode bicycles up and down the street, monitoring activity closely. The bathroom ceiling inside the apartment was black with mold. The whole place was exposed red brick on the inside, even the shower cubicle; the walls, close and impenetrable. On the day I inspected the property, a cockroach was swimming weakly in the dripping kitchen sink, and when I tried to flush the pathetic creature down the drain the real estate agent assured me he'd be back—he was a permanent housemate. I was about to shake hands with the agent and leave when a troupe of children came out of the apartment next door, each carrying a guitar case the length of their body, letting the screen door slap shut behind them, to the grumblings of the old man inside. From the lawn, after the real estate agent left, I watched the children waiting for their rides, saw a teenager arriving for her guitar lesson, a bright-red electric guitar slung over her shoulder. I called the agent and took the apartment right there.

The day after the robbery at the Pump'n'Jump, I was standing at the kitchen counter drinking a coffee and watching the morning news on the TV when a small, familiar knock came at my door. I crossed the apartment in five strides and found my usual Saturday morning visitor: a small Asian boy named Quincy, clutching his ukulele.

"Are you ready?" he asked, as he always did. I leaned in the doorway, still half listening to the news. Something about an elderly couple and a cop attacked and bitten by a crazed drug addict. Typical Los Angeles stuff.

"I'm always ready for you, Quince," I said.

Quincy hefted his ukulele against his small chest and played "Somewhere over the Rainbow" haltingly, skipping the part about bluebirds completely. Upon finishing, he flashed me a set of big white teeth and bowed. I put my coffee on a shelf beside the door and clapped.

"Boy, when you're a super-cool solo performer doing gigs downtown, I'll buy you a martini," I said as I retrieved the box I kept on the shelf. "But right now all I've got is chocolate."

"What's a martini?"

"It's a special drink for grown-ups."

"My dad drinks beer and my mom drinks wine. *Lots* of wine." He rolled his eyes.

"She's my kind of woman."

"I'll just have chocolate, please."

"You got it, buddy," I said. He dug around for a while in my collection of goodies, trying to decide on a reward, making the wrappers crinkle. "What's for homework this week?"

"'What a Wonderful World,'" he said, selecting a Twix.

"Good song," I said. "Can't wait."

Quincy waved and ran to the corner to wait for his ride. I stood in the sunshine for a while, still watching the news. I knew that bribing kids to give me mini-concerts on my doorstep after their guitar lessons was weird, and potentially dangerous. It would only take one parent who heard I was a violent ex-con paying for child interactions with candy, and a world of trouble would erupt. The old guy next door who taught the classes would face a downturn in business. My parole officer would get a call. But being around children reminded me that I had been a good person once, and that one day I might be a good mother to my own child, who I saw once a week for a couple of hours. It reminded me that somewhere deep inside me, the head surgeon who had sweated and labored over the bodies of tiny infants in the operating room, who had stayed up all night reading stories to cancer-riddled toddlers, who had cried with parents for hours in waiting rooms, was still there. She was still alive, just buried. Even though I had taken a life, "shockingly and viciously," as the newspapers had claimed, I was not completely irredeemable, because children still liked me.

The news stole back my attention.

"*Outrage this morning following an announce-*

ment regarding the three million dollars that was found by construction workers developing a property in Pasadena last September," the newsreader said. I retrieved my coffee and looked up to see an image of dirty suitcases on the screen, lying at the feet of police officers in a crowded conference room, footage from the find a few months earlier.

"A spokesperson for city hall told reporters that investigators have found no physical evidence to support claims the buried hoard of cash once belonged to famed bank robber and murderer John James Fishwick. Fishwick is a current inmate of San Quentin State Prison and has not commented publicly on whether the exhumed money was indeed his."

A photograph of a long-jawed man in his sixties flashed on the screen. The deadened, stale look of all mugshots. Denim prison shirt.

"Lawyers representing the families of some of Fishwick's victims have expressed dismay at the government's decision to withhold the money under penal code 485 rather than use the funds to compensate those who lost loved ones during Fishwick's criminal reign."

I closed the door and drained my coffee. Then another knock came, harder this time, definitely not Quincy. When I opened the door and saw who it was I dropped the coffee mug on the carpet and slammed the door in her face.

"Oh, *fuck*!"

"I hate to break it to you, but that's not going to work," Sneak said. "Open up, Neighbor girl."

I winced at the name. I hadn't been called "Neighbor" in a year, not since I left the gates of Happy Valley, the California Institution for Women. Prison is full of unclever nicknames like that. I was Blair Harbour: Neighbor Killer, aka Neighbor. I had met car thieves called Wheels and jewelry thieves called Jewels and gunrunners called Bullets in my time inside. I looked down at my straining knuckles gripping the door handle.

"You can't be here," I called through the door.

"Well, I am, so deal with it." She barged into the door, causing it to smack me in the forehead. Sneak's steps jiggled her huge white breasts as she shoved her way past me into the apartment.

"Jesus Christ." I scanned the road outside. "What the hell do you want?"

Sneak smelled the same as she had back in prison, of candy and fried food. Her leather miniskirt was squeaking, trying to contain her big rump as she headed for my kitchen.

"I need your help. But before that, I need something to drink, all right? I've been out all night. What time is it? You got any ice?" She began fishing in my fridge. Sneak talked fast, even when she wasn't high. She was like a storm blowing into my world, knocking things over, filling the air with noise and chaos.

"Whoa, whoa, whoa." I slammed the fridge door shut, almost on her fingers. "We're not doing this. You've got to get out of here. I'm on probation. *You're* on probation. It's real nice to see you but you've got to go. Known association with convicted criminals or fellow parolees will get us both thrown back inside. It's one of the main conditions."

"Oh, come on." She shoved me away. Her words were slurred, running together. "Unless you've got a parole officer hiding in your freezer, we'll have to risk it. I need help here." She poured herself a vodka from the big bottle in my freezer and pocketed two mini Jack Daniel's bottles from my cupboard. The movement was quick, but not quick enough to escape my eye, because I expected the theft. "You were robbed last night at the Pump'n'Jump gas station, am I right? You lost your car and some cash?"

I stood back. "Yes. How—"

"That was my kid, Dayly." Sneak gulped her vodka shot. "She called me up and told me she hit the Pump'n'Jump. I've known you worked there for a while. Now she's gone. The last person who saw her was you. So I need your help getting her back."

I worked my temples, looked at the front windows, dreaming of escape from this. The day outside was just beginning, full of potential. I longed for it. Jamie was on my mind again. Something stupid like this could break us apart.

I went and drew the curtains. Someone was playing "Hotel California" almost perfectly next door. Sneak sloshed herself another vodka, probably pocketing items from my kitchen drawers with the hand I couldn't see below the counter. I grabbed a picture of Jamie in a nice silver frame from the shelf near the door and stuffed it under a couch cushion. I stood uncomfortably in the center of my mostly bare apartment.

"She was in trouble." Sneak turned to me. "Big trouble."

"She told me someone was after her," I confirmed. "She was injured. Looked scared. But that's all I know, okay? Whatever this is, I can't get involved, Sneak. I'll lose everything. If I go back to prison I'm facing another five years." Sneak wasn't listening. I took my wallet from the counter. Throwing money at problems was still a reflex, even after so many years away from my life as a Brentwood medical celebrity. I had been very wealthy before I was locked up. I treated the kids of the stars, drove a Mercedes-Benz, vacationed in La Jolla. Once, I went to Oprah Winfrey's house in the middle of the night to treat the child of a friend of hers who was staying over, suffering a fever. All that was before I shot my neighbor in cold blood and stood watching him bleed out on his dining room floor, doing nothing, while his girlfriend screamed at me.

"I don't even have any money to offer you to—"

I stared into my empty wallet. I'd had a twenty-dollar bill, all that was left to my name after I'd paid for Sneak's daughter's theft. Now it was gone. Sneak had probably snagged it when I went to close the curtains. I tossed the wallet on the counter.

"Okay, I'm good now." Sneak swallowed her third vodka, gasped, and exhaled hard. "Let's get rolling."

"We're not—"

"We can talk on the way."

In the cab I leaned against the window and wondered how on earth I'd let myself be abducted into a fellow ex-con's personal troubles, and how I could best extract myself. Sneak rambled beside me and wrung her hands. The confidence and determination I'd seen in my apartment was draining away from her. She had me now, and was gearing up for the next challenge. Prison does that to you: gives you the ability to put up a tough front to get what you want, but then it burns out and moves on, like a grass fire. I was looking now at the face of a terrified mother, something I'd seen in hospital hallways and in the mirror plenty of times. Sneak was drunk and high, but she was wavering on the edge of screaming panic.

"You never even told me you had a kid," I said.

"I'm not lying. Not this time."

"All that time in Happy Valley together. All those hours you listened to me talking about Jamie, you never once mentioned it."

"We only just got back in touch." Sneak shifted in

her chair. "I gave her up as a teenager. It was kind of embarrassing, okay?"

Sneak had been a good friend of mine on the inside. Good enough that I'd overlooked her constantly stealing my things, coming up with grandiose lies to entertain herself, waking me up in the winter with her ice-cold hands on my face. I could feel those hands now, slapping at my cheeks and brow. Her big blue eyes peering at me over the edge of the bunk. *Hey. Hey. Neighbor. Wake up. I'm bored. That cute guard on seven just got here. Come be my wingman.*

"She called me from a pay phone," Sneak said. "This morning, maybe one a.m. She said she fired a gun at the woman behind the counter. I figured it had to be you. There couldn't be too many women stupid enough to work a night shift in a place like that."

"*Desperate* enough, I think you mean," I said. "It was the only place that would—"

"She would hardly let me speak."

"I know the feeling," I sighed.

"She said I should watch my back, that someone was coming, something real bad was going down." Sneak chewed her nails. "Then we got disconnected. Like, fast. She went quiet suddenly and the line went dead."

"Why did you wait so long to come get me?"

"I had to see what the street was saying first. Get a feel for what Dayly was telling me about someone being after her. But nobody's heard anything. Usually if there's some kind of hit out, people will know."

"Where are we going?"

"To Dayly's apartment." Sneak blocked a nostril, inhaled, made a snorting sound. Irritated sinuses from bad coke. "I've been there a couple of times. Like I said, we've been trying to make good with each other. She looked me up. She's angry, I guess, but it wasn't my fault, her childhood. My parents made me give her up."

I knew some things about who Sneak had been before she turned to a life of drugs and prostitution. Walking by her bunk one day at Happy Valley, I'd spotted a newspaper cut-out on the floor. A yellowed picture of a lean young girl in a gymnast's outfit. The resemblance to Sneak was minimal—the girl was fresh-faced, grinning broadly, blonde ringlet curls held up in an elaborate scrunchie, and a sculpted, muscular frame shining in spandex. The headline read "Dreams Shattered." Sixteen-year-old Emily Lawlor had been warming up for her performance at the 2000 Olympics in Sydney when she landed wrongly after back-flipping off a floor beam. She suffered a traumatic fracture in one of her cervical vertebrae. I'd stuffed the newspaper article back under Sneak's pillow, where I assumed it had come from. Another inmate told me Sneak had got hooked on oral Vicodin after the accident, then moved to heroin when her insurance ran out.

"I don't know who the father is," Sneak said. "I was knocking boots with a lot of bad guys. Some of them are in jail now. Like, forever."

I watched my former cellmate from across the cab. She looked older than her years, her mouth downturned with worry. I realized she and I had both given up our babies unwillingly; her as a teen being pushed by disappointed parents, me in the Happy Valley infirmary only an hour after giving birth to him. Though Sneak and I hadn't been able to be there for our kids, the idea that they might fall into peril still throbbed, in the back of my mind, at least, like a burn that never really healed. From the moment our children had left our hands they'd fallen into the big, bad world, and it looked as though Dayly was in the grasp of some of that badness.

"What do you think your daughter's into?" I asked.

Sneak pursed her lips and looked away from me. "I don't know. It can't be drugs. She's so disgusted with who I am as a person, she'd never go there."

"Don't bash yourself up so much, Sneak," I said. "That sort of thing won't help right now."

"She's a good person." She thought about it and shrugged, bewildered. "I don't know how she ended up that way. She was preaching to me about rehab. She's really smart. Likes animals. Wants to do something with that. Study them or whatever. This thing is completely out of character. Dayly is not like me. I was never around her long enough to stain her that way."

Dayly's apartment building was a stucco and terracotta-tiled place near the Warner Bros. lot. I watched the billboards roll by, prime-time television shows I was never at home to watch, Ellen DeGeneres's cartoonish eyes peering over a cut-foam letter *E*. Sneak headed up the stairs before me and stopped abruptly. There were people on the landing. Residents of the building, it seemed, four or five of them hanging around looking bemused. One man was wearing a blue bathrobe. Sneak went directly to a young woman, a thin redhead wearing a T-shirt that read *Be Kind To Bees*, standing in the open door of one of the apartments.

"What happened? What happened?" Sneak asked the girl. Her voice was higher now, almost shrill. She didn't wait for an answer, went inside the open apartment. The girl turned to me and the crowd.

"We should call nine-one-one."

"What's going on?" I asked.

"I was just telling these guys," the girl in the bee

shirt said, gesturing to the people around us. "I was out last night. I had an audition. I stayed with my boyfriend. This morning I came back and the door was open and the place is . . . There's blood in there. Hey! She shouldn't go in there. That's Dayly's mom, right? She should come out. I think . . . It might be, like, a crime scene. What if it's a crime scene? Do we call nine-one-one?" The girl fell into tears. No one seemed game to hug her.

I entered the apartment. There were droplets of blood on the carpet just inside the door. An over-turned chair on the way to the tiny kitchen, a little table knocked askew. There was smashed glass on the floor, papers brushed off the front of the fridge where they had been arranged with colorful magnets. It was the sight of all the lights on in the apartment that made my stomach plunge. Whatever happened here, it had happened in the dark hours.

Sneak had been right—her daughter had been doing well for herself. The apartment was cluttered and small but obviously shared between two young women who worked hard at their dreams and lived busy lives. A dying peace lily on the kitchen window-sill told me they were rarely home. Dust on a maga-zine near the couch. There was another blood smear and a picture knocked from its hook in the hallway. I found Sneak in Dayly's bedroom, standing by the desk.

"Her bag's here." Sneak pointed to a handbag on the floor by the messily made bed. The bag flopped open, showing the usual things a woman kept in her everyday carryall: tissues, a notebook, some makeup. I knelt and went through the bag, moving things about with my knuckle when I could to avoid leaving prints.

"No phone," I said. "Did she have a car?"

"No," Sneak said.

"Well, she does now."

There was no blood in this room, no signs of disturbance. I noticed a laptop charger peeking over the edge of the desk, leading to a clear space where the laptop must have belonged among the papers, takeaway coffee cups, and pieces of stationery that covered the surface.

"Laptop's gone," I noted. "So she's somewhere, and she's got her phone and her laptop. But no bag. Or a different bag than her usual one."

"You see a bag on her at the Pump'n'Jump?" Sneak asked.

"No," I admitted.

"So what did she do? Put the laptop on the ground outside before she robbed you?"

"I don't know, Sneak."

"Whoever attacked her has got the laptop, probably the phone, too."

"We don't know she was attacked," I said.

Sneak didn't answer. We stood quietly together, locked inside a bubble of dread. I tried to take Sneak's hand but she pulled away from me, went to the little desk and picked up a flyer that was sitting there.

"Parachuting?" She showed me the brochure. A flight school in a place called San Jasinte was advertising tandem parachuting adventures for $200 per drop. A windswept, grinning couple was leaping out of a plane on the cover. Sneak pocketed the flyer and went to a table by the door, which held a fish tank. I picked up a strangely shaped piece of plastic from the desk. Layers of sticky tape rolled into a small tube, cut and unraveled, like snake skin. There were notes pinned on the backing of the desk. Reminders, it seemed, from Dayly to herself. *STAY ON TRACK! CHIN UP!* I dropped the tape and peeled off a small yellow note that was stuck to the edge of the shelf above the desk.

BIRDS ONLY.

When I joined Sneak at the fish tank, I noticed the thing had no water, just a layer of sawdust and a blue plastic wheel.

A small, brown, ratlike creature was huddled in the corner of the tank, licking its small pink paws and brushing them against the backs of its tiny ears.

"Oh, wow. What is it?" I asked, whispering in case I startled the animal. "A hamster?"

"A gopher." Sneak picked up the little creature from where it crouched and cupped it in her hand. "She found it sitting in a driveway, poisoned."

"So she brought it here?" I asked. I'd had gopher men to my house in Brentwood more than once to poison dozens of the creatures that were digging holes in my lawn. I'd never seen one, only their small round tunnels and the devastation of my expensive landscaping. The gopher ran across Sneak's palms as she made an endless track for it, putting one hand in front of the other.

"She's like that. A bleeding heart," Sneak said. "Always picking up wounded and stray things. I was the same when I was her age. I picked up a few birds. They all died." I looked at the *BIRDS ONLY* note on the desk and wondered if it was somehow connected.

"Sneak, we should go," I said. I could hear voices in the living room. "This might be a . . . It might be important for the police to see the place untouched."

"I knew a guy once," Sneak said, focused on the gopher. "His daughter was kidnapped down in Mexico. Young kid, like seven. They grabbed her out of a playground toilet block, asked the family for money. The cartels, they've got this rule—sometimes they let you switch out another family member for your kidnapped loved one if, like, they're too vulnerable or whatever. The guy I knew, he tried to give the cartel his wife and his sister in exchange for the daughter, just while he drummed up the money."

Sneak had been renowned for her "I knew a guy once" or "I knew a chick once" stories in prison. Either they were all elaborate falsifications or she alone had somehow befriended all of the wildest, most eccentric and misfortunate people who ever lived. Most compulsive thieves I had known in prison were also gifted liars. Sneak's "I knew a guy once" stories always ended in tragedy.

"What happened?" I asked, regardless. "He get the kid back?"

"No. The cartel took the wife and the sister as well and tripled the ransom demand."

"We can't think like that right now, Sneak," I said. "And we can't hang around here much longer. We'll get caught together."

"We can go." Sneak nodded, replacing the gopher and taking Dayly's bag. She wavered, the vodka and whatever she'd taken before it hitting her suddenly. "Wherever my baby is, she's not here."

JESSICA

The house on Bluestone Lane was still, unnaturally quiet, cast in yellow morning glow. At every other house on the row, gardeners in wide-brimmed hats worked, dragging tree trimmings toward their battered trucks or sweeping hoses over colorful garden beds. The house Jessica watched was empty, almost posing, like a real estate photo. *Imagine entertaining your rich and famous friends here.* Cocktails by the pool. Intimate dinner parties on the back deck. Bentleys parked on the enormous river stone drive (designer landscaping by Exotiq Impressions). Jessica waited, watching a group of deeply tanned women powerwalk by. French-polished nails and expensive cheekbones. A little dog that cost more than the Suzuki she was sitting in was going mad behind a fence covered in ivy.

Brentwood on a Saturday.

Rachel Beauvoir's arrival interrupted the third drive-by of a private security car, nervous about a Latina woman sitting idly in her shitty vehicle. Jessica got out of the car and smelled desert plants. Something was ticking in her temple, a tiny trapped animal under the skin, suffocating in the heat. Rachel stopped in the big double doorway, her key out and ready.

"My god." Rachel's right hand fluttered at her chest. "What happened to you?"

They'd met before, briefly. A cursory interview early in the investigation about the victim, Bernice Beauvoir, Rachel's niece. Rachel had been aloof and skeptical, but Jessica found all rich white people like that. Jessica and the elderly woman had exchanged a nod at Stan's funeral a month ago, but now her wide eyes wandered over the bandages on Jessica's neck and arms, the bruising on her face.

"I had a run-in with a zombie," Jessica said.

"That was *you*?" Rachel pointed at her like an accuser in court, her mouth hanging open. "I saw the news report. A man *bit* you?"

"It's over," Jessica lied. "I'm fine." Really, it would be approximately forty-eight hours before it could be fine, before Jessica received the results of her HIV and hepatitis screenings. "Let's just get on with this."

The slender, birdlike woman unlocked the door to the sprawling mansion.

"Well, here it is," Rachel said, as if Jessica hadn't seen the place before. In reality both women knew that Jessica had spent days here, altogether, sitting with Stan Beauvoir, looking at pictures of his murdered daughter, listening to his stories, searching the girl's room over and over. It wasn't the first murder Jessica had worked in the area. She recalled one three streets away, a shooting, a dispute over neighborhood noise gone horribly wrong. Neighbor on neighbor, highly strung rich people with guns.

The women stood together before the stairs in the massive foyer. The house was empty of furniture, recently cleaned, the carpet spotless and fluffy, and the air hanging with citrus scent.

Jessica put her hands in her pockets. "Look," she said. "I didn't come here to see the house. I came to say this is all a waste of time. This is not happening."

"You said that on the phone." Rachel walked through the foyer and into the vast living room. "'This is not happening.' Thing is, Detective, it's already happened. You're named as the beneficiary. It's on paper. You can't take that back. Stan's dead, so he's not undoing it, and I'm not challenging it in court. Lord knows I don't need another real estate portfolio heaped into my lap."

Jessica had no choice but to follow the woman through the living room toward the deck as she spoke.

"Now you get to decide what's done with the place. You can sell it. You can split it with your"—Rachel waved her hand dismissively—"your partner. You can toss the keys in the gutter and walk away. Let the house rot to the ground. I don't care. But until you make a decision, you're in this, Jessica. It's not going away."

The two women stood on the massive, empty deck overlooking the glittering pool. Above them, two more stories of the house yawned upward. Huge sheets of glass and artistically laid stonework. Jessica sighed loudly without meaning to. She walked to the edge of the deck, sat down with her legs hanging over the manicured lawn, and rubbed her ticking temple.

"I had an appraiser come through on Thursday." With difficulty, Rachel Beauvoir sat on the edge of the deck beside the detective, smoothing her skirt over her knees, a woman lowering herself beneath her usual standards. "It came in just under seven million."

"I don't need to know things like that."

"I've got to tell you, Detective Sanchez, I'm a little surprised by your reaction to all this. You're LAPD. What have you been making the past two decades of your career? Eighty grand? That ridiculous car out front makes me think a windfall like this is beyond anything you'd ever have imagined."

A windfall like this will turn the entire Los Angeles Police Department against me, Jessica thought. *It will destroy my relationship with my family in blue.*

"How long have you been riding around in that beat-up old car? It's embarrassing," Rachel sighed.

"Leave my car alone. It's got a hundred and seventy thousand miles on it and it runs like a dream."

"I'm just saying, this could change your life."

"It's already changed my life." Jessica pointed to the bandaged bite mark on her shoulder. "You see this? This happened because of this house."

"I don't understand."

"My partner didn't back me up last night because he was so pissed about the inheritance. He was assigned to the case too. He thinks he deserves half."

"I notice you say *assigned to* the case, rather than *worked on* the case." Rachel gave a wry smile. "If he didn't back you up when you needed him, he doesn't sound like a man who particularly likes doing his job."

"You weren't there. You don't know."

"I only ever heard Stan talking about you." Rachel shrugged. "*Jessica* is coming over to show me some footage. *Jessica* called again. *Jessica* might have a new theory."

Jessica said nothing.

"Stanley wanted this." Rachel turned to her. "It's all he wanted, in the end."

Jessica watched the morning light flickering on the surface of the pool.

"When the Silver Lake Killer . . ." Rachel trailed off, then cleared her throat. Swallowed hard. "I refuse to say his name. I just call him the killer. When he took my niece, Stan told me that his time thinking of himself as a man ended. He was a father who could not protect his daughter. Bernice was gone and he—well, he was impotent. There was no revenge, there was no closure. He was helpless. Then you came into our lives and you worked and you worked until Stanley almost felt like you were haunting him."

Jessica smirked.

"You were showing up here in the dead of the night trying to track down an item of her clothing. Pulling up the floorboards. Clambering around in the attic. Searching her room for the eighteenth time. He told me all about it. You sounded obsessed."

"That's what it takes," Jessica said.

"Not everyone would agree with you, it seems," Rachel said. "Not the officers who were on the case before you. It had been thirteen years, for Christ's sake."

"I was just doing my job."

"Stanley didn't believe that," Rachel said. "He believed you went beyond the call of duty. And though he couldn't do anything for Bernie, he felt as if he was doing something when he decided to pay you back."

Jessica didn't reply.

"If you refuse to take this house," Rachel said, "you'll be denying my brother his—"

"Stop." Jessica held up a hand. "I don't want to hear that shit."

Rachel pursed her lips, wounded. She took a set of keys from the pocket of her skirt, and held them in the air before them, counting off the keys one by one.

"Front, back, deck, pool gate, side gate, pool house." She pointed. "Garage."

Jessica felt a stab of pain in her chest. She didn't want to enter another garage, maybe ever again. Just the thought of one was unsettling.

"You've got my number," Rachel said. She left the keys on the deck between them and stood, walking out without another word. Jessica looked at the keys for a long time, but didn't touch them.

There was a kid watching her.

Jessica became aware of him in the yard behind the Bluestone Lane house as she lit her cigarette, wondering if smoking was even allowed in Brentwood, if a private security guard would turn up and hose her if the smoke carried too far on the wind. She noticed a shape moving behind a lattice gate in the back wall, covered with vines. She ignored him. When the cigarette was gone but the boy was still there Jessica went to the gate, skirting the huge, humming pool behind the glass fence.

"Are you our new neighbor?" the kid said before she could offer a greeting. Jessica stopped in her tracks.

"No."

"Oh." Disappointment.

"I'm just sort of . . . taking care of the place. For now." She felt a strange obligation to comfort the child she could barely see through the leaves. She caught a glimpse of sandy blond hair and a wide blue eye.

"Mr. Beauvoir was a really nice guy," the boy said, gripping the gate so that his fingers wiggled through on Jessica's side, curious worms. "I'm kind of sad he's gone. He died, you know."

"I know."

"He used to let me help him with the garden sometimes. See those purple flowers over there? The big ones? They've got thorns. Don't go near them. You've got to wear gloves and long sleeves or they'll get you."

"Okay." Jessica lit another cigarette, nodded. "Good advice."

"If you want someone to help you with the garden, I can do it."

"I don't think it'll come to that."

"Mr. Beauvoir used to give me five bucks every time."

"I can see why you miss him."

"You were sitting there for a long time. Were you thinking about something?"

Detective Sanchez looked back toward the house, the sweeping windows and the deck. "People are usually thinking about something, kid," she said. "You make it your mission to spy on people?"

"Sometimes."

"And what about asking a million questions to people you just met. You do that a lot?"

"Yep."

The woman and the boy stared at each other through the leaves. A squirrel scaled a tree nearby, scuttling upward fast.

"Did Mr. Beauvoir's daughter get killed?" The boy gripped the wood tighter. Jessica laughed awkwardly at the question, punched by the sudden severity of it. The kid couldn't know all that his question entailed. The years of work she'd put in to answer it completely.

"Yeah." Jessica craned her neck and tried to see the house the boy belonged to, looking for parents to interrupt the neighborly interrogation. "She was killed."

"Murdered?"

"Yes."

"He told me she died but he wouldn't say how."

"It's nothing for you to worry about."

"I'm not worried."

"Okay, good." Jessica laughed again, bemused.

"Sometimes, people who kill other people—it's, like, an accident, you know?" the boy said. "That happens sometimes. It's not on purpose and they're really sorry afterward."

Not in this case, Jessica thought, but said, "Sure."

"My mom killed someone."

Jessica reeled. She put a hand up against the daylight and saw the boy watching her carefully for a reaction.

"Jesus. That's . . . That's sad," she offered. "Is that something you tell a lot of people?"

"Sometimes."

"Right."

"It was an accident, but she went to jail anyway."

"What do you mean?"

"She wasn't supposed to go to jail. It was a mistake. The police made a mistake."

Jessica felt something twist in her stomach. Her cigarette suddenly tasted like bile in her mouth. She dropped it on the wet grass, stubbing it out carefully. She remembered the shooting three streets over. The pregnant woman with the long face and sad, wild eyes reflecting the blue lights of the cruisers. It had been Jessica who'd cuffed her. You never forget people like that, the ones you escort from their everyday lives into their personal hell. She was afraid to ask her next question, even as the words left her lips.

"What's your name, kid?"

"Jamie Harbour." The boy smiled.

"Oh, fuck my life," Jessica sighed.

BLAIR

At the Denny's on Crenshaw Boulevard I took a booth far from the front doors and any windows, close to the bathrooms so that I could duck in there if I saw anyone who remotely looked like they worked in law enforcement. I wore sunglasses, used the menu as a shield, and kept one eye on the patrons around me. Sneak was drawing looks in her skimpy tank top and skirt as she perused the menu.

"It's too big," she said finally, slapping the menu down. "I'm not used to this kind of choice. There are fifteen types of pancakes. I can't do it."

"Just get the Grand Slam and a coffee," I said.

"You look more suspicious acting like that than you would if you just sat there like a normal person, you know." She picked her teeth with a folded straw. "If a parole officer or someone catches us together, you just offer them something."

"Offer them what?"

"Money, idiot."

"I don't have any money."

"A blow job, then."

"Jesus, Sneak." I shook my head. "Let's try to focus, here. Last night: You get the call from Dayly. It gets cut off. You ask some people what they know. Then you reported her missing, right?"

Sneak fiddled with a napkin, didn't answer.

"Are you telling me you didn't go to the police?" I shifted in my seat. "Okay, we need to go there right now. That's the first step."

"We don't have to. The housemate will do it. You heard her. They were going to call nine-one-one."

"But you have to go in and tell them what you know." I settled back in the booth. "Tell them about the phone call."

"I can't."

"Why not?"

"You know, I knew a guy once who robbed a Denny's," she said, looking at the menu. "It was like that scene from *Pulp Fiction*. He swung a gun around, yelled and threatened everybody, had all the customers put their wallets in a trash bag."

"Sneak."

"He even went into the back and started hitting up all the chefs for their wallets and jewelry and stuff." Sneak sniffed. "But this fry cook got so scared she dropped a big bucket of cheese sauce on the floor and the guy slipped in it. Fell right on his ass. Dropped the gun and the bag and everything. That was the moment to grab him and make a citizen's arrest. But the guy kept trying to get up on his own and slipping over in the sauce again. It was so funny everybody started laughing. They let him go. He ran out the back door covered in cheese sauce. Left the gun and the bag of goodies behind."

"Sneak, are you avoiding going to the police about Dayly because you're wanted?" I asked.

Sneak laughed, smoothing back her greasy, tired curls. "*Wanted*. You make me sound like Jesse fucking James."

"They can help us. This is your daughter we're talking about here."

"I *could* be wanted," Sneak said. She gave a heavy sigh. "I don't know. I heard they were looking at me for some stolen goods that may or may not have been found in a storage container with my name on it."

I held my head. "You're just a barrel of problems, you know that?"

The waitress came and we ordered. Sneak wrung her hands on the tabletop.

"I can't go in. If I get locked up now, I won't be able to find my kid," she reasoned. "The cops know me. They'll pin whatever they can on me. Then it'll be all up to you."

"Me?" I scoffed. "Why me?"

"Because you're the only person I've got on this," she said. She watched me carefully. "You are with me on this, right?"

"Look." I chose my words carefully. "I'm . . . I'm not sure what we have here yet. I'm willing to bounce ideas around about where Dayly might be. But I've got my own kid, you know. I can't risk getting taken away from him again."

Sneak watched me silently weighing up my options.

"I owe you," I admitted.

"You sure do," she said. "I was waiting for you to get to that."

"You dragged me up out of a pretty dark hole in the Valley."

"I didn't just come to you because you owe me," she said. "You're tough. You're good in a tight squeeze. You used to be a big important surgeon, and that makes you the smartest person I know. So now's the time to tell me if you're in or you're out, because if you're out, I've got to find another running mate."

I thought about Jamie. Pictured myself telling him goodbye for another five years, trying to explain to him that I'd been doing something good for a friend when I sacrificed my relationship with him for another half a decade. It had been hard enough to pitch my story about my crime to him when I was released; that I'd done something terribly wrong that I hadn't meant to do, and that despite my acting with the best of intentions, the police had put me away. It seemed impossible for a kid to understand. Impossible still that I would risk all that for Sneak and her daughter, a girl I had known for mere seconds while she stuck a gun in my face.

But the fact was that Sneak had been the key to my survival in prison. She'd got me out of my stupor, and then she had simply been there—a woman sadly adjusted to the institutionalized life, someone who knew the routine, the language, the rules. She was my prison life tour guide. Sure, Sneak was bad company. She was constantly high, often embroiled in a feud with another inmate or an attempted romance with a guard, and she was so sticky-fingered that I had to keep anything I absolutely couldn't afford to have stolen stuffed into my bra—emergency panty liners, pictures of Jamie, my postnatal medication. But every time she finished her stint at Happy Valley and disappeared from my life, I felt the ground crack underneath me. When she inevitably reappeared months or weeks later, it was like welcoming home my long-lost sister. Sneak never got down, no matter how long she was sentenced for, no matter how fruitless her attempts to go back into the real world seemed. She believed that if she let prison life break her, she might break others in turn, so she kept her head high. I admired that.

I also recognized a desire in me to join Sneak in

the search for her daughter as the same kind of desire I'd felt during my time in the operating room. I wanted to sew Sneak and her child's relationship back together. Patch it with neat white bandages. I had the chance to save a child here. Help a mother. Be a hero. It was what I had been doing before I was locked up. This was a sign, a test, that, if I passed, would mean I still was the woman I had been before I was dumped in a jail cell. It would mean I was still good on the inside.

"I'm with you," I told Sneak.

She smiled.

"Tell me what you found out last night about Dayly. The word on the street," I said.

"She's been slipping." Sneak took out her phone and brought up something on the screen, pushed it toward me. "Friend of mine who works as a webcam girl showed me this. I'll let you watch it. I need a cigarette."

Sneak left and I examined her phone. She'd checked into a website called Rareshare-Hx.com. At the top of the screen a slick, shiny cartoon woman was giving a cartoon man a blow job in a dark room. Her head bobbed in an endless loop, big eyes locked on his, while a banner encouraged the viewer to "Try not 2 cum." There was a list of categories above a collection of videos of real girls doing similar acts. In the thumbnail for the first video, the girl who had robbed me at the Pump'n'Jump was curled in the corner of a blue couch, a glass of wine in her hand. I tapped on the thumbnail and Dayly came to life, flapping a hand at the camera.

"*Stop*," she said playfully. "*This is so dumb.*"

I watched for a while. The camera was set down, and from behind it emerged a small, lean man with a head of close-cropped black hair and an unreadable blue tattoo on his neck. Dayly and the man started making out on the couch. I scrolled down the screen and read the caption below the video.

Busty amateur teen blonde gets hammered hard on boyfriend's couch.

The man in the video was peeling off Dayly's shirt when a voice above me spoke.

"Refill?"

The waiter was muscular and tanned, the green Denny's polo clinging to his chest. I snapped the mute switch on the phone and slammed it down, screen to the table.

"Yes, please," I managed.

I toyed with the nice stainless-steel salt and pepper shakers that were on the table as he went away. It had been a decade since a man had touched me intimately. That included everything from full-blown sex to a pat on the shoulder, a warm hug. The closest I had got to a hug was from Henry, Sasha's husband, when I left prison, and I had come no nearer to the act than its imagining in my mind: the slow, deliberate mental repeat of his arms closing around my shoulders, his breath on my neck, his hips against my hips. I imagined it for weeks on end as my release date neared. But he never actually hugged me. Sasha and Henry had picked me up at the prison gates, and Henry had stayed in the car, turning and smiling in greeting as I slid into the back seat. The waiter leaned over now and filled Sneak's cup, and I caught a whiff of his deodorant, saw the thick tendons move in his neck. Big hands and forearms.

"Thanks," I said when he was done. "Could we maybe get some ice water, as well? If it's not too much trouble."

The waiter nodded, smiled, and walked away. Sneak slid back into the booth with me.

"Did you just try to pick up that waiter?"

"I . . . What? No! No, I didn't. Of course I didn't."

"You had a look on your face like you were gonna drag him home to your sex dungeon and chain him to a rack."

"Please," I laughed. "I asked for ice water."

"To throw all over your steaming crotch?"

"Sneak!"

"You haven't broken the curse yet, have you?" She shook her head at me. She seemed grateful for something to latch on to that wasn't her missing daughter. "You've been out a year and you haven't been dicked."

"Can you just . . . Don't say 'dicked.'" The waiter came and deposited our meals and the ice water, and I completely ignored him. "And put the salt and pepper shakers back."

Sneak rolled her eyes and produced the items from her handbag, shoving them back onto the table.

"This video of Dayly," I said. "It's amateur porn."

"From a paid site." Sneak nodded as she spoke. "Viewer pays a fee to watch. The poster gets a cut of the profits. Maybe she was hard up for cash and did something stupid. Maybe her boyfriend filmed them and posted the video, hoping she'd never find out about it."

"This guy is her boyfriend?" I asked. "Or is he just some douchebag?"

"Boyfriend, apparently. I've got the name, the address. Dimitri Lincoln. He's bad people. We need to talk to him, see what he knows. But he lives out in Temple City. If Dayly was willingly doing amateur porn, she was starting to circle the toilet. It's how I started in the industry. I let a guy take some pictures of me to get money for Vicodin. Then I was giving blow jobs. Then I was out on street corners. If she was mixing with the wrong crowd, I want to know who was in that crowd."

"Okay." I nodded. "Sounds like a good lead."

"But Temple City is a hell of a cab ride. We're going to need money and a car."

"Right," I said.

"I spent some of last night trying to get hold of a car," she said. "No luck. Money's tight. What about you? What about that woman who's got your kid? Will she loan you a car for a couple of weeks?"

"She might, but I don't want to do that," I said. "I look like enough of a fuck-up already. I can't have her and her husband thinking I can't handle myself, or they'll never agree to increased custody of Jamie." I tapped the tabletop with my fork. A thought that had been pushing its way into the back of my brain was now surging toward the front, and try as I might to suppress it, it was demanding to be acknowledged. Sneak seemed to know it. She was watching my face.

"I have to go see my kid," I said. "We'll meet up after that."

"You got an idea?" she asked.

"Yeah," I sighed. "But I really, really don't want to do it."

Dear John,

My name is Dayly Lawlor. You don't know me, but if you've got a good memory, maybe you'll recognize my last name. A week ago I was sitting watching the news in my apartment with my mother, and a report came on about three million dollars cash found in suitcases, buried in the desert in Pasadena. Some builders found it, I think. (I have no idea why they involved the police and didn't just run off with it.) The report said the money probably belonged to a San Quentin death-row inmate named John Fishwick, who buried it there for safekeeping before he was arrested. Some criminologist they dragged on the show said he agreed. I'd never heard of you before, but my mom laughed and said she slept with you a long time ago. Actually, she knew exactly how long it had been: twenty years. I'm 19 years old in February.

You probably get a lot of letters from people you've never met on the outside. Crackpots and weirdos who want to know about your crimes. I've actually written to a couple of other guys who my mother was hanging out with around the time that I was conceived, and two of them are currently incarcerated, like you. She has always been a rough sort of person. Fell in with the wrong crowd really young, I think. She is an addict who gave me up when she was sixteen. I

*have mixed feelings about her, but I don't want
to bore you with all that. I wonder if you remember her? You must have been hanging around
a lot of bad people. At the time, you were at
the height of your career. That was just before
Inglewood. My mom said you would turn up
to parties at clubs and throw cash around, then
leave before the police arrived to get you. I can
see the attraction, I guess. You were probably
thought of as a kind of Robin Hood. But I have
to say before I go on that what you did on May
11, 2001, in the Inglewood Chase Bank was
truly shocking to me. I read everything I could
find about you and the massacre, and the internet these days has all the grisly pictures available if you happen to take a wrong turn and
stumble upon them.*

*I'm not writing to interrogate you about your
crimes. I'm sure you get enough of that. I'm
writing to see if you remember Emily Lawlor,
who some people called "Sneak." Is there any
truth to her saying that the two of you were together around that time? Has she ever contacted
you to tell you that you might be my father?
Have you had any contact with her at all over
the years?*

*I realize I've written this whole letter so far
without saying anything about myself, in case
you were interested. I guess it's weird to think
that I'd be curious about you and you wouldn't
be curious about me. I live in Toluca Lake,
near the studios, because my housemate is an
aspiring actress. I'm taking community college
classes in animal studies, and I like to rescue and
rehabilitate animals when I can. At the moment
I'm raising a juvenile Botta's pocket gopher, if*

you've ever heard of one of those. They're native to the Northwest. Lots of them in Texas, too. I found it poisoned. He's a very sweet animal (I'm guessing it's a he—it's extremely hard to tell). A couple of months ago I had a pigeon that I found on the Ventura Freeway that had been buffeted by a car, and luckily it recovered quickly, because my housemate was pretty grossed out with me for having it here. She was convinced she was going to get bird lice. There are sadder parts to my life, too. I'm not a saint. But I'll spare you those until I see if you ever reply to me.

I've enclosed a picture of myself and my gopher, Pockets. The internet is pretty vague about the photograph restrictions for death-row mail at San Quentin, so I hope they get through.

Kind regards, and hope to hear from you soon,
Dayly

JESSICA

The street was crammed with squad cars, officers finding excuses to stay in the air-conditioned West LA police department building as the heat of the day grew. Jessica had spent the evening in her cramped apartment on Alameda, thinking about the house and the Harbour boy. She'd showered awkwardly, protecting her bandages, and dreamed of being chased by zombies. At midnight she'd got up, taken the keys to the Bluestone Lane house from the coffee table, and thrown them into the trash. In the morning, she'd retrieved them.

At the station, two bored-looking officers she didn't recognize were manning the desk under the huge framed photographs of chiefs past. Jessica didn't alert them to her presence, instead buzzing quickly through the door to the back offices with her swipe card. To be ignored on this mission would be a joy.

She was not so lucky inside the open-plan office of the first-floor bullpen. The familiar smell hit her, of body odor, coffee, and cigarettes. She felt the gaze of every person in the room drift toward her. Some of them held phones to their ears, or were leaning over cluttered desks, examining photographs, reviewing

CCTV, staring at notes. But Jessica's presence was like a low siren rising, hitting each officer separately. She cleared her throat and headed for the elevators.

She was only seconds at the elevator doors, punching the button repeatedly, before she heard the words whispered somewhere behind her. *Brentwood. Mansion. Millions.*

Nothing about her injuries. Nothing about Wallert and Vizchen. On the third floor, she didn't stop to assess her impact on the room. She found Wallert in the coffee area, dumping sugar packets into his paper cup. She waited until he turned away from the counter, then slammed her palm upward into the bottom of the cup, spraying coffee all over his face, the coffee machine, the counter, the wall. Before her partner could clear his eyes she drew back and punched him hard in the mouth.

"You piece of shit," she snarled.

"Oh my god! What the fuck!"

"You fat, fucking traitorous piece of shit!"

She hadn't composed her words, hadn't considered anything more articulate or cutting, something that people would remember in years to come. The insults just exploded out of her like barks. Officers were on her before she could land a second blow. Romley from Narco squad and some woman she didn't recognize were hooking her arms and dragging her back. A crowd had formed, ostensibly to break up the violence but really to have front-row tickets for the showdown of the month in Homicide.

"I could have been killed, you motherfucker!" she howled at Wallert. "That guy picked me up and put me on the ground like I was a child. If you'd been there I wouldn't have had to kill him. I *shot someone* because of you—"

"You'll get over it." Wallert's shirt was stuck to his

front with coffee, showing the outline of the black hairs on his pudgy chest. He wiped blood from his chin. "You've got all the money in the world to spend on therapy now."

"Are you hearing this?" Jessica wrestled herself free from arms that held her, looked around at her colleagues. "Are you all *hearing* this? This guy bailed on his partner." She pointed at Wallert. "That's not what we do here. That's not us."

She examined the faces in the circle, expecting to see her fury reflected back at her. But many eyes were downcast, or locked awkwardly with one another, having silent conversations, judging, weighing. She was surrounded by her people, and yet the word *us* rang in the air thinly, like a squeak. Suddenly, Wallert seemed to be a part of them, of The Great Us, and Jessica was standing there wondering what had happened in the twenty-four hours she'd been away from the office, what discussions had been held, what decisions made, to draw a line in the sand between them.

"This is unbelievable." She was suddenly out of breath. "This is—"

"Sanchez, why don't you pipe down." Some guy from Personnel division put a hand on her shoulder. Jessica felt the bite wound come alive. "Making a scene isn't going to help your case."

"My *case*?" She shoved him away.

"What Wallert did wasn't right," Romley from Narco said, shrugging. "But me and some of the guys have talked about it. Everybody's been talking about it. From the initial reports, it sounds like you went off on your own. Sure, Wally and Vizchen should have backed you, but you made that decision, Sanchez. And this house in Brentwood thing—this is some incredible bullshit, if I'm honest."

"Sure would have pissed me off," someone said.

"You're not gonna take the house, are you?" It was Veronica from West Homicide. "Someone said you were. But you can't."

"I heard it's worth nine mil."

"Talk about bailing on your partner."

Romley handed Wallert a bunch of napkins and Wallert smiled beneath them as he dabbed his bleeding gums. Jessica turned and glimpsed Vizchen at the back of the gathering, expressionless, watching. The bodies around her suddenly seemed to be radiating heat, making her wounds burn. Jessica thought of fever, infection, HIV. She gripped her head, tried to tell herself that this was all an act, an office joke gone wrong. That any minute someone was going to push through the crowd and put their arms around her and tell her everything was okay, that she was still a part of this team, that she wasn't the enemy in their midst. But the person who pushed through the crowd was Captain Whitton, and there wasn't anything friendly about his expression.

"Sanchez," Whitton said. "Let's talk in my office. Now."

Jessica sat in her captain's office, thinking about how Andrew Whitton was a man stamped out of the mold of leadership in the Los Angeles Police Department. He was tall, serious, grave. Emotionless slate-gray eyes and broad shoulders constructed specifically for carrying the weight of responsibility, shoulders that looked dramatically stooped at solemn police funerals and old but powerful when he worked them alongside the boys at the station gym. On his desk sat a picture of his wife, Karen, curly-haired and eager-eyed in colorful spectacles, and their three sons, all cops. Sailing shots dominated the other frames.

"It's decision time," the boss said as he sat down.

It was probably always time for something like that in Captain Whitton's life. A decision. A recommendation. A request. A determination. Things that required paperwork and stamps. "You taking the house or not?"

"I've known about this goddamn house for exactly forty-eight hours," Jessica said. Her tone was dead. "In that time I was injured on the job and I killed a man."

"Sure. And I don't want you to think I don't care about that." Whitton held up a placating hand. "My understanding is that a union rep and one of our health people came and saw you at the hospital straight after. You've got your trauma leave paperwork taken care of, haven't you?"

"They did. I do."

"Good. Then Internal Affairs Group will set a date with you about the officer-involved shooting. So the process of dealing with your injuries and the events related to the shooting have started," Whitton said. "You used your gun. They have to look into it. And aside from offering you my condolences, and my full support as your captain, mentor, and friend, all of that has nothing to do with me. What isn't being handled yet is the potential shitstorm that's going to come from this whole thing with the Beauvoir inheritance."

Jessica pinched the bridge of her nose. An ache was spreading through her face, backward across the top of her skull. She thought about viruses again. If only she had been more careful, more discreet. But the phone call she'd received from Rachel Beauvoir in the locker room two mornings earlier had left her so stunned she'd repeated the conversation to a woman she barely knew, Fiona Hardy from the Firearms training section, who was standing nearby in a towel. From there, the news had spread.

"A couple of guys from patrol said you were there yesterday," the captain said.

"Yeah, I went to look at the house." Jessica shifted in her chair. "I went directly from the hospital. Is that what's happening now? Patrols are doing sweeps to see if I'm hanging around?"

"They're curious," he said. "Wouldn't you be?"

"No," Jessica said. "What other officers in this precinct do with their personal time is none of my fucking business."

"Hanging around the house sure makes it look as if you're taking it."

"A man left it to me in his will," Jessica snapped. "His dying wish was that I have it. The very least I could do is go look at it, see the gesture in person."

"But you'd been to the house a million times during—"

"Did you bring me in here just to bust my balls?"

The captain leaned back in his chair and looked Jessica over. She could see him reminding himself that this wasn't her doing, that she was the victim, at least of the fallout of the inheritance.

"You must be tempted, surely," the captain said. "It's twelve million dollars."

"Every time I hear about this place the property value has gone up. There must be an oil spring underneath it that nobody told me about."

"Here's how it is, Sanchez. The truth." The captain glanced at the door as though to make sure it was closed. "You deserve all the recognition you can get on the Silver Lake case. I know Wallert slacked on that investigation."

Jessica remained silent.

"Wallert's promotion to detective was an overestimation of his character. A decision made before my time," Whitton said carefully. "And I expect you not to repeat that outside this office."

Jessica still said nothing.

"I feel as though I should make it perfectly clear what's at stake here." The captain opened a drawer beside him.

"I know what's at stake, Captain," Jessica sighed.

"And it's my responsibility to confirm that, officially."

Jessica slumped in her chair. As she had done many times throughout their time together as detective and captain, Jessica sat in Whitton's office and watched while he traced a finger under the words in a battered copy of the Los Angeles Police Department *Policies of the Personnel Department* handbook.

"If you were to accept the house in Brentwood as a reward from Mr. Beauvoir in exchange for your work on his daughter's case," Whitton began, finding his place in the text, "you could be disciplined under section 33.2." He read, "'Misconduct, on or off the job, seriously reflecting on city employees or employment,' whereby 'employees must perform their duties in a manner that earns and maintains the trust and respect of their supervisors, other employees, and the public.' Your offense would be 'Accepting favors or gratuities for services required on the job.'"

"Uh-huh," Jessica said.

"You could alternatively be disciplined under 'Fraud, dishonesty, theft, or falsification of records,' whereby 'employees must demonstrate personal integrity and honesty both in securing employment and in the performance of duties.'" He paused for effect, his finger resting on the page. "Here, Jessica, you'd come under soliciting, accepting, or offering a bribe. That's an immediate discharge."

"There was no talk of the house being offered to me by Mr. Beauvoir for working his daughter's case when I was first assigned to it," Jessica said. "It wasn't a bribe. The first I heard of his reward was when I was called by his sister, the executor of his will."

"You were obsessed with that case. People were getting concerned around here."

"This is exactly my point." Jessica threw up her hands. "You give a case everything you've got and people start getting *concerned*."

"You lost weight. You lost sleep. You never went home. You tried to walk out of the locker room to attend an all-staff meeting without a shirt on."

"I was tired."

"Just tired?"

"I felt it." Jessica paused, trying to find the words. "I felt the . . . the heat."

"The heat?" Captain Whitton asked.

"You know when you're in the dark." She struggled with her words. "And, uh, someone's there. You can't see them or hear them but you can feel, like . . . a kind of heat? Like a body heat?"

The captain stared at her.

"I felt him. I felt how close I was to catching him."

"Do me a favor," the captain said. "When you leave here, don't tell anyone else you caught the Silver Lake Killer because you felt his metaphorical body heat in the dark. You sound crazy."

"What can I say?" Jessica said. "The guy's in jail now. You want to talk about crazy? Let's talk about me sitting here getting chewed out for doing my job too well."

"Look, all bullshit aside, I don't think IAG will believe, given the circumstances, that you were just overeager on that case," Whitton said. "The investigators are going to say it was more than simple passion for the job driving you. Some people are whispering about a relationship between you and Mr. Beauvoir. One that would contravene other LAPD policies."

"I didn't fuck the seventy-five-year-old father of one of my victims, Captain."

"I'm just telling you what people are saying, what IAG might bring up."

Jessica shrugged. "I stopped giving a shit what IAG thought about me a long time ago."

"Nevertheless," he said, "if you take that house, Sanchez, you're out of the LAPD. One way or another, they'll see you out that front door and you'll never be welcome here again. I think that would be a shame. You belong here, Detective. This is your family."

Jessica left Whitton's office quietly, the throbbing rage she'd felt when she'd entered it slightly dissipated. Members of her LAPD family watched her make her way to the elevator. They watched her standing there, and in the burning quiet her eyes wandered to the records room door to the right of the elevators.

She felt a surge of defiance hit her. A great, silent wave of anger. While a pressure was forming behind her, a will to see her pushed out the door among the men and women she had once trusted, she was grasping at anything to try to stay where she belonged, where she felt safe.

The police made a mistake, the boy had said.

I don't make mistakes, Jessica thought. *I was right then. I'm right now.*

She broke away from the elevators and back-tracked to the records room. Jessica found the book for the Harbour murder, a thick blue binder stuffed with papers. She tucked it under her arm and walked down the fire stairs.

BLAIR

When I gave birth to Jamie, one of my wrists was shackled to the bed in the infirmary at Happy Valley. I strained against the chain as the contractions thundered through me, feeling something like a wild pig in a pen waiting for slaughter, trying to break free. I got to hold my child for an hour before the social worker came. I didn't feel anything in that moment, handing him over.

Looking down at Jamie on my chest in the room in which I'd birthed him, I'd thought how beautiful he was, how appropriate it was that this perfect little thing should be on his way out of the ugliness of that institution in only moments. I hadn't been sad for me. I'd been relieved for him.

The deliberate peeling away from the present I'd been doing from the moment my fate was sealed meant I spent the next few months swimming in a fantasy of my own creation. The other inmates had little to do with me. I was generally considered too "spaced out" to bother with. I lay silently on my bed most days, dreaming my incarcerated sisters and I had been abducted from Earth by aliens, and the prison was a kind of holding facility for humans under observation by the extraterrestrial overlords. I'd given up my baby so that he could go back to Earth, where it was safe.

I didn't see Jamie in person for the first nine years of his life. It had been a necessary choice for me. The decision meant I didn't have to watch him grow up behind glass, and that I could imagine him romping around the green fields of the Earth in my imagination, carefree and joyous under endless blue skies. He would be untouched by my imprisonment when I was finally released, a perfect boy, ready to welcome me as his mom, his only living kindred spirit. We would continue on the plan I'd made for us before the murder.

It had been a good plan. Measured and calculated, almost clinical. My relentless pursuit of my career after med school had meant I'd fallen into a pattern of casual dalliances with men—usually other doctors, who were as neurotic about their careers as I was. I'd had no desire to get serious about finding a man when I realized I wanted to be a mother. Signing up for a sperm donor hadn't been weird. I'd had a vision for Jamie and myself, the son that wanted for nothing and the mom who would make him proud. Until I was released, all I had to do was survive. Things would resume like a play after an intermission when I finally came home to my son.

But now a year had passed since I was released, and our lives were not nearing the ridiculous ideal I'd constructed at all. Jamie loved his foster mother and father, friends from my former life, and he was awkward at best and scared at worst with me. I'd stayed out of his life to protect myself, but in doing so I'd landed him with a mother he didn't know but was forced to make space for in his already confusing and tumultuous young world.

As I lifted my hand to knock on the door of Jamie's house, I heard the boy somewhere inside the spacious home, his voice a high whine. "...want to go to Benny's house! It's not fair! Everyone is going except me!"

"There will be other parties, Jamie. This is more important."

"It's not important! It's stupid!"

I knocked, swallowing hard. Sasha opened the door, wearing a paisley apron. Perfect bangs. She was that kind of housewife, the kind who ran a blog where she taught other bored white mommies how to make cookies in the shape of action heroes and cartoon characters. Something was baking in the house somewhere, the scent of cinnamon and vanilla wafting out the door. Jamie was in the hall, his face dark with dread.

"Hello, buddy!" I said, smiling.

"Hey." He sighed and wandered off.

"Someone's having a little tantrum this morning." Sasha hugged me with one arm, made a *mwah* noise next to my ear. "It'll wear off. There's a party down the street and he wants to go, but a boy needs to hang out with his mother."

I was the "mother" and Sasha was the "mom." I didn't like it but I didn't have the right, or the power, to change it, and Sasha had been good about leaving Jamie's surname as Harbour, as I'd requested. Sasha had raised Jamie since he was an infant. She and her husband had unquestioningly accepted my baby so that he didn't fall into the hands of strangers in foster care, strangers who might have adopted him and insisted I never see him again. Accepting that I was Jamie's mother, but that he would call me "Blair," was just one of a million heartaches I'd had to face following the moment I pulled the trigger of a gun and took a man's life. You don't tell your mother you love her, or confide your secrets in her, or go to her for help. That stuff belongs to the mom. I followed Sasha into the high-ceilinged home, looking for my son, my chest tight with the anticipation of holding him.

"Jamie, we can drop in to the party if you want," I said, finding him slumped on a leather couch. "Let's go get ice cream and then pay a visit on the way back."

"Whatever," he said. "All the good food will be gone by then, probably."

"That's your last 'whatever.'" Sasha pointed the finger of doom at the boy. "You get one per day and you've just used it, bucko. Now get up and hug Blair, then get your stuff. And if I find a Nintendo Switch in your pocket when you come back out here I'm going to put it in the lockup."

The "lockup" was Sasha's underwear drawer, a place for overused electronics and confiscated forbidden magazines. I received an awkward hug from Jamie and then stood, face burning, while Sasha saw to her Iron Man cookies in the huge kitchen.

"Oh my god," she said suddenly, while adjusting the temperature on the high-tech oven. "You'll never believe this. I've been clearing out some old stuff from the basement. I found some photos of us." She pointed with an oven mitt to a stack on the counter. "Such a blast from the past."

I went to the stack of photos and looked through them. Pool party shots. Some extravagant drunken gathering or another. Brentwood society ladies liked expensive white wine and deep, devastating conversations poolside while the children played, and we'd find any excuse to do it. Someone's promotion. A kid's graduation. A marriage, a divorce. We'd had a party for a dog's birthday once. I spotted myself at Sasha's side in the cabana in her yard, laughing, drinking sparkling water with lemon, my baby bump hardly showing. I tried to guess how many days passed between the taking of the photograph and the night I murdered a man. Maybe two months. I put the photos down.

"Look at my hair." She leaned over. "Crazy, right?"

"I need to talk to you," I said.

"What about?"

"I was robbed two nights ago." I glanced at the hallway to make sure Jamie was out of earshot. "They got my car and all my cash. Every cent. I snuck onto a bus to get here."

"Jesus Christ." Sasha jerked away, as though from an offensive odor. "How is that even possible?"

"It's a long story."

"Blair," she sighed. "Honestly. This is not the kind of behavior that fills me with confidence about you getting more one-on-one time with Jamie."

"Maybe you didn't hear me correctly," I said carefully. "I was robbed. It's not *my* behavior we're talking about."

"You're the one who insists on living in the badlands," Sasha said, waving in the general direction of the southeast. "I've told you before, someone up here would let you live in their guest house, where it's safe. I could make some calls."

"Accommodation is great but I've got to eat. No one within miles of here would hire me."

"They'd hire you *in the house*, Blair." Sasha rolled her eyes. "It would have to be someone I knew, but I could swing it."

"That sounds hellish for me," I said. "And you. What are you going to say? 'This is my murderous ex-con friend, mother of my child. Will you have her as live-in help? It might be dangerous, but imagine how fun it will be, staring at her and whispering about her while she brings us drinks.'"

"So what do you need?" She looked me over. "Cash and to borrow the car to take Jamie to the pier, I suppose."

"I can pay you back in a couple of weeks."

"It's fine. I'll have to tell Henry something. Perhaps I won't mention the robbery. We need to make a time to discuss the custody arrangement and I don't know how something like this will sound to him," she said, going to her handbag, on a chair by the windows. She started extracting notes from her pocketbook. "He's hardly ever here at the moment anyway. Work has got him run ragged."

A sparkle of terror hit my brain. The "talk" Sasha was going to have with Henry, about my having shared custody of Jamie, had been mentioned but not executed three times already. I wondered if this was going to blow it all out of the water. I wasn't asking for fifty-fifty. I just wanted days, not hours, with my son. I'd met all my parole conditions. I was being visited and interviewed once a month by Child Protective Services agents, two prim and stiff-backed women who sat together on my couch and looked down their noses at my scuffed secondhand coffee table and the worn industrial carpet in my apartment. I was doing everything I could.

I pushed down the ache in my chest as the boy re-emerged from his bedroom, a smile full of effort and strain on his face. Sasha gave him the Nintendo pat-down and kissed him goodbye.

"Let's go!" I chirped, like a cartoon adventurer about to set off on a treacherous mountain climb. I squeezed his shoulder on the way to the door, maybe too hard.

* * *

The Santa Monica Pier Ferris wheel carriages swung gently as the machinery clunked between stops. Jamie bumped into me at one of the intervals, shifted by the movement of the carriage, and then slid across the seat away from me, awkward. It always took him a long time to warm up.

"So, what's so great about this Benny kid and his party?" I asked.

"Someone said they were going to have a magician," Jamie said. "Or an acrobat. I don't know. Me and the guys have been trying to learn how to do backflips and I thought he might teach us."

"I like how you say 'me and the guys' like you're a bunch of twenty-year-olds."

"We're kind of half twenty-year-olds," he mused.

"I knew a chick in prison who could do backflips," I said. "She could do a handstand on one hand too."

"Why was she in prison if she was so cool?"

"Drugs. Theft," I said. "In fact, I saw her yesterday morning, out of the blue." I shoved away the sudden wave of anxiety that rose at the thought of Sneak and her child. "Hey, guess what?" I said.

"What?"

"I love you with all my heart and soul."

"Oh, god." He clapped a hand over his eyes. "You've said that, like, a million times before, you know that?"

The sun was sparkling in Jamie's hair. I wanted to stroke it so badly that I had to turn away.

"What was your jail friend visiting for?" he asked. "Was she just saying hello? Do you ever, like, hang out with all the people you knew in there?"

"No. Actually, we're not allowed to hang out."

"Well, that's pretty stupid."

"It's the law," I said. "It's complicated."

"Were there any other murderers in jail or was it just you?"

I flinched at the question.

"Sure," I said. "There were plenty."

"I didn't know girls could be murderers before Mom told me about you."

"They can."

"Were they scary? The ones in prison?"

"Some of them were," I said. "Most of them were just like me. I'm not scary." I waited for a response. There was none. "Am I?"

He thought for a moment. "Nah," he replied eventually. I took a chance and patted the back of his head.

"So, get this," he said suddenly. "We've got a new neighbor at our house."

"Oh yeah?"

"At the back. I met her last night."

"You like her?"

"She seems pretty cool," he said thoughtfully. "But she smokes a lot. Smoking's bad for you. Gives you cancer. That's what happened to Mr. Beauvoir. He got cancer. Maybe everybody who moves in to that house will smoke and get cancer and die."

I watched my child, wondering how he could turn something as exciting as the arrival of a friendly new neighbor into something so dark. I supposed it seemed to Jamie as though there was murder and unexpected death all around him, stories of it happening in a past he was not a part of, events that permeated his present reality. No matter what I did, I would not be able to protect Jamie from what I had done while he was curled, unborn, inside my body. I fiddled with my phone, and a desire to indulge my addiction rose and fell. I thought about Dayly's blood on the wall of her apartment, the upturned chair. I saw the desperate young woman behind the gun in the Pump'n'Jump, the way her arm shook with a terror that radiated from deep within. Sneak's child, out there somewhere, dead or alive. Our carriage was almost at the bottom of the wheel.

"Can we get ice cream now?" Jamie asked.

"Anything you want," I told him.

It was about three weeks after I gave birth to Jamie in the prison infirmary. The hazy, dense mental fugue I'd fallen into, complete with alien overlords and space battles for Earth, had complete control of my waking minutes. I was lying on my bed looking at nothing when she came by.

"Bitch," she said, putting an elbow on the bed beside me, leaning in. "I gotta ask you. How long you planning to lie there pretending you're dead?"

I blinked myself back into reality, looked at her.

"Leave me alone," I said.

"No way. You know why?" She turned and pointed. "Because that's my bunk over there. The one in the corner. I sleep on my left side, which means every morning and every night for the past month I've gone to sleep and woken up looking at your bugged-out, drooling face. I'm tired of it. It's bothering me. It's offending me now. If slapping the shit out of you is going to bring you back to earth, I'll do it."

"Go ahead," I said.

She leaned in closer. "Here's what you need to understand," she said. "We're all sad in here. We're all angry. You think you're the only one who's ever had to give up a baby in this place? There was a crazy woman in here last summer who had to sleep with a doll. Not just sleep with it but carry it around everywhere, pretending to go off and breastfeed it, talking to it and changing its diapers. You think you're the only one who's ever had to stare down the barrel of a decade or more in this shithole? You're trippin'. We're all in this together, and you lying there cracking up is going to start making other people wonder if they shouldn't be doing the same. We all get through it or none of us get through it, you understand? Weren't you a doctor? Didn't I hear that?"

"Yeah," I muttered.

"So you're supposed to be all about helping everyone else," she said. "Snap to it, bitch."

I thought about Sneak's words as I led my son into the police station.

"What are we doing?" Jamie asked as we entered the dull brick building. "Is this where you went to jail?"

I hushed him. It was, in fact, the police station I had been escorted to on the night of the murder. But it was the only station I knew, and while I had Sasha's car I had to act.

"We're just making a quick report."

The boy looked around excitedly at the framed pictures of police, collections of badges, and the polished brass trophies from police sporting events in a big cabinet before the brick wall. The smell of the place was the same as the night I had been brought here. Leather, gun oil, trouble, pride.

The thin male officer behind the front desk was clicking idly at a computer. "Yep," he said by way of address.

"Hi." I put my sweaty hands on the counter. "I'm here to report a stolen car."

The officer sighed and began leafing through sheets of paper on a shelf below the counter. He set a form in front of me.

"Fill that out."

I filled out the form. The officer took it, signed it,

and slipped it behind the desk, somewhere I couldn't see, probably onto an enormous pile.

"I'm also . . . uh." I stared at my hands on the counter, thinking, deciding. "Yeah. I'm here to see if a missing person report has been filed."

"You're here to file a missing person report?" He frowned.

"No." I swallowed. "I'm here to see if one *has* been filed. I . . . I'm trying to find out . . . If one *hasn't* been filed, you see, I may want to file one. Or have someone come here and file one. If that's okay. The girl . . . I'm hoping her roommate might have, uh . . ."

The officer stared at me. His badge said *McAuley*.

"Could you please just see if a missing person report has been filed for Dayly Lawlor?" I said. Sweat was rolling down my ribs. I flapped my shirt away from my skin. "L-a-w-l-o-r. I don't know if it's 'Daily' like every day, or otherwise."

McAuley looked over my shoulder at Jamie and then back at me. There was a deadness in his eyes that didn't lift as he turned to the computer and started typing. He ran a finger down a list of names that was laminated and taped to the desk, then picked up a phone and dialed. The officer said "Front desk," and then replaced the receiver.

I stood, hoping whoever was being called to the front desk had nothing to do with me. That McAuley would return to the computer, check for Dayly, confirm that she wasn't my problem, and let me go. But a man in plain clothes appeared through a door beside the counter and looked right at me.

He glanced at Jamie then beckoned me sharply with one hand. "You can leave the boy where he is."

Hallways, corners, sudden vast offices full of cubicles, eyes, posters, racks of uniform hats. I was tracing steps that I had taken ten years earlier, each one taking me further and further away from my child. I was inside. An interview room door was shutting behind us. An air-sucking sound.

I realized I hadn't looked at the man before me. Like the well-trained inmate that I had once been, I'd focused only on his shoes. Brown leather boots, worn, scuffed, under jeans. I caught a glimpse of a neat blond buzz cut and a questioning look. Heavy, stubbled jaw. I turned away.

"Sit." He gestured to a chair. There was no table in the room to hide behind. I sat, clasped my hands, and he sunk into the other chair.

"What's wrong with you?" he began.

"What? Nothing."

He stared at me.

"Nothing." I straightened. "I was just here to check on a report."

"You're nervous."

"Police stations make everybody nervous."

"Your name," he said. It wasn't a request, it was a statement.

"Blair Harbour."

The man took out his phone and started typing. I was in too deep. Trying to regulate my breathing, avoid drowning. I struggled in the silence.

"And yours?" I asked, just to break it.

"Detective Al Tasik."

A detective. I gripped my chair. "What division are you in?" I asked.

More silence. He was in control, an elbow on the arm of his chair, chewing a nail as he surfed the internet or looked at his texts or whatever the hell he was doing. The calm of a person in a doctor's waiting room. Casual.

"You're lying," he said finally.

"What?" I said again, laughed stupidly. "No, I—"

"You're Blair Harbour. Killer. Convict. Parolee." He showed me the phone screen, a second-long flash of my own face. "But you sit down in front of me just now and the first thing you say is you're nervous because everybody gets nervous in police stations. That's a lie by omission. When were you going to tell me you're a convicted criminal?"

"Look." I took a deep breath, swiped a stray hair out of my face before it stuck to the sweat beading at my temples. "I'm just here to see if my friend—if a person who I think may be missing—has been reported as such. That's all."

"Dayly Lawlor is your friend?"

My heart was hammering. I wondered if he could see my jugular ticking. "No. I don't know her."

"You just said she was your friend. Are you avoiding saying she's your friend because she's a criminal, too? You have particularly strict parole conditions, Ms. Harbour. I'm sure you've been made aware of those. They specifically state that interactions with anyone who has been convicted of a—"

"I know," I said. I needed to take back control of the conversation. Interrupt him. He didn't like it. His jaw twitched.

"When was the last time you saw Ms. Lawlor?"

The Pump'n'Jump. The gun in her hand. The blood on her fingers.

"I've never seen her," I said. "I'm telling you Dayly Lawlor is not a friend. I've never met her. She's related to someone I know."

"Someone you know? Who?"

"Just a person."

"Tell me their name."

"I don't have to do that."

"So you're just here checking on the missing person report of someone you don't know and have never met." He nodded slowly, smirked at an empty corner of the room as though he was so used to sharing a smirk with his partner that he did it even when they weren't there. "Ms. Harbour, I'm going to ask you now, are you currently under the influence of any drugs?"

My mind leaped ahead, sizzled and snapped through a series of horrific visions. A drug test. A formal interview while we waited for results. A call to my parole officer. A call to Sasha and Henry from McAuley at the front desk, telling them to come get Jamie, that I was going to be detained for an undetermined amount of time due to a sudden unfolding of circumstances on which he could not elaborate. The thought pressed again that the only person who was going to get me out of this room was myself. The way I had got myself out from under the gaze of the robber's gun two days earlier, the way I had talked and schemed and lied my way out of rapes, assaults, and shankings in prison a million times across the decade I had been inside.

Take back control.

"I'm leaving now." I stood up.

"No, you're not."

The man had me before I saw him move. He was out of his chair, his hard hand twisting my right forearm and locking it into my back. I smacked against the cold concrete wall, my head, my ribs, my hips. We stopped. His hands were on my wrist and my shoulder. Our breaths were hard. That was something to focus on. That was a clue. Hot breath. Agitated. Why was he agitated? I waited to be read my rights, but he said nothing.

Because he was thinking.

I realized I had a chance. "I want my lawyer," I said.

"You don't—"

"Lawyer, lawyer, lawyer," I said. "Now. Right now."

"You don't need a fucking lawyer." He pulled my wrist away and shoved my hand into the wall, then lifted my other arm and flung it upward. "I'm going to conduct a routine body search for weapons or other restricted items."

I closed my eyes, held the wall, and prepared to be briefly sexually assaulted. The camera was on us, but I was sure he'd do as the guards in Happy Valley had done more times than I could remember—reach too high, too deep, linger for too long. He didn't. The man swept his hands over my clothes and pulled me off the wall, jabbed me in the shoulder to get me to move toward the door.

"Get going," he said.

I walked stiffly back the way we had come. In time I looked behind me and realized he wasn't following. I walked faster, and hit the door to the foyer at a jog. Jamie was slumped in the chair I had put him in, his Nintendo upright on his chest, thumbs dancing on the buttons. I yanked him up and walked fast with him out of the building toward the car.

"What happened? What's wrong?"

"Nothing," I told him, laughing too loud. "Where the hell did you get that Nintendo? Sneaky, sneaky, sneaky. What a sneaky kid."

"Are you okay? You're all red."

"It's hot. We're just late, that's all. Gotta get you home or we'll be in trouble."

Trouble. I breathed the word, hardly able to give it sound. My head was throbbing, hands shaking as I opened the car door. Wet handprints on the steering wheel. It took me longer than it should have to figure out what I was supposed to do with the keys in my hand, where I'd even got them. Jamie was watching me, the Nintendo playing looping music, bouncing sounds. We sat in silence while I tried to remember how to put the car in reverse.

"Hey!" he said in time. I looked over. He was smiling, pointing through the windshield. I followed his aim and saw Detective Jessica Sanchez walking across the street before us toward her car, her gaze bent to her phone, a thick binder of papers under her arm. The sight of the woman who had arrested me for murder sent a bolt of pain through my chest.

"That's her. My new neighbor," Jamie said.

I looked at him, then back at Sanchez, who was pulling open the door of her Suzuki, her black hair caught in the hot afternoon wind. I let my hands fall into my lap.

"Mother*fucker*," I said.

Jamie laughed.

I walked to a quiet street five minutes from Jamie's house after dropping him off, sat down on a low brick gate outside someone's house. My fingers were trembling as I tried to dial. I didn't even look at the numbers, just listened to the tune they played. The phone rang three times as I tried to regulate my breathing.

"Hello?"

"Hi," I swallowed. My mouth was bone dry. "My name is Blair, and I need someone to talk to."

There was the usual pause. A shuffling sound. "Huh? Who is this?"

"I just want to talk to you for a minute," I said. "What's your name? Where are you? What are you doing?"

I already had some of the details I needed. Deep voice. Not old, but it was hard to tell—he hadn't said much yet. I formed an image of his face quickly. Closed my eyes to see it better. The man sounded as if he was in a quiet, enclosed space. No background noise. A car? His house? An elevator? The possibilities were endless. I could picture him taking his phone from his ear, looking at the screen. Unknown number.

"Sorry, *who* is this?" he insisted.

"Who is *this*?"

"It's Steve."

"Steve," I said. "I'm Blair. Are you at home right now?"

"Woman, whatever you're sellin', I can tell you I don't want it."

"I'm not selling anything," I said. My breaths were slowing. I could see Steve's face. A kind face. Big hands. I added a ball cap. Blue. Dodgers. "I just want to know what you're doing."

"Me?" he said. "I'm waitin' on somebody."

"Who?"

"I drive Uber. Some guy. Is this Rebecca?" Skeptical. I could see him narrow his eyes.

"It's Blair," I said. I wiped my sweaty hand on my jeans. "What kind of neighborhood are you in? How long have you been driving Uber?"

"A year. What . . . Oh man. What do you want?"

"I just want to talk."

"This is so weird." A smile in his voice.

"I know. I'm sorry."

"You just some random chick calling people looking for someone to talk to? About nothin'?"

"That's right," I said. "I do it all the time."

"Hell, why?"

"Because it makes me feel good."

"It makes you feel good to know it's Steve here, sittin' on his ass in a car outside some goddamn house in the middle of nowhere, waiting for some dumb fuck to come get his ride." His voice rose and rose until it cracked with laughter. "That's stupid, girl."

"I know," I said again. "But it's a thing now. It's something that I do. And I'm real grateful you answered."

Steve the Uber driver laughed again and hung up. I closed my eyes and felt the sun on my face, focused on him sitting in his car, watching as his passenger emerged from their house. As always, I inserted the details I needed to latch on to the dream—the passenger's suitcase rumbling as he wheeled it along the concrete drive outside his meager home. The smell of Steve's car, cigarettes behind a wall of hibiscus air freshener. A dancing plastic sunflower on the dash. A scar on Steve's wrist, old, from a fence nail. In time, my fantasy was as real and vivid as it would have been if I'd been sitting next to Steve in his vehicle. I forgot all about Jamie, Dayly, Sneak, the detective at the police station, the feel of his hard hands running up my thighs, over my shoulders. I sat and watched Steve greeting his passenger, putting his car into drive, adjusting the air-conditioning, putting his phone into the holder and tapping the screen to tell the app he had his man.

I'd been dialing random numbers and speaking to strangers for six years. The addiction had started in prison, when Sasha had forgotten to tell me that she and Henry were taking Jamie camping and I'd called their house a hundred times, trying to get an update on my child. The whole weekend I'd called and called, receiving nothing but her calm, authoritative answering message, the prison common room around me swirling and crashing with activity. I'd imagined fires. Home invasions. Sudden fatal accidents, illnesses. I'd imagined Sasha and Henry had taken my child and run off to Australia. I'd dialed a random number by mistake, my finger slipping onto an eight instead of a five. An elderly man's voice croaked through the receiver. As I'd ached and burned and shaken with terror at the fate of my child, the old man's confused voice had disrupted the violence my mind was inflicting on my body. He'd never received a call from a correctional facility, he'd said. He was curious to know who I was. We'd talked for fifteen minutes, and my addiction had begun.

JESSICA

She had never before arrived unannounced. Never in the bright light of day. But Jessica pushed a discreet gold button beside the ornate stained-glass door of a house nestled in a leafy street in Beverly Hills and waited in the shade. Her every limb was burning with tension and hatred. She was buzzed in and she crossed the small foyer of the home, climbed the stairs.

The house yawned around her, still and silent beyond her crashing thoughts. She always came here with a loaded mind, noticed the quiet. Right now she was screaming internally at her colleagues. The truth was, this was not the first time she'd felt abandoned by other police officers.

The Sanchezes were an auto family. They had been for decades. There was no need to change things, her abuela warned Jessica and her brothers as they grew up. You worked with what you were proven to be good at, and they were good at cars. The Sanchez men fixed and serviced and reupholstered cars, either in their own oil-slicked, sunbaked shops or in the shops of cousins or friends. The women went into sales, worked the cracked concrete in heels, toting clipboards, haggling over prices with customers. Jessica had been trained in negotiation tactics since she was a kid standing in the shade of beat-up vans in their lot in Vernon, listening to her mother talk smog checks with men in big, dirty boots.

It was here in the lot, at five years old, that she had encountered her first police officers up close, when two white patrol cops came in for a quick replacement tire on a squad car. Jessica had watched in reverent awe as the men exited their vehicle, leaning around her mother's legs to look into the car at the shotgun installed in the front cabin. As her mother went to assist the officers at the counter, Jessica heard the taller one mutter to his partner.

"We gotta make this quick, bro."

"They're brothers," little Jessica had proclaimed to her cousin Hernan, who was also watching from the auto shop break room doorway, but with the feigned disinterest of a twelve-year-old.

"No they're not," Hernan had replied.

"Yes they are. I heard him say it."

"Okay. Sure." He'd rolled his eyes. "They're brothers. All cops are brothers. They're one big happy family."

Jessica had taken the boy literally, had believed from that day on that all police officers were biologically related, that an enormous family encompassing thousands of people of different races composed the city's uniformed law enforcement. She'd learned the truth with quiet embarrassment at twelve, when a newspaper article about a Mother's Day picnic with the moms of police officers from the local station had appeared in the newspaper. Though she'd felt like an idiot for believing all cops were actually brothers and sisters for so long, an excitement had stirred in her chest, a door formerly closed now wide open. Her destiny didn't have to be spark-plug replacements and wheel-alignment deals. It could be the uniforms, guns, and flashing lights she had so admired of the police who came into the shops and those on TV. Jessica didn't have to be born a cop. She could become one.

She'd signed up to the force at nineteen, sitting in the recruitment center looking at posters of cadets standing in lines in ceremonial uniform. The men and women in the pictures had all looked the same. Shining buckles. Sharp, peaked caps. Stern faces. Jessica had assumed donning the uniform would allow her to slot right in with her fellow officers. She'd felt a yearning to be a part of something so large, so welcoming. A perfect fit, the snug and warm hole in which she'd always belonged.

It was at the academy that she realized her new family would require her to earn her place. She'd found her room in the featureless brick accommodation block on her first day and noticed right away that the entire floor was populated by other Hispanic recruits. They were being segregated from the rest of the intake. She wasn't pure cop blood after all. That blood was white. There were cops, and then there were *Hispanic* cops. Above the bathroom door of the dorms, someone had nailed a sombrero, and apparently nobody had ever been defiant enough to tear it down.

It had taken her reaching detective rank for the jokes about wetbacks, taco trucks, and siestas to fade out. Snide remarks about ethnic quotas and questions about her quinceañera. Had she worn a huge dress with big balloon sleeves? Were there pictures? When she made detective, she'd finally been let in, and all the racist bullshit had stopped.

And now she was out again, just like that, over a stupid house. Wallert and Vizchen were white. They were male. They were older than her. Card-carrying boys club members. "Bros." Of course her colleagues were going to side with them over the Beauvoir inheritance. Jessica should have seen this coming. Should have known she was always a foster sister, and never a real part of the family.

Goren met her in the doorway of the second-floor bedroom now, filling most of it with his muscular frame. He was wearing a black T-shirt and jeans. She'd never seen him this way. It was usually suits, tailored Hugo Boss, sometimes a bare chest if he was running clients back to back. Jessica thought for a moment that perhaps she'd caught him on a day off.

"Jessica." He smiled warmly. The corner of his mouth twitched a little as he took in the bandages, the bruises. He never asked. It was part of his policy. You brought to him what you wanted him to see, and he probed no further. "You know I need you to make an appointment."

"I was hoping you'd make an exception, just this once." She heaved a sigh. "Everything is . . . Everything is so completely . . ."

"Come in." He led her into the bedroom. She sat on an overstuffed leather ottoman at the end of the bed and he stood behind her. The view out of the windows was blocked by foliage, gentle afternoon light illuminating some of his equipment. A massage table was set in one corner of the room with its candles, oils, and bottles of aromatherapy ingredients. On the wall by the door hung the stuff of very different experiences: a rack of chains, straps, belts, and buckles. Another rack of whips, paddles, knives. A glass cabinet full of masks, both cloth and leather, ball gags, blindfolds. There was a long trunk against the wall filled with things she had explored with him more than once, devices of pleasure in every conceivable shape and color. Goren took the back of her neck in his big hand and she let her weight fall there while he gently slid the tie from her hair. He worked the fingers of both hands into the soft recesses between the hard cords and bones at the back of her neck.

Jessica had met Goren Donnovich more than fifteen years earlier. She'd been a patrol cop, participating in an unsuccessful raid of his property for drugs. She'd come down the stairs and locked eyes with the man in the foyer as he was questioned by a detective. They'd held each other's gaze for mere seconds, but when she'd arrived a month later for an appointment, he hadn't been surprised to see her.

"You're injured," he said now. She explained, as vaguely as she could.

"Have you been tested for the bug?" he asked.

"Got the text this afternoon. We're all good."

"Text." He laughed. "They're doing texts now? Well, that's going to save me some time, at least."

"Mmm."

"What kind of experience are you seeking today, Jessica?" he asked.

"Gentle," she said. "I'm hurting."

He peeled off her T-shirt, lifted it over her head, and folded it neatly, placed it on the ottoman beside her.

"My whole world is upside down," she said.

"Let's get it all out of you." Goren worked his hands down her spine, avoiding the bite mark on her shoulder. "We'll begin on the table, and then I'll bathe you. We'll wash it away together, the pain, the tension. Then I'll hold you in the bed for a while, and if you decide you'd like to advance into an intimate experience, we can do that."

"How long have you got?"

"I can do three hours," he said.

Jessica sighed again, her whole body releasing, exhaustion shuddering through her. "That sounds great."

He guided her up, drew her to him, kissed her on the mouth, hard and long, the way he knew she liked. She could feel his cock, erect already, through his jeans.

"Let's reverse the order, though," she said.

He smiled and lifted her off her feet.

BLAIR

Ada Maverick's strip club, The Viper Pit, opened at 5 p.m., in time to catch the after-work crowd. Sneak and I waited on Olympic Boulevard, squinting through the low afternoon sun at the big iron doors, trying to find refuge from the heat in a bus shelter that reeked of urine. There were four men waiting outside the doors for opening time, glancing at their watches or phones, rolling their shoulders, and wiping sweat from their brows. After a while, as we watched, a preacher in a black shirt and trousers arrived and started counseling each of the men in turn, appealing with his hands out. Before long a huge white man in a suit came out of the iron doors and seized the preacher by his collar, lifted him off the ground, and dropped him a few yards down the street, shoved him so hard to get him going that his head snapped back as though on a spring.

"This is your big idea, huh?" Sneak asked. "I can see why you didn't want to do it."

"I'm still iffy about whether we should or not." I shifted uncomfortably, watching the club. "It might be a bad idea."

"You've got to risk it to get the biscuit, I suppose."

"Hmm."

"Tell me about this alert thing before we go in," Sneak said, trying to light a cigarette in the warm breeze.

"As soon as I asked the counter cop about Dayly, I was whisked away into a back room by some detective, Al Tasik." I told Sneak about Tasik's behavior. The roughhousing and the questions about how I was connected to the case. "There must have been a flag on the file. He was called up when I said Dayly's name. Tasik didn't sound like a guy who wanted help. He was . . . kind of angry."

"Did you get the feeling he's looking for Dayly, too?"

"Maybe."

"Maybe the scene at the apartment was an arrest gone wrong." Sneak gave a worried sigh. The thin, hesitant sigh of a mother pushed to the edge. "They came for her. She fought them and escaped. Bailed out of town. Maybe she kicked this guy Tasik in the nuts on the way out and now he's got a hard-on for her."

"You said she wasn't that kind of kid. The running-from-the-law kind, I mean."

"We'll soon find out. But this. *This* is a terrible idea," Sneak said, gesturing to the club with her cigarette. "Mav's a raging psychopath. Like, she's got a diagnosis for it and everything."

"Are you allowed to have a name like Ada Maverick and not be a raging psychopath?" I wondered.

"I heard Ada isn't her first name." Sneak exhaled cigarette smoke into the wind. She looked hard-faced and cold despite the sunshine. "She changed it because her mom gave birth to her in a courtroom and called her Custa'd."

"The courtroom? Like, in front of the judge?"

"Yeah."

"Sounds like jailhouse bullshit to me," I said.

"I heard that when a girl I knew asked her about it, if it was true or not, Ada threw her off the second tier in B Block. Nearly broke her neck."

I'd known Ada in Happy Valley. The beautiful, shaven-headed Black woman never went anywhere except the visiting room without a cohort of followers, like most criminal overlords inside the prison. Dangerous women with heavy tattoos and severe cornrows, women who cleared the halls of looky-loos and beggars and potential threats before Ada arrived. At the time, Ada had been doing a stint for dealing guns, but all that followed her were tales of extreme violence, lines crossed and bones broken, warnings like the one Sneak had just given me about questioning her given name. I'd heard my fair share of dorm rumors about Ada. That she'd set a cell on fire with two women in it. That she'd kicked off a riot and killed a guard who was trying to blackmail her. I knew not all of it could be true, but the sheer number of rumors about her spoke of danger, of a menace much bigger and more powerful than me. Looking at Ada brought a tight, shallow feeling to my chest.

I'd been waiting for my lawyer to arrive in the visitor's center one day, sitting with other inmates in a row of cubicles behind glass, when Ada arrived to visit with someone who I would later learn was her cousin. My lawyer was chronically late, so while I waited, trying not to listen to the conversations around me, I'd shuffled my chair back to the wall to get a better view of the women coming and going on visitor's row. I'd heard a baby wailing and saw Ada's cousin bend down and retrieve the infant from a stroller parked out of my view. She'd heaved the heavy baby to her chest, joggling it in a failed attempt to stop it crying.

The baby was wriggling in its mother's arms, trying to get free, sweaty cheeks and brow glistening as it shied away from the overhead lights. I watched as, presumably, the cousin explained the baby's symptoms, pulling up the leg of the baby's pants to reveal a swelling rash on the child's thighs to Ada through the glass.

"Oh no," I'd said. Before I realized what I was doing, the dangerous waters I was hurling myself into, I'd grabbed Ada Maverick on the shoulder. "Tell her to—"

Ada had my hand in hers, like a rattlesnake seizing a mouse, in a movement that was so fast I didn't even see it. She twisted my hand backward toward my wrist and came around at me, out of her chair, suddenly closer and taller and more terrifying than I could ever have imagined. My wrist cracked and my fingers ached. She forced me down to one knee.

"Hands off, bitch," she seethed.

"I'm a doctor," I yelped. "Oh god. Oh, please let go. I'm a doctor. The baby is sick—"

"The baby is sick, yeah." Ada forced me down further. "It's none of your business."

"She shouldn't be here," I managed. The pain was searing up my arm. I imagined my veins bursting. Bones splintering. A guard was watching from the end of the row, arms folded, doing nothing. "The rash. The purple rash! It's—"

"It's what?"

"I'm not sure, but if there's bruising—"

"You better speak faster, bitch, before I break your arm."

"She might have meningococcal disease. It can be deadly. She needs to get to a hospital now."

"What is she saying?" Ada's cousin was pounding her fist on the glass, her voice muffled from the other side. We both looked at her. The distraction caused Ada to go too far. I felt two of my fingers pop, dull heat, broken proximal phalanx bones. My mind grabbed at deep, detached thoughts to try to drag me away from the pain. I thought about my hands. About how once they'd been the fine instruments of my craft as a surgeon, and now a criminal overlord was using them as her tools of punishment in a filthy prison visiting room.

Ada reluctantly released me on her cousin's command and I slithered pitifully to the bench, dragged myself up so that I could see the child in its mother's arms. I took the receiver from where Ada had dropped it and held it to my ear with a trembling hand. As I asked the mother about body stiffness and the child's reaction to food, Ada breathed in my ear, hot and menacing, the whisper of a devil.

"You better not be tellin' me my cousin's a bad mother, little whore," Ada said. "You better not be sayin' she can't take care of her own kid."

"Take the baby to a hospital," I told Ada's cousin. "Go now. Show them the rash and the bruises and tell them about the fever and the sensitivity to light. You haven't got much time."

Ada's cousin disappeared with the baby. I tried to turn around but Ada slammed my head against the desk and pinned it there with a hand like a steel claw. Her thighs were against mine, trapping me in a painful, humiliating crouch in the cubicle.

"Either you're right about that kid, or you're dead," she told me. "Nobody interrupts me on a visit."

I never heard from Ada Maverick directly if I'd been right about the child. But as word of the incident spread throughout the prison, I waited hour by hour to receive a brutal punishment from the terrifying and beautiful gangster or one of her minions. None came. I made myself scarce, slept with my shank, and discouraged anyone I heard speaking about the event from spreading it further or developing it into something it was not. After a few weeks I assumed, right or wrong, that Ada had forgotten completely about me. She and her crew breezed past me in the prison halls without even a glance in my direction.

Now I stood outside Ada's club, waiting for a break in the traffic so that Sneak and I could follow the men in the line into the darkness.

"Just follow my lead," I said as we approached the doors.

Following my lead turned out to be impossible. As we stepped into the small foyer, I had just enough time for my eyes to adjust to the dark, to see the glossy black tiles on the walls and the velvet curtains hanging before the entrance to the club. Then an arm swept around my neck. I felt suit buttons against my back. The man yanked me into an embrace against his chest, and from the corner of my eye I caught sight of Sneak being similarly grabbed by another huge, suited man.

"This way, ladies," the man who had me said. He shoved me through a small side door padded with leather and ornate gold studs. I was blind. The narrow hallway was pitch black. Only his guiding hand on my shoulder got me to the end of the passageway and into Ada's office.

We arrived in a grand, windowless room lit only by huge gold candelabras and a diamond chandelier the circumference of a four-seater dining table. Ada sat behind an enormous oak desk, her elbows splayed, a bottle of what looked like whiskey at one and a huge red leather notebook at the other. She was dressed in black lace, pushing closed a small gold laptop, through which I assumed she had watched us approach the club from the road out front. The suited men shoved Sneak and me into wooden chairs before our queen.

"Just follow your lead?" Sneak sneered at me. I frowned back.

"There's only one explanation for this," Ada said. Her voice took me all the way back to Happy Valley. My fingers burned as though broken anew. "You two must be high as fuck."

"I'm kinda high," Sneak agreed, nodding. The man behind her whipped out his big hand and slapped her on the back of the head.

"This ain't In-N-Out Burger, bitches," Ada snapped. "You don't just roll up here unannounced and come strolling through the doors. This is *my* house. Last person who decided to come barging in here without calling ahead and requesting a meeting left half a set of teeth on the floor before Fred here showed him out."

I looked at Fred, the goon standing behind me. There was a tattoo of a woman being raped by a devil on the side of his neck. He looked down at me and I straightened in my chair.

"I'm really sorry, Ada," I said. "I didn't know the protocol."

"I'm not surprised, punk-ass Brentwood girl like you." Ada sniffed at me. "But this fat little meat puppet here should have known the rules. I'm shocked to see you here after you ripped me at Happy Valley."

"You what?" I turned to Sneak, who was reddening around the neck while the fingers that gripped the arms of her chair were turning white.

"I stole a pair of earrings from her on my last day," Sneak said.

"Sneak! You think you could have mentioned that *outside*?" I cried.

"I forgot!"

"*You forgot?*"

"They were really nice earrings," she huffed. "This cute dude I met through the inmate pen pal program was picking me up. I wanted to look nice."

The man behind Sneak stepped forward. I thought he was going to slap her again, until I caught a flash of silver in the dim light. I failed to stifle a yelp of terror as he grabbed Sneak expertly by the ear and sliced off her earlobe in one swift, seamless motion.

"Oh my god! Oh my god!" I tried to rise but Fred pinned me in my seat, his hands on my shoulders like steel.

"You sure look nice now." Ada smiled as Sneak bled. "Red is a good color for you. You should say thank you. I've done you a favor. From now on, it's half-price on earrings for you."

Ada leaned her chin on her fist.

"Mike's ex–Special Forces, Iraq," she told me, watching Mike deposit what he'd cut from Sneak into a chrome trash can by the desk. "He's the one you hear unfolding his toolkit while you sit tied to a chair with a hood on your head."

"Listen." I shifted to the edge of my seat. "I know we shouldn't be here. It was a mistake to come the way we did. I promise you, Ada, we didn't mean any disrespect."

"So tell me what the fuck you're doing here," she said. "And I get bored real easy, so make it interesting."

I told her about Dayly, the robbery at the Pump'n'Jump, the blood in her apartment, and the phone call to Sneak in the middle of the night. I told her about Dayly's boyfriend, and Al Tasik roughing me up. Sneak wasn't making a sound. There was blood running down the side of her neck as she sat rigid in her chair, staring at the floor.

"We need some help," I concluded.

"Why are you in on this?" Ada jutted her chin at me. "Surely this idiot has stolen from you, too. Thieves are the worst kind of people. The sex trade is full of them. When I started up this place here, every third girl I hired was a thief. It took a while to get the message out around town that you don't steal from me. There was so much blood on the floor in those days, I had a rug dealer on speed dial."

"Look, you're right. Sneak has stolen from me," I said. "She steals from everyone. But I looked her daughter in the face and that kid was scared, and I've got a child myself. I want to help."

"You're risking a lot," Ada said. "You're throwing more jail time on the table to help this walking trash bag and her scum-sucking kid. Why?"

"Sneak is my friend. She's always been good to me. And I . . . Well, I'm trying to do something with my life," I said. "I was a good person once. I was happy. I was respected. Now I work at a gas station and my son's afraid of me. I live in a shitty apartment and I can't afford the basics sometimes. I just want to do something good."

It was the first time I had put my reasons into words. It sounded weak, and behind my meaningless utterings my mind unveiled subtext, the words between the words, my real reasons. Being around Sneak and Ada, the two of them together, reminded me of conversations in my dorm with other inmates. Plans for the future. For redemption. We were a trio of people who had experienced the sheer terror and crushing demoralization of prison. Though I was horrified with what Ada had done to my friend, there was a familiarity to being in the presence of these women that was comforting.

Dangerously comforting.

I'd felt it first when Sneak turned up and shoved her way into my apartment. Now it was in full force. I felt at home around these underhanded, dangerous people. My feet were on the floor—steady, safe—for the first time since I had left the prison gates. I knew the rules here. Some of them, anyway. And I was no better or worse than either of these women. I gripped my wooden chair and thought about that. About letting myself be led, step by step, into something criminal and dangerous, and risking the life I had spent a year building, just because I felt safer and more comfortable in prison than I did outside.

"Tell me about this boyfriend," Ada said. "The video."

I went to the desk and put my phone before her. I had the video Sneak had sent to me on the screen. Ada took the phone and leaned back in her chair, put her feet, in black python-skin boots, on the desk. She looked at the screen and recognition came onto her face. She smiled, gave a small, dark laugh.

"Look who it is," she said, beckoning Fred. Fred went and looked at the phone, gave a quarter-smile.

"You know Dayly?" I asked as Fred returned to his station behind me.

"I met this bitch," Ada said, nodding.

"Where? How?"

"Never mind." Ada waved me off. She tapped the phone and watched the video. The whole video. Sneak, Mike, Fred, and I were silent for twelve minutes and fourteen seconds as Dayly and her boyfriend had sex on camera in front of Ada Maverick.

Eventually, Ada put the phone on the desk and I dared to creep forward and take it back.

"I don't like this," Ada said.

Sneak looked up.

"You think this guy posted the video without her knowing?" Ada asked.

"We don't know," I said.

"So you want to go put his head in a toilet, ask him," she concluded.

"That was sort of the plan . . ." I said, looking to Sneak for help. "Maybe not with the use of a toilet. I mean, that wouldn't be our . . . first strategy."

Ada yawned, looked at her goons as if her curiosity had been piqued and had settled again, and she was about to order them to throw us out. I drew a deep breath and counted to three.

"You owe me, Ada," I managed.

Ada stiffened, her gaze locking onto mine.

"Don't pretend you don't know what I'm talking about," I continued, surprised by my own daring. "I saved the life of a member of your family. People know that. They might know that you never paid me back."

"You've got some balls, Neighbor girl," Ada said quietly.

"I know you're curious," I said. "You owe me, and this case makes you curious. You know Dayly and you don't like what's happened to her. I can see it on your face. You're just afraid of doing a nice thing, what people will think of that. You have a reputation to maintain. Well, I can promise you, Sneak and I will never tell any—"

"You think I sit here all day long sweating my perfect ass off about what people think of me?" Ada asked, her voice heavy with menace. "You think I'm that fucking pathetic?"

"No." I struggled with the word, every muscle in my body tensed with terror. "No, Ada."

She fell quiet. I held her gaze, but only just. A minute passed, maybe the longest minute of my life.

I counted the seconds and wondered what piece of me Ada might order her goons to chop off when she finally spoke again.

"I can give you five thousand dollars and a reasonable car," Ada said.

Sneak made a sound, like a shocked exhalation. I felt the dread fall over me like a blanket.

"That's too much." I put a hand up. "We couldn't possibly pay back anything like—"

"We could use some guns," Sneak said.

"No we couldn't," I snapped. "We don't want any guns. We don't even want—"

"Get these assholes out of here." Ada waved at the men behind us. I was dragged out of my chair by my arm, Fred's fingers digging into the tender flesh under my bicep. I tried to call to Ada as we were ushered out, but she ignored me, taking a whiskey glass from her desk drawer and pouring herself a nip.

Fred and Mike shoved us down another dark hall and out the back doors of the club. I lifted the hem of Sneak's shirt and pressed it against her ear, pushed her hand against the wad of fabric so she would hold it and stem the bleeding.

"Why did she do that?" Sneak asked.

"Because she's crazy," I murmured, in case there were cameras with audio around us in the parking lot. "I shouldn't have brought us here. I'm sorry. We'll go back to my place and I'll fix your ear."

"No, I mean why did she agree to help?"

"She likes things to be even. And I challenged her pride," I said. "What was all that about guns?"

"We could use them," she said. "We don't know what we're up against here."

"I'm not hanging around you while you're armed,"

I said. "The only time you're sober is when you have to go to court."

"Should I give this to you, then?" She pulled an enormous black gun out of the waistband at the back of her skirt.

"Jesus! Where did you get that?"

"I lifted it off Mike. I got his wallet, too." She produced the wallet from her cleavage.

"Give me those."

Fred and Mike emerged from the club doors again. I presented Mike with his gun and wallet, and the big man snorted in surprise and anger, patting his coat pockets as though he was sure they were replicas I was offering. Fred put a banded stack of cash in my hands, as thick as a sandwich, and handed Sneak a single car key attached to a key ring with a miniature eight ball on it. He pointed to the back of the lot without taking his small, mean eyes off me.

"In the corner," he said. "The black one."

"Now fuck off," Mike said.

Sneak and I walked numbly to the back of the parking lot. In the furthest corner, parked with its wide rear against a chain-link fence, was a 1988 Chrysler Fifth Avenue, its glossy black paint job lit with red highlights from the neon sign of The Viper Pit. The car had been fitted with huge chrome rims and a hood ornament of a rearing cobra. I opened the car and looked in at the interior, which seemed to be crocodile or caiman leather. Huge black scales rolling over every surface, including the dash and steering wheel. The car screamed drug dealer. Arms dealer. Killer. Thug-for-hire. It screamed Ada Maverick. It was a Gangstermobile.

Sneak opened her mouth and I shook my head before she could speak.

"Just get in," I said.

JESSICA

On Thursday, January 1, 2009, at approximately 2:25 a.m., Blair Gabrielle Harbour left her house at 1109 Tualitan Road in Brentwood through the front door and turned right to walk down the steep driveway. Across the street, at 1108 Tualitan Road, fifty-one-year-old Derek McCoy and his wife, forty-nine-year-old Teresa McCoy, were arriving home in a taxi from a New Year's Eve party organized by Derek's workplace. Derek McCoy spotted Harbour as the sensor light at the bottom of her driveway illuminated her on her path toward the house next door to hers, number 1107. In his witness statement, McCoy described Harbour's walk toward the house next door as "determined." "I wouldn't go so far as to say angry. But she had a long stride and she didn't look happy. I knew she'd been having some troubles over there with noise."

Harbour had indeed been having trouble with the couple at number 1107 and their noise for a period of thirteen months. In that time there had been three complaints made to police from the Harbour residence about music coming from 1107, synthesized dance tracks that had heavy bass and were played after 10 p.m. and before 7 a.m. above the allowed forty-decibel limit set by the Los Angeles Municipal Code. The couple at the residence, Adrian Orlov, the property owner, and his girlfriend, Kristi Zea, had been confronted by LAPD noise enforcement officers in response to each complaint. Harbour had complained to two other witnesses in the street about the music at 1107 within the thirteen-month period. She was pregnant, lived alone, and had described experiencing difficulties sleeping due to the unborn child and the noise activity at the adjacent property.

According to Zea's witness statement, Zea had consumed approximately three to four standard alcoholic beverages throughout the night while Orlov had consumed five to seven standard alcoholic beverages. The two had taken what Zea described as a "small amount" of cocaine. They were dancing on the second floor mezzanine of the property when Harbour opened the front door, which had been unlocked and was in full view of the mezzanine. Zea testified that Harbour shouted for the pair to come downstairs and turn off the music. It was obvious to Zea that Harbour was hostile, due to her aggressive stance and a threat she issued to call the police if the couple did not comply with her demands. In her haste to get downstairs to acquiesce Harbour, Zea lost her footing on the stairs and fell, causing minor injuries to her leg and upper arm. Orlov became agitated that Zea had injured herself in her attempt to appease Harbour and shouted angrily at Harbour. In response, Harbour raised her fist and struck Zea twice in the face. Orlov came down the stairs and the three became engaged in a physical struggle.

On the dining room table in the next room, approximately fifteen feet from where the trio fought, lay Orlov's registered Smith & Wesson 625 revolver, which Orlov had been cleaning that afternoon and had not returned to its case in the upstairs bedroom. According to Zea's statement, Harbour disengaged from the fight in the foyer and ran to the dining room, where she took up the pistol and pointed it at the pair. Zea's statement said of the incident:

> She was crazy. Like, wild, crazy eyes. She told us she hadn't slept in days and started rambling about all this stuff she thought had been done to her, like we'd stolen from her and scratched her car. I thought she might have been high but I wasn't sure. She said she knew we had been poisoning her and, like, trying to drive her insane. I think she thought we were sneaking into her house and putting stuff in her food. She told us to get on our knees. Adrian made a grab for the gun but she cocked the hammer and backed away. We got on our knees saying we were sorry and we wouldn't do it again, you know, with the music. She wouldn't listen.

According to Zea, Harbour shot Orlov in the chest at a distance of approximately five feet. Zea took refuge under the dining room table, and while she hid there, Harbour stood silently over the body of Orlov for an unknown period of time. Harbour then went to the kitchen with the gun and proceeded to wash her hands and the weapon in the kitchen sink. At no time while at the 1107 property did Harbour attempt to call 9–1–1 or instruct Zea to do so. It appeared to Zea that Orlov had died instantly, and though she wanted to render assistance to her boyfriend, she was too afraid of Harbour to come out from cover. Zea, in distress, watched Harbour construct a cheese sandwich from supplies she found in the couple's refrigerator, which she partly consumed before leaving the premises through the front door, closing it behind her.

Jessica scraped the oily red clumps of rice from the bottom of her Poquito Mas takeout container as she browsed the reports on the Harbour/Orlov case that lay on her lap. A crimson sunset loomed overhead, making purple flickers on the surface of the pool. The pool filter at Stan Beauvoir's home hummed gently by her side, her feet and ankles cooling in the water.

It was in sheer, petty defiance that she had returned to the Brentwood property after leaving Goren's house. If she had been even pettier, she'd have taken up residence on the expansive front porch to read the file she'd retrieved from the station that day, so that street crews doing drive-bys would see her. She thought about flipping them the bird as they went. What pissed her off most about the Beauvoir inheritance was the assumption by her LAPD "family" that she would take the reward. It was seven million dollars. She'd never make that kind of money as an LAPD officer, not even if she made it to chief of police and became the most corrupt person to ever hold that seat. From the moment Wally had heard about the inheritance, he'd assumed she would cut him out, make a fool of him for slacking on the Silver Lake case, walk out the front doors of the West Los Angeles office triumphantly, leaving him to wallow, to dream. Now deadbeat patrol cops she didn't even know were checking in on her, trying to catch a moving van in the driveway, Jessica herself visible through the huge windows, instructing decorators. Only Captain Whitton had bothered to ask her directly if she was going to take the reward or refuse it. The crazed drug addict who had attacked her and almost eaten her alive, a man she'd only fallen victim to because of the inheritance, seemed like an afterthought. Everyone assumed she would spend her trauma leave living it up in her new mansion.

Jessica wasn't taking the house. She was sure of it. Yes, it was more money than she'd ever imagined possessing. Yes, she understood Stan Beauvoir's feelings of impotence at his daughter's loss, his desire for something good to have come of what the slain young woman had left behind. But Jessica was a cop. She had been doing her job, not at a level that was "obsessive" or "unhealthy" but to her normal standard. She expected the same kind of commitment from her colleagues. Okay, she'd lost weight and some sleep. She'd become befuddled. She'd pestered witnesses and the victim's family, put in hours she didn't necessarily log as overtime. But how the hell did anyone get anything done without doing that?

Taking an extraordinary gift would mean admitting she'd done an extraordinary thing, and doing whatever it took to solve a goddamn murder wasn't extraordinary. It was required.

She shuffled the papers on the Harbour/Orlov case and tried to focus. She remembered Derek McCoy, the neighbor from across the street, vividly. Jessica had just made detective, and she'd taken too many notes on McCoy's description of Harbour's walk to her neighbor's house, the detective and witness standing on McCoy's porch with red and blue lights flashing on them. In a squad car nearby, Blair Harbour sat with her hands cuffed behind her, staring straight ahead through the windshield, her face passive and her lips pressed together. From the outset, Jessica knew Harbour was a woman who had simply snapped. She'd seen it before. Psychologists at the academy had talked about a parting with reality, a deepening crack that slowly filled with strange ideas, like water seeping into treated wood, eventually rotting the layers underneath until the piece of wood gave way. Jessica had really liked "shrink week" at the academy. She'd paid particular attention to delusions associated with schizophrenia. Persecution and poisoning were common among them. Harbour had likely constructed her own world in which Orlov and Zea sat next door at all hours of the day and night planning her demise, escalating pranks like the unexplained scratch on her BMW and a strange tint to the color of her orange juice all precursors to violence on the horizon.

Jessica took a photograph of Orlov's body from the file and held it in the falling red light. Zea had been right about her boyfriend's death. It had been painful, but almost instant. The man was slumped on his side, one arm folded over the wound, his mouth open in shock against the marble floor. A tendril of blood curled from his lip. Jessica flipped to the picture of the wet gun by the kitchen sink, a forensic photo of Blair that had been leaked to the newspaper the next morning, her hands spread open for examination, the beginnings of a pregnant belly pressing against the chain between her wrists. A photograph started to slide out of the pack and Jessica caught it before it could get completely free. The infamous cheese sandwich sitting on the cluttered kitchen counter in the Orlov house, one bite taken from the corner.

Jessica realized only when pain zinged through her finger that she'd chewed too hard at a hangnail. She shook herself. There was a tension running through her, a wire so taut it was ticking, and she knew exactly what it was. She'd begun questioning the case against Blair Harbour. *Her* case against Blair Harbour. It was undeniable now—Jessica liked the kid next door. He was smart, funny, weird. And if Jessica was wrong about Blair being a killer all those years ago, Jessica had kept the kid's mother from him for his entire life. If she'd overlooked even the slightest detail, she'd have put an innocent woman in prison.

All this, she told herself, was just her tired, fractured mind picking at seams, trying to unravel herself faster than the drugged zombie attack and the surprise inheritance were already doing. She did this when she was down. Kicked herself. She reminded herself that this time, she was right. That she'd done nothing to warrant the abuse she was getting from her colleagues, Wallert and Vizchen abandoning her at the scene in Lonscote Place. She was a good cop, and deserved her title as detective. If she was right now, she knew she was right then, when she arrested Blair Harbour for murder. She would have checked all the boxes. Made sure she was covering all bases. She was that kind of officer. Thorough. Sure.

"What's that?"

Jessica turned and looked. The boy was at the gate again, a blue silhouette behind and to the right of her, beyond the glass wall bordering the pool. She found herself smiling, and wondered if it was in pity at the boy's fate or amusement at his stealth and unapologetic nosiness. Jessica had known a few cops in her time who had been inspired to enter the force because of murders in their family history. The child might have a bright future in blue ahead.

"Work," she said.

"What kind of work?"

"None of your business, kid."

"Have you decided if I can help you with the gardening yet?" the boy called. "Or do you still need more time to think about it?"

Jessica packed the file back into its binder and laid it upside down beside her with a sigh.

"Get over here."

She watched the water and listened as the boy vaulted the six-foot-high wooden gate, rattling the latch he'd decided to simply ignore, rustling the vines that almost blocked the view between the two properties. He landed on the grass with a dramatic grunt of effort and appeared at the poolside, hanging his wrists over the glass fence, almost casually but not quite.

"Are you a cop?" he asked.

"What would make you say a thing like that?" Jessica frowned, shifting the file to the other side of her. "Get in here, for god's sake. I'm not having this conversation across the yard."

"I'm not allowed in there."

"Why the hell not?"

"Because I can't swim."

Jessica stared at Jamie. He stared back.

"You know you're in California, right?" she asked. She regretted it instantly. The boy looked away in feigned aloofness, gave a weak shrug.

"My mom doesn't like the beach. She hates sand. And we don't have a pool."

Jessica stood and went to the glass.

"Come here. If you fall in, I'll only let you flounder around for a little while before I pull you out," she said, lifting the safety latch. The boy skirted the glass fence to the pool stairs, stood four feet back from the edge. Jessica put her feet back in the water and sat with her thigh pinning the file on the child's mother shut. "Why do you think I'm a cop?"

"I saw you today outside the police station."

"Oh, great." Jessica nodded. "That's just great." She reached out a hand. "I'm Jessica. Nice to meet you."

The boy shook her hand. When he did she dragged him toward the pool edge and forced him down beside her. He grabbed a handful of the waist of her shirt, then put his bare feet nervously in the water.

"I've got to talk to you about something important."

"Okay." Jamie huddled in, letting go of her shirt with effort. "Sure."

"You've probably heard adults say it's bad to keep secrets from your parents, right? If anyone ever asks you to keep a secret, it's bad news, and you should tell them right away."

"Yeah," Jamie said. "They taught us that at school."

"Well, I actually am a cop. So it's . . . um. It's okay in *this* case to keep a secret. But this is the one and only time, okay? These are what you call special circumstances."

"Special circumstances." The boy nodded again, wiggling his toes in the water. "Got it."

"You ever talk to your mother?" Jessica watched the boy's face carefully. "The one you were telling me about the other night? Who had the accident?"

"Sure, all the time." He shrugged. "We have ice cream."

"What do you mean, you have ice cream? At the prison?"

"No, at the pier."

"She's out?" Jessica turned her body and the Harbour/Orlov file almost slid into the pool.

"Yeah. She got out of prison like a year ago."

"Oh, this just keeps getting better and better." Jessica massaged her brow. "Look, it's really important, under the circumstances—the *special circumstances*—that you don't tell your mom that I live here."

"My mom or my mother?"

"Blair."

"Oh." Jamie pursed his lips.

"I mean, I don't actually live here . . ." Jessica

glanced toward the house. "I just hang around here sometimes. And I'm going to stop doing that. But you can't tell her about me at all. Not my name, not that I'm a cop, not what I look like. Nothing. All right?"

The boy was silent.

"You haven't told her already, have you?"

"Nope." He looked away. "How come I can't, anyway?"

"It would just be easier all round, for everyone."

"Why?"

"It just would."

"But why?"

"Boy, you don't need to know everything that's going on in the world," Jessica said. "I know you think you do, but you really don't. It's a life lesson I'm giving you here. Sometimes the Earth just turns a little more smoothly on its axis when a person shuts up and does what he's told."

"Okay." The boy tested the water with his fingers. "I won't tell, then."

"Good kid."

"So are those papers police papers?" he asked, leaning over. "With, like, scary photos of dead bodies and guns and stuff?"

"Sure are."

"Can I see them?"

"I could show you," Jessica said. "But then I'd have to drown you."

BLAIR

I fixed Sneak's ear at my apartment, telling the crew of kids who came to the door to play me a group rendition of Ed Sheeran's "Castle on the Hill" that the blood on my shirt was tomato juice. When I'd showered and changed for my evening shift at the Pump'n'Jump I'd expected her to be making moves to leave, but instead she was standing by the front windows, talking on her phone and chewing her nails.

"I'll be here for a few days at least," she said, and gave my address.

"Who was that?" I asked when she hung up.

"Girl who takes my mail."

"Did you just tell her you'd be staying here for a few days?"

"Don't freak out. I need a home base," Sneak said. "I haven't had a fixed address lately."

"What does that mean, exactly? Are you homeless? Where's all your stuff?"

"I was living with a dude, kind of casual. We had an arrangement. All my stuff's there," she explained. "It was going great, but I think he got possessed by a demon, so I scrammed."

"Sneak, honestly."

"He was totally normal, and then he went out one night and got a tattoo of a weird symbol on his chest." She sniffed, rubbed her nose. "Couple of days later I find him naked in the kitchen at midnight. He was, like, wriggling around on the floor, clawing at the tattoo and groaning. He started shouting, 'You can't take him! He's mine! He's mine!' If that's not demonic possession, you tell me what it is."

"A drug-induced hallucination."

"You weren't there." She waved me off. "I know a demon when I see one."

"Sneak, you can't stay here." I went to the window and drew the curtain. "If you're found in my place—"

"I won't be," she insisted. "Come on, Neighbor. You're in this far."

She was right. I was in dangerous waters up to my waist. Walking in further, letting the water rise to my neck, seemed like a small compromise. I knew the moment I left her there unattended she was going to ransack my possessions for anything valuable, and once she'd secured her stash she was probably going to pop some pills or snort some cocaine off my coffee table. But I was tired and anxious about Jamie, and the fight seemed more than I had the strength for. I went into the bedroom and packed the silver-framed picture of my son into my work bag, and hid Ada's money in a shoe inside a box at the top of my wardrobe.

I went to the freezer to get a scoop of ice cream, a small treat before my venture into the night. The plastic tub–style ice cream container was on the counter. I sighed and picked it up, thinking Sneak must have got into it while I changed. It was too light, almost empty. I noticed the holes punched in the top of the lid at the same time I felt the shuffling movement of something alive inside it.

"Oh, Jesus!" I dropped the container on the counter.

"Damn," Sneak said as she came into the kitchen. "I should have warned you. Sorry."

"Is that the goddamn gopher?"

"It is."

"What the hell is it doing here?"

"I brought it from Dayly's." Sneak peeled the lid carefully from the ice cream container.

"How?"

"In my handbag."

"That thing has been in your handbag all this time? What the hell is wrong with you?"

"I'm a nice person," she said. "The cops will have looked at Dayly's apartment by now. You think they're going to feed and care for this thing during their investigation? You think Dayly's housemate will? I know how she was about the pigeon Dayly rescued. She threw a fucking fit."

"Having you here is bad enough, Sneak. You can't have that thing here, too."

"Well, it's here."

"Get rid of it."

"Just hold it, Neighbor." She scooped the creature out of the box. "You'll see it's just—"

"No, Sneak! No, I don't want—"

"Just hold it, for fuck's sake! It doesn't bite!"

Sneak snatched my hand and held it flat. I winced as I felt the warm, furry weight fall into my palm.

"Oh god. Oh god. Oh god."

"Look at you. You're pathetic. How could you be afraid of something so small and cute? This thing is straight out of a goddamn Disney film. Open your eyes."

I looked at the creature in my palm. Its pink nose was snuffling at the base of my thumb. A splinter of terror shot through me at the sight of the bucked yellow teeth pressed against the tiny, furry chin. I had one eye open, my face scrunched and arm trembling.

"It's going to bite me."

"No, it's not."

"Do you know how they test a human for rabies? They have to drill into your skull and take a brain sample."

"It doesn't have rabies." Sneak rolled her eyes. "Pat it."

"I'm not going to pat it."

"Pat it or I will slap you down right here in your own kitchen, bitch."

I brought the little creature closer to me. With the index finger of my free hand I tentatively stroked its oversized head. The thing seemed to enjoy the attention. It rose up on its hind legs, and Sneak and I watched while it scratched at the white fur of its belly like a fat old man waking, yawning. I stroked its tiny pink tail, rolled my finger over its back.

"It's very soft," I conceded.

Sneak was smiling.

"Now take it away, please," I said.

"Just hold it another second."

The gopher turned and started walking up my wrist, its little pink paws padding over my forearm, fast, toward my elbow.

"Grab it, Sneak! Oh god! Oh god! Grab it!"

Sneak plucked the animal from my arm. I watched her return it to the ice cream tub and secure the lid. I had no words for her. I gave her a withering look and went to get my work bag.

There's a comfort in work. In blessed, mindless routines. Wiping sugar granules from the countertop of the coffee station, slipping bottles of Mountain Dew into the fridge in neat rows, checking off the bathroom cleaning roster. I watched cars move in and out of the lot in waves; cab drivers stocking up on water and aspirin for the long shift ahead, frat boys in juiced-up cars grabbing Red Bulls before heading out for a night on the town, film agents paying for gas for their Maseratis without breaking the conversation on their Bluetooth earpieces. In the quieter moments after the red and violet sunset I did the crossword in the newspaper behind the counter.

A no-show: *Absent*.

I thought about Jamie, how many events in his short life I'd been a no-show for. Birthday parties. School awards ceremonies. Baseball games.

My phone rang, a welcome reprieve from the dark thoughts.

"I'm sending Fred around there," Ada said, without any sort of greeting. "Don't run when you see him. I haven't told him to whack you. Yet."

"What?" I shook my head, bewildered. "You're sending him where? Here?"

"That cholo hangout where you peddle Twinkies."

A cold chill ran through me. I looked out at the street, the last whispers of white sky being slowly crushed by night. I didn't like Ada knowing where I worked, didn't want to think about how she'd acquired the information. "What are you sending him here for?"

"I'm giving you a gun. Sneak was right. You might need one. But I wasn't going to give it to you with that walking train wreck around. She'll take it and sell it, or she'll pop you with it while she's high. She's dumb as shit, Sneak. Her mama was a hill person. You can tell. One of those types that has a baby and lets the cow feed it from its udders in the barn while she goes about making the next one. She's probably lifted most of the cash I gave you already, am I right?"

"No, I hid it pretty well."

"You might think so. I bet you're wrong."

"Ada, I don't want a gun," I said. "Please don't send one. I get caught with it and I'm going back to prison, guaranteed. If I'm found in Sneak's company, maybe I can argue my case. But they'll throw away the key if there's a weapon discovered at my place."

"But I thought you liked guns, Neighbor girl." I could hear the smile in her voice. "You certainly seem to be a natural with them."

"How do you know Dayly Lawlor?" I asked.

"Never mind how I know her."

"Come on." I leaned on the counter. "Help me understand why you're doing this for us. You laughed when you saw her picture on my phone. Was she one of your dancers at some point?"

There was silence, then a small, sinister laugh, and I heard Ada sigh as if she was giving in.

"I was sitting on Ventura trying to get to a meeting with an associate of mine," she said. "This was maybe six months ago. Traffic was backed up. I mean, it was at a standstill. I'm sitting in the back of my Lincoln—I got Fred driving—and I'm looking out. We're stuck under this freeway overpass and there are these pigeon nests all clustered up under the concrete ledge. Dozens of them. Shit dripping everywhere. Feathers. Really nasty, nasty business."

"Okay," I said.

"While I'm sitting there, a girl gets out of a cab in front of us," Ada said. "Pops the back door and walks over to where the wall is all filthy with pigeon crap. She takes her hoodie off—her own damn hoodie, that she's wearing—and she starts chasing around this goddamn pigeon that's minding its own business there on the ground. I mean, holy shit. I'd never seen anything like it. She's trying to catch this disgusting little bird and it's squeaking and flapping. Nobody else could believe it, either. We were sort of a *captive audience*, I guess you'd say—all the other people in the cars. Dudes start honking their horns, yelling, hollering."

"Did she get the bird?" I smiled, seeing where this was going.

"Yeah," Ada laughed. "She got it all right. Snatched it up like, uh, like a crocodile you see on the nature channel grabbing a bird off the side of a lake. She'd done it before, you could tell. I was so curious I rolled down my window. I said, 'Hey bitch! What the fuck you think you're doing? You going to eat that thing?' I mean, I couldn't understand it—woman has got enough money for a cab but she's taking a skyrat home for dinner. So she comes over to the window of my car to show me the damned bird all wrapped up in her hoodie like a newborn baby."

I laughed.

"She says it's a juvenile," Ada said. "Baby pigeon fallen from the nest. It's been blown around by cars going by. It's bleeding, hungry, dehydrated. She shows me how you can tell it's a baby from the feathers and the beak and all that. This bitch is giving me a nature-channel lecture right there on the side of the road. She says if she leaves the bird there it'll starve to death or get hit by a car, or a hawk will come down from where they sit up on the light poles along the freeway and eat it. Turns out pigeons are terrible parents. They won't go down and help it."

I listened, watching the night.

"I tried to tell this girl," Ada said. "'Honey, that's what happens in life. Birds fall from nests and get eaten alive or run over or whatever the fuck. They suffer and they starve. That's life.' And you know what she says? She says, 'Not this one. Not on my watch.'"

I heard two clunking sounds, imagined Ada putting her boots up on the desk in her office.

She continued. "So, anyway, she turns away and tries to get back in the cab she came out of. Well, the cab driver is having none of it. He's yelling about lice and disease and infection. So I called the girl and I told her to get in my car, and me and Fred gave her a ride to Sunset."

"That's hilarious," I said. "You had that bird in your car?"

"Oh, I had the car taken away and crushed right after," Ada said. "Shame. I liked that car. But I ain't riding around in something that's had some sick fucking vermin bird in it. I had Mike burn all the clothes I was wearing at the time, and Fred's too."

"Why did you do that?" I asked.

"I got body lice in juvie once. Fat girl like Sneak brought it in. Everybody got it. It was hell."

"No, I mean why did you give Dayly a ride?"

"I don't know." She sniffed. "Crazy ho amused me, I guess."

"I think it's more than that."

"Excuse me?"

"I think you recognized the fact that if someone had said 'Not on my watch' about you when you were a baby bird, then maybe your life would have been different," I said.

There was silence.

"Are you kidding me?" Ada said eventually.

"What? You think I'm wrong?"

"I know you're wrong," she said. "I'm not some scabby fucking highway pigeon who needs rescuing. I'm one of the hawks. I'm a bird of prey, bitch."

I felt the smile drift from my face.

"You tell anyone that story or your bullshit back-yard psychoanalysis of it and I'll cut you," she said.

"I won't," I answered, but she had already hung up on me.

Dear Dayly,

You're right, I do get a lot of letters from crackpots and weirdos, but "Are you my daddy?" is a subject that had not, until your letter, appeared among their writings. Regardless of the answer, your letter was a breath of fresh air in what is for the most part a monotonous stream of public grumblings and pleadings. Most people write to tell me how awful my crimes were, particularly the Inglewood massacre, in case the idea hadn't occurred to me. Rarely if ever are these letters from actual victims of the crime; mostly grief tourists wanting to vent their supposed pain. Much of what I've received lately has been people writing to see if the $3 million you mentioned was mine, or if indeed there are other caches of my stolen money buried across the state. The find has tripled my mail intake.

It's true, your mother Emily Lawlor and I had a brief thing around 2000. She was a bit of a young punk. Smart-ass, but sweet about it. People called her "Sneak" back then because she was real light-fingered, but she mainly stole to support what I thought was a rather minor drug habit. I'm sorry to hear she is an addict now. I'm not surprised you have "mixed feelings" about her. It's a hard life, having been given up. My mother was a prostitute, and I was raised by my grandparents in Utah. Most people don't bother looking into my history to try to figure out why I did what I did, but that was a big reason; the abuse and neglect I suffered at the hands of my grandparents and the feeling of abandonment when my mother dropped me on their doorstep at age six and drove away forever. You might be interested to know that I've been seen by plenty of psychologists over the years, and have been tested to have an IQ of 142. There have been no findings to support a brain malfunction or tumor or psychological condition to account for me killing all those innocent people that day in Inglewood. I'm just a broken man who was pushed too far.

So, yes, it's possible you may have some claim to my DNA. Whether or not you want to confirm that is something you should probably think hard about.

I've never had contact with Sneak in here, and I'm surprised by that, now that you say she's an addict. There are a lot of former and current addicts in here, and all they ever want to ask me about is the money. I hit a lot of banks over a long stretch of time. The theory is that if I was stockpiling money from all my different jobs, surely it would be stupid to put it all in one place. But even if there was, say, another large cache of money hidden in Los Angeles or its surrounds somewhere, none of these guys would be able to spend a fraction of it in here. There's only so much commissary you can eat, and they'd be relying on someone on the outside to take care of the rest of it for them without running off. A lot of times these guys just want to know the answer to a question. Questions and secrets can eat away at you in prison, with us all sitting in our cells twenty-three hours a day with nothing to do.

Most guys on the row are indigent, meaning they live off what the state provides for them in postage, commissary, and phone call allowances. Some of the more notorious inmates, serial killers for example, smuggle out pieces of themselves to a broker to sell online. My neighbor on the left gets about $50 on the internet for a lock of his hair. He's got about six rape/murders under his belt. I have a broker who sells my letters for a lot more than that. People are convinced that one of these days I'm going to drop a hint about more hidden cash, disguised somehow in a letter. They think perhaps I'll write a message in the first letter of every line, or gradually leak numbers that translate into longitude and latitude. I've heard you can leave invisible messages in paper with lemon juice. But I'm not that stupid. The first person to notice something like that hidden in a letter would be a guard. They read, scan, and chemically test our mail, and there's no way I'd risk one of those bastards getting any of my money. If I wanted to give some secret information to someone, it would have to be in person.

This is all hypothetical, of course, based on the public presumption that there's more of my money out there. I stole a lot more than I ever spent or gave away, including what was found. But you know how ignorant the public are. They'll latch on to an idea just because it's exciting and romantic.

I hope you write back, but, like I said, think about whether or not you really want to know the truth of your parentage. I can tell you, some parents aren't worth knowing. And think about selling this letter on the internet. A smart cookie like you should be able to figure out where. Some places, you can get up to $500 for them. At least, that's what my broker tells me, but there's no way for me to know if he's holding back.

Take care,
John Fishwick

P.S. Why anyone would rescue a gopher or a pigeon is totally beyond me, but your photo is cute. You've got my eyes. Tell Sneak I say hello, next time you talk to her.

JESSICA

Jessica sat at her desk in the Homicide department, ignoring the eyes on her, scrolling through the six-hour initial interrogation of Blair Harbour over the Adrian Orlov shooting. She had not seen Wallert or Vizchen on her way into the building, but her shoulders ached with tension at the inevitability of their arrival, a feeling that mingled with the dread of someone pointing out that she should be nowhere near the station on account of her trauma leave. On the screen, Blair Harbour seemed shrunken in her chair, the forensic body suit ballooning around her, a smear of blood still in her hair. Jessica had always liked to do that, to get the first interview with the perp as soon as possible after the crime, make it as long as she could. Adrenaline from the crime makes them chatty, and the ensuing exhaustion makes them stupid. She liked to make the perp stare at the blood and dirt under their nails and try to explain it all away. Jessica was leaning forward in her chair in the video, while her partner at the time, Nandermann, stuck to the corner, a silent sentinel. Jessica pressed the right side of the headphones closer to her ear, watched the blurry image of Harbour's face as she spoke.

HARBOUR: I had nothing against them. They seemed nice enough. It was just the noise that bothered me. Aside from speaking to them about the noise I really didn't know them terribly well.

SANCHEZ: So the only interactions you ever had with Orlov and Zea were negative ones. You complaining about the noise, they defending themselves. You were in that pattern already.

HARBOUR: Yes. I guess so. But look, you don't shoot someone because they're being noisy.

SANCHEZ: Well, most people don't.

HARBOUR: I shot Adrian because it was him or her. He was on top of her when I walked in and he'd already hit her once and that big fist was coming down again and again and I thought *He's going to kill her* and I tried to get in there and—

SANCHEZ: To get in there?

HARBOUR: To pull him away. I fought with him a little but he just threw me off like I was nothing. He was in a rage.

SANCHEZ: Uh-huh.

HARBOUR: And then I saw the gun and I just . . . You know. I just—

SANCHEZ: What you're saying doesn't make much sense, Dr. Harbour, if I'm being honest. You say you intervened in a domestic argument between these people who you barely knew, a violent domestic argument that you just happened to walk in on. That's not what Zea is saying.

HARBOUR: What?

SANCHEZ: She's saying you shot Adrian over the noise.

HARBOUR: No, she isn't.

SANCHEZ: Yes, she is. She says you had it out for them. That the relationship was dire. That you walked in, confronted them about the noise, shot Adrian, and went into the kitchen to wash the gun and make yourself a snack. If what you're saying is true, Harbour, and you just popped around to number 1107 to say hello and found yourself compelled to save Zea's life, why the hell would she cook up this elaborate tale about you shooting her boyfriend over a noise complaint?

HARBOUR: I don't know. I have no idea whatsoever why she would say that. I didn't pop around about the noise. I looked out my kitchen window and saw them through their bathroom window. I saw him hit her.

SANCHEZ: And you just charged over there like Wonder Woman to help the girl out.

HARBOUR: You're not listening.

Jessica sat back in her seat, looked at the aisles of cops around her. On the screen ten years earlier, and now, she was silent, thoughtful. Harbour's words rang in her ears, and she winced now. The doctor was right. She wasn't listening. She'd listened to the victim, Zea, already, and that seemed like enough. She watched herself in the interview and knew exactly what she was doing—pushing. Squeezing. Trying to massage a confession out of Harbour.

SANCHEZ: Zea says you snapped. That you were completely out of it. Talking crazy.

HARBOUR: Not . . . Not at that moment. Afterward, maybe, after I'd shot him. I was stunned and shocked but I wasn't crazy. I had my wits about me. I was trying to think of what to do. I've never killed anyone before and I was horrified and for a few minutes I . . . I couldn't think straight. But I'm not crazy. I've never been crazy. Can I talk to her?

SANCHEZ: No.

HARBOUR: But—

SANCHEZ: Why did you wash your hands and the gun?

HARBOUR: That was . . . I've been trying to figure that out. I think I'm just so used to doing it as a part of my job that it happened as a sort of reflex. Whenever I do anything at work I wash my hands. Before and after. I must wash my hands fifty times a day. I didn't wash the gun, I dropped it in the sink. That's what I do with my instruments. It must have got wet.

SANCHEZ: Bullshit.

HARBOUR: It's not bullshit.

SANCHEZ: Making yourself a snack in the kitchen is crazy, Dr. Harbour. Don't you think?

HARBOUR: I didn't do that.

SANCHEZ: Why the hell would Zea tell us you made a goddamn sandwich if you didn't?

HARBOUR: I have no earthly idea. I don't know why she's saying any of this. It's possible she has a brain injury from being hit. If I could just speak to her for—

SANCHEZ: Why didn't you administer first aid to Orlov after you shot him?

HARBOUR: Well, because he was dead. He was *clearly* dead. He died instantly. I shot him right through the heart.

SANCHEZ: Your statement is that you did absolutely nothing to try to bring him back. Am I understanding you correctly?

HARBOUR: There was no bringing him back.

SANCHEZ: Are you laughing, Dr. Harbour?

HARBOUR: I'm . . . I'm laughing at the absurdity of it. Of—what—doing chest compressions? On a heart with a giant bullet hole in it? He bled out in . . . in seconds. I'm not laughing at . . . It's . . . Oh, god. This doesn't feel real.

SANCHEZ: Can you answer the question? You did nothing to assist Orlov after you shot him?

HARBOUR: I feel like I'm on another planet right now.

SANCHEZ: You feel out of touch with reality?

HARBOUR: No, I mean I don't know how to make you understand. He was going to kill her. I couldn't let him kill her. You don't just let a person die in front of you.

SANCHEZ: Well, most people don't.

Harbour's story had originally been that she had gone to 1107 Tualitan Road, the house next door to hers, after seeing Orlov strike Zea through the couple's bathroom window. On arrival, she said, she had found Orlov beating his girlfriend savagely and, after making unsuccessful attempts to separate the two, had grabbed the gun from the dining room table in desperation and shot the man dead to protect Zea. The story explained the injuries to Zea, Orlov, and Harbour, but it didn't explain why Zea wouldn't back up Harbour's version, why a young woman would tell the kind of lie that sent a woman to prison, presumably to protect the honor of her dead boyfriend, or as revenge for all the noise complaints. For Jessica, the story didn't explain Harbour's bizarre movements after the shooting, why she'd washed her hands and the gun in Orlov's kitchen sink, why she'd made a cheese sandwich and taken a single bite, then wandered out the front of the house without dialing 9-1-1. By the time Harbour employed her first lawyer, her account had changed, become simpler under the guidance of a legal professional. She had indeed charged over to the Orlov household to confront the couple about the music, and Orlov had grabbed his gun in a rage and pointed it at Harbour. In a vicious struggle for the gun, which included Zea, the weapon somehow got turned around, went off, struck Orlov in the chest. That explanation didn't wash with Sanchez and Nandermann either. Ballistics had shown Orlov was hit from a distance of five feet, and Harbour's bizarre behavior after the crime didn't indicate an accidental shooting.

Harbour had been psychologically assessed by specialists from both the prosecution and defense. She was perfectly sane, and showed no signs of a hidden, lingering mental illness that might have peaked during the altercation. There were no signs of perinatal depression or mania that the defense could lean on.

Jessica paused the video and sat back in her chair, looking at the image of Harbour. She wondered again what she was doing, why the Harbour case was drawing her back in. It was open and shut. Neighbor snaps, kills neighbor. Just because Harbour had a cute kid, Jessica reminded herself, that didn't mean she wasn't a stone-cold psychopath. Plenty of vicious serial killers had normal, well-adjusted kids. Jessica saw a write-up about one every now and then in the *Times*: *My Mom, the South-Side Baby Killer*. She closed the Harbour video and was about to rise when a hand fell on her shoulder.

"You're not supposed to be here," a voice said.

Jessica winced, but it wasn't Wallert or Vizchen standing over her. It was a man in his sixties whom Jessica hadn't personally encountered in her brushes with IAG, but nevertheless knew well. Detective Cheng Woo slid a buttock of his gray trousers onto Jessica's desk, forcing her to retreat backward in her chair, bumping into the divider between her desk and the next. Already she could feel the eyes of her colleagues on her again, people glancing around computer monitors or taking conspicuously brief trips to the coffee area to see what was happening over the cubicle wall.

"Detective Woo." Jessica nodded in greeting. "I was just checking on some open cases, making sure they've been taken up in my absence."

"Everything's fine, Sanchez. You'll find all your cases have been reassigned. Running like clockwork without you, as difficult as you might find that to believe."

A snicker from nearby. Jessica didn't bite.

"In fact, I've already begun seeing to the two internal investigations that feature your name," Woo said. He was talking loudly enough for a group of people at the end of the row of desks to hear.

"Two investigations?" Jessica said.

"The officer-involved shooting and the Brentwood inheritance."

"Ah," Jessica said. "You guys over there in IAG are so quick, I thought you'd have figured out by now that the two are related."

"It's a very curious set of circumstances, the Lonscote Place shooting in particular," Woo said. He eased more of his bulk onto Jessica's desk, nudging aside pencils and papers. "I can't really get my head around it. To me it seems that either two diligent, capable, and committed officers like Wallert and Vizchen failed to back up a fellow officer in life-threatening circumstances—"

"I'm sorry, did you say 'capable'?" Jessica asked.

"—or you, a decorated officer with some regrettable disciplinary marks against your name, someone who had only just learned of a life-altering change of fortune, stormed off on your own to try to play the hero cop."

There it was again. *Hero cop.* Vizchen had said it the night of the shooting. Jessica bit her tongue.

"So which is it?" Woo held out his hands.

"I think it's completely inappropriate for me to comment here," Jessica said.

"Why?" Woo looked around. "We're just talking informally. I'm not wearing a wire." He laughed. "Our interview is scheduled for next week."

"You're trying to get me to—"

"From some initial reports I have seen, there's a suggestion that Wallert might have been under the influence of alcohol," Woo said. "His judgment might have been impaired, and it might have caused him to fail to follow you on your pursuit of the suspect. Is that true, Sanchez? Was your partner drinking that night?"

Jessica's hands formed fists in her lap. The knuckles cracked. No one was doing much to disguise their interest now. A group of officers had moved in from the coffee area and were standing, cups out from their hips like guns, in the middle of the aisle, only feet away, waiting to see if she would betray her partner to IAG. If she would betray them all.

"I'm not . . ." Jessica took a deep breath. "I'm not talking about it here."

"And then there's the house, of course," Woo said. "We need to talk about that when we meet. You said just now it was connected to the shooting. In what way was it connected? I'm so curious about all this. Was your judgment compromised by the news, perhaps? Were you so filled with confidence from receiving such a substantial reward for your services that you—"

"I said I'm not talking about this here." Jessica rose from her seat so fast that Woo shot backward, almost falling off the desk. The two stood in the tiny cubicle, chest to chest, everyone watching them. Jessica locked eyes with her adversary. "So hold on to your fucking curiosities for the interview room."

Woo smiled and raised his hands in surrender as Jessica slid past him into the aisle and walked stiffly to the bathroom.

Jessica kicked over the trash can in the women's room, relishing in the huge clanging sound it made, a noise that rippled off the tiled walls. The bathroom had been the wrong choice. Women went to the bathroom after an argument to cry. She did not cry, but instead grabbed handfuls of paper towels from the dispenser and wadded them into a dense ball, pressed the ball against her mouth, and screamed. The scream came out as a gruff howl, but it felt good. Jessica went to the sinks and washed her face. Her whole body trembled with fury. Panting, she looked at herself in the mirror and noticed blood spots peeping through the fabric of her white T-shirt from the big bite on her left shoulder.

"Goddamn it," she whispered, lifting her shirt.

She was standing in her bra, peeling away the bandage tape carefully when Oliver Digbert walked in. Digbert always used the female bathrooms on the third floor, because the forensic pathologist had determined them to be the cleanest in the building.

"Diggy," Jessica grunted. The last thing she felt like doing was talking, but the plump, freckled pathologist had come through for her on a rape case years earlier that meant she had been able to snatch an innocent suspect out of the clutches of a life-in-prison term a day before the jury went out on his trial. Digbert liked pleasantries, and she watched him smile in the mirror as he headed to the stalls. His shirt was a shade of fluorescent pink with tiny black teapots patterned all over it like polka dots.

"Someone's having a rough day," he said as he closed the door behind him. The toilet seat creaked as he sat down. Jessica listened to him pee as she examined the red and blue mess that was her shoulder, guessed peeing sitting down was cleaner and more efficient, which was very like Diggy. When he emerged to wash his chubby hands, the pathologist hit the soap dispenser five times. "I heard about the inheritance. I presume your distress is due to Whitton giving you a hard time because you told him you'll take it."

"You think I should take it?" Jessica smirked. She could feel her pulse slowing. "You'd be the only one in the building."

"It would be the only sensible economic decision," Diggy said, frowning as he scrubbed the webbing between his fingers. "The property value is considerably above anything you'll ever make in your current role, even projecting out to consider future pension and long-service compensation versus property fluctuations and—"

"I get it." Jessica patted his shoulder. "It's not that. It's the betrayal. Turning my back on the team. On the job."

"I don't understand." Diggy dried his hands. "Your job is solving crimes. With that kind of money, you could open your own private detective agency. Employ a slew of top-notch investigators. Delegate your cases based on your interests, and not on the woeful backlog-versus-urgency system. Your considerable monetary advantage would provide you with plenty of opportunity to test forensic material privately and in a timely fashion."

Jessica leaned in to the mirror to look at the bite

wound and dabbed at the wet spot with a paper towel. Diggy nudged his glasses back onto his nose.

"I heard about the house, but not the assault," he said.

"Yeah, zombie got me," Jessica said. "You don't watch the news? It made the top stories."

"Modern current affairs journalism is a diabolical slurry of political corruption and the flimsy whims of narcissistic millennials," he said.

"Flimsy Whims," Jessica said. "That's your porn star name."

"Who was the guy?" Diggy asked, looking at the wound in the mirror.

"How do you know it was a guy?" Jessica turned to him.

"Well, a layman might have guessed a female aggressor," Diggy said. "Statistically, women are more likely to bite in a fight. But, luckily, this observer was raised from a young scientific larva to gifted specialist by Dr. Richard Rhodes of the Virginia Commonwealth University."

"Gifted, huh?" Jessica smiled.

"Dr. Rhodes's research focused on determining gender and ethnicity through odontometric analysis of the maxillary arch and maxillary and mandibular teeth. He used mesiodistal, labiolingual, buccolingual, and distobuccal measurements to determine the characteristics of biters in a range of medico-legal case studies. I tended his lab and basked in his unquestionable greatness," Diggy said.

"So you're saying you can look at this and tell me it's a male bite mark?" Jessica pointed to the wound on her shoulder.

"Within a certain range of probability." Diggy leaned over, studied the bite mark. Jessica noted he had not glanced at her chest even once. "Remember,"

Diggy said, "I was the apprentice, not the master. But what I believe I'm looking at is a bite from a male of Caucasoid ethnic heritage. Am I correct?"

Jessica stared at the man in the bathroom with her. She folded the bandage back down over her wound and pressed the tape tight against her shoulder.

"Come with me," she said. She grabbed her shirt from the edge of the sink and threw it on. "I want to show you a photo of a sandwich."

Dear John,

Thanks for writing back. Crazy stuff. Especially about the guy selling his hair. What you'd even do with a serial killer's hair once you got it is a pretty creepy prospect. I did what you said—I looked online and toured through the "murderabilia" sites. A lot of Charles Manson stuff is going for a mint because he's dead. The guy sure did a lot of crappy artwork. Gacy, too. You were right, there are a couple of your letters going for upward of $500. The seller says "strong suspicions of clues to hidden cash" for each. Everybody's got to have their side hustle, I guess. I might sell the letters. I could use the money.

At first when I read what you wrote about how having a terrible childhood and being abandoned had an effect on your decision to kill, I thought—that's bullshit. There was a seven-year-old kid in that bank. I put the letter down and walked away. But I guess now I'm thinking more about it. I haven't come to a decision, but I'm thinking. It's because who I am as a person is so tied up in where I've come from, what Sneak did to me. I don't want to get too heavy with you, but from the moment you learn you were abandoned there's a kind of break inside you. Like you become disconnected from everyone else, everyone who grew up loved and wanted.

Everyone who wasn't a mistake, an accident, something that was not meant to be. Sometimes I wonder if I'm a black hole. A vacuum in space. I'm the plus-one, on the waiting list for my shot at belonging in the world. Maybe that's why I never feel satisfied or settled.

If I wasn't meant to be here, then a weird twist of fate happened when I was born, you know what I mean? A rule was broken. And so why in the hell do I spend so much time and effort and heartache trying to be something or someone when I'm no one and nothing? I don't feel like I count. Don't get me wrong—I had great foster parents. They had a child who died so they kind of felt like they'd replace their minus-one with a plus-one: me, the figure outside the equation. The extra. Once I got past childhood I think they kind of forgot that there was supposed to be other stuff. Adult to adult parent–child relationships. Sometimes I don't hear from them for nine months, maybe longer. It's like I served my purpose for them and now they're just bored.

I don't think that translates into an excuse for panicking during a bank heist and killing a bunch of people. But for me maybe it translates into an interest in the same kind of "break free" mentality. Separation from the real world, from everyone else. Sometimes I wonder what would happen if I just took off. Packed a backpack and just went away. Anywhere. Nowhere. I could leave behind everything that is Dayly Lawlor and find a space in life where I'm not the outlying piece of the jigsaw puzzle. I could find or build a whole new puzzle where I fit.

But all that requires stuff I haven't got. Cour-

age. Worldliness. Money. A car. A fucking back-pack, ha ha. I think I would want to understand where I came from properly before I went. All of the different pieces and elements. Because for me there'd be no coming back.

Sorry, all of that got really heavy, when I said at the outset that I wouldn't let it. I suppose I'll just send this letter anyway and see what you think.

Chat soon,
Dayly

P.S. Sounds in your last letter like you're try-ing to hook me into the whole mystery about there being more money out there somewhere, but I'm not buying it. Yes, I've looked at all the articles and conspiracy theories online. Been to all the subreddits about it. Plenty of experts agree, there is more money missing from the robberies that were attributed to you than was ever found or spent. But I also know how many marriage proposals guys on death row get. Surely you've found someone to give the money to, over the years, if there ever was any.

JESSICA

The Blue Room was close to home, only a stroll down Alameda from her small apartment. For Jessica, it held comforting memories. She'd sat here alone every year for five Super Bowls, most of the patrons wedged into the huge round booths upholstered in bright, plasticky teal, while she watched from the bar as they leaped from their seats or paced the sticky floor, grabbing their heads as teams scored or fumbled. The blue lights above the bar reminded her of the brick public toilets on Santa Monica beach with their anti-injection bulbs, her early days on the job hustling hobos off the sand or chasing bag-snatchers along the windy esplanade. She lingered now over a second Manhattan with two cherries, the bartender having forgone the fancy glass and given her a napkin to tear to shreds, the way he had a thousand times before.

She needed a distraction from what she had learned about the Blair Harbour case from Digbert. The cheese sandwich bite, the pathologist had asserted, was distinctly male. Jessica couldn't think about that now, what that meant about her, her work, the boy behind the vine-covered gate. She retreated from one growing storm in her mind into the chaos of another.

It's decision time, she thought. The words that rattled in her mind were in Captain Whitton's heavy tones. Though she'd never liked being forced into a corner to decide on anything, she needed to make a call. Rachel had wanted to read the letter Stan left in his will, written on his deathbed in the company of his lawyer, over the phone for Jessica on the morning she broke the news about the house. But she couldn't have that man's voice in her mind, not then, not when it had taken so long to scrub his daughter's crime scene photographs from her memory.

Now, she could no longer ignore the letter. She opened the photos app on her phone. Rachel had sent a picture of the handwritten letter, wanting to keep one of the last things her brother had created before he slipped quietly from the world. She scrolled to the picture and zoomed in.

Dear Jessica,

I am writing to you to inform you of my decision to bequeath my house in Brentwood to you. The finer details of the arrangement will be presented to you by the executor of my will, Rachel, who you know, and my lawyer, Martin Astley of Astley, Rich and Pine.

In the years after Bernie's killer took her away from me, all I had been able to do was measure and endure the ways in which I could not act. Bernadette was only there at the Ralphs supermarket in the first instance because I'd forgotten some ingredients for dinner and had her stop there on the way home from work. It was my fault that she was available to him in the parking lot. I was unable to find her the night she went missing, or in the days after. I was unable to save her from her fate. I was unable to exact my revenge on the man who did this. I will never be able to hold her again and tell her she is finally safe.

But there is something that I can do. I hope that my house, where Bernie and I shared so many beautiful memories, goes some small way to demonstrating to you how grateful I am for your service. It's just a house, and you'll come to understand that. But please understand that, to me, it is not just a building where I shared the greatest years of my life with my child. The house represents the only powerful act I have been able to exercise after what happened to her. I couldn't help her, but I can thank you for helping her.

I hope that it becomes a place of beautiful memories for you too. Maybe you'll raise a family there. But if you should sell it, or give it away, please know that I am happy with your decision. This gesture is undeniably selfish of me. I realize it will cause problems for you with your job. But I ask you to bear it, as you have done so much already.

With my deepest regard, and eternal gratitude,
Stanley Michael Beauvoir

The phone rang in Jessica's hand, startling her. Rachel Beauvoir's name appeared on the screen, as though she had been summoned by Jessica casting her eyes over the woman's name in the letter. She answered, and heard a rush of breath on the other end of the line: relief.

"Jessica, I've just got off the phone with Sal Eriksson at 915 Bluestone Lane. He says there are flashlights sweeping around Stan's hou—your house. Is that you?"

Jessica gripped the phone. The napkin she had been given lay in tatters on the bar before her. She knocked back the rest of her drink, thinking.

"Flashlights?"

"Inside the house. He's concerned there are prowlers. Should we call the police? Security?"

"No, no, no." Jessica pulled a bill from her wallet and left it on the bar. "That's me. I tripped a circuit and I'm just looking for the breaker. Oh, yep. Yep. I think I've got it. No need to worry."

She hung up, pushed through the door of the bar into the street, and ran back toward her apartment, still gripping the phone.

There were indeed flashlights roaming through the house when Jessica arrived on Bluestone Lane. She parked her car and drew her weapon, skirting a thick hedge to reach the front of the property. The sight of an unmarked police car in front of the house gave her pause, then filled her with dread. A heavy weight flopped into the pit of her stomach like a stone.

Jessica went to the front door and found it ajar. She pushed it open. Blackness cut through with slices of light from the back of the house, the windows lit by the pool. She heard something break upstairs, a crunch and the tinkling of glass. Laughter.

"Whoops," someone cackled. A familiar voice. "So clumsy of me."

"Get down here, assholes," Jessica called. There was silence, then footsteps on the floating stairs. Vizchen appeared first, a thin outline with his characteristically hunched shoulders and immaculate military-style haircut, before he blasted the flashlight into Jessica's face. Wallert came slowly afterward. Jessica could smell the bourbon on him from where she stood in the foyer. She saw Wallert's gun was out of his holster, then noticed Vizchen going for his.

"Put your guns down!"

"*You* put *yours* down," Vizchen said. He raised his weapon. "We've had reports of a break-in at this property. We're securing the scene."

"You're pointing your weapon at a fellow officer!" Jessica snarled. "How fucking dare you? Wally, drag your bitch into line!"

"No can do, Sanchez. You're on leave. A civilian. For your own safety, we'll have to disarm you."

"Hey, hey! What the fuck?" Jessica was shocked at the desperate sound in her voice as Wallert batted away her pistol and shoved her into the wall. She heard the jangle of his cuffs. "You're drunk. This is . . . Wally, stop!"

She twisted out of his grip and scraped a boot down his shin, extracting a yowl that filled the house. Vizchen's arm slid under hers, wrapped around the back of her neck, a sudden shove downward locking the hold into place. Outrage was paralyzing her. She needed to think about escape routes, counter-maneuvers, words and threats that would stop them. But the surprise that they dared touch her at all was so all-consuming that she could only stand there, held like a suspect.

"What do you fuckheads want?"

"We just wanted to come see the place." Wally walked into the living room. Vizchen pushed Jessica in after him. "Half of this was supposed to be mine. Look at the pool. It's fucking beautiful. I can see myself out there, margarita in hand. It's like a postcard. Look at the pool house, Viz. They store their fucking surfboards in something bigger than my apartment."

"Every house in Brentwood has a pool," Vizchen chipped in. "I told you so."

"Listen to me," Jessica said. "Whitton will have

your badges for this. This is break and enter, and assault on a police officer."

"We were conducting routine drive-bys and we saw evidence of a prowler." Wallert shrugged. "Just like you did on Lonscote. What are you going to say? We struggled with a suspect who subsequently fled, some shit got broken. It's part of the job, Sanchez."

The big man pulled an arm back and threw his flashlight through the plate-glass wall separating living room and deck. The glass split and shattered in a fantastic explosion of electric-blue light and falling shards. Vizchen laughed while Wallert went to retrieve the flashlight. Vizchen's chest was hot against Jessica's back, her twisted arm. She finally came to herself, aroused by the gunshot sound of the glass smashing, and drove her foot into Vizchen's ankle.

"Oh, Jesus!" He fell and she landed a boot in his ribs. She went for his gun and felt the air leave her body as Wallert barreled into her side, a heaving black mass reeking of sweat and alcohol. Vizchen had recovered enough to pin her to the plush carpet, twisting her arm again, his fist clamped in her hair.

"You better get used to this, Sanchez," Wallert huffed. He dragged himself to his feet. In the huge, bare living room, the man stood above her while Vizchen drove his knee into her back.

"If you take this house," Wallert said, unbuckling his belt, "someone's going to be here every goddamn night. Tapping at the windows. Ringing the doorbell. Smashing through the back gate. I'll bring a fucking special response team down on you, Sanchez. I'll bring them down on every family in every house on this street. They'll drive you out of here with pitchforks."

He unzipped his fly, and for a moment Jessica's body seized in terror, every joint locking, her mouth snapping shut, and her eyes bulging against the dark.

She had a piercing vision of Wallert grinding on top of her, his hand around her throat, his thighs slapping against hers, Vizchen nearby, watching, waiting his turn. A camera phone recording. And then, in an instant, the fantasy had morphed into something more real, not a vision but a memory. The soft carpet beneath her was the cold concrete floor of 4699 Lonscote Place. The suspect. His slobbering, drug-slack mouth wrapping around her bicep, his teeth clamping down. Impossible strength. A bite on her shoulder, deeper this time, tearing. It was almost a relief to shake herself back into the impending double rape.

But she heard the sound of liquid pattering on the carpet, and her horror-blindness cleared to show her Wallert not climbing on top of her but standing and pissing in the middle of the living room. She watched while he emptied himself, hips rotating this way and that, piss foaming on the cream wool, Vizchen's body on top of hers jittering while he laughed. She lay flat against the floor as they left, too mortified to do anything else.

In time a blessed breeze, sea air stroking its way through the city toward the mountains, came and lifted the stench of Wallert's piss out of the room and through the smashed back window.

Jessica was sitting with her feet in the pool again. She had only just stopped shivering when she heard the boy climbing the lattice, the characteristic "Oof!" that announced his landing.

"I heard glass smashing," he said as he rounded the pool fence. He stood looking back at the house, gripping the glass. "What happened? Did you have an accident?"

"Don't your parents wonder about you sneaking around in the middle of the night?"

"They're having people over for dinner." He waved dismissively at the fence. "They think I'm playing my Nintendo."

The wind was warm. Jessica wondered if the boy could smell the urine carried on the air, or if the smell just lingered in her nostrils, a part of her for the indeterminable future. She beckoned him and he came. She stepped down the stairs, the cool water rising up over where her jeans were pushed up to her knees. She put out a hand and the boy stepped back.

"No way," he said. "I told you, I can't swim."

"Come on," she said.

"My clothes will get wet. Your clothes are getting wet!"

"Live a little, kid," she said.

It was all he needed. The kid stepped down into the water, slowly at first, then launched himself at her, thin arms grabbing at her neck and shoulders. For an instant she felt the arms of her attacker at Lonscote Place, the brutal embrace of Vizchen, and then she was back in the moment again, just a woman struggling with a panicked boy in a pool. His floundering brought a smile to her face. She turned him over, hooking her arms under his.

"Look at the sky," she said. "Relax. I've got you."

"This is crazy," the boy was huffing. "I'm gonna drown. I'm gonna die. I'm dead. I'm dead!"

"You're not gonna drown," Jessica said. "You've got this."

She walked backward through the water, dragging him gently along, their arms locked. The bones in his ribcage swelled as he gulped air, the water pooling around his face.

"I'm going to teach you how to float," she said.

"I can't."

"Yes, you can. Everybody floats. Arch your back.

Stick your belly up. Higher. Higher. Stick your butt up. Lift your chin and just look at the stars. I'm not going to let go of you."

"Promise?"

"Promise."

"Really promise though!"

"I do," she laughed. "I do."

She wandered. Jamie watched the stars. Guilt and comfort swirled in Jessica. She had grabbed the child and forced him into a difficult position, taken control, so that she could have something more vulnerable than herself to play with, to take her mind off what had just happened to her. To make her feel strong again. If the boy hadn't been around, she might have reached for anything: a stray cat, some lonely deadbeat sitting in a bar. Anything would do. She wanted to see fear in something else's eyes, to know she was not alone. She wanted to watch that fear dissipate. The boy in her hands laughed, bringing her back.

"I'm floating."

"Put your arms out."

He spread his arms and legs, giggling, his strangely round belly protruding from the surface of the water. In the blue light it seemed like a taut, smooth island of spotless sand.

"What happened to your arm?" he asked. Jessica looked. The sleeve of her T-shirt had been pushed up over the ring of bite marks in her upper arm.

"Dog bite."

"Whoa! A police dog?"

"No, just a normal dog."

"Like a Labrador?"

"Does it really matter?"

"Why did the dog bite you?"

"It was crazy."

"Crazy how?"

"Just concentrate, would you?"

She slipped her arms out from under his and held the back of his head, pulling him gently along.

"Don't let me go!"

"I'm not what's holding you up, kid. I've just got your head in my hands. That's it. Look."

She dropped her hands. The boy floated on his own, drifting slowly away from her like a child-shaped log, silently at first, then giggling again. His laughs made ripples in the pool and the island of his belly quake.

"I can do this!" he told the stars.

"Seems so," Jessica replied.

BLAIR

Sneak looked terrible in the morning light. She sat on the stool on the other side of my kitchen counter, her chin on her folded forearms, watching me top up the gopher's food. I rinsed out the bottle cap we were using for his water bowl. There were big, dark circles under Sneak's eyes and a bloody crust at the side of one nostril, probably from a night spent snorting bad coke.

"We need a better arrangement for the gopher," I announced, shifting the little animal from one side of the box to the other so I could take away the shredded mound of paper towel that served as a bed, and replace it with fresh stuff. "There are scrapes and scratches inside the container here as if he's been trying to chew his way out."

"Hmm," Sneak grunted.

"It's cruel, him being in a container all day, where he can't see out. Must be like being in a padded room in an asylum."

Sneak looked at the coffee I'd made her, but didn't touch it.

"Did you hear me?" I asked.

"Is Dayly dead?" she responded. I picked up the

gopher and held him in my palm. The animal took up a seed stuck to my thumb and pushed it into its furry mouth, sat crunching happily.

"Sneak," I said. "I don't know how to answer that."

"I'd have heard something by now if she wasn't dead," Sneak said. "I'm not her favorite person in the world, but she wouldn't leave me hanging like this. Is she dead or not?"

"I can't give you an answer," I said.

"I know," she said. "I just need to say it out loud. It's been three days. The question keeps rolling around in my skull. *Is she dead? Is she dead? Is she dead?* If I don't say it out loud it'll be me in the asylum."

There was a knock at the door. Sneak sat upright on her stool. "Who's that?"

"I don't know. I'm not expecting anyone."

I saw the badge immediately when I opened the door, hanging on a chain around her neck. *County of Los Angeles Probation Dept.* The image seared into my eyes like a blast of sunlight. I didn't get a look at the woman. The clipboard and the badge hit me, left me blind, stunned.

This is what you wanted, isn't it? a voice inside me said. *You wanted it all to be over. You wanted to go home. Well, it's happening now.*

"Blair Gabrielle Harbour?"

"Oh god," I said.

"Not god." The woman smirked, flipped the badge on her hefty chest. "Jasmine Bahru, Probation. May I enter the premises, please?"

I held the door open, my limbs already seizing with terror and dread. When I turned, I saw that Sneak was gone from the stool by the counter. She'd disappeared like an apparition; her bag had vanished from the couch. I listened but heard nothing at the back of the apartment. There was no way out that way, no back door into the shared courtyard like other apartments had.

"I'm here to conduct a routine inspection of your living arrangements, Blair." Jasmine dumped the clipboard on the coffee table and went straight into the kitchen. "Could you please sign here to indicate that you've permitted me access to the property?" I'd had routine inspections from parole officers before, but never an unannounced one, and never one so straightforward and determined. Usually there was small talk. An almost apologetic stroll around the kitchen, the offer and refusal of coffee. Jasmine started pulling open cupboard doors, shifting aside bottles and cans. She peered into my refrigerator, bent to see what was on every shelf.

I signed the document on the coffee table without looking at it. "There's alcohol in the freezer. A bottle of vodka. Alcohol is not one of my restrictions."

"I'll check up on that," Jasmine said. "Is there anyone else living here in the apartment?"

"No, just me."

"So why are there two coffee cups here on the counter?"

"One's from last night. I haven't done the washing-up yet."

Jasmine lifted my empty coffee cup and held it in her palm, testing its temperature. We stared at each other. An icy tension rung in the air, the unspoken knowledge that she had come here to get me, and that I could do nothing but allow it to happen, roll over like a dog and let her put her teeth around my throat. I wiped my sweating palms on my jeans.

"Anything you want to know?" I asked.

"Everything I need to know is right here." She gestured to the apartment. "What's with the birdseed?"

I went into the kitchen. The gopher's box was not on the counter. My tongue felt heavy in my mouth.

"I like to feed the birds. At the park."

"You feed them dried grass?" She picked up the container on the windowsill.

"Some birds like that," I wheezed, thumped my chest. "Pigeons?"

"It's a public nuisance to feed pigeons."

I swallowed. "Is it illegal?"

"It's a municipal code thing. Depends on where the park is. Where's the park?"

"I don't know," I said.

"You don't know?"

"I don't remember."

She stared at me for a while and then went into the bedroom. I winced as she opened the closet. I expected she'd find Sneak there, crouched behind a row of Pump'n'Jump polos. I stood in the doorway while Jasmine conducted a thorough search of my drawers, my dresser. She looked under the mattress, in the hall closet. I silently thanked past-Blair for refusing Ada's gun. In the bathroom doorway she took a plastic cup from her bag and handed it to me.

"Let's go." She gestured to the toilet. I sat and urinated into the cup in full view of her, as I had a hundred times before in front of parole officers, police officers, prison guards, and a variety of other law enforcement officials. She slipped a drug-test strip into the cup on the counter and I watched the colors turn in my favor. The corner of her mouth twitched, red lipstick on dark brown skin. She headed for the door.

A rustle. Jasmine turned toward me. I fixed myself and stood, my face burning.

"So that's it, then," I said.

She pushed past me to the bathroom vanity and wrenched open the doors. The gopher's ice cream container rattled as she threw it on the counter, seed spilling inside.

"What the hell is in there?" she asked.

"A gopher," I said grimly. She peeled a corner of the container up and peered inside, shut it tightly.

"Right." She sighed and left the room. In the living room, I watched her snatch up her clipboard.

"Having pets is not one of my parole restrictions," I said, my throat tightening.

"No," she said. "But maintaining steady accommodation is. This building is rent-controlled. Pets are prohibited. I'm putting it in your report that you have deliberately sabotaged the conditions of your parole."

"Wait," I said. "Look, it's not my—"

"There'll likely be a review of your circumstances following this revelation, Ms. Harbour." She wrote something on the paper with a flourish. "You can expect a call from the department within the next twenty-four hours."

This is what you wanted, I thought. A mixture of dread and sweet, sweet relief flooded over me, warm honey sliding down my neck and shoulders. This is what I had been playing at all along, creeping softly into dangerous territory, following Sneak's siren call. This was why I had let a possibly wanted lifelong criminal sleep in my house, sit on my couch and do drugs. Why I had gone with her to visit a crime lord. Why I had accepted dirty money and a gangster car from that crime lord, why I continued to pursue a dangerous investigation that was none of my business. It was this moment, the instant it all came crashing down. The fall. The backward plunge. I'd felt it when I was arrested, the sickening ease of knowing my life and freedom were no longer in my hands. My job was gone. My child was gone. My friends were gone. In a few days I'd be back in Happy Valley, where nothing mattered, where I was required to do and think and be nothing.

You don't have to jump off a cliff. You just have to lean back, put your arms out, and let the gravity take you. Float away.

I found my fists clenching as Jasmine walked to the door and closed it behind her.

Give up, my mind said.

"Fuck you," I said aloud.

I went to the bedroom and ripped the sheet back from the mattress. They always look *under* the mattress, but they never pull off the sheets. The stack of notes Ada Maverick had given Sneak and me was fanned under the spot where my pillow would rest, some slipping down the bed. I gathered a handful and folded it as I ran to the front door and out across the lawn.

Jasmine Bahru was sitting in her red Kia, writing more words on her clipboard. I knocked on the window and she wound it down.

"Don't hand in that report," I said. She stared at me. I steadied myself against the car with one arm, my hand hanging down in Jasmine's view, and let a couple of the notes fan from my fingers. Jasmine looked at the notes, then at me.

"Are you offering me a bribe, Ms. Harbour?"

"You came here to fuck me," I said. "That much was clear from the moment you walked in. The gopher in the bathroom is a stretch, and you know it, but you were determined to catch me on something. I don't know what you've got against me, but let me try to even things out."

Jasmine sat, watching me. I stood on the curb with nothing to lose. She could see it. The emptiness, the wildness. She reached up and took the notes from my fingers, counted them. Eight hundred bucks. She peeled the page off the clipboard and handed it to me. I watched her drive away, feeling tremors start in my fingers and feet.

"Sneak?" I called when I got back to the apartment.

"Help!"

I rushed to the bathroom. Sneak's legs and ass were hanging out of a manhole in the ceiling, her skirt caught on the edge of the opening. Rippling cellulite, white butt in a purple G-string. I grabbed her legs and did little to help her flop to the ground.

"How the hell did you get up there?"

"I'm a gymnast," she reminded me. "And a drug addict. The easy part of both jobs is getting up. It's coming down that's hard."

I pondered the deeper philosophical meanings of that while I examined the paper Jasmine had given me, sweat-damp and smeared from my hands. It was filled out in full. She had been citing me for breach of efforts to maintain stable accommodation, as she declared she would.

I was familiar with parole reports. What I was looking for was not the report's breach contents, but a line close to the top of the page. I usually did little to arouse the suspicions of authorities. I lived a good, clean life. There was a box that normally remained empty. But this time, there was a name in the section that read *Recommending officer*, the space to record the police or prison authority who had called the parole office, recommending someone check up on me.

"Detective Al Tasik," I read, touching the page.

My phone rang. I went to the counter and picked it up. An unknown number. Ada Maverick's voice was unmistakable.

"I'm gonna give you an address," Ada said. "Meet me there."

"Why?" I asked. "Is everything okay?"

"I got your boy here," she said. I heard a whimpering sound in the background, like a dog makes when someone treads on its toes. "Dayly's boyfriend. Come help me play with him."

JESSICA

Jessica had been on hobo detail plenty of times as a patrol cop. Things had been different back then. Most of the ragged, windswept men she herded out from behind dumpsters or off the sides of busy, dusty highways had been crazy somehow. She'd heard every possible rendition of the world's coming demise from the alcohol-reeking street-dwellers—tales of asteroids approaching from galaxies far away or electromagnetic pulse bombs from North Korea soaring across the Pacific.

These days there were both men and women in the camps on the rugged hillsides beside the freeway, and their tents were equipped for long hauls, sometimes concreted or hammered into place and sometimes equipped with large pieces of furniture. Tents and shacks were fed power from nearby warehouses and some lit by television sets or battered laptops. The people who lived here weren't crazy, but were mothers and fathers who had been thrown out of foreclosed McMansions, and young people who turned to crack in college to try to stay awake and ended up on ice because it was cheaper and they were hooked. They were protesters, activists, children of the earth, the awakened, the oppressed, the misunderstood. Sometimes they rented space to travelers in their tiny, misshapen hovels, and some Christmases they hung them with lights. The homeless people Jessica saw now as she walked up the shoulder of the I-10 could afford guns, had a code of conduct, and knew their rights when it came to territory and police intervention.

But if there was one thing that hadn't changed in all the time Jessica had been a member of the LAPD, it was the way homeless men pissed. For all the sophistication that came with being homeless these days, running water was not included, so men from the camps still pissed in soft-drink bottles, and threw those bottles down into the tree-lined ditches separating the highway from the businesses alongside it. They did this to keep the smell away from the camps. Urine stink was the silent enemy of the panhandler. One whiff and the businessmen trapped in their cars on the way into the city rolled up their windows and looked straight ahead.

She crossed the top of the embankment, pulling nitrile gloves onto her hands. She headed toward a camp made from colorful slabs of a ruined billboard, stained bedsheets, and blue tarpaulins. Through a doorway made in what she was sure was a slice of Matthew McConaughey's nose, she could see an old man sleeping on a thin, green mattress. It was early, but haze lingered permanently over the city beyond, a rusty gauze speared by the buildings of Downtown.

A man was standing by a tree, shirtless, the backs of his jeans brown from hours of sitting and ragged at the ends. Jessica stopped a few feet away from him. He turned as he was screwing the cap on a Gatorade bottle filled with foamy yellow liquid.

"I'll pay you a buck for that," Jessica said.

The guy stared at her.

"For this?" He held up the bottle of piss. Jessica nodded, took the garbage bag from her back pocket and shook it out, held it open. The man dropped the bottle into the bag, his face twisted in confusion.

"Know where I can find any others?" she asked.

The man pointed down the hill, and as expected Jessica saw dozens of bottles lying scattered or grouped together in the shade, like oil barrels spilled across the surface of the sea.

"Help me collect them all," she told the man. "A buck for each one that goes in the bag."

The man nodded and made his way down the hill. Jessica followed him carefully, stepping over a pile of broken glass and rotting food.

JESSICA

Diggy sat in the passenger seat of Jessica's Suzuki, watching the house on Tualitan Road that had once belonged to Blair Harbour. Jessica glanced at him now and then, the morning sun bouncing off Diggy's yellow shirt like white light on water. The shirt was covered in blue rubber-duck images, each the size of a quarter. The forensic scientist rubbed his hands together nervously, his brushy hair almost touching the roof of the vehicle.

"I don't understand why my presence is required in this particular situation," Diggy said.

"It's Brentwood," Jessica said. "Most of these people have only seen cops on TV. They'll be expecting two nicely dressed men. We might get away with one Latina and a guy wearing . . . whatever the hell it is you're wearing."

He looked at his shirt. "I designed this shirt."

"Don't give up your day job, Diggy."

"My shirts are terrible. It's deliberate." He smoothed the front of the shirt, making the small blue ducks dance on his chest. "The disparate colors and novelty images are supposed to confuse the eye, distract the brain. That's because there's actually a Fibonacci golden spiral hidden in each of these shirts."

"A what?"

"It's a nerd thing."

"Where's the spiral?"

"There." He pointed to his right nipple.

"I don't see it. I just see ducks."

"That's because you're not the love of my life."

"Are you telling me you wear those terrible shirts because you're trying to attract the love of your life?" Jessica scoffed.

"I'm confident she'd see past the distractions and recognize the sequence. She'd be looking at me long enough, and would be of the kind of mind, to do so."

"Have you heard of Tinder?"

"You're not serious."

"This is a weird clash of romantic fantasy and science, isn't it?"

"Not really. Lots of animals use visual or auditory performances to attract their mates. Male pufferfish, and some other types of cichlids, construct geometric patterns on the sea floor to attract females, such as radially aligned ridges and valleys made from sand, rocks, and sediments. If the female sees a design she likes, she goes there to lay her eggs."

"I sure hope a female human lays an egg on your shirt very soon, Diggy, because my eyes are burning out of my skull."

"I don't want to do this." He sighed, looking at the house across the street.

"Well, we're here now."

"Is it possible you just want me here because you prefer working with a partner?" Diggy asked. "The brain likes patterns, particularly symmetrical ones. You've been working with an assigned partner for more than a decade, usually a male one. You might feel lopsided without a Watson to your Sherlock."

"Fuck you, Diggy," Jessica said. "I don't need a dick within arm's length to do my job, and I don't know a woman who does."

"It was an untested hypothesis." He shrugged. "Based on cognitive neuroscience. I was just saying that maybe there's a party in your striatum, which is housed in your basal ganglia, when you work with a partner. And when you're working alone perhaps there's not."

"I'm gonna kick you in the basal ganglia if you don't start talking like a person soon."

Diggy considered this.

"Get in that house." Jessica pushed at him. The two got out of the car and walked across the leafy street, up the driveway toward 1109.

This was where it had happened. Jessica could see it clearly now, put sights and smells and sounds to the memory that reading the report on the Orlov murder had been unable to evoke. She remembered Blair Harbour now the way she had found her, standing in her driveway with her mobile phone in her hand, watching the squad cars approach with the stunned, shaken look Jessica had seen so many times, the look of one who has just taken a life. She remembered patrol cops standing on the wet, slightly overgrown lawn, smoking and laughing about Brentwood females and their tempers, about dragging drunk rich girls off each other at parties here during vacation season when the parents were in the Bahamas. As she approached the door, Jessica remembered plastering the crime scene tape here herself, sealing off both the Orlov and Harbour houses as a paramedic briefed her on Orlov's state. The thought pulsated in her consciousness, a ticking, returning rhythm: if she had made a mistake in the Harbour arrest, this was where that mistake had begun.

The Japanese housekeeper, Yume, made three phone calls before letting Jessica and Diggy through the door. Though she stood out of earshot, peering over her shoulder now and then at the two of them standing on the stoop, Jessica was sure the woman mentioned the shirt to the house's current owners. After fifteen minutes they were admitted, and the woman went back to vacuuming the downstairs bedrooms.

"This way," Jessica said. She led Diggy up the wide, carpeted stairs to the second-floor kitchen, a sprawling space dominated by huge slatted windows looking out over the forestlike backyard. Jessica remembered when it was Blair Harbour's things adorning this room. A "Kiss the Chef" apron hanging from a rail on the navy-blue six-burner commercial oven. A ceramic chicken with a succulent growing from its back on the windowsill by the sink. There had been an unopened box containing a baby bottle sterilizer on the island in the middle of the room, Jessica recalled. Mummy getting ready early, nesting, checking off her list. She went slowly to the windows that faced north and looked out toward 1107, gripping the edge of the marble counter with white knuckles.

She didn't realize she was holding her breath until it gushed from her lips with relief.

"What is it?" Diggy stepped up beside her.

"You can't see the bathroom of 1107 from the kitchen window," Jessica said. She took another deep breath, let it out slow. "That's all I needed to see. We can go."

"At least explain to me what we're looking at," Diggy said. Jessica rummaged in her shoulder bag and brought out the Harbour/Orlov murder book. She flipped through to a section of notes near the middle of the book.

"Blair Harbour's statement about what happened on the morning of January 1, 2009, changed a bunch of times before trial," she said. "But in the first rendition, she said she went to 1107 because she saw Orlov strike his girlfriend, Kristi Zea, in the face, through her kitchen window. She said she looked out when the music started because she was annoyed by the noise, and she saw Orlov and Zea standing in the bathroom, arguing. He hit her. Harbour went over there to intervene."

Jessica leaned forward and pointed left toward a window inset on the side of what had once been the Orlov house. The window was twenty feet away and seven feet to the left of where they stood. All that was visible was a slice of window frame.

"You can't see in," she said.

"I concur. You cannot," Diggy said.

Jessica nodded, smoothed her hair back. "This is a good enough hole in the story for me. Harbour was very clear in her first statement. She was standing in her kitchen, and she saw them in their bathroom."

"Did she say where in her kitchen she was standing?" He shuffled sideways, trying to find an angle on the bathroom window. He went into the dining room and back. Jessica watched, satisfied. He went to the furthest corner of the kitchen and stopped.

"What's that?" he asked.

Jessica went to his side. He was pointing to a window at the back of the Orlov house, lower and wider than the bathroom window. It was on the first floor, not the second.

Jessica flipped through the murder book to a floor plan of the Orlov house. She found the room and tapped it with her finger.

"That's the laundry room."

"You can see into that room a lot better."

"Doesn't matter. It's the laundry."

"It has tiles on the walls."

Jessica leaned over the counter and looked. "So what?" she asked.

"Is it possible Harbour saw tiles and assumed it was a bathroom? Had she ever been in the Orlov house before? Was there any reason she would be able to discern one tiled room from another?"

Jessica realized she was cracking her knuckles for the third time in a row. Her fingers ached. She shook her hands out.

"No," she said. She went to the murder book and took out a sleeve of photographs, slapped them on the countertop. "She said she hadn't been in the Orlov house before. But that window wasn't visible either."

She shuffled the pictures frantically and spilled some in the sink.

"This is a series of photographs of the Orlov house taken from these windows back in January 2009," she said, spreading the images on the counter. "They were taken from this very spot. You can't see in the second-floor bathroom because of the angle, and you can't see into the first-floor laundry either, because the view is blocked by vegetation."

"Just stay calm." Diggy put a hand on Jessica's shoulder. "If there's been some mistake, we—"

"I am calm." Jessica tapped the photographs too hard. "There's been no mistake. I don't make mistakes. Look at the photos, Diggs."

Diggy looked at the photographs in turn. He examined each closely, then went to the window and looked at the first floor of the house next door. He repeated this process three times.

"Would you just agree with me so we can go?" Jessica wiped sweat from her brow. "Jesus fuck, I thought you didn't want to be here."

"There's foliage in front of the laundry window in this picture," Diggy said, selecting the photograph and presenting it to Jessica as though she'd never seen it before. "So the laundry window was not visible. It was blocked."

"I just said that."

"There's a problem."

"What?" Jessica gripped the picture hard, crumpling the corner.

"The bush that was down there blocking sight of the window, in the picture; it's not there now." Diggy pointed.

"It's been ten years. Who keeps a bush for ten years?"

Diggy stared at her. "Plenty of—"

"I know. I know. I'm panicking. Go on."

"If the bush was there today, perhaps we could examine it."

"Examine it! For *what*?"

"Hear me out." He took the photograph from Jessica's hand and placed it on the counter. "The time stamp on these photographs is three weeks after the shooting."

"Yes, we took them after the prosecutor briefed us on what we'd need for trial."

"Exactly." Diggy nodded. "So perhaps three weeks *earlier*, when Harbour looked out her window, she *could* see into the laundry. Maybe by the time these pictures were taken the bush had grown up over the window, blocking the view."

"No." Jessica shook her head. "No. We checked it."

"*You* checked it?"

"My partner at the time. He checked it. Once I

heard the story in the interrogation room, I sent him up here to check the angle. It was maybe twenty-four hours later. You couldn't see in the bathroom window."

"Would he have considered the other window? The laundry window?"

"He . . ." Jessica couldn't answer. She stared at her hands.

"Who was your partner?"

"Ira Nandermann."

Diggy pursed his lips, looked away. Jessica knew what he was thinking. It was the same thing she was thinking: that Ira Nandermann was not a cop who paid attention to details, who tested hypotheses and considered angles or nuances or possibly misinterpreted laundry room tiles. He was a dreamer. A dullard. She had once seen him pour dishwashing liquid into his coffee instead of milk on a late shift. It had taken three sips before he'd realized. He'd been fired from the West LA station years ago for stealing toilet paper from the men's room. If he'd been told to look out the kitchen window of the Harbour house and determine if it was possible to see through the bathroom window of the Orlov house, he'd have done just that and nothing more.

"A bush couldn't grow that high in three weeks," Jessica said. "Not in winter."

"Depends on the bush." Diggy shrugged. "It might have grown right up to the bottom edge of the window on the night of the murder. Depending on a thousand different variables, it's not impossible it might have continued growing and blocked the window by the time it was photographed."

"What variables?"

Diggy sighed, opened his hands. "The species of plant, its germination and heritage, the nitrogen and acidity levels in the soil, sunlight, watering and fertilization, pruning history, fluctuations in the weather patterns in the area, humidity, elevation, the effects of climate change—"

"Stop," Jessica said. She covered her eyes. "Stop."

Diggy didn't speak in the moments she stood there, staring at the terrifying dark of the backs of her eyelids, a darkness pregnant with the crushing possibility that she had sent an innocent woman to prison for a decade. In time she dropped her hands and walked back out to her car.

They were silent all the way back to the station. When she parked in the underground parking lot of the West LA police station, Diggy held the handle of the door but didn't get out.

"What are you doing, poking holes in this case?"

"Trying to find the truth." Jessica held on to the steering wheel, stared straight ahead.

"I mean, what inspired it?"

"I found out the Harbour kid lives directly behind the house in Bluestone Lane."

"So?"

"So I talked to him. I like him. He's a good kid."

"Plenty of murderers have good kids," Diggy said. "It doesn't mean you were wrong about his mother. Why did her story change so many times at trial, and before it, if she was innocent?"

"She got an expensive lawyer," Jessica said. "A Brentwood-woman's lawyer. The guy bled her dry in legal fees, took the house and everything, and he did that because he could—because he had a zero-loss score at trial. The only way you get a zero-loss score is by making your clients plead out. He pitched every story under the sun to prosecutors so they'd bump the charge down to manslaughter. Self-defense. Accident.

Provocation. Insanity. Nothing worked, and Harbour was half-hearted about the alternative stories. She was backing herself. She said she was defending Zea and she believed that."

"Well, it's possible she was lying," Diggy said.

"It's starting to look like she wasn't, Diggs," Jessica said. She could hear the terror in her own voice. "The cheese sandwich."

"Okay," Diggy said. "So we looked at a photograph of the cheese sandwich Harbour allegedly made and partially ate after the killing. We determined that it was most likely made by Orlov. Male bite mark, definitely not female. But that doesn't mean anything. Just because Zea lied or was mistaken about a sandwich at the crime scene doesn't mean the rest of what she said isn't true. She might have panicked and her brain constructed the tale. She might have seen Harbour go into Orlov's kitchen, seen the crime-scene photos later and assumed that's what Harbour did in there. She might have deliberately bolstered her story with the sandwich detail simply because she was angry and wanted to make sure Harbour went down."

"You might be wrong about the bite mark being male," Jessica added.

"Unlikely, but possible." Diggy shifted in his seat. "And the bush under the window today. That's another minor detail that could be explained in a thousand different ways."

"Something's wrong," Jessica said. "As soon as I met that kid I started getting whispers in my mind that something was hinky about this case. Now that whisper is a scream. What are the odds that the kid lives there behind the house that I inherited? It's fate."

"Jessica," Diggy sighed.

"Harbour is back in my life because I made a mistake. I have to keep looking."

"Why?"

"Because I don't fuck up like this." Jessica turned to him. Her face felt tight, almost bruised with tension. "This is not me. I'm a good cop. I check things. I make sure. I don't take babies from their mothers unless the moms are violent killers."

"The kid was a newborn when he was taken away," Diggy said. "He wouldn't have had the core neurodevelopmental capacity at that age for the absence of his biological mother to have affected his psychological and emotional well-being—"

"Diggs," Jessica said.

"Look at the bigger picture." Diggy put his hands out. "The whole equation. You're not picking at the edges of a scab here. You're cutting into something that is already completely healed. If you reopen and disprove your own case you'll leave yourself exposed to appeals from any and all of the scumbags you have put away in the past ten years, or longer. A real killer might be released from prison simply because you want to find the truth."

"You say 'find the truth' like it's a bad thing," Jessica said. "Like it's stupid."

"It is," he said. "In this particular case, it isn't reasonable or viable. Blair Harbour has already done her time. Obtaining an exoneration for her would not be worth what you risk in doing so. You risk ruining your career and further damaging the reputation of your partner on the case, Ira Nandermann. You risk opening old cases and setting guilty people free. You'd bring public disgrace on the department and gouge its resources thanks to a huge compensation claim by Harbour and her lawyers. The sacrifices outweigh the payoff here, Jessica. It's simple math."

Jessica said nothing.

"Sometimes you have to conduct an experiment and

find the truth, yes," Diggy said. "But sometimes you have to consider that you might burn the lab down in the process."

Diggy looked at her eyes. What he saw there made him sigh.

"We're building a new lab," Jessica said.

"I assumed as much," Diggy said. "What do you want me to do?"

"Work on the bush theory. Calculate some of the variables, as many as you can. Have your professor double-check the bite mark photograph."

He saluted and got out of the car. Jessica watched him go, then drove to the lower level of the parking lot, rolling slowly toward the southeast corner, where Wallert's Mustang stood parked against a concrete wall in its usual place. She got out and went to the back of her vehicle, popped the trunk and took out a towel, which she wrapped around her neck. She thought about how grateful she was to have Oliver Digbert on her side, as she hefted a huge plastic tub full of sloshing, jostling materials to the side of Wallert's car. Good investigative company had been hard to find lately.

Jessica went back to her car, opened the glove box and extracted her crime-scene kit. She pulled a mask over her nose and mouth, and gloves onto her hands, then returned to the tub by the Mustang. As she lifted the lid a wave of feral, fetid stench enveloped her, making her gag. The smell of the urine bottles was strong enough to penetrate the garbage bag they lay in, but not the tub itself. She took the towel from around her neck, spread it over the driver's-side window of Wallert's car and smashed the window with her elbow, a soft crunching sound emanating across the lot. She cleared the glass away, glanced around the interior of the car. Wallert spent a lot of time on his car, she discerned. The leather interior was shiny, oily, smelling of eucalyptus. She took the first piss bottle from the bag in the tub, unscrewed the cap, and leaned away from the car as she emptied it into the front seat.

She bent for another, thinking about the Harbour kid, about truth, about guilty men roaming free. The hobo urine sloshed over the center console and onto the floor of Wallert's car. She dropped the bottle into the vehicle.

Thirty bottles to go, she estimated.

BLAIR

Sneak hung an elbow out of the car, the desert winds rustling her curls. She was not a desert person. Two bright-pink blotches had emerged on her cheeks at the northern edge of Lancaster city, and there they remained, slick and round, as we drove through the brown, sandy nothingness. The Chrysler had no working air-conditioning. I wiped the condensation from a bottle of water we'd bought from a Native American kid running a roadside stall in Mojave across my forehead.

"It'll be a body," Sneak said. I didn't need to ask her what she meant.

"If it's a body, we play it nice, nod and smile, and get the hell out of there," I said. "We say, 'Thanks very much for dealing with our little problem, Ada. Have a great day.' Then we step on the gas and get to the nearest police station."

Sneak didn't answer. That wasn't her plan. I knew that if Ada Maverick had killed Dayly's boyfriend I'd turn around and find Sneak gone, and I'd be stuck trying to explain to the police that she and I had only wanted to question Dimitri Lincoln when we made the mistake of sharing our predicament with a psychopath. We were headed for a pin marked on a map, well away from any paved roads or structures. I glanced at the phone as we rolled through California City, a lonely row of shopfronts in the middle of a vast, flat void three hours from Downtown LA.

Like the planned and failed utopian community partly built and now rotting by the Salton Sea, California City was marked out on Google Maps as much bigger, grander, and wider than it was in real life. We drove past ghost streets, working our way north through a dream that never materialized. I turned off the main road onto a strip of dirt cutting a path through low, sparse desert scrub, heading toward the flat, hazy horizon. Wind-scattered piles of trash rolled past the car. A rusted oven resting on its side. A clump of children's toys and clothes half buried in sand. Sheets of corrugated iron making shelters for snake families in the boiling sun.

I saw Ada's car two miles before we arrived at it. A candy-pink Porsche Panamera gleaming so brightly I couldn't look directly at the paintwork. Ada was standing ten yards ahead of it with her foot resting on an upturned blue plastic bucket. Her black leather pants and boots were dusty, and she'd stripped down to a black singlet top. There was a leather jacket on the hood of the car, which told me she'd been out here since the chill of morning. The shovel on the ground beside the car nailed it. The guy was dead and buried. I stopped but didn't put the car into park.

"Should we just go now?" I asked Sneak.

Sneak got out of the car. I parked and joined her. That voice was whispering at me again, the one that told me I had gotten myself into this mess, that I was getting deeper and deeper with every second I hung around these women.

Ada flicked her cigarette into the wind and jutted her chin at me.

"You're late."

"We left when you called." I shrugged.

"What's the matter with you? You got a vat of soup in the car?" she said.

"That's just how I drive."

"Is he dead?" Sneak broke in. I looked and saw that her fists were clenched. "Did you at least get something out of him before he died?"

Ada stepped off the bucket, kicked it so that it flipped off a human head sitting on the desert floor.

I reeled away, pressing my fingers into my eye sockets.

"Oh, Jesus. Oh, god!" I cried.

"Help!" A man's voice cut through my blindness. "Help me, please. Please! This bitch is crazy!"

The human head was talking. The man from the video was buried up to his neck in desert sand. It was Dimitri Lincoln. His tightly cropped crown of black curls was covered in dust, and his mouth was crusted with sand and blood. Sweat was running in stark lines through the dust on his face, rivers cutting paths toward the ground. The absurd, decapitated head turned and looked around him, took in the sight of Sneak and me standing casting shadows over his situation.

"Listen to me," he said. "My name is Dimitri Lincoln. I've been kidnapped. I—"

"We know who you are," Sneak said.

"Dimitri has been trying to figure out what all this is about for six hours now," Ada said. She sat on the bucket and put a boot up against Dimitri's temple, pushed his head at a painful angle. "He's got some very interesting guesses. He owes a lot of money to some pretty heavy gangs. He's fucked a lot of connected women, the wives of some important people. Cops. Drug dealers. This isn't a very surprising scenario for you, is it, Dimitri? You've been expecting something like this for a while."

"Fuck you," Dimitri snapped, wiggling his head and neck madly in the sand. "You bitches are looking at twenty to life for this. This is kidnapping. Conspiracy. Assault."

"Cut the lawyer bullshit," Sneak said. She yanked her phone out of her pocket and showed him the page for the video of him and Dayly. "See her?"

Dimitri squinted in the sun. "I see her."

"That's my daughter."

"Sounds about right." Dimitri looked Sneak up and down, which was an interesting move from his position. "She said her momma was a junkie whore."

"She's missing," Sneak said. The veins in her neck were standing out. She was edging closer to Dimitri's head, and I could see her thighs tensing as though she might deliver a fatal kick. I grabbed her arm to hold her in place. "Tell me where she is or I'll back that big fucking car over your fat, stupid head."

"I haven't seen her in weeks."

"This video was posted"—Sneak checked the screen—"eleven days ago."

"Yeah, I posted it. Dayly cheated on me, and I had the video. I needed cash. So what, huh? She took off, and the video was just one thing she left behind. Too bad. I made good money from it on the site."

"I don't like that," Ada said, her lips twisted in distaste. "Revenge porn, they call it. I don't like it."

"I don't give a fuck what you like, bitch," Dimitri scoffed.

"Well, you better start, baby." Ada's voice was soft, terrifying. "You better start real quick."

"Did Dayly know you took the video of her?" I asked.

"Yeah, sure."

"Bullshit," Ada said.

"She did." Dimitri turned with difficulty and looked at Ada. "Maybe she would have been into selling it, too, if I'd asked her. She liked getting freaky. She was playing with fire, that girl. When I met her she was uptight. Wouldn't say 'dick' if you paid her. Then suddenly she wants to know about drugs, wants to go out and party. She was a fairy princess. Wanted to come over to the dark side. I was happy to show her. I introduced that bitch to a bunch of things. She had one of the tightest asses I ever—"

Ada shot out her foot and kicked Dimitri in the mouth. His head snapped sideways.

"Fuck!" Some of Dimitri's bravado drained away. I saw the sand around him expanding as he drew long breaths. "I'm gonna kill you, woman. You hear me? I'm going to come back from this and kill you slow. I'll film that, too."

"Do you know what happened to her?" I asked. "Tell us what else you know so we can end this, for god's sake."

"Fuck you." Dimitri spat blood on the sand.

"Dimitri, come on," I said.

"Nah. Fuck all y'all," he sneered. "You want to kill me, go ahead and kill me. I'd love to be the reason you didn't find her. I hope she's dead out here somewhere with her bones baking in the sun like fucking breadsticks."

Ada stood and I cried out for her not to strike or kick Dimitri again, but instead she went to her Porsche and brought out a small black backpack. From it she extracted a bottle then walked back to Dimitri's head.

I watched in quiet horror as she squeezed a syrupy liquid all over him. I smelled honey on the wind.

"Stop! Stop! What the fuck is wrong with you!" Dimitri tried to tilt his head out of the stream. The honey gathered in folds and slopped over his ears, making thick brown beads on the sand.

"You know what kind of ants they got out in the desert?" Ada said to me. She scooped the excess honey off the side of the squeeze bottle and licked it off her finger. "You're the smart one. You might be interested. I was googling them while I was sitting in the car waiting for you slowpokes to arrive. They got about fifty different types of ant around here. There's the harvester ant. The carpenter ant. I guess those are the working ants. The guys who get shit done. But then there's the fire ants. They just fuck shit up. There's the regular fire ant *and* the red imported fire ant. They're the ones that inject venom into you. By the time anyone finds this guy, his head will be the size of a beach ball."

"Ada," I sighed.

"You know what eats ants?" She bent and looked Dimitri in the face. "Tarantulas. You know what eats tarantulas? Rattlesnakes."

"She was seeing some cop," Dimitri said. "That's all I know."

Sneak and I glanced at each other.

"She was having an affair?" I asked.

"I caught her with a second phone. She tried to deny it. Say it was a friend's."

"This cop," I said. "Was his name Al Tasik?"

"I don't fucking know, man," Dimitri said. "I never knew his name. I saw him with her once. He had a stupid-ass military cut, like a flat-top."

"Blond hair? Fifties?"

"No, brown hair. Young. Like twenties."

"How'd you know he was a cop?" Ada leaned on the hood of her car.

"I'm from the hood—I know a goddamn cop when I see one. He walked like he had a stick up his ass. And one time I caught her on my laptop looking up a police station. San Jasinte. I figured that's where he worked."

I beckoned Ada and Sneak to our car. Ada slid into the driver's seat, which didn't surprise me. The air was stifling inside the vehicle. I wound down my window and tried to suck air in from outside.

"Who the fuck is Al Tasik?" Ada asked, watching me in the rearview mirror.

"A cop in West LA. He's been very interested in me since I came in asking about Dayly. I don't know why."

"You got another cop on the inside who can tell you why?" Ada asked. "A cop might be useful in all this. Track the guy with the flat-top. Tell you where the investigation lies, if there is one."

I said nothing. My stomach was stirring.

"You said Dimitri is gang affiliated." Sneak turned to Ada. "He might have found out about the affair and had some of his friends come after Dayly. We should question him about that next."

"I don't think we should question him about another goddamn thing," I said. "We need him out of that hole before he gets heat stroke, or a collapsed lung from the pressure of the sand on his ribcage."

"Your tone sounds a little like you think I've done the wrong thing this morning." Ada's eyes in the mirror were like fireballs. "I came out here and labored in the sun for hours to help you."

"You dug that hole yourself? I thought it must have been your goons." Sneak glanced out into the desert, looking for them.

"Girl, you think I can't dig my own fucking hole?" Ada shifted in her seat to take Sneak in. "What the hell you think I was doing before I was rich enough to have goons do that for me? This is my bread and butter. I love this shit. I don't need Mike and Fred coming out here kicking heads for me, ruining my fun. Why the hell do you think I'm here? Because of you shitbirds? I'll take any excuse to make a fool scream for his life."

"That aside," I said, "your tactics, while much appreciated, are a bit aggressive for our taste."

"Speak for yourself," Sneak said. "I say we rev the engine a little. Make him shit his pants."

"He's not wearing pants." Ada smiled.

"We need to check out the San Jasinte lead," I said. "Find the guy with the flat-top. See what he knows. San Jasinte is the same place on the front of the parachuting pamphlet. It's not a coincidence."

"Where the fuck is San Jasinte?" Sneak asked.

I was scrolling on my phone, looking at maps. "East. Miles from anywhere. Another day. Right now we pull Dimitri out of that hole," I said.

"You two idiots get out of here," Ada said. She was leaning forward, smiling at him through the windshield. "I'll get him out in a few minutes. I think I can see a big ol' ant headed his way."

Dear Dayly,

In your last letter, you were talking about my reasons for killing all those people in the Inglewood heist. You said, "I don't think that translates into an excuse for panicking during a bank heist and killing a bunch of people." By that you meant having a crappy childhood, feeling abandoned. But that's just the thing—I didn't panic. I'd already cut away, the way you're imagining doing. It might sound scary to be out there, floating around, without all the things that tie people down—consequences, guilt, fear, panic. But if no one teaches you those things, if no one ever instills in you a sense of guilt, then there's nothing riding on your shoulders, telling you to be a good person. The first sense of guilt you get is from your parents, for disappointing them. If you never get that, you never get the rest.

I killed all those people because it was the smartest way to get out of the situation I was in. That's it. The cops showed up. A couple of hostages inside the bank got confident, started getting fresh with me, so I did what I had to do.

I knew an inmate who had a cell next to Manson's in protective segregation at Corcoran. Pretty self-obsessed man, but very convincing, so I heard. A few times guards got shifted out of there because they got sucked into his teachings. A gifted bullshit artist both inside and outside of prison, it seems. I don't know why everyone's so obsessed with the guy. He wasn't even there the night of the murders. Who organizes a party and then doesn't go?

It sounds to me like you're slipping, Dayly. You're asking what it's all about. I'm not the kind of guy people should take advice from, not in my current situation (although if I'm really your father maybe you should take it—maybe it's fatherly wisdom). But I wouldn't fight it. See where it takes you. If you packed a bag and just left, "broke free," as you said, you might end up somewhere great. It doesn't take worldliness and a car and all that bullshit to do it. Those things will come when you need them. But breaking free can be something different entirely. It's like an experiment. Just say "fuck it."

The first time I ever said "Fuck it!," I was about ten years old, I think. Me and a couple of boys from school were out riding our bikes and we headed up to the school, which was closed because it was a Sunday. This is in Utah, where I grew up. We found a dumpster full of shredded paper and cardboard, and I wanted to light it up, because I always carried a lighter around and was always tinkering with it, lighting things. One of the boys with us gave a big speech about crime and badness, and the other two kids who were with us went along with it, so I got argued out. But I was dying to light that thing. I could feel it in my bones, the hunger. So I went back after we'd finished riding around and lit it up. The smoke was black and thick, almost like liquid rising up. I bolted right away, and after ten minutes I could see the smoke from the front door of my house.

The next day at school I heard some teachers talking about the fire, and they said there'd been a homeless man at the bottom of the dumpster who was using the cardboard and paper to stay warm, kind of like a nest. Another kid might have been horrified by that, but I was different. I figured I'd made a choice to try something, and sure, maybe it turned out bad, but I'd tried. I'd done something spectacular with that fire, something that could be seen from suburbs over, and making a decision like that when you're just a little kid is kind of crazy. Maybe grand. In here, I hear the guards talking about their kids—it's all they can think to do while they're sitting around watching us, now and then getting off their fat asses to stop us passing notes up and down the row. Their kids sound like pussies. Their faces are buried in computer screens all day long. They don't know the smell of free air, let alone the taste of smoke drifting on it. If I had a small kid these days I'd give them a lighter and send them on their way. Once you light a fire, you've committed to something, good or bad. I think kids need that.

You might think the guards are going to be angry at what I've said when they read this letter, but they know what I think. I've told them before. And as for the homeless guy, they could never pin that on me. The lawyers would put it down to jailhouse bragging. I've said it in interviews to journalists before. But it's true, I did do that, and I've had to live with it all these years. If you're worried about it, don't be. The fact that he was hanging around the school should tell you something about the kind of guy he probably was, and the smoke would have got to him well before the fire anyway.

How's your gopher? Surely you wouldn't leave him behind when you went on your adventure. More pictures would be great, if you've got any—of you, not the gopher. I promise I'm not selling them around the block, though I probably could and get a good price. A guard said yesterday that you have my lips, but he's an idiot.

Take care,
John

P.S. I've had one marriage proposal since I've been here. Maybe it's my face! I have found that those kinds of ladies, the ones who fall in love with killers, tend to go for the more "traditional" serial killers—the rapists and abductors. I'm someone who's only ever killed out of necessity (or accident), so I guess I don't have the mean streak they're looking for. If there was more money of mine out there, it would be stupid to tell a prospective love interest where it was. She'd just run off with it. What would be the fun in that? Whoever I tell, or whoever I would tell if indeed there is any money, would have to be someone I'd be happy to see fly away like a bird into a new life with it and never look back. Hey—sounds a little bit like you.

BLAIR

Sasha and Jamie were at my apartment. I recognized them standing on the lawn under the bright-orange streetlight, Sasha bent over her phone, Jamie kicking at the unmown grass. One of the men in long shirts who patrolled the street on a BMX bike was circling at the nearest intersection, probably made curious by the unfamiliar sight of Sasha's Prius and now fascinated by the sight of my pimped-up Chrysler. Sneak and I exited the car to the familiar chorus of pit bulls behind chain-link fences and Chicano rap that heralded the fall of night.

Sasha took one look at us and her mouth fell open. We were desert-dusted and slightly sunburned, and Sneak had been picking at her amputated earlobe on the ride home, as much as I warned her not to. The wound had dribbled blood in a thin line down the front of her white tank top. Sneak had also ingested something from her handbag of mysteries as we reached the city limits and was nodding, her eyelids drooping unevenly.

"My god," Sasha breathed, a hand to her chest, like a Southern belle startled in her parlor room by an unannounced visitor.

"This is Sn—Emily, my friend. She's fine, she just . . ." My face was burning with horror, embarrassment. "She was mugged yesterday, that's all. She's also on medication."

"Mugged?" Sasha looked at Sneak then me. "You were robbed and she was mugged . . . in the same week?"

"Go inside," I told Sneak, giving her my keys. Jamie was wide-eyed with excitement at my side, watching her walk away. "What are you guys doing here?" I asked.

"We brought you cookies." Sasha gestured to Jamie, who held up a bag. "I made a batch of Captain Americas that were supposed to go to a bake sale and didn't. And I brought you this." She thrust a wad of papers at me. "This is a little collection of materials I compiled on my neighbor five doors down, Roger Wardel. He's an MIT graduate. Works in stocks. He's looking for a housekeeper. Please tell me that's not your new car."

"It's Sneak's car," I lied.

"*Sneak?*"

"Emily."

"My god," Sasha breathed again, shook her head. "Blair, honestly."

"You want to come in? I can make you a coff—"

"I want to go in!" Jamie announced. "I want to see the blood again. Mom, can I?"

"No, Jamie, you can't," Sasha said. She glanced at the man on the bike, who had been joined by a friend on another lowrider. "It's not safe around here."

"He's safe in my apartment," I said. "He's safe on my street. He's safe anywhere I am." I put a hand on Jamie's shoulder and guided him toward the apartment block. "You can come or you can stay out here, Sasha."

My son had been to my apartment before, so he knew about the box of chocolates on the shelf by the door. He went for them, but I grabbed his hand. "Come with me. I want to show you something I think you'll like."

We went to the kitchen. Sneak had left a pile of bloody clothes in the hall—Jamie ogled them as we went by—and I heard the shower running. The ice cream container was where I had left it on the counter. I pried it open. A whiff of animal smell met me, the dry, husky scent of the birdseed and grass Sneak had bought for the gopher to eat. The creature was propped up on its hind legs, looking expectantly up at me with oil-drop black eyes. I swallowed the prickling fear that rose in my throat and scooped the gopher into my palm.

"Look at this." I presented it to Jamie.

"Ohhhhh." His hands rose to his face and made fists of excitement over his mouth. "Oh wow. Wow. Wow! It's a rat. You have a pet rat?"

"It's a gopher. A Botta's pocket gopher, in fact. I looked it up."

"Who's Botta?" Jamie asked.

"The guy who invented gophers."

"Maybe it was the guy who invented pockets."

"Could be."

"Can I hold it?"

"Of course you can."

I tumbled the warm little body into my son's cupped hands. The gopher snuffled at its new fleshy surroundings, tiny pink paws gripping Jamie's index finger. The gopher seemed to realize it was free to roam after being stuck in a box all day, and started walking up Jamie's wrist, then forearm, toward his shoulder. He giggled and brought it back, only to have it do it again.

"Jeez, he sure likes you." I folded my arms and watched, my heart big and heavy. "Look at him go. He wants to kiss you."

"What's his name?"

"I don't think he has one . . ." I thought about it. "At least, not one that I've heard."

"Can I name him?"

"Be my guest."

The boy thought for a moment, looked at the bag of Captain America cookies he had dumped on the counter.

"Hugh Jackman."

"You want me to call the gopher 'Hugh Jackman'?" I laughed hard. "Why?"

"He plays Wolverine."

"So why not call it Wolverine?"

"Because Hugh Jackman is way better."

"Not Hugh? Not HJ? Not Jackie?"

"Hugh Jackman."

"All right." I shrugged. "You got it. Is he your favorite Avenger or something?"

"Oh god." Jamie slapped a palm over his eyes. "Wolverine is an X-Man, not an Avenger. Jeez, Mom."

My breath seized in my chest. Jamie didn't seem to realize his mistake. He stroked the gopher on the top of its head.

"Well, this is the most awesome thing that has ever happened in my whole life," the boy said.

"That's a hell of a claim. I'm glad I could be a part of it."

Sasha beeped her car horn from the front of the house and I went to the door to wave at her. "All right, buddy, put Hugh Jackman back. Make sure you close the lid tight."

I dug in the chocolate box for a Reese's Peanut Butter Cup, his favorite. As Jamie headed for the doorway he took it from me, turned, and wrapped his arms around my waist.

"See you, Blair," he said as he bounded out into the night.

"See you, baby," I said. I pressed the door closed and burst into tears.

I dreamed about Dayly. We were standing with the counter of the Pump'n'Jump between us, crowded closer than we had been in reality. The jumble of chips, candy, fried goods, and magazines that stocked the store had somehow festered and grown like jungle vines all around us, almost blocking the windows. There was only a hole the size of a dinner plate in the window over the cash register through which I could see the parking lot. I knew someone was out there, looking at us from the darkness. Someone bad.

"He's coming," I told Dayly. "Hide."

The raw panic ripped up through the center of my chest into my throat as I was torn from dream to wakefulness by my phone. I grabbed it and answered in the still blackness of midnight.

"Get. Your ass. Over here. Right. Now," Sasha growled.

"What? What?"

"Jamie has a rat in his room." The fury coming down the line was like nothing I'd ever heard from her before. She seemed to be forcing the words out through clenched jaws. "A *rat*! A fucking *rat*!"

"What . . ." I sat up, gripping my head. "What the hell does that have to do with me?"

"*He says he got it from you!*"

A coldness flooded over me. I tore off the sheet and stumbled out of bed. In the kitchen, the ice cream container on the counter felt sickeningly light as I snatched it up.

"Oh, Jesus."

"You gave our kid a pet rat?" Sasha wailed. "Without asking me?"

"No," I said, reminding myself to later celebrate her reference to "our" kid. "No, I did not. He's taken . . . uh. I don't know. Something's happened. There's been some mista—"

"I have Francine Readley over here," Sasha snarled. "Do you understand? Governor Readley's wife. *Everyone* is here. Everyone who is fucking anyone from the neighborhood is here and my son has *a rat* in his—"

"I'm coming," I said. I grabbed the keys to the Gangstermobile. Sneak was collapsed on the floor between the coffee table and the couch, a pillow under her head and pills all over the table, snoring loudly. The stitches I'd put in her earlobe looked like tiny spiders in the dark. In the background of the call I could hear Jamie's frantic voice, but not the words. "Listen, don't do anything," I told Sasha. "The rat isn't a rat. It's a gopher and it's not mine. It's a very important animal, okay? It belongs to—"

"You better haul ass, Blair," Sasha said. "I'm putting a rat trap in the room and blocking the door. You get here and it's dead, that's on you."

Dialing, dialing, dialing. Too late for anyone to answer an unknown number. I crushed the caiman-leather steering wheel cover with one hand and dialed frantically with the other, the breath caught in my chest, refusing to go in or out. Night walkers on Jefferson eyed the car from the shadows outside closed clothing stores and cafes. I passed a homeless camp under a bridge, watched the shapes moving inside tents draped with clothes and towels. My thumb danced over the phone screen. Finally, an answer.

"Wassup?"

"Who's this?" I asked. There was a lot of noise in the background of the call. People laughing, the pop and tinkle of a bottle shattering on a road. The thumping of bass.

"Huh?"

"Who's this?"

"This is Miranda," she said. Her voice high and crisp, a little slurred.

"This is Blair."

"Bear?" She laughed.

"Where are you?"

"I'm outside the Pig Pen," she said, sniffed hard. When she spoke next, her mouth was away from the phone. "Get me a vodka! Ice! Ice! *I said ice!*"

"Sounds like a fun night."

"Not so far, we're stuck in the damn line."

"I hope you get in soon."

"What the hell do you want? I don't even know who this is."

"I'm no one," I said. "I just wanted someone to talk to. Someone to listen to." I knew the Pig Pen in Culver City, had passed it on my bus ride to work a hundred times. The interior was painted all pink, pink neon signs out the front, pink shag carpet stapled to the front of the bar, worn and dirty from a thousand thighs and knees passing it by. A young people's place. Chalkboards out the front advertised cocktails in colorful plastic cowboy boots. My eyes left the dark road ahead and I imagined Miranda standing in the line with other girls in shiny miniskirts, pink lights making their platinum hair look like cotton candy. I felt the thump of the bass in my chest, smelled beer on the road, vomit in the bases of potted palms. The ringing of Sasha's voice in my ears was replaced by security guards waving people back.

"This ain't a suicide hotline, Bear," Miranda said, and hung up as I climbed the winding hills into Brentwood. The night walkers disappeared, the only eyes peering from the shadows now the scopes of security cameras and motion sensors.

Sasha's house was full of people. Women in formfitting dresses and towering heels. I saw the faces of a couple of the women I'd known from the time before my great fall, pool-party buddies and ladies I'd jogged the streets with, lamenting the closing of our favorite boutique coffee-roasting house and the price of a good car detailer. A troupe of women bent in the window of the sitting room to watch me walk up the drive in my slippers and Walmart sweatpants, covering their mouths, holding their wine glasses to their breasts. Oh, what I had become. I didn't have to knock on the front door. Sasha wrenched it open.

"You have got *a lot* to answer for," she seethed. I put my hands up in surrender.

"Go back to your party," I said. "I'll get the gopher."

"No." Sasha followed me to Jamie's room. "Bette Davis Eyes" was playing on the Sonos system and people were singing along in the yard. My slippers slapped on the marble tiles. "I want you to tell me how the hell this happened."

Jamie was sitting on his bed, wearing only Super Mario boxer shorts. I'd never seen my child look so beaten, so exhausted with shame. I gathered him in my arms as Sasha closed the door behind us.

"What did you do, you silly little thing?" I asked.

"I'm sorry. I'm sorry. I know it was stupid," he sobbed.

Despite everything, a laugh escaped my lips. "What happened, buddy?"

"I put Hugh Jackman away in a shoebox before

I went out the back . . ." He was racked with sobs. "And when I came back he was gone. I just wanted a pet."

"We've discussed this." Sasha stood in the corner with her arms folded. "You can have a dog when you're sixteen, depending on your grades. You don't go stealing rats from people's houses! Rats are not pets!"

"I'll find it." I stood and took Sasha by the shoulders and shifted her toward the door, trying my best not to shove her, though every fiber of my being told me to. "Get out, Sasha. Go back to your party."

The rat trap wasn't set. It was closed and unbaited, placed under the dresser, probably a baseless demonstration of Sasha's anger serving only to terrify the boy. I picked it up and put it on the shelf, lay down on the carpet, and looked under every piece of furniture. Jamie sat on the floor next to me while I searched, his head in his hands. I opened his wardrobe and began checking every shoe, wincing as I slid my hand into the toes. In the right shoe of a pair of Nike Air Max 1 Ultras, my fingertips hit warm fur.

"I've got good news," I said. Jamie lifted his head. I shook the shoe until Hugh Jackman rolled into my palm, a flailing ball of brown with pink paws gripping for purchase. Jamie crawled into my arms and I kissed his head.

"I'm so stupid!" he cried.

"You are not stupid," I told him. I held his cheek and looked at his eyes. "You just did a stupid thing. Everybody does that sometimes. Including me. Hell, I'm the queen of doing stupid things. You can't compete with me on thoughtless acts, Jimbo, so don't even try."

He hugged me. I rocked him a little until his sobs subsided.

* * *

Sasha was standing outside the door when I left Jamie's bedroom. There were women at the end of the hall staring at us. Erin Gaille, my old tennis partner. Willow O'Leary, a former fellow wine-and-cheese-club member. The famous Francine Readley. I waved. They turned away, huddled together like startled birds. I slipped Hugh Jackman into the pocket of my hoodie and pulled the zipper shut on him.

"I'm going to have to get Jamie a tetanus shot tomorrow morning," Sasha said.

"Was he bitten?"

"Does it matter?" Her eyes widened. "This is not something you take chances with, Blair."

"Look," I said. "I get it. Really, I do. I was freaked out by the gopher when I first held it. It's very ratlike. And the feeling of it crawling on you takes a minute to get used to. But it's kind of cute if you give it a chance. And think about it, Sasha. If it doesn't bite you in the first thirty seconds, what the hell is it waiting for?"

"You're nuts," she sighed. "You're just . . . Urgh."

"I get why you—"

"No," she snapped. "See, this is what you don't *get*. Parenting—*real* parenting—is all about this shit. It's about saying, 'Hey, bringing a wild, flea-and-parasite-riddled piece of vermin trash into my house sounds like a fun idea, but I'm not going to do it because my kid might get rabies and die.'"

"Have you looked at the recorded human deaths attributed to gophers?" I asked. "I bet you have."

"What the hell was his plan?"

"He didn't have a plan," I said. "He's a child. He wanted a pet, saw one, and brought it home."

"And what the hell was *your* plan?" She gestured to my pocket. "What is a rat doing in your house?"

"I'm babysitting it. It isn't mine. It belongs to a friend."

"The friend I saw you getting out of that hideous car with?" she asked. "The one who was covered in blood?"

"Where's Henry? Maybe I can explain it to him."

"He's away." Sasha glanced at the women at the end of the hall, tugged at the front of her dress. "On business. Just forget it. You can explain in the morning. I'm done with this." She waved her hands around me like a magician summoning a rabbit out of a hat, indicating me, my life, my friends, my gopher, the dense cloud of problems I presented on the horizon of her neat, perfect world. "Just go."

The troupe of women at the sitting room windows was bigger when I left. Expensively sculpted bodies against the gold interior lights. I stopped halfway down the driveway and looked back at them, waiting for them to flee into the house in embarrassment, but they didn't. They just stared. I flipped them the bird, and all their mouths fell open at once. I smiled as I walked to my car.

JESSICA

Jessica tried to think of nice things that were yellow. Sunflowers. Lemon gelato. Beaches. But the stink of Wallert's urine rose and rose from the stains she scrubbed at, a heady, feral smell, and all she could think of was his shriveled, limp penis in his chubby hand, the way the stream twisted as it poured out and pattered on the carpet like the footsteps of a small animal. His arc had been wide, so she shifted on her knees to a new spot, working the carpet cleaner into a pale-yellow foam, pushing the soaked cream fibers this way and that. The T-shirt she had tied around her nose and mouth was damp with sweat. She settled back on her haunches and finally faced the fact that there was only one mental project that would take her away from this moment, from the little yellow stars crowding the cream universe beneath her. She let go, and thought about Blair Harbour.

She'd been wrong about the cheese sandwich. It was looking as though she was wrong about the view through Harbour's window into the Orlov house. Like Diggy had said, it was possible these were meaningless variables in an otherwise solid case. But Jessica could feel the heat in the darkness. A strange, rising fever that wanted to envelop her. Jessica dried her hands and slid her phone out of her back pocket. She searched for Kristi Zea, Orlov's girlfriend, the only witness to the murder. There was no social media profile, no links to any information on Zea that didn't originate from news sites covering Orlov's murder. That was strange. Zea had been a prolific social media user before the killing, with multiple accounts on different platforms. Jessica guessed the young woman had changed her name, tried to move on to a new life.

She stood and went to the smashed back window, decided to give the piss stains a rest for a while and see to the broken glass. It wasn't a good idea to leave it lying here with the Harbour boy jumping the back fence and strolling over any time he wanted. She looked back at the meager supplies she had bought for the clean-up job. She hadn't factored in the glass, too revolted by the urine on the carpet. She wondered if there was a broom and trash bags in the garage. She went there, unthinking, and opened the internal door.

It was the lights that did it. Fluorescents blinking to life, white eyes waking, reflecting on the polished concrete surface of the big, bare space. She remembered different things every time the flashbacks hit her. A sign above the door to the Lonscote Place garage, soldered into pine and lovingly polished—*Garage-mahal*. A joke gift from a family member, probably. The old battered red couch. Beer fridge. Rug. Framed photographs on the walls, hot rods and football teams, a lime-green Chevrolet parked in a field. The rippling shock of panicked pain that seemed to pass from her head to her toes as she turned and saw the man crouched over the old woman, bending to take another bite.

Jessica realized she was on her knees in the middle

of the garage of the Bluestone Lane house when the doorbell rang. Her hands were gripping at her own throat, where air refused to pass. She staggered toward the front door, wiped at invisible creeping, itching feelings crawling up her arms and neck. Taking the gun from the counter was a thoughtless action. She didn't expect any friendly visitors here.

She wrenched open the door and lifted the gun.

"Motherfucker," Jessica sighed, shook her head. The anger was instant, washing over the terror that had gripped her in the garage. She had the gun pointed at the woman on the doorstep, out from her hip, cocked. "What the hell are *you* doing here?"

Blair Harbour paused, looked at the gun, then glanced into the street, where a group of women in jogging Lycra were standing on the corner, talking. The Harbour woman was older than Jessica remembered. Prison time was etched on her face. Ten years without proper food, sleep, or exposure to sunlight. Her chocolatey hair was pulled into a bun at the nape of her neck and her shoes were worn sneakers, the T-shirt and shorts combo something she could probably slap a cap on and call a uniform at whatever shitty job she'd managed to acquire since her release.

"It's complicated," Blair said. "Can I come in?"

"You must be lost. Your son's house is over the back. I have nothing to say to you. I'll give you thirty seconds' head start, and then I'm calling the cops." She flicked the gun sideways. "Go now."

"Look, I just want to talk to you."

"Beat it. This is your first and only warning."

"It's not about my case."

Harbour held her hands up. Her eyes were big, full of emotion. Jessica remembered her at the defense table. How those soulful eyes had wandered through the jury, assessing faces as they looked at the crime scene photographs. The big blue eyes of a curious deer, like her son had.

"It's not about my son, either," Harbour said when Jessica didn't answer. "He seems to like you living here."

"I don't live here."

"Can we just talk?" Harbour glanced at the Lycra women again. "We're causing a scene. And you're not going to shoot me, because I'm not a threat to you. I come in peace."

Jessica thought there was something pretty ironic about the Neighbor Killer's stance on shooting people who were not a threat, but she didn't have the sense of humor to make it. She went inside but kept the gun hanging, ready, by her thigh. Blair followed her through the living room to the first-floor kitchen, glancing thoughtfully at the pile of soap suds slowly dissolving on the otherwise empty living room floor that was visible through the large passageway.

"Here's what's not happening," Jessica said when they arrived. "I'm not reviewing your case so you can seek exoneration and a payout from the state. I'm not appearing in a true crime documentary about you, and I'm not saying nice things about you to a judge so you can get custody of your son back. If you're here to apologize as part of some bullshit twelve-step circle-jerk then do it and get out."

"It's not about any of those things."

"Then what the hell do you want?"

Blair looked around for somewhere to sit or lean, but there was nothing available, only a kitchen bench that would have left her standing far too close to the cop who had arrested her. So she stood in the empty space, alone. The detective didn't answer when Blair had finished telling her story about Dayly Lawlor and the amateur investigation she had launched with Dayly's mother. She just stood there, her hand on the gun resting on the counter between them.

"We're not *completely* out of our depth," Blair went on. She cleared her throat, winced in the stinging silence. "We've found some good leads, I think. But we're getting to the stage where someone in law enforcement on our side would be really helpful. Invaluable, actually."

"This friend of yours, Sneak," Jessica said. "I understand her coming to you to question you. You were the last person to see her daughter alive. But why is she hanging around? You're not a private investigator. You're a doctor."

"Not anymore," Blair said. "They canceled my medical license."

"Thank Christ," Jessica said. "Why doesn't she just go to the police?"

"She may be . . ." Blair gave a big sigh, paused for a long time to weigh her options. "She may be wanted."

"Are you kidding me?"

"She's not sure."

"Oh, great." Jessica nodded. "That's just great."

"Dayly's disappearance is with the police. That much became clear when I went to inquire about it myself. I was handled . . . aggressively."

"I'd probably have handled you aggressively, too, if it was me," Jessica snapped. "You're a killer. Not just that, you're a parolee hanging out with a known criminal. How the fuck are you not behind bars again right now?"

"I've been lucky," Blair said. "But the aggression wasn't related to that. The detective on the case is named Al Tasik. Do you know him?"

"Maybe."

"He treated me as if I was fishing around in something that was off-limits." She shifted uncomfortably and looked out at the pool. "And he's since made a play at getting me thrown back in jail."

"*Made a play?*" Jessica asked. "You mean, *did his job?*"

Blair folded her arms, stared at the carpet, seemed to consider something. Jessica watched, the heat burning in her cheeks, her neck. The heat that told her something was wrong here. That she was fighting for the wrong side.

"I'm asking you not to follow the same course of action," Blair said. "As a kindness."

"You can ask all you want."

"Maybe it was a mistake to come here," Blair sighed.

"You think so?"

"I wouldn't have done it if I wasn't desperate. Believe me, you're the last person in the world I'd want to see again after what happened."

Jessica's hand tightened on the gun.

"But I'm willing to set aside our history and work with you on this," Blair said carefully. "Sneak is my friend, and I believe her daughter is in real danger. And maybe you were just doing your job the best way you knew how when you put me away. You were wrong about me, of course. I didn't kill Adrian Orlov because I was paranoid or angry. I did it because I had no choice. I believed he was going to kill his girlfriend right there in front of me, and as a doctor I was trained to protect life. You didn't believe me, but everybody makes mist—"

Jessica shook her head. "There was no *fucking* mistake, Harbour."

"But like I said"—Blair put a hand up—"I'm not here about that. I came because Dayly Lawlor put a gun in my face, and that gun wasn't as scary to me as the look in her eyes. She looked like a hunted animal."

Jessica watched her visitor across the wild, hot, empty space between them, the burning knowledge of what they had once been to each other. Hunter and hunted. When Blair met Jessica's gaze, it was all Jessica could do not to look away.

"Will you at least see what's going on at your end?" Blair asked. "Where the investigation stands and why Al Tasik—"

"I don't know what I'll do," Jessica said. "Right now my only plans are to watch you get in your car and drive the hell away from here."

She walked out of the kitchen. Blair followed her to the front door. There was some kind of drug-dealer special parked in front of the house. Jessica marveled at it, the glimmering chrome rims and hood ornament. She could only imagine what stories might be cooked up at the station the next day if a patrol drive-by spotted the car parked next to hers out front. Blair Harbour was hardly out the door when she slammed it shut, twisting the deadlock closed.

Three seconds.

She watched helplessly as her own hand twisted the lock back again. With a will that was not her own she wrenched open the door. Blair paused on the stoop.

"The Orlov bathroom," she said. "First floor or second floor?"

Blair looked back at her, her features a mixture of confusion and fear.

"What?"

"You said you saw Orlov and his girlfriend fighting in the bathroom that night," Jessica said. "You saw them from your kitchen window. Was the bathroom on the first or second floor?"

Blair searched her memory, her eyes roving the ground at her feet. "I don't know."

"What do you mean, you don't know? It's a simple question."

"It's been ten years. It was a horrible night. I've tried not to think about it."

Jessica smirked, was surprised by the nastiness of the sound. "You ever go into the Orlov house before that night?"

"No," Blair said.

"You sure?"

"Positive."

"So how do you remember a thing like that, and not what floor the bathroom was on?"

"Why are you asking me this?" Blair asked. Jessica opened her mouth to answer, but whatever had been controlling her had fled. She shut the door and locked it again.

Jessica watched through the glass panels beside the door as the killer she had once arrested walked down the driveway toward her car.

BLAIR

I hadn't dreamed of the murder in many years. The dreams had always come unexpectedly, surprise attacks that arrived in the middle of a good week, when my mind was furthest from the night filled with blue lights and red blood. Sometimes I was pregnant, the way I actually had been when I killed Adrian Orlov, and sometimes Jamie was a small child tucked into a crib in the beautiful nursery I'd made for him. I was standing at the kitchen window of my house, watching gold explosions dazzle on the horizon toward the coast, young revelers getting rid of their after-midnight fireworks. Dark landscape burning. I'd never been an enthusiastic New Year's reveler, and, being unable to drink, I'd decided to spend the evening by myself watching *Sex and the City* reruns in my cotton pajamas instead.

It was on one of my frequent nighttime trips to the toilet that I'd stopped in the kitchen for a glass of milk. Almost as though its inhabitants could feel my exhausted presence, music started up at the Orlov house. I sighed, leaned, and looked at the house next door. Gold light in a tiled room. Kristi Zea storming in, thrusting open a cupboard that was immediately slammed shut by her boyfriend's hand. His wide, boxy fist pulling back as if he'd drawn a bow, snapping forward, smacking into her temple with a noise I figured I could hear from where I was standing.

My mouth fell open. Next came the moment that changed everything. Not so much a decision, but an instinct to turn toward the stairs and run down them rather than heading back to my bedroom to grab my phone and call 9–1–1.

Stupid. Arrogant.

Later I knew what it was: sheer, ridiculous bravado. I was wild with instant adrenaline, with the belief that I was untouchable. That because I could somehow manage to create a thriving human life inside my body from nothing at all, that I was clearly some kind of god. I was a doctor. I created life. Sometimes I brought life back to the dead. Miracles. The week before the killing, I'd performed surgery on a five-year-old girl who had been paralyzed in a horrific pileup on the I-10. Her nerve endings had been as fine as hair. I'd saved her from a lifetime of paralysis. Intervening in a fight between a man and a woman at the house next door seemed like child's play. I'd march in and know exactly what to do, just like I did in the operating room. I was heading down the driveway toward the Orlov house, shattering my own life one self-righteous step after the other.

Then a hand was on my mouth.

Weight on my back.

I was suddenly not in my old driveway in Brentwood eleven years ago but here, now, in my bedroom in my apartment in Crenshaw. The dream fell away like a dropped curtain and I felt stubble against my cheek, my ear. He didn't say anything. In the nightmares shown on true crime television, they always say something. *Don't scream. Don't move. Don't panic.* I bucked and felt his hips against my buttocks. An animal scream ripped loose from me, high and primal, full of shock and outrage.

I called Sneak's name, though some cold corner of my mind told me that this man and I were alone in the apartment. I thought about the gun I'd refused from Ada, about the gun I'd once killed a man with, how easy it had been. My mind raced through a list of humans in proximity. The man with the guitar school whose name I didn't know, probably snoring loudly in his bed only feet away. Celeste, the kid who had visited me that afternoon to play Pearl Jam at my door for treats, long gone hours ago. The men on the bikes. Was he one of them? All of this mental chaos crashed into my mind in mere seconds as he found my arm and dragged it behind me.

Once he has you tied up, I thought, *that'll be—*

I didn't need to finish the thought. I snapped my head backward, hopeful but off with my aim, glancing him on the jaw. It was enough to startle him, to loosen the hand on my mouth, which was pressed so tight against my lips it was crushing them against my teeth, making them bleed. I caught a minuscule roll of calloused skin between my teeth and bit down hard. A yowl. He mashed my head into the pillows. He was turning me, trying to roll me over, maybe to punch me, subdue me. My arms were free. I punched and kicked, wailing with effort and terror, the man easing back in the darkness just enough for me to slither off the bed.

He went for my hair. In prison, that's the first and easiest mistake a fighter can make. A big wad of an opponent's hair makes a good handle to control their head, but you leave their arms and legs loose, the primary weapons. With enough adrenaline pumping, a fighter can lose a chunk of hair and not even feel it tearing away. I struck out with a punch in the darkness, caught thigh, denim. My knee hit a boot on the carpet. I aimed again and hit pay dirt. The man folded in two above me, slammed into my bedside table, all the wind leaving him as my fist sank into his balls. His hands released my hair, flying away to cover his tender parts. I scrambled out from beneath him, grabbed what I could on my way to the door and hurled it back in his direction. My work bag. A laundry basket. A shoe. In the hall I was hit with a wave of nausea, dizziness, my brain failing to keep up with my fighting, fleeing body. He was there. He caught my ankle as I steadied myself in the doorway to the kitchen. I hit the floor with a whump.

JESSICA

"What kind of experience are you seeking tonight, Jessica?" he asked.

Jessica stretched, suppressed a shiver as his hands worked into her hair, tugged the tie away gently as he always did, began to smooth and knead the taut muscles at the base of her skull. Goren had taken another last-minute appointment. He didn't seem perturbed, but Jessica knew she was pushing her luck. Still reeling from the Harbour woman's visit, on the doorstep of the three-story terrace she'd received a text from Wallert.

I'll fucking kill you, bitch.

She'd known then that she needed this, that without Goren's treatment she'd never sleep, never be able to escape the trauma of her day. Sometimes it was her only source of release, distraction. To let go, to have someone take her away from herself without the guilt or awkwardness of mutual affection. She paid the money, he opened the door to sweet relief. She left, feeling warm and light and tired. It was a good system.

"I want to play the game," she told Goren. Jessica

looked behind her and saw a wry smile on his face as
he knelt on the ottoman at her back.

"It's been a while," he said.

"I know."

"Will you be in charge, or will I?"

"You," she said.

Jessica thought she saw the whisper of some kind
of excitement run through him, but it was probably
just an act. This is what he did, and the women and
men who came here would be looking and hoping for that same excitement, dreading the slightest
slump of his shoulders or look of reluctance in his
eyes. Everyone wanted to be desired. Yearned for. She
stood while he stripped her gently, running his hands
up her ribs as he pulled off her top. He went to the
large dresser and took a blindfold, slipped it expertly
across her eyes, and tied it. He led her to a room that
was warmer and somehow felt smaller, even in the
dark. She had been in this room before, knew the red
walls and dark velvet curtains. Sometimes it had been
her fitting his ankles into thick leather straps on the
vertical table, him behind the blindfold. The big table,
she knew, could be adjusted into a range of positions
with the flick of little gold switches.

As was his routine, he stood her against the table
and pulled the straps tight on her ankles, then worked
the belt at her hips extra tight, as she liked. Jessica
could feel the tension falling away from her muscles
immediately. The simple pull of the straps took the
weight of her worry over the Harbour/Orlov case,
her guilt about the boy next door, the fury and hatred
boiling inside her for Wallert and her colleagues.

The strap across her ribs was her favorite. It con-
stricted her breathing just slightly and forced her to
focus on her own heartbeat. Goren guided her left

wrist into place and pulled the strap tight there. She could feel his breath on her face. His crotch, hard and warm against her own. Intrusions attempted to break through the rapidly falling relaxation. A distant siren. The screech of tires. She gave a sigh that pulled the strap around her ribs tight as he guided her other hand into place.

Three car doors slamming nearby. Very nearby. At the front of the house. Jessica felt him pause. They both waited.

"It's nothing," he said, looping the strap over her right wrist.

A pounding at the door, three thumps, a noise she had heard a million times.

"Police! Open up!"

"Oh, shit," they said in unison. He let go. Jessica reached out, expected to find him there, bent, unstrapping her. Nothing. She swung wildly. Felt only vacant air. His footsteps in the hall, heavy, running. The cold emptiness of losing him sliced through her. She ripped off the blindfold. He was gone.

"Goren! Goren! Fuck!" She was panting. Near screaming. "Come back! Come back! Don't leave me like this!"

She knew it was no use. Jessica began frantically working her trapped wrist free of the buckle when she heard the downstairs door slam open.

BLAIR

A punch to the back of the head. Effective. Dulling. My face smacked against the chipped linoleum. My brain told me to sleep. Concussion slipping over me like a hood. A voice pushed through—my own voice, the words I'd spoken to hundreds of kids who'd fallen out of trees or down cliffs, had been pulled from crushed vehicles, were sinking into fever. *Stay awake. Stay with me. Listen to the sound of my voice.* He stood above me, one foot on either side of my ribs. In a single, surging move, giving it everything I had, I sprang upward, toppled him into the wall and was immediately wrapped in his embrace. We wrestled in the kitchen, clawing, snarling. I heard Hugh Jackman's ice cream container hit the floor along with a set of knives, a coffee mug, papers. I palmed at my attacker's face, used the momentum to shift around him, felt the drywall crunch as he smashed me into an embrace again.

"Get off me! Get the fuck off me!"

The howling, snapping words were unrecognizable, even as they flew from my lips. A dog that never barks, never growls, suddenly backed into a corner. We tumbled into the counter. I grabbed what came under my hand, a jar of sugar I kept for guests' coffee, and smashed it against the top of his head.

It was enough. He slumped sideways in the dark. I danced past him, sprinted across the living room, and threw myself at the door, unlocking it with slippery, shaking hands.

I ran out into the night and didn't look back.

JESSICA

Footsteps on the stairs. Two men. Jessica's hands were numb, unusable, all the blood in her body rushing to her heart and her head. She managed to get the buckles at her wrist, ribs, and waist undone. But as she reached for the straps at her ankles the door to the room burst open. She sank into a crouch to protect her naked body, the table too close at her back, tipping her forward so that she had to steady herself against the floor with one hand. The buckles cut into the front of her ankles, painful, a distraction she tried to savor as she felt their eyes wander over her.

"Police! Let me see your hands!"

"I can't," Jessica cradled her breasts with one arm, her face turned away from the men at the door. "I can't."

"Let me see your hands right now!"

"Turn your body cams off!"

"Ma'am, I won't ask you again!"

"I'm a cop, you assholes! Turn your body cams off!"

She heard the sound of a stun gun being pulled from its holster. The distinctive snap and flick of the safety. Devastatingly clear images whirled through her mind, of her body twitching and writhing under the electric pulse of the Taser, all of it recorded on the patrol officer's body camera. Being naked on video was better than being Tasered and naked. She let go of the floor, released the cradle she'd made for her naked chest, and rose up slowly. She wasn't going to put her arms up. That would be an indignity she couldn't bear. She stood there, strapped in place, finally turning her face to meet the men she didn't recognize standing in the doorway with their Tasers out.

"I'm a cop, you *complete—fucking—assholes*," she said.

One of them was staring at her crotch. The other, her breasts. They both looked at her eyes at once. Jessica could see the two little red lights of their body cams still blazing in the glowing mood lighting of the room. Somewhere downstairs, other officers were dealing with Goren. Doors were slamming open and drawers were being pulled out. She could hear him yelling in protest.

"If you're a cop, what the hell are you doing here?" one of the men in the doorway asked, a tall, young patrolman with a thick black beard.

"It's none of your business what I'm doing here," Jessica said.

"We have reason to believe there are drugs and activities involving prostitution occurring on these premises," the officer said. He paused, looked at his partner, and the faintest hint of a smile played at the corner of his mouth. "You'll be placed under arrest pending further investigations. Ma'am, would you please, uh . . . free yourself from . . ." He pointed at the straps. "Or maybe you need help—"

"I don't need any goddamn help," Jessica said. She bent to undo the buckles at her ankles. Her whole body was submitting to trembling waves of humiliation, the stinging sensation of the cameras, their eyes, recording her every move. When she rose again she caught them smiling, laughing silently, the smaller one turning away. More officers were arriving in the hallway. She cupped a hand over her crotch and covered her breasts with the other arm.

"Can I retrieve my clothes from the other room?" she asked.

"Of course." The tall officer finally had a hold of himself, his face barely straight. "Guys, let her through."

The officers in the hall parted. She couldn't look at their faces. She dressed alone in the bedroom, listening to their laughter.

BLAIR

"Hello?"

"Hi. I'm so, so sorry to call you at this late hour. I just . . . I need . . . I'm really, really sorry, but—"

"Well, for god's sake, tell me who it is."

"My name is Blair. You don't know me."

"Are you calling from a pay phone?"

"Yeah. I'm sorry, sir. I just need someone to talk to. I feel so bad for waking you up."

"Hell, you didn't wake me up, darlin'. I don't never sleep these days. My house is full of gremlins every second week. Are you okay? You sound all puffed out."

"I'm fine. I'm okay. I'm . . . Did you say gremlins?"

"My sister's kids. She got a second job workin' night shift at a sawmill. Place runs all day and all night. That's why I'm talkin' quiet. I only just got them little bastards to sleep. Kids don't know what's good in the world. They don't like sleep. They don't like food. They don't know what great skin and hair they got. I went bald at fifteen. Smooth as an egg. Took me two weeks. Like somethin' scared it right out of me."

"How old are the kids?"

"John's seven and Maggie's three and a half. So what is this? Is this like one of them survey calls where you win a prize?"

"No, no. I'm sorry. I don't have anything—"

"My aunt got a call in the night like this once. Said she won a four-day cruise. She told everybody. Turned out it was a whole lot of bullshit. They just wanted her credit card numbers. Oh, Lord. Oh, shit. Go back to bed, Johnny."

"Oh, no."

"It's nothin'. Nothin'. Just one of them survey calls. Go back to bed or . . . Ah, shit. You woke the baby. Now it's a party."

"I'm so sorry."

"It's all right. Don't worry about it. Hell, it's always a party at Uncle Shane's place. Ain't that right, Mags, huh? Who wants milk?"

JESSICA

Diggy was signing forms at the front desk of the Wilshire Community Police Station when Jessica was brought out from the cells. This morning's Fibonacci golden spiral shirt was a vibrant blue and covered in pictures of tiny men in top hats curling their villainous mustaches. The female officer behind the counter was examining it closely. Jessica imagined that having to stand at the counter enduring Diggy's ultimate encounter with true love might be more than she could bear, so she caught his arm and turned him away from the woman's gaze.

"I have a question," he said, his finger raised.

"What?"

"Where do you get three gallons of human piss at short notice?"

"Was it really three gallons?"

"According to the bottles that remained at the scene, assuming each was full or close to."

"Hobos," Jessica said.

"Ah." Diggy nodded. "That was my guess. A colleague at the lab said they must have been yours, but I did not concur. You seem sensible about hydration, and it smelled like whoever provided those samples was distinctly otherwise."

"You smelled the car?"

"Everybody did. It stank up both floors of the parking lot. Some people went down to look when Wallert came into the office shouting and making a commotion about what had happened, but I deemed a viewing unnecessary."

Jessica smiled. Her face felt stiff from the dread of the past few hours sitting in a holding cell.

"He'll have to dispose of the whole vehicle," Diggy said as they walked to the doors of the station.

"I know you're just trying to make me feel better about the footage of my arrest." The day was stingingly bright. Two officers were already unloading a van full of gang members scooped up from the streets into the side entrance. "Is it across the department yet?"

"I was forwarded it by email." He had his head down, watching the road pass beneath his feet. "So was my colleague. So you can assume if it's reached the forensics office . . ."

She nodded.

"Jessica," Diggy said as they slid into his immaculate car together. "Erotic practices that involve BDSM are surprisingly common, and in the current sociosexual climate—"

"Don't." She held a hand up.

"Okay."

They drove for a while in silence. Jessica smelled her armpit, grimaced. The jailhouse had stunk of the bodies of sweating, sobering women, herself included.

"Tell me where you are on the Harbour investigation," she said.

Diggy straightened in his seat. A pair of young

actors were crossing the street before them at the traffic lights, their noses buried in scripts, gesticulating wildly to each other. Jessica looked at her phone and saw that there were five missed calls from Captain Whitton and eight from female colleagues she had known across her career. One of the women, she knew, worked out in Glendora. The video was spreading like a wildfire from cop to cop, embers carried across the country, heading east.

"The bush in question outside the Orlov house is a Baby Bear manzanita, or a species of *Arctostaphylos*, for the connoisseur. That much I worked out for myself. Then I consulted a botanist. Not just any botanist—*the* botanist. Dr. Ramona Bulle. President of the Botanical Society of America. She's taken the inquiry seriously. Extremely seriously. It appears to me as though she's spent every waking moment on the case study since I presented it to her. I'm receiving reports on the hour." As if on cue, Jessica heard Diggy's phone ping. "She's currently analyzing vehicle smog patterns in the area at the time to try to determine their effect on the growth of our particular species."

"Jesus," Jessica said.

"Yeah." Diggy glanced at her. "There are scientists and then there are obsessives. Frankenstein types who fall down into deep investigative wells and go mad."

"Can you tell anything from what she's provided so far?"

Diggy paused. "I hate to draw conclusions based on incomplete—"

"Diggy."

"It could have grown that high." He looked at her. "Yes. I'm calling it. The bush could indeed have grown high enough in three weeks to cover up the view of the first-floor laundry window."

Jessica was silent.

"So it's possible you were wrong about the bush. And you were indeed wrong about the cheese sandwich," Diggy said. "My mentor got back to me. It's definitely a male bite mark. But Jessica, these things are—"

"I get it. They're just pieces of a puzzle."

"Should we get breakfast?"

"No, I'm going to freshen up, get changed, and start looking for Kristi Zea. I want to hear the story again from her mouth." Jessica sighed. "But first, just drop me at the Bluestone house. I want to make sure Wallert calling the Wilshire cops on me wasn't act one in a longer, grander performance."

They drove through Brentwood, silent, watching teams of gardeners unloading equipment from their trucks onto immaculate lawns, dog walkers in bright vans carrying precious furry bundles. Jessica sat up in her seat when she spied the private security car two driveways down from the Beauvoir house. There was a man in the front seat using his radio, watching the porch with binoculars. Three ladies were there, waiting. Jessica recognized Ada Maverick leaning against the front window, tapping cigarette ash into a potted plant. Blair Harbour was sitting on the steps, nursing a battered and bloodied face. Jessica didn't know the third woman, who was pacing the porch, talking to herself.

"What the . . ." Diggy let the car roll to a stop outside the house. "Who are . . . Is that . . . ?"

"Thanks for the ride, Diggs," Jessica said as she opened the door.

"Is that *Harbour*?"

Jessica shut the car door on Diggy and walked toward the house.

BLAIR

Jessica Sanchez walked past me as I rose unsteadily on the porch. She unlocked the front door of the house and went inside before I could offer an explanation. Sneak followed her without even looking at me. We gathered in the kitchen, Ada taking her time, wandering over to the huge windows, one taped with paper where the glass had been blown out and swept into a pile on the porch. When I had called Sneak at daybreak, I knew it was a mistake instantly. She was still high now, rolling her tongue across her front teeth beneath her dry lips, her eyes restless, strings of muttered words escaping her that I barely caught in the huge room.

"Really, really nice house. Expensive. Too expensive for . . . I'm talking millions. Millions and millions. But who knows? Who . . . Who knows something like that? It could be—"

"What the hell happened to you?" Jessica asked. She looked exhausted. Her long black hair was out and tangled. I'd expected another snarl of abuse about turning up unannounced on her doorstep only hours after I'd done it the first time, this time with the backup of two other criminals. I looked at Ada and Sneak, and wondered how to begin defending myself.

"I was attacked in my apartment," I said. "I escaped and didn't know where else to go. I called the others just to tell them where I was headed, that I was alive. I didn't tell them to come here, but—"

"Blair says you can help finding Dayly," Ada said. "I'm here to find out how."

There was a blistering silence, broken only by Sneak's pacing footsteps. Jessica watched Sneak for a while, squinting at her missing earlobe.

"Jessica," I said hesitantly, gesturing to Ada. "This is—"

"I know who Ada Maverick is," Jessica snapped.

"Everybody knows." Ada gave an icy smile.

"Have you guys . . ." I began.

"Last time I saw Detective Sanchez, she was part of a squad trying to pin me with possession of some guns," Ada said.

"A *shipping container* full of guns," Jessica corrected.

"One of my many hobbies is importing and trading rare antiques and domestic fineries," Ada explained to me, shrugging innocently. "A simple shipping manifest mix-up has left Sanchez here with the unfortunate misapprehension that I'm some kind of international arms dealer."

"'Terrorist' might be another word," Jessica said.

"How dramatic." Ada rolled her eyes.

"I guess that's Dayly's mom." Jessica jutted her chin at Sneak, who was staring out at the pool.

"*Millions and millions*," Sneak said.

"She's not handling things very well right now," I said.

"I can't help you women." Jessica put her hands up. "I'm in enough shit right now as it is."

"Your cinematic debut not sitting well with the captain?" Ada asked.

Jessica's neck flushed with red. "Where did you see it?"

"YouTube."

"Wonderful."

"What are you guys talking about?" I asked.

"Nothing." Jessica scratched her neck. "Blair, if you've been the victim of a home invasion, you should go directly to the police. Your apartment is a crime scene. They'll send a team out."

"I've told you why we can't do that," I said, covering my nose and mouth. I was infuriatingly weepy. For fifteen minutes after I'd bolted from my apartment, leaving my attacker inside, I'd hidden in an alleyway crying and hyperventilating in turn, trying and failing to shake myself out of it. When I had gone back to my apartment after a few hours waiting in the dark, I had found the door open, the place empty, and Hugh Jackman's container on its side in the kitchen, lid off, the creature long gone. The sight of it had thrown me into more tears. I drew a deep breath now and clenched my fists. "Look. When I left here yesterday, you hadn't said no to me. You said you didn't know what you'd do. I hope that's because you wouldn't turn away from the case of a missing girl just because it was brought to you by someone like me."

Jessica gave a tired sigh, and I saw my opening.

"Ada and Sneak and I are ex-cons," I said. "We're bad people. But we're trying to do something good here. Dayly needs us."

The clang of the locking mechanism on the pool fence outside drew all of our attention. We looked out the unbroken kitchen windows and watched Sneak stripping off slowly at the water's edge. She had more tattoos than I'd imagined, prancing pixies and butterflies around her hips, a set of paw prints on her white, round butt. She walked into the water and pushed off as if she was about to do laps in a public pool, heading for the deep end, her chin above water. She was still muttering to herself. Jessica bumped my shoulder with hers.

"I want to talk to you alone," she said.

I followed her out onto the deck, past the pool, toward the back garden gate. I could see Sasha's house through the foliage, and gripped the gate that surely gave my son access to Jessica for their little visits. So close to the world I desired, yet impossibly separated from it, the way I had been when there were bars and walls between Jamie and me instead of leaves and lattice. Jessica lit a cigarette and exhaled hard.

"You didn't tell me Ada Maverick was involved in this," she said.

"I left that part out," I confirmed.

"Let me make something absolutely clear," Jessica said. "You need to expend every effort you can from the moment you leave here today detaching Ada from yourself and this case."

"What? Why? She's been very helpful to us."

"She can smell money," Jessica said. "That's why she's here."

"She gave us five thousand dollars to help our cause," I scoffed. Ada was standing on the pool deck, out of earshot, smoking and watching Sneak cutting laps across the smooth surface of the water like a cat watching a fish in a tank.

"That cash was an investment," Jessica said. "Trust me. I know that woman. She doesn't do things out of the goodness of her heart. If she's helping you it's because she thinks it'll be worth it to her in the long run. You can see where she's coming from, can't you? If Dayly's got herself mixed up with gangs and drugs, that's money. If there are corrupt cops somehow involved in this, that's money. If she's been kidnapped by someone for ransom, that's money."

"You've got it wrong," I said. "She's helping us because she owes me. I saved a member of her family. A baby. She couldn't get even with me in prison and she doesn't like the idea of people knowing that."

Jessica laughed humorlessly.

"Yes, okay, she's a violent lunatic," I pressed. "But she knows when she needs to pay her dues."

"It's your funeral." Jessica shrugged.

"Are you going to help us or not?" I asked.

Jessica looked at me. Really searched my eyes. I stood there, not knowing why, not knowing what she could possibly see in me but a killer who had returned to her world only to wreak more havoc, to bring yet more darkness than I had last time. I didn't want her looking at me, trying to decide if I was worth helping. It was Dayly she needed to think about. Sneak, sitting on the edge of the pool, was staring at the wispy marine layer slowly creeping over the neighborhood toward the base of the mountains. Jessica threw her cigarette into the lush garden and folded her arms, seeming to have made a decision.

"Who was this guy who attacked you?"

"I don't know," I said. "It was pitch darkness. For all I know it was Tasik. He already set a parole officer onto me."

"That's a big leap. The guy did what any sane police officer would do—order a check on a parolee who's acting strange—and then suddenly he's trying to rape you in your apartment?"

"I don't know if rape was the goal."

"Might it be someone connected to Sneak? Or Ada? You invite these types into your life, you're going to get—"

"You didn't answer my question," I said. "Are you going to help us?"

Jessica wouldn't look at me.

"I'll see what they have on your stolen car," she said finally. "And I'll check in on Tasik, see why he's so determined to crawl up your ass. But that's it."

It seemed too dangerous to celebrate in any way as I stood there, but inside my chest an explosion was happening, of relief, of excitement. I felt an urge to hug Jessica, then an otherworldly repulsion at the idea, a sudden prickle of fury and hatred at this woman and what she had done to me, the necessity of her in my life both a decade ago and today. Outwardly I stiffened, determined not to do anything to let her know how grateful and confused I felt.

"What would you recommend we do?" I asked.

"I'm curious about this parachuting thing," Jessica said. "You said the pamphlet was on top of the desk. You didn't have to dig for it."

"Right."

"So it's recent."

"I guess so."

"Go check that out," she said. Sneak was standing naked at the pool fence, her breasts and belly pressed against the glass like flat sugared doughnuts. Jessica turned to me. "And try to get your little posse of jailbirds under control."

I heard rapid, thumping footsteps on grass but didn't have time to turn before the gate beside me lurched violently as Jamie scaled it from the other side. I looked up to see my son hanging over the top of the leaf-covered lattice, wearing a halo of morning sunshine.

"Whoa!" I laughed, shading my battered face with my hand.

"Whoa back," he said. "What are you doing over there?"

I remembered Sneak standing naked at the pool fence, but when I looked back she seemed to have submerged in the water again. Ada was watching Jamie with interest. I expected Jessica to answer my child but the detective was examining her fingernails, leaving me to it.

"I was just, uh, visiting." I gestured weirdly at Jessica. "Visiting my, um . . . friend?"

Jessica looked up at me. Her eyes blazed.

"Are you having a party?" Jamie asked. "Who's that near the pool?"

"Shouldn't you be getting ready for school, kid?" Jessica asked.

"Shouldn't you be out solving crimes?" The boy wobbled his head, sassy and proud of it. I bit my tongue as I watched the cogs and wheels in his mind working. He pointed at me. "Hey, wait a minute. Do you guys know each other from—"

"Jamie, just—"

"From jail?"

Neither Jessica nor I spoke.

"Because *you* put people in jail," Jamie said, pointing at Jessica now. "And *you* used to be—"

"Knitting class," Jessica blurted. Everyone stared at her. "We met each other at knitting class. We both knit. Toys. Sweaters. So do they." She jerked her thumb at Ada and Sneak. "It's a knitting circle." Sneak was at the deep end of the pool, seemingly engaged in a whispered conversation with the filter box.

"I didn't know you knit stuff." Jamie looked at me, skeptical.

"I'm not very good," I said. I reached up and rubbed his arm. "Now go get ready for school, buddy."

Jamie thumped away like a happy rabbit, up the lawn toward Sasha's house.

"I love you!" I called. He made a vomiting noise in response.

"He usually says 'I love you back,'" I assured Jessica. She said nothing. "Knitting circle, huh?"

"Fuck you," Jessica sneered.

"I actually can knit," Ada chipped in with a smile, waving her cigarette. "It's useful to know a variety of knots and ties. Good life skill."

A cold shiver ran through me. If Ada had heard our conversation with Jamie clearly enough to comment, perhaps she had heard Jessica warning me to get the dangerous woman off my team. Jessica seemed to be thinking the same thing. She sighed and walked away, into the house.

Dear John,

I don't know what to say to your confession about the homeless guy. You're telling me to go with it, to follow my instincts, that voice inside that's saying "Fuck it!," and then you tell me the first time you did, you killed an innocent person. That's hardly an endorsement of the free life, if I'm honest. But you're right. I'm slipping. I missed (skipped!) a class at community college the other day so I could go to a party with my douchebag boyfriend. He doesn't have a lot of respect for me but I'm hanging in there anyway. That's the first class I've skipped. Ever. At the party, I enjoyed the sense of recklessness. I enjoyed it so much, in fact, I got crazy high and have no idea what I did for a while there. I remember that this guy was walking around with a big yellow snake on his shoulders. We left the party in someone's car, went somewhere, into the mountains maybe. The rush of reality creeping in heavily the next morning was sickening. Like a big monster that came lumbering through the door. I'm so angry all the time. Why do I have to do this? And why do I have to do it alone?

I feel terrible for talking about how caged and hunted I feel when you're sitting there in your cell twenty-three hours a day. I just watched a Louis Theroux documentary on San Quentin. I didn't realize you have steel mesh on the front of your cell. *You can't even see out properly. I guess I thought there might be bars, a view of something, people going by. Maybe a window. It occurs to me that if you did have a secret bag of cash out there somewhere, you might try to find someone who would take it and share the adventures they had on your dime with you. It would kind of be like you're along for the ride. They could send you postcards. But you know how that goes, don't you—they send you a few then they get bored and stop, and you can only wonder what they've done, whether they've got themselves killed in Colombia while chilling out on the beach, and now some cartel scumbags have got your cash. Sounds like torture. While you know where the money is, you have the power. The potential.*

I'm supposed to go to class again tonight, but I have a bag of weed here and no sense of panic or fear in my chest about not going. There's another party tomorrow night, and another class. Some dangerous people are going to the party, apparently. Sounds fun. I feel no real guilt about the trouble that will come if I keep sliding. Am I turning into you? Following in Daddy's footsteps? If I stop going to school completely I'll lose my place in the course, lose my scholarship, probably end up out on the street like my mother. What am I supposed to do to turn all this around? Am I fighting destiny?

You should just come right out and tell me if you have the cash buried out there somewhere or not. I'm sick of thinking about it.

Talk soon,
Dayly

BLAIR

I needed sleep. It was dangerous, with the probable concussion, but I had a shift at the Pump'n'Jump that night, and every limb weighed twice what it should. I left Sneak, still damp, in the kitchen, searching every cupboard and drawer for Hugh Jackman. I knew the creature was gone, but it seemed cruel to tell Sneak so. The thing was tame, but it had almost certainly walked out the open door when my attacker and I left the apartment. I tried not to think about its tameness likely making it easy prey for cats, hawks, or coyotes out there. Him. Making *him* easy prey.

I woke to the sound of furious scratching and leaped out of bed, hoping the sound was the gopher trying to make its way under the door to my bedroom. It was not. When I found Sneak she was in the shower, and the scratching noise was my toothbrush working a chemical foam back and forth in the grout between the floor tiles. The whole house smelled of bleach. She had cleaned every surface. I opened the oven and stared at the gleaming interior. She had cleaned the collected gunk off the little plastic ring around the red "on" light. The curtains had been steamed and were still blotchy. I thought about cocaine or ecstasy or whatever the hell she was on, and how easily I would be able to get through a night at the Pump'n'Jump on it. I saw myself cleaning the fine cracks in the slushie machine of crusty blue sugar crystals with a toothpick and a sponge.

Sneak came down while we drove out of the city, as we turned off the I-10 and onto the I-85 toward San Jasinte. She watched the vast, flat suburbs of Redlands recede into sun-bleached farmland at the base of the mountains. Road signs to Big Bear Lake encouraged drivers to speed through our destination without bothering to stop and look. There was little township to speak of. A yellow minibus outside the school was waiting for students as we drove by, half of the driver's face masked by enormous aviator sunglasses and a ten-gallon hat. The only bar in San Jasinte had a horse post out the front. Inconceivably, a surf gear shop dominated the corner of one block, blaring loud rock music, a chalkboard reading simply *SALES! SALES! SALES!*

On the edge of town, Sneak perked up as we followed signs to the airfield.

"I can't believe you asked the cop who arrested you to get involved in all this," she said.

"She's the only cop I know."

"Well, I appreciate it. It must stir up a lot of stuff."

"It'll be worth it when we find Dayly."

"Why the hell is she doing this for you?" Sneak asked. "You're her old collar. It doesn't make a whole lot of sense."

"I think there's something terrible going on there," I said. "I'm afraid to ask what it is. But she looks awful compared to when I knew her a decade ago. She's thin and exhausted. That house isn't hers. Can't be. And the broken windows? What the hell is that? I think I saw bandages under her shirt. Maybe she's trying to distract herself from all that trouble, whatever it is, with a side case."

"It doesn't matter. If she's going to help find my child, that's all that counts." Sneak picked at her wounded ear. "I want to know what's happened to Dayly, even if it's bad. Even if it's the worst."

I didn't know what to say to that, so I said nothing.

"It has to be bad," she said. "The gopher's gone."

"The gopher's gone because of me. I knocked it off the counter."

"It's a sign."

"It's not a sign, Sneak."

"I want to know if it was my fault, whatever happened to her. I showed her the dark path," Sneak said. "If she turned and walked that way and got mixed up with some drug dealers or pimps or bad cops or whatever, then I've got to know. I can't wonder forever."

We arrived at a windswept field full of long, dry grass. A squat, plain building stood surrounded by large sheds, small aircraft lit yellow and orange by the falling sun. I pulled over in the parking lot and grabbed Sneak's arm before she could get out.

"Sneak," I said. "In Happy Valley, you slapped some sense into me when I was lying there pretending I was on another planet for days on end. Remember that? You might not. It was early on. You told me that if I cracked up, everybody would wonder why they weren't doing the same."

"Sounds a bit deep for someone like me." She shrugged.

"You said 'We all get through it or none of us get through it.'"

She looked at the buildings beyond, didn't reply.

"It doesn't matter why Ada and Jessica have come along. They're with us. You're not alone. We're going to get answers. We're all going to get through it together."

She turned away and opened the car door, but in the side mirror I saw a flicker of a smile on her face. I tried to stop her outside the office doors.

"We need a game plan," I said.

"I got one," she said, continuing ahead. "Your turn to follow *my* lead."

The man behind the counter was small and lean, wearing a khaki uniform with little winged badges on the lapels. He was cleaning a glass display case full of aeronautical objects—antique-looking goggles and old maps, a leather helmet with long, dry straps and buckles—that served as a counter. Sneak strode up to the display case and put her forearms right where he'd just finished wiping.

"Sir, I'm Detective Tanya Morello and this is my partner, Detective Frances Levine. We're here to ask you a few questions."

I kicked Sneak in the ankle but she didn't look at me. The man behind the counter took in her greasy T-shirt, which seemed to be from a tattoo shop called "Death Punch" in Las Vegas. He looked out the window at the Gangstermobile, and then at me with my mom jeans and bruised face.

"You guys are cops?"

"We've just come from an undercover job," Sneak said.

"What job?"

"Fentanyl shipments coming across the border. We have reason to believe a gang from south of here is using small private airports east of Los Angeles to bring dangerous drugs into the country from Mexico. You watch *Dateline*?"

"I do." The man straightened. "I saw the episode last week about fentanyl. Crazy stuff. Have you two got any identification?"

"Identification?" Sneak shook her head, baffled. "You think we'd risk carrying identification around these creeps? My partner and I have just spent three days holed up with a crew of psychopathic drug smugglers in Long Beach, in an attempt to get information on their leader. These guys are lunatics. We saw a guy get his hand chopped off with a chain saw."

"Jeez." He swallowed. "And they're in this area now?"

"This is an epidemic we have on our hands here, man," Sneak said. She started taking leaflets from a stand at the end of the counter and making a stack of them. She tucked the stack into her handbag. "A national crisis. Millions of lives are at stake. You think you've asked enough time-wasting questions yet?"

"Okay, okay." The man put his hands up. "Sorry. I don't know how I can help you. There's nothing like that coming through here. We're a family business. We log every landing, and we take ID, and we have ground surveillance twenty-four seven. I have the manifest right here." He leaned behind the counter and hefted a book onto the glass that was so big I was worried the display case would give way.

"Mr. . . . ?" I said.

"Danny Rieu," he said. He looked at me as though asking for help. "It's French Canadian."

The man's glance awakened me. I thought about interrupting Sneak's lies before they went too far. Then I realized how much was at stake, and how well Sneak's plan was working from the attention Danny was giving her.

"Mr. Rieu, we're looking for any information you have on a particular couple that might have been inquiring about parachuting in the past few weeks," I said. "We think they might be mixed up in all this."

I showed him a picture of Dayly on my phone that I'd taken from one of her social media profiles. Rieu hardly glanced at it.

"I saw the report on CNN about the airfield outside Odessa," he said to Sneak, his eyes big, earnest, eager. "The ground controller who was letting guys through with night flights full of fentanyl. Eleven years, he got." He wrung his hands. "Eleven *years*. Just for turning a blind eye. He wasn't even the one who—"

"Danny." Sneak tapped the counter. "Try to focus. We've got to find these people before they skip town and head for Panama."

"Right." Rieu went to the computer by the windows and started clicking. "I've got all the footage here for the past six months. I'll put it on a USB drive for you. I'm really tight on security. That's how I know there's nothing to worry about. Nothing I've overlooked. Nothing criminal. I don't remember your girl specifically but a lot of couples inquire about parachuting. It's the quintessential twenty-first birthday gift. A wholesome, thrilling adventure at a reasonable price."

He gestured to a poster behind the counter by a window looking out onto the field. The couple from the pamphlets, faces smashed with wind, howling with joy. The slogan beneath that read *Wholesome, thrilling adventures at reasonable prices!*

Sneak and I stood back from the counter while Rieu clicked and dragged files onto a thumb drive.

"This is not what I had in mind," I told Sneak quietly. "Getting caught impersonating police officers would be about as bad for us as sticking a gun in the guy's mouth."

"I thought you were anti-guns."

"I am."

"So it's the police officer route, then." Sneak shrugged.

"Sneak." I rubbed my brow. "Why didn't you just tell him the truth?"

"Because this is faster and more fun. Just relax." She rolled her eyes. "I've done this a million times before. I learned from the best. I knew this guy who used to play a cop for truckers hauling goods out of the Port of San Diego. He'd pull the trucks over and threaten to write them up for some bullshit infringement, let them buy him off with whatever was in the back."

"Sneak, we don't have time for this."

"He'd get all sorts of goodies," she said. "Cameras. Fur coats. Golf clubs. It was a great gag. But eventually it went bad, as all good grifts do. A trucker he'd pulled over gave him some DVD players as a payoff, and one of the boxes was full of chameleons. They're smaller than you think, chameleons. Expensive on the black market. There were about a hundred of them in the box and they'd traveled all the way from Africa so I guess they were pretty excited about getting out. They crawled all over the inside of his car. The guy freaked out and drove into a tree. Car exploded in a giant fireball. Crispy little chameleons on the ground everywhere."

"Mr. Rieu," I said, pushing Sneak toward the counter. I needed to get Rieu away from Sneak to give her time to search. "Perhaps we could leave my partner to look at your logbook and you could show me some of your aircraft?"

"Sure," the man said, smiling brightly. "I'll give you a proper tour. Come this way."

Long grass was growing under the wheels of unused planes in the shade. Sun-bleached rubber and faded seat belts. There was a nest of swallows in the roof of a long hangar, the birds swirling out, going for fast, extended sweeps of the field before returning with tiny bugs in their beaks. A fire was burning in the mountains somewhere, smoke trailing thin and black against the white, blazing sky.

I should have known something was wrong by the speed with which we walked by the rows of small aircraft sitting like ready white birds, ticking with the heat of the sun. Rieu wasn't giving me a tour. He was leading me. I didn't question our path. I was thinking about Dayly, what she might have wanted out here, who the possible cop with the flat-top haircut was.

I was in the hangar before I really had a sense of the danger around me. Perhaps it was the sun beating down on my head, or the shock of the past twenty-four hours, but I looked at the three men in front of us almost pleasantly, as though Rieu was going to introduce me to them and we were all going to have a friendly chat about aviation fuel types. It was the sight of the bags on the table that brought me to. Large, clear plastic ziplock bags stacked in an enormous pile, some already packed into cardboard boxes marked with a brand of ramen noodle that I recognized from my time in prison. The bags were full to bursting with little white pills. Rieu pushed me forward and the men froze, two pausing in packing the boxes, one slowly lowering his phone from his ear in shock at the sight of me.

"There's another one in the office," Rieu said.

"Whoa." I put my hands up carefully, trying to force my screaming brain to focus. "Okay. Let's everybody just stay calm."

"They're cops." Rieu dragged a chair from beside the table full of pills. "I don't know if they're wired up or not."

I glanced around the huge aluminum hangar. There were more aircraft here, tables of parachuting equipment and coiled ropes, random parts of planes under restoration—the aileron of a Cessna lying on a tarp covered with fresh white paint. I could see stencils of letters lying in a stack on the ground by one of the planes. These men had probably been switching the tail numbers every few months as they moved drugs across the border.

The sight of the setup was so terrifying I almost gagged. I was grateful when Rieu shoved me into the chair before the men, my legs unsteady, tingling as the blood rushed to my head.

"We're not cops," I managed. No one heard me.

"Fuck, fuck, fuck." A big guy with long, dark sideburns rounded the table and grabbed Rieu by the shoulders. "How did this happen? How did . . . Aw, fuck!"

"They're not here looking for us." Rieu was panting, wringing his hands. "They're after some chick and a guy who might have come out here a couple of months ago. Don't panic. We can contain this."

"We're not cops," I repeated. The men who had been packing the boxes were still frozen, bags in their hands, watching Rieu and Sideburns try to work out the situation with the big-eyed stillness of frightened cats. "Listen to me."

"Go get the other one," Sideburns stammered. He drew a black pistol from the back of his jeans. "Is the parking lot empty? Are they the only ones here?"

"We're not cops!" I snapped. The men looked at me. I was gripping the chair for dear life. Words started spilling out of me. "We're just regular people. We're here looking for our friend. She's missing. I swear to God, we don't care what the hell you're doing here. All the stuff about fentanyl was a—"

"They know it's fentanyl." Rieu's mouth was down-turned with horror. "They know about the Long Beach guys."

"Jesus." I gripped my hair. "That was all bullshit! It was a lucky guess! My friend was lying her ass off, trying to get you to give us a look at your books. Just . . . We . . . You have to listen to me! Please!"

"Who would lie about being a cop?" Sideburns asked me. "Why wouldn't you just tell the guy your friend is missing? Ask to see the tapes?"

"Because she lies about everything. She's just that sort of person. We're not cops, I swear to you. Let us walk away from here and you'll never see either of us again."

Sideburns looked at Rieu, at the men behind the table, at me. He actioned the pistol. As it swung up toward my head, I felt the seconds begin to lag with shocking clarity, my brain frantically trying to catch up to the situation I had found myself in. My pulse was beating so hard in my head I was seeing disjointed glimpses of the movements around me. The gun coming up. All the men turning toward the sound of an engine roaring outside the hangar. The east side of the hangar collapsing inward, bursting open as the Gangstermobile smashed through it and into the table where the pill bags were piled, sending the men there flying for cover. I sat rigid in my chair as Sneak hung out of the driver's-side window and leveled a gun the size of her forearm at Sideburns, her aim hardly fixing before she blasted the weapon at him. The noise hammered off the sides of the building. Sneak fired twice more, and I felt the percussion wave of the bullets sailing past my left and then right shoulder as she fired wildly at Rieu and Sideburns, sending both of them scattering.

"You just gonna sit there?" she shouted at me. I

scrambled off the chair and ran numbly to the car door as Sneak backed the vehicle awkwardly out of the hole she'd made in the hangar.

JESSICA

Wallert wasn't at his desk. Jessica made like she was just swinging by to pick up some papers, shuffled things around the keyboard while the few officers at their desks got over the shock of her presence. She took the boxed bar of soap from her pocket, unpacked it, and set it on the desk. Jessica took Wallert's keys from the little tin cigar box he kept beside his monitor and selected a gold key with a black rubber rim from the collection. She pressed the gold key into the soap bar, making a careful impression, then reboxed the bar of soap and returned it to her pocket, the keys to their rightful place. She ran a finger down the sheet of printed paper taped to the back of the cubicle that read *Roster*. Jessica was almost at the elevators when someone hooked a finger into the back of her shirt, tugging her to a stop.

She smelled the bourbon before she saw him. Jessica turned and stood chest-to-chest with the sour-breathed man, so close she could see the pockmarks on the end of his nose.

"Have you got the call yet?" Wallert smiled.

"From who?"

"Justin Helger from *LA Magazine* rang here, trying to reach you. They put him through to me. He's running a story about the video, wanted you to comment." Wallert's smile had grown into a wide grin. "I gave him your cell number."

"A psychic once told me I'd make the national news one day," Jessica said. "I bet she didn't see this in her crystal ball, though."

"Take the house," Wallert said. He glanced around the cubicles, his voice low and threatening. "Take the Brentwood house. Sell it. Give me half. Say you'll do it now, and I'll stop."

"Your breath smells like a fucking dumpster, you know that?" Jessica spat.

"If you think the video was a low blow, you've got no idea what else I have in store." Wallert's eyes were wet, pale, desperate. "I've shown you that I'll use cops to get to you."

Jessica sighed.

"I'll use other people, too," Wallert said.

"Wally"—Jessica edged closer to him—"I'll burn that house to the ground before I give you a dime of what it's worth."

Jessica spied Vizchen making his way toward them along the aisles. She backed off. Two of them were more than she had the energy for. She punched the elevator button and slipped inside, watching the doors close on the two men with relief. At the first floor, the doors opened on Captain Whitton, standing with his arms folded, obviously having known she was in the building. Jessica tried to punch the "door close" button but he stuck his long arm through the gap.

"How many times did I call you?" he asked.

"I don't know." Jessica exited the elevator. "Twenty?"

"Thirty-one," he said. They stood by a poster of a patrol cop cleaning his gun on a spotless gray tabletop. *Never trust a badly maintained weapon!* "You don't ignore calls from your superior officer. Ever. That's policy."

"Give it to IAG. They can add it to my file."

"What the hell are you doing here?"

"I came looking for you. I figured you'd called so many times it would be rude to just suddenly answer. You deserved a face-to-face."

"That's a pile of horse shit," Whitton snapped. "This thing between you and Wallert has got to stop. It's reflecting poorly on the department now." He leaned in a little, glanced down the hall. "I don't care what your sexual proclivities are, Sanchez. That sort of thing between consenting adults is . . . well, it's unusual. Untraditional. Un*conventional*. But it's fine. It's really fine."

"I don't need you to rubber stamp it for me, Captain," Jessica said.

"I had this girlfriend in college—"

"Please don't."

"Anyway, look, that video appears to capture you engaging in solicitation, which is a crime. A fireable offense."

"It was solicitation," Jessica said. She looked the tall man right in the eyes. "I've been going to Goren for years. I like what we do together. I need it. It takes me away from the troubles in my personal life, and it's a hell of a lot less emotionally taxing than maintaining a real relationship."

"Would you keep your goddamn voice down?"

"But convicting me on solicitation is going to rely on a conviction of Goren for prostitution, and you won't get that," she continued. "He's been dodging that charge for more than a decade. The man has friends, clients, in high places. Much higher than you, boss."

Whitton shook his head, looked distant, as if he was trying to see reason approaching on the horizon, a cavalry of cooperation and sense.

"You and Wallert leave each other alone." He pointed a finger in her face. "Make a decision about the house so we can all move on from this."

Jessica walked off, waving as she went, ending the meeting with what she hoped was a noncommittal but friendly goodbye.

The first-floor bullpen seemed less personalized than the third floor. There were few if any photographs in frames on desks, novelty posters stuck at the back of cubicles, cut-out comic strips pinned to dividers. While she was used to the coffee station on the third floor, with its leaning towers of coffee mugs and snack plates, and wet huddles of spoons at the bottom of the sink, the station here was spotlessly clean and didn't seem to require the tattered printed signs about clearing up. Through large, tinted windows at the end of the space she could see patrol officers coming and going to squad cars with their go-bags of weapons, logs, personal equipment. She saw Al Tasik at the end of a row of desks, looking at his phone as he slowly rose from his swivel chair.

"Tasik," Jessica called. The man hardly glanced at her, heaving a backpack onto the desk and sliding some paperwork into it.

"Tasik," she said again as she arrived. "I'm Jessica Sanchez. Third floor. We did our weapons cert together last November?"

"Oh, right." Tasik looked down at her, at the people around them who were slowly waking to her presence. "I remember. Commiserations on the . . . uh."

Jessica waited, forced him to finish.

"The video." He shrugged. "Complete bullshit.

Nobody needs to be caught out like that. Those guys should have turned off their cameras."

"Thanks."

"You looked good, if you don't mind me saying," he added. "It might be some consolation. Everybody agrees. You were red hot."

"It's no consolation," Jessica said. "At all. Can we get down to business? I want to talk to you about a missing person. Dayly Lawlor."

"Oh, yeah." Tasik turned and sat on his desk, rubbed a hand over his blond stubble. "Isn't that a mess."

"What kind of mess?"

Tasik shook his head. "That was a good girl, you know? Some kind of animal studies person. Steady job. No jacket. Then she falls off the wagon for some reason and gets all wrapped up with a bunch of low-lifes. Probably daddy issues. It usually is."

"Which lowlifes?" Jessica sat beside him.

"It's like this. A few months ago I was doing a ride-along and write-up on a young patrol officer going for a promotion. I'm in the back of a wagon and my guy pulls over this rolling hotbox on Sunset jammed with idiots. We got Trammon Willis and Sean Sykes in that car, a couple of other meatheads, and this kid I've never heard of, a girl. Dayly Lawlor."

"Willis and Sykes are Crips."

"Yah," Tasik said.

Jessica thought, watched the officers going by outside the window.

"So the guys all eat whatever drugs they've got on them as we're pulling up behind them," Tasik continued. "The driver's bugging out, hard. I was sure it was all just a waste of time. But then my guys look in the trunk and they find a duffel bag with two AR-15s in it."

"Jesus Christ."

"Yeah." Tasik nodded. "The driver tried to do a runner. Bolted, got taken down by some teenagers standing outside a boxing gym in a citizen's arrest. They split his head open like a coconut on the pavement. Hilarious. We look, and there's worrying stuff in the bag besides the guns. Wads of cash. Five ski masks. Five kids in the car; five ski masks. That doesn't look great, does it?"

"What does Dayly say about it all?"

"Well, when I finally get her to stop crying, she tells me she knows nothing about the bag. For once, I believe what I'm hearing. She says she was just catching a ride from one gathering of bottom-dwellers to the next. Says she didn't even know she was at a Crip party."

"All the blue do-rags didn't clue her in?" Jessica asked. Tasik rolled his eyes.

"Anyway, the kid is losing her mind. Keeps telling me she's never been in trouble before. She's right to freak out, too. They booked the four guys. They're going to trial. Sean Sykes was on probation. He'll go back for seven years if they pin this on him."

"So, what, you think the morons in the car have asked her to take the rap for the guns because it's a first offense? She said no and now they're after her?"

"Everybody but Sykes bailed on the charges." Tasik shrugged. "It's one of the theories I'm working on. Pinning the bag on Dayly would be an easy out for them."

"What other theories have you got?"

"What's your interest in this case?" Tasik glanced at his watch.

"You had someone come in and inquire about it. Blair Harbour."

"Right." Tasik nodded. "That was weird. She's that

rich bitch who popped her neighbor over in Brentwood. You know her?"

"I bagged her," Jessica said.

"Yeah, well, she's friends with Dayly's mother, I think. Came in trying to make anonymous inquiries. I told her to fuck off."

Jessica waited for more. There was none. Tasik picked up his backpack.

"And it was Dayly who stole Blair Harbour's car that night." Jessica watched Tasik carefully. "You knew that, right?"

"What? No. Harbour didn't mention that. I'll have to track that down, see if the car has been found," he said. "Who told you that?"

"Harbour."

"You're talking to her?"

"She came trying to make inquiries. I told her to fuck off." Jessica smiled.

"Wise choice."

"So what did you do with the kid on the night you picked her up in the car full of douchebags?"

"I didn't book her," Tasik said. "I told the guys to hold off. She seemed to me like a kid walking the line, you know? So I didn't want something stupid like this to be the thing to tip her." He rubbed his face, tired. "Maybe I was being too soft. Just a week earlier, I had a real tear-jerker dropped on me. This kid I'd been watching circling the drain for a while got pushed in front of a train by his supposed best friend. It was over a bag of dope. Victim had just got accepted into Harvard. Can you believe that?"

"Crazy."

"These people"—he shook his head—"they're animals. Once you get in among them, you're part of the group. There's no escape. You start limping and the rest start moving in, wanting their share of meat.

They'll pick off their own if they have to. They've got the herd mentality *and* the scavenger mentality."

"Right," Jessica said. She was thinking about predators and prey, about Ada Maverick watching Sneak swim laps in the pool.

"Harbour and the mother will only have popped up to get their share of whatever Dayly's into before the girl goes off the radar completely. Me? I think the kid's probably dead in the desert somewhere. But you never know. Maybe she's in New York or something, starting over."

"Can I have a copy of the file? Just so I can put it to bed."

"Be my guest." Tasik handed her a stack of papers from the desk. "But let me warn you. You don't want to get involved. Nothing good can come from these people. It's not in their nature."

BLAIR

I couldn't speak. Not as I sat clutching my seat belt while Sneak sent us screaming across the tarmac toward the road in the Gangstermobile, bullets tinking off the paintwork, splitting the back window, raining glass over the back seat. Not as we burned through San Jasinte and the next two towns, trailing dust, Sneak's hands gripping the wheel until her knuckles were white. Not as she parked in an abandoned lot connected to what once must have been a drive-in movie theater, the big screen torn and whipped by wind, emblazoned with a huge spray-painted penis, no doubt the work of local youths. When I could finally put my thoughts in order, Sneak was clicking away at a laptop she'd obviously stolen from the airfield.

"Why the hell didn't you just tell the truth, Sneak?" I growled. "You almost got us killed."

"The truth is lame," she said.

The gun she'd blasted at the men in the hangar lay on the dashboard. It was a long-nosed silver revolver with a handle so thick I wondered if I would be able to get my fist around it. I thought about Adrian

Orlov's gun bucking in my hands, the textured grip of the handle wet with my sweat.

"Where did you get that gun?"

"Where I get everything. The street."

"We need to talk about strategy," I said. "About your lies. About how much deeper I'm willing to get into this mess."

"You can give me the third degree later," she said. "I've got something here." She pointed to the screen. "Didn't take me long to find it. The camera in the reception where we were only comes on when it's triggered by the door. See? There are separate video files for each visitor. Dayly visited three weeks ago. It's not great quality, but it's her. And some flat-top guy. He's tall. Looks young and cute. They come in and they take two flyers away. I checked the video against the pamphlets I took from the counter. Looks like they took the parachuting one and this one."

She fished a leaflet out of her handbag and showed it to me. On the cover was a picture of a small white plane. Sneak opened the pamphlet and began to look through it.

"*The star of our extensive fleet of personal-hire aircraft, the Cessna 172 is a deluxe four-seater, single-engine, high-wing, fixed-wing aircraft made by the Cessna Aircraft Company,*" Sneak read. "*The engine capacity—*"

"Four-seater?" I said.

Sneak checked the pamphlet. "Yeah."

"Why?"

"I don't know." Sneak shrugged. "Does it matter?"

"Yeah," I said. "I saw two-seater planes on the field. Plenty of them. One was even done up on the inside with all sorts of Valentine's Day stuff. Red velvet seat covers and a little heart hanging off the roof.

Couples must hire them for romantic weekends. So if that's what Flat-Top and Dayly were doing, why the four seats?"

Sneak sat quietly, watching the video on the laptop. The mountains were rimmed in gold light beyond the old drive-in screen.

"They don't hold hands," she said eventually.

"Huh?"

"Flat-Top and Dayly. They don't touch each other. I've got footage of them parking her car, walking into the office, making the inquiry, and taking the pamphlets and leaving. They don't touch, not even once. So is he a boyfriend, like Dimitri said, or not? And if not, what are they doing hiring a plane together?"

I leaned over and watched the footage of the young man and Dayly entering the office at the airfield, taking the pamphlets, wandering around, and leaving.

"How do we know they were going to hire the plane?" I asked. "Maybe they took that pamphlet for cover, in case they were asked, and the real inquiry was about parachuting."

"The same is true in reverse," Sneak said.

I sighed.

"Did you look at the record book before you almost got us murdered and forced us to flee?" I asked.

She twisted in her seat and hefted the logbook off the back seat and onto her lap. I shook my head. In the back seat were two other logbooks, another laptop, a cash register, and a silver model plane.

"Did you steal all that stuff before you knew I was in trouble, or after?"

"I was just making my second trip to the car when I heard you yell." She rubbed her nose. I could see sweat beading at her temples. "I'm not seeing the name Lawlor anywhere. But if we find out who the guy is, maybe he's in here, if they did end up booking something. Here, you keep looking. I've got to get back to the city."

She threw the book into my lap and started the car. There was sweat on her upper lip. Withdrawals. As she took us back to the highway, we fell silent. I realized as night grew that I had pushed aside my terror at the feel of the man who had attacked me in bed, his stubble against my cheek, his weight on my back, all day. Now I had new nightmare fuel, the men in the hangar and the sound of the pistol actioning, the car crunching through the wall across the room from me. I was disassociating, the way I had in prison. Riding the chaos from moment to moment. I didn't want to be alone when all the terror of the past twenty-four hours caught up to me.

"Are you staying in tonight?" I asked Sneak.

"I might have to run some errands."

"Don't run any errands," I said. "Just do me a favor this one time. Stay in. I want someone there when I get back from the Pump'n'Jump."

"You got it," she said. I knew she was lying again.

I unlocked the door to my apartment and pushed it open, and Sneak followed me through it only to bump into my back as I stopped suddenly in front of her. On the coffee table, sitting on the remote control as if it were determined to turn on the TV and engage in an evening of viewing, sat a small, round gopher. I pointed at Hugh Jackman, and for a long moment Sneak and I could do nothing but stare at the creature perched on its hind legs, its front paws fiddling with a button on the remote. My friend and I broke into laughter and fell into each other's arms.

Sneak said she wasn't going out, but there was

another four hundred dollars missing from the cash pile, which I'd hidden between papers in a box of personal files in my bedroom. She twitched and paced and pretended to watch the television while I dressed for work, then caved and said she was going to take a walk around the block to clear her thoughts. She didn't come back. It seemed somehow important to keep the gopher near me, my relief at his reappearance forbidding me to leave him alone. So that night I stood behind the register at the Pump'n'Jump and tried to ignore Hugh Jackman's scuffling and scratching about in the ice cream container under the counter while I served customers. Business fell away near midnight, as it always did, and I pulled a stool toward the register and filled in some of the day's crossword in the newspaper.

My phone rang as I was watching the headlines scroll across the bottom of the television above the Coke fridge. Jittery footage of stairs in a beautiful house, a hallway, a red room, some sort of table flipped on its side. A naked woman crouching, her hair covering her face. *LAPD officer caught in the act!*

I answered the call distractedly.

"They haven't found your car," Jessica said down the phone.

"Damn it."

"There are a few cars on the list, however, which haven't been examined," she said. "Burned-out shells in the mountains, in the desert, one in Malibu. I'll go check those out. Some of them I can rule out right away. They've been sitting there for months waiting for the municipal council to come get them. But this one in the mountains was only reported three days ago. I'll start there."

"That's great," I said. "Well, not for me. Not for Dayly, either, if it is the car. But a good lead."

"There's no activity on Dayly's phone, bank accounts, or social media accounts," she said. "She's completely blacked out. Tasik is pursuing the angle that she might have some Crips after her to take a bullshit charge on a bag of guns."

"What?" I watched a cat skitter across the empty parking lot, pursuing a cockroach. Jessica told me the story she had heard from Tasik. "But what about the guy? Flat-Top? Sneak and I have him with Dayly at the San Jasinte airfield looking at hiring a plane."

"Not everything means something in an investigation like this. Sometimes things are just parts of the puzzle. All I've got on Flat-Top is a vague lead about an officer out there," Jessica said. I heard papers shuffling. "I searched the internal database, the personnel files for the San Jasinte police department. Marcus Lemon is your guy, I think. Weird name. Badge number 994901. Officer Lemon is a newbie straight out of the academy, just posted into San Jasinte in January. He's pretty clean. Young and square. Has that stupid haircut."

"Sneak and I can check him out," I said. "Did you ask Tasik why he went for me like he did?"

"I didn't need to, Blair. You're a criminal. You should be used to being treated like shit." The silence hung for a beat. "He wanted you to back off, that's all. That doesn't matter. If Dayly has pissed off some Crips then she's either dead or she should be hiding under a rock on Mars, because they'll come after her. Killing Dayly to get two of their lieutenants and one of their footmen off a guns charge would be no problem for them."

"Great," I said.

"It would make sense for one of them to bust into your apartment and try to grab you. It probably means they don't have her yet, and they're looking for anyone who might know where she is, and you stuck your hand up when you went into the police station, or maybe when you turned up at her apartment."

"So where do we go from here?" I asked.

"Tasik will probably be working on confirming the Crips angle. We should work on something else. Three weeks ago we have a weird payment into Dayly's bank account. I can't figure it out," Jessica said. "Eight hundred bucks. The money came in from one of those crypto websites that keep the payer anonymous. It'll take some tracking down. Tasik doesn't seem to be onto it."

"Okay," I said.

"Dayly also flew to San Francisco two months ago," she said. "Landed at five a.m. on a Saturday and hired a car from the airport. Dropped the car back six hours later and flew home."

"Six hours?"

"Yeah."

"Why the hell would she do that? What can you do in San Francisco for six hours?"

"No idea," Jessica said. "You can ask your friend Sneak. See if she knows what her daughter was up to."

"Look," I said as I sensed her tone easing toward the end of the call. "I want to say thanks fo—"

"Don't."

"I'm serious," I said. "It was a big ask. I don't know what's going on with you right now, but—"

"Why would what's going on with me be any of your fucking business?"

"—but things seem to be a little hectic in your life, and you were good to listen to me, to *us*, when we came knocking."

There was silence on the line. The tautness of it made me restless. I looked out the window and saw a huge black Escalade pulling in to the lot, parking without stopping near the gas pumps. I recognized the license plate and a bolt of fear sizzled through me.

"Blair," Jessica said. "That night. In Brentwood. Why didn't you—"

"Oh, Jesus, I've gotta go. I've gotta go." I ended the call and hurled the phone into the messy space beneath the counter where Hugh Jackman's container lay. I tossed the newspaper in after it.

I had never met the cartel men who owned the Kangaroo Gas Pump'n'Jump, but I had seen them talking to my boss out in the parking lot once. I'd seen the sheer menace in their eyes and the nervous, rigid gait of my boss as he walked toward them, and had stood at the counter with my hand on the receiver of the phone, ready to dial 9–1–1 and stop him from being beaten or mugged. He'd explained who they were when he returned, but I'd still written down the license plate. The men had poured out of the Escalade that day dressed uniformly in black, finely cut clothes with thick gold chains hanging from their wrists and necks, tattoos winding like blue and black vines up their necks and into their hairlines, dappled across knuckles and fingers. They'd looked like a collection of bit actors waiting to audition for the role of violent goons in an upcoming HBO narco drama.

Now as they headed toward the automatic doors, I glanced anxiously out into the darkness beyond the lot, imagining Jasmine the parole officer there in her car, ready to photograph the men and me standing under the fluorescent lights.

They were here about the robbery, I knew. The bullet hole in the Marlboro dispenser, my abject failure to do anything to counteract the shame such an incident would bring upon their gang. I felt my body shrink as I tried to calculate the odds of surviving hostile encounters with two gangs of criminals in one day. The two biggest men ducked their heads instinctively as they came through the door, easily exceeding the limits of the colored height strips inside the entrance. The four men came right for the counter. One of the two human-height guys came and leaned on the surface before me under the light, so I could see down the hollow made by his shirt, which was unbuttoned to the navel. A pierced nipple winked at me in the shadows.

"Blair Harbour," the man said.

"Yeah," I managed.

"I'm Santiago Cruz. You've probably heard of me."

"Of course," I lied.

"I'm here to talk to you about—"

"The robbery," I blurted, wincing as I interrupted him. "I know. I'm sorry. It was . . . I didn't . . . I wasn't sure what to do, and I'm sorry about the . . . the dispenser. I can replace it. It's my fault. The robber didn't take any money, so that's something."

"That's the weird thing. She did take some money," Santiago said. He straightened up. "For some reason, you replaced it with your own."

I froze. I had always believed there were no cameras inside the Pump'n'Jump or the office behind it. My boss had let slip once that the cartel sometimes held meetings at the gas station on the rare evenings in winter when it wasn't worth opening the store. I assumed they didn't want the hassle of proving to their associates that the cameras weren't on when they came together. Santiago could read my thoughts. He smiled, flashing gold teeth.

"You think I don't have cameras in my own store? I see everything that goes on here. I see you doing those puzzles all night long."

"Shit. Sorry."

"I don't give a fuck." He sniffed. "I just want to know why you would give up your money to cover a chick who just stuck a gun in your face." He made a gun with his thumb and index finger and popped an imaginary bullet at my nose. "I can't figure it out."

"Well, I . . ." I looked around at the men. Santiago's sideman was watching me closely, leaning on a stand full of cheap phones. He had the relaxed, predatory gaze of a lion in the sun watching cubs play, above the drama. I felt a stirring in my stomach at the sight of him. Big, hard hands. I shook my head to focus myself. "Look, it's hard to explain. I guess I just saw someone who was in a bad place, and um . . . I didn't want you guys to, uh . . ."

"To hunt her down and kill her?" Santiago raised his eyebrows. "Maybe kill her family, just to send a message?"

I said nothing.

"Because we're those kind of people, right?" he continued. "Sicarios. Pandilleros. Monsters. We'd find her, bust into her house, tie her family to lawn chairs, and toss them in the swimming pool one by one. That's what you see when you look at us."

I opened my mouth to reply, but nothing came out. The air was like fire all around me, flickering with danger. My hands were wet with sweat, white-knuckled, gripping the counter. When a big smile broke over Santiago's face, my throat tightened almost to closing.

"You're right!" he laughed. It was a hard, deep hacking. "We are those kinds of people!"

The San Marino 13s gang leader leaned over and thumped my shoulder, grabbed my arm, and shook my whole body with it. The men around him smirked. The sweat on the back of my neck had turned cold.

"That's exactly what we would have done." Santiago grinned.

"Okay." I swallowed, looked at his sideman or lieutenant, the one who wasn't a towering beast. He seemed frighteningly calm.

"So who was the chica with the gun? Do you know her?" Santiago asked.

"No," I lied again. "Seemed like some street girl, maybe. A nobody. I'd never seen her before. Haven't seen her since."

"You wouldn't tell me if you had," Santiago reasoned, shrugging. "If you're going to cover her ass with your own money, you're not going to then give us her name. Not unless we tie *you* to a lawn chair. Put *you* on the edge of the pool."

I stared at his grinning teeth.

"Anyway, I can let it slide this time," Santiago said. "You covering for her was a nice thing to do. You're a nice person, Blair Harbour. Nobody on the street has been talking about the hit. I try to let one go every now and then. It's like a tribute to Santa Maria." He thumped his chest.

"Thank you." I exhaled. "I really appreciate—"

Hugh Jackman shuffled loudly in his box. A stab of pain hit my ribs, seizing my breath. Santiago leaned on the counter again, curious this time.

"What the fuck was that? Don't tell me we got rats in this place."

My hands were numb as I brought the ice cream container up onto the counter. The men all crowded in.

"I'm so sorry," I said. "It's just my pet. I, uh . . . See, I've been having some trouble at my apartment. My friend . . . My friend's daughter . . . It doesn't matter. Look, it was just for the one night and he hasn't been out of his box at all. I would never let him out. None of the customers have noticed. He's not a rat. He's a gopher. Some people have them as pets. I'm sure they do."

"Open that thing up." Santiago pointed at the box. My throat felt ragged now. Torn. I was about to feed my gopher to a pack of wolves. I took Hugh Jackman out of the box and held him in the light. The gopher stretched, its rump in the air, then put its head up and yawned, baring two long front teeth. The cartel members watched as he did a circle on my palm and headed for my wrist.

Santiago snatched the animal.

"Please don't hurt him." I made a grab for the gopher. "Please. Please just—"

"Look at this thing." Santiago held the gopher in his fist like a microphone, Hugh Jackman's round, furry head poking out from the choke chain of the man's thick thumb and forefinger. The men all leaned in to look. I couldn't bear to watch the gang leader crush the life out of Dayly's pet, so I stared at my own terrified reflection in the windows.

I squeezed my eyes shut and waited for a pained animal squeal, the crunch of broken bones. Nothing came. When I looked back, Santiago was stroking Hugh Jackman's head with the index finger of his free hand.

"It's like a hamster." Santiago was smiling. "Only smaller."

"I like the nose. It's twitchin'," one of the big goons said. "See it twitchin'?"

"Look at the ears. They're so small. So stupid."

"Can I have a hold, boss?"

Santiago tipped the gopher into the big man's hand, which was the size of a baseball glove. Hugh Jackman ran over his palms and the men watched and laughed.

"Does it bite?" Santiago's lieutenant asked me. I wiped my throbbing face on my palms.

"No, he's friendly," I said.

"What's it doing in this little box here?" Santiago said. "That's no place to keep a pet."

"It's a long story," I said. "The arrangement was supposed to be temporary but it's gone on longer than I anticipated."

The two big goons put their palms together to make a big platform and watched the gopher run between them, almost giggling with delight. Santiago picked up the gopher and put it in the pocket of his shirt, showed his crew how the gopher popped out again, looking over the hem of the pocket like a kid going for a ride at the fairground.

"Alejandro here is gonna bring you a nice hamster cage," Santiago said, nodding at his sideman. "One of those ones with the tubes that go in and out. The tunnels. You know? So the gopher can run around. Can he use a mouse wheel? Get one with a mouse wheel, Alejandro. Two mouse wheels."

Alejandro nodded once, smiled warmly at me.

"You don't have to do that," I said.

"I like this thing," Santiago said, ignoring me. He was making a tunnel with his fists now, the restless Hugh Jackman wriggling through one hand and into the other. "I like its stupid little ears. I might get one for my *sobrina*. Do you have a name for it?"

"Ye—"

"You will call it Santiago Mateo Nicolas Cruz," he said, passing the gopher back to me.

"Of course, I will," I said.

Santiago gave Alejandro some instructions in Spanish. I returned the creature to its box and tucked it safely away. When Santiago nodded, the men started to file out. The gang leader pointed back at me as he left.

"You're a nice person, Blair Harbour," he said again.

JESSICA

Jessica stood on her balcony and stared down at the vehicles backing up at the traffic lights on Alameda, panhandlers ducking between cars with their cardboard signs. She could see a helicopter circling the streets south of Downtown, its blue-white spotlight stabbing down, stirring, looking for someone in the murk. She had taken a flight with one of the bird crews once, just out of curiosity. She'd sat rigid in her seat, gripping the frame of the shuddering aircraft, sweat rolling down her belly under her uniform. They'd flown over one of Johnny Depp's houses, so low they'd rustled the treetops. The unbroken view of the glittering city had been ruined when her pilot started up with a story about how the chopper had been shot at as it flew over Compton once. A bullet had pinged off the left landing skid. Another half an inch and it would have hit the fuel tank, turning the machine into a fireball rocketing toward the earth. She'd thrown up for fifteen minutes straight after her feet hit solid ground.

The time had come. Jessica held her phone in one hand and a piece of paper with a number on it in the other. A phone number for Kristi Zea had been difficult to obtain. Zea filtered her calls through a website that specialized in masked numbers—generic phone numbers with an area code of the client's choosing. According to the piece of paper, Jessica would be dialing Missouri. However, she would bet that the call would be diverted through the website's algorithms and back to Los Angeles, where Kristi Zea was still living. People were creatures of habit, and trauma tied them to a location. She dialed the number and waited with little hope that the woman would pick up.

Someone did. There was a shuffling, as if the phone was dropped and retrieved. "Yeah?"

"Kristi?"

A pause. Jessica gripped her balcony rail and watched the night, listening hard.

"She's not here," the woman on the line said. "You can leave a message."

"I'm Jessica Sanchez. West LA. I was hoping to talk to Kristi about a case she was involved in some years ago. In 2009. Adrian Orlov."

"She doesn't talk to any journalists," the voice said. "Bye."

"Wait. I'm not a reporter. It's Jessica Sanchez—*Detective* Jessica Sanchez. West LA *Homicide*."

"Oh."

"Do you remember me?"

"I . . . Look, Kristi already knows that the woman got out. The shooter. She doesn't care."

"I'm not calling about Blair Harbour's release," Jessica said. "I want to ask you some questions about the case itself."

More silence. Jessica tapped the balcony rail, chewed her lip, bracing for the disconnect tone. She heard a dog barking in the background of the call, close.

"Kristi's not—"

"I know it's you, Kristi."

"Yeah, well, I don't want to talk about it," Kristi snapped. "And I don't have to."

"I just have a couple of things to clear up, and I hoped we could meet," Jessica said. "It's nothing official."

"What the fuck does that mean?" Jessica was surprised by the sudden desperation in Kristi's voice, which had gone up in pitch. "I mean—what—clear up what things? The case is closed. Adrian is dead. That Harbour bitch did her time and she's out now. It's over. What the fuck could you possibly want to know?"

"Can I just meet you for a drink?"

"You said it was nothing official. Does that . . . What does that even mean?"

"I don't want to cause you any distress," Jessica said carefully. "I just want to talk."

"Well, I don't want to talk, okay?" Jessica heard a glass clunk onto a firm surface on the other end of the line. Kristi swallowed hard. "I don't know why the hell you would think I'd want to talk about my dead boyfriend who got shot right in front of my eyes."

"It's just that—"

"Don't call this number again," Kristi said. "I'm changing this number. This number is dead now. Don't call me. Ever."

The line clicked off. Jessica looked at the screen, the red circle with the *X* emblazoned on it, and felt the last dregs of hope draining out of her.

BLAIR

Sneak wasn't home when I arrived. There was a note on the counter that just read, *Sorry, Neighbor.* I scrunched it up and put it in the bin, changed Hugh Jackman's water bowl, and was just clicking the lid of the ice cream container into place when there came a knock at the door.

Alejandro was standing there in the night with a large box in his arms. A shudder of strange emotions rushed through me, terror and desire and joy and dread, a wave that left me feeling light-headed.

"Right now?" I laughed. "I didn't think he meant—"

"He always means right now," Alejandro said. I shut the door behind him and followed him to the counter. I expected him to dump the box and leave, but he took a butterfly knife from his back pocket, flipped it open, and started slicing down the side of the box. I stood back and watched. A man cutting open a box. Muscles working in his forearms. His eyes downcast, dark lashes. Box falling open, defeated. Half my thoughts were desperate screams at how pathetic my sex-starved brain was being about this man's presence. The other half were blazing, primal fantasies. There hadn't been a male person who wasn't a parole officer in my apartment since the real estate agent who had shown me the place. I broke away out of sheer necessity, opened the window by the sink, and sucked in some cool night air.

"You like it?" Alejandro asked when the hamster cage was unveiled. It was a sizeable plastic tank with multicolored attachments, curling tubes that went from level to level, spiraling up a tower to a kind of pod with a dome where the creature could look out from on high. There were indeed two mouse wheels. Alejandro peeled clear protective tape from a number of hatches where the different floors could be accessed for food and water and cleaning.

"It's very elaborate," I said. "A grand estate for a rodent bachelor."

"It's like Santiago's house. Big. Over the top. I sent photos from the Walmart. He didn't like the first few I tried. Too small." We both laughed. I took Hugh Jackman from his box and put him inside his ridiculous hamster mansion, and we watched him taking tentative steps around the first floor, snuffling curiously at the mouse wheel.

"You also get this," Alejandro said, taking a roll of money from his pocket and unclipping it from a diamond-studded fixing.

"Oh, no." I put a hand up. "I don't need it."

"I've got to give it to you," he said. "I have no choice."

I watched him peel four hundred dollars from the roll. He put it on the counter. "That's about right, isn't it? Four?"

"That's fine," I said. There was a long, awkward silence.

"So, you're hot right now," Alejandro said. "You know that?"

I felt fire rush up my throat. "Oh, well, thank you. I—"

"No, I mean like you're running hot." He grinned. "You got a guy on your tail."

"What guy?"

"There was a guy out there"—he nodded toward the door—"when I arrived. He's gone now. He was watching you at the Pump'n'Jump, too. Al Tasik. He's a detective. You know him?"

My stomach dropped. "Yeah. You too?"

"He's well known to us," Alejandro said. "Not a nice guy. He picks on young cholos. Little homies who ain't blooded yet. He planted a bag of weed on this kid from Santiago's neighborhood and the boy got his skull fractured in a holding cell while he was waiting to clear the bullshit charge. Now one of his eyes don't work right."

"Did Tasik see you?"

"Nobody sees me."

"Right. So if your guys hate Tasik so much, why don't you just, uh . . ." I struggled.

"The lawn chairs?" Alejandro laughed.

"Yeah."

"He's a cop," he said. "And not a boot, either. He's got rank. It would be a big deal. Lots of negotiation required. Takes time. You get what I'm saying?"

"I do."

"What's he after you for?"

"A friend of mine is missing." I shrugged. "That's honestly all I can think of that is driving him after me. I guess he thinks I know where she is, that I'll lead him to her. Thanks for telling me."

My whole body was tingling with physical desire for Alejandro. I imagined myself giving off visible waves of steam or heat. He knew it. The few times I dared to catch his eye, he was smiling knowingly.

I locked my gaze on the floor and told myself that I would not sleep with a San Marino 13s gang lieutenant, as another seemingly huge awkward silence swept over us.

"Would you like a glass of wine?" I asked.

"Sure," he said. I only had one nice wine glass. I filled it and a water glass, tried to hand him the nice one. He took the water glass of wine and sipped it, trying not to laugh.

"Is it that obvious?" I asked eventually.

"It's like a big neon sign," he said.

"How wonderful."

"How long were you inside?"

"Ten years," I said. "One year out."

"Eleven years." He nodded appreciatively. A silence, broken only by our embarrassed giggling. He fell quiet in time and took a step toward me, reached up and touched my cheek. I twitched with anticipation at the contact, a jerky movement, rusty gears and pistons grinding to life inside my mind, sparks flying. Just to be touched at all was nearly intolerable.

"We better take it slow," Alejandro warned as I started unbuttoning his shirt.

Dear Dayly,
I think it's time you came and saw me. I've enclosed the visitation forms.

John

BLAIR

Sneak was awakened by the clinking of my teaspoon in my coffee cup. She sat up on the couch and looked at me standing at the counter.

"So, that was not a San Marino 13s guy I saw walking out of here at sunrise," she concluded.

"It wasn't?" I suppressed a smile.

"No, because you'd be dead if it was."

"I see."

"Unless he wasn't here to kill you. Unless he was here for something else." She watched me carefully. I focused on my coffee.

"Huh! I thought I smelled burning pubic hair." Sneak shook her head. "What the hell are you thinking, mixing with those guys? You can't lick those tattoos off. Don't let them tell you any different."

"I'm not *mixing* with them, Mother Teresa. I slept with one," I said. "It's not going to be a regular thing. It was an accident."

"No it wasn't. You know how I know? Because of the gopher palace. Look at that thing." She gestured to the tank by the window. "It looks like Disneyland. You didn't buy that. That's what a guy brings a woman with a gopher so he can make friends with her beaver."

Sneak waited for me to defend myself. I sipped my coffee instead. The simple fact was that the hours after Alejandro had arrived at my door had been indefensibly good, a selfish, devilish indulgence I couldn't possibly justify rationally. It had been something I couldn't connect to the real world, to legal or emotional or physical consequences, to predictions of it happening or not happening again.

There was a knock at the door. Quincy. His apparently alcoholic mother was waiting for him at the curb, the engine running, the woman leaning forward over the wheel to eye me curiously. Obviously the child had decided that she could wait—nothing was more important than performance and chocolate. Sneak sat on the couch with her arms folded, decidedly miffed.

"Can you play 'Desperado' by the Eagles?" I asked Quincy wistfully.

"How 'bout 'You're No Good' by Linda Ronstadt?" Sneak asked.

"I've never heard of either of those songs," Quincy said. His mother beeped the horn.

"Just take a chocolate, honey. Your mom's waiting." I offered the box. My phone rang as Quincy bolted away across the lawn to the waiting car.

"You need to drop that cop. Sanchez," Ada barked down the line.

"Everybody's lecturing me this morning." I set my coffee down. "I'm going to go back to bed in a minute, if you're not careful."

"I don't lecture," Ada said. "I don't 'ask' or 'advise' people to do things. People do the shit I tell them to do or they get a squeezin'."

I didn't need to ask what Ada's idea of "a squeezin'" was. I assumed it meant having body parts chopped off, bones broken, or significant parts of oneself submerged in desert sand, perhaps permanently.

"Sanchez rubs me the wrong way, so you're gonna get rid of her."

"You rub her the wrong way, too," I remarked. "Just in case you were curious."

"I wasn't."

I put Ada on speaker and told her what Jessica had told me about Marcus Lemon, my car, Dayly's bank and phone accounts, Tasik's concern about the Crips gang. Sneak sat watching me, listening, from the couch.

"What does a woman sell for eight hundred bucks?" Ada mused. "To someone who doesn't want to be traced. You should ask the flabby ho-bag you've got crashing on your couch. She'd know."

"You're on speaker," I said.

"Hey, skanky ho-bag!" Ada said, louder. "What does a person get from a dirty chicken-header in your gene pool for eight hundred clams?"

"I don't know, why don't we ask your daddy what he paid last time I stuck my thumb up his ass?" Sneak snapped.

I hung up before Ada could reply, and grabbed the keys to the Gangstermobile.

The I-110 freeway. Homeless camps, factories spewing steam into the yellow sky, the desert, and the scrubby brown mountains beyond. I watched billboards for casinos on the way to Palm Springs. Neil Diamond in silver sequins. Rod Stewart's blazing white teeth poking out from his turmeric-orange face.

"San Francisco," I said.

"Hmm," Sneak agreed, taking a hit of cocaine or

the like from her handbag then dumping the bag on the floor.

"What can you do within three hours of San Francisco airport?"

"Three hours is not what we're looking at," Sneak said, checking her face in the mirror. "If she was there for six hours total, she'd only have been able to stop for a few minutes wherever she got to three hours away. So, what—she drives three hours, spends two minutes picking up a lobster roll and hightails it back?"

"Maybe not a lobster roll," I said. "But maybe she picked up something else. Something that could only be collected in person, by her, and then turned around. Maybe it was something someone paid her eight hundred dollars to go get."

"It's just as likely she went somewhere an hour away from the airport, stayed for four hours and then drove back."

"Okay," I sighed. "I'm just trying to—"

"That's not accounting for traffic on the highways, or foot traffic in the airport. Plane delays on the tarmac."

"You can stop now," I said.

"I saw a psychic last night," Sneak announced.

"A psychic? Like a medium?"

"I've known her for a long time. She helped cleanse me after the demon stole my roommate's body. We did a sage ritual."

I quietly considered Sneak's ultra-logical dismissal of my San Francisco time theory next to these new pieces of information and chose to say nothing.

"She said Dayly's under the ground. Deep under the ground. Where it's dark."

"Well, I place about as much stock in that as I do in your roommate's demon problem, Sneak," I said.

"But if she's right, she might have been seeing Dayly in New York catching the subway. That's deep underground and dark."

"Hmm," Sneak said again.

"Underground parking lot. Someone's wine cellar. Basement. Storage unit. Dodger Stadium has tunnels underground."

"Shut up," Sneak sighed. I watched her for a moment, then jerked the wheel and took an exit off the highway. "What are we doing now? Don't give me another pep talk. I'll smack you the fuck out."

I took the off-ramp under the overpass.

"Al Tasik was watching my apartment last night. If he's following us now I want to lose him," I said. I popped my door. "Swap with me."

"Why?"

"Because you're the street girl," I said. "I'm the Brentwood bitch. You'll know how to shake a tail much better than me."

Sneak got into the driver's seat. A small smile crossed her lips. I was expecting her to have some fun winding around the streets, but she slammed her foot down on the accelerator and sailed through the red-lit intersection, causing a pickup truck to veer dangerously close to the bridge pylon. She was heading for a field of warehouses, dusty dirt roads between huge steel walls, that stretched as far as the eye could see. Sneak blindly swung the car down an alleyway between the warehouses and I shuffled up in my chair, grabbing my seat belt.

"Jesus, Sneak! There could be people in here!"

"Well, they better get out of my way," she said, flooring it. The dust cloud behind us lifted and swirled as we cut wildly between the warehouses, ramming the car sideways into turns, grinding in the dirt. Sneak started laughing and wailing after a while and, despite myself, I joined in. We passed a storage facility auction, where groups of men and women stood bidding on the contents of a row of units yawning open in the blazing sun. I caught a glimpse of old furniture, tubs of toys spilling out over stripped-down motorcycle bodies and stacked boxes. Hands raised to bid. We covered the crowd in dust as we sped past. Sneak was laughing her head off, tears running from her eyes.

The San Jasinte police station had art deco leanings, might once have been a pizza restaurant when prospects for a bigger population out here were imagined. It was beige, surrounded by bushes, and set on the corner of a block between squat, neat houses. Sneak parked a block down from the station and we swapped positions again, sat watching the police station as though expecting Officer Marcus Lemon to emerge and head directly for us to submit to an interview.

"I don't think we should go in," I said. "Not in the least because we can't legally be seen together. But they'll also have cameras. Jessica thinks whoever's after Dayly might have broken into my apartment because I made myself known when I went in to report my car stolen."

"We don't have to go into the station to find out if he's there," Sneak said, drawing her phone out of her handbag. "That's amateur hour."

She googled a number, dialed and waited. I sat beside her and watched. When she spoke it was with an old crone's voice, high and gravelly and dry-throated, a voice so convincing I was struck dumb at the sound of it.

"Hello? I'm calling with the intention of contacting my grandson, Marcus," Sneak croaked. "Lemon is the name, Officer Marcus Lemon . . . I'm calling because the young man in question is supposed to pick me up this evening at my home to take me to a dance class at the local hall, six o'clock sharp. I'd like to know if he's still coming . . . What's that? You'll have to speak up . . . Well, I didn't suppose in the first instance that a man would be allowed to have his personal cellular phone on him while serving and protecting the community . . . My, my, yes, I'll do just that."

She hung up.

"He's not in there," she said. "He's out on patrol."

"That was simply amazing," I said.

"I do the sex hotline in winter when it's cold out," Sneak explained. "The old-lady voice is quite popular. I can also do innocent schoolgirl. Horny single mom. Lonely female trucker. The president's bored secretary left all alone in the Oval Office while the prez is out on the campaign trail."

"Jesus, that last one is a rather elaborate fantasy. Why does she have to be the *president's* secretary in particular?"

"So she can do stuff to herself on the president's desk while portraits of important historical guys watch on."

"Okay," I said regretfully.

"You asked."

"Well, I wish the performance just now could have helped us find Lemon. We know he's not here. But he could be anywhere."

"*This* will help us find him," Sneak said. She bent and pulled a heavy gray radio unit out of her handbag and heaved it onto the dashboard. She plugged it into the car's cigarette lighter socket and flipped it on.

"A police radio scanner?"

"You thought I was out all night getting high,

suckin' dicks, stocking up on energy pills? That was the night before, Neighbor. Last night I got this, and a few other useful bits and pieces."

We sat and listened to radio calls coming through. It was warm in the car, getting warmer. Desert heat carried between the mountains on a heavy breeze. The voices were too old or too female to be Lemon for the first twenty minutes.

"How are we going to know when it's him?" I wondered aloud. "They're all reporting car numbers, not their names or badge numbers."

"Here's a contender," Sneak said, holding up a hand to silence me as a young male voice came on the line.

"*Dispatch, this is L81, I'm stopping for a possible 11–25 on Wilson and Harlow. No assistance needed. Over.*"

"*Copy that, L81. And did your grandma get on to you? Over.*"

"*My grandma? Over.*"

"That's our boy." Sneak smiled.

On the corner of Wilson and Harlow Streets, not far from the San Jasinte surf shop, a large pane of glass had slid from its holdings on the side of a truck and shattered on the road. Sneak and I watched from a distance as Officer Lemon put out road hazard cones that he extracted from the trunk of his cruiser.

"He certainly looks like the guy from the video," Sneak said.

"So what's our play here?" I asked. "One of us just goes up and starts questioning him?"

"I don't know about that. I mean, all he's got to say is, 'We were dating. She dumped me and moved to Alaska,' and where do we go from there?"

"He doesn't even have to say that," I reasoned.

"He could just say 'fuck off' and we're in the same position. We've got to get this right, because the moment we let him know we're snooping around, we've played our hand. We have to know that if we speak to him, he'll talk."

"We don't have anything on him to make him do that," Sneak said.

"Well, I'm not putting him in a hole in the desert, if that's what you're thinking."

Sneak tapped the door of the car, a rhythmic strumming. Lemon was standing in the middle of the sunbaked road, adjacent to his cruiser, lazily directing traffic.

"Look at that ass," Sneak said suddenly.

I frowned. "Are you checking out your daughter's possible boyfriend or killer right now?"

"Look at his ass, though," she said. "Those pants are tight. I don't see the outline of a cell phone in that back pocket."

"So?"

"So if the phone's not on his body, it's in the car." We watched Lemon for a while before Sneak unclipped her seat belt.

"All right, here's the play," she said. "You pull out, drive past him slowly, drift over, and ram the front of the car into that traffic light."

"*What?*"

"Don't ram it hard. Just bunt it. Enough to cause a distraction. The front's already scratched up from me busting into that hangar." She was pulling wads of tissues from a packet in her purse. "You ever faked a car crash before? Bite down on these as you make impact but try to let the rest of your body go limp. A good bump can rattle a tooth out real easy at your age."

"I'm two years older than you!"

"Get out and make a scene if you can. Maybe cry. Yes, definitely cry."

"This is—"

"Just do it." She got out and I watched her walk to the surf shop and browse the windows, only feet from Lemon's car. Seconds ticked by in which I waited for her to return to the vehicle and admit that her idea was ridiculous. She turned around and looked at me, raised her eyebrows. I shook my head. She made a menacing fist.

"I'm the best friend in the world," I told myself aloud, pulling my seat belt tight across my chest. "I'm the best possible friend a person could have."

I pulled out into the street, slowed by the hazard-cone ring Lemon had made in the right-hand lane. I made eye contact with the young man so that he would know I was gawking at the scene. In the rear-view mirror, I saw Sneak push off the surf shop window, heading for the cruiser.

The car behind me beeped at my slowness as I passed the glass crash zone. The perfect form of encouragement. I stuffed the wad of tissues into my mouth, bit down, and hit the accelerator as I aimed for the traffic light pole.

A whump, dull and heavy in my center mass, like a punch to the sternum. The air left me and I doubled over, slamming my head into my arms, which I managed to cross over the steering wheel at the last second. The car had hopped the curb unevenly, the left-side tires still on the road. I flopped into the passenger seat and spat out the napkins.

Shrill, all-consuming pain hit me. It was not only my tensed muscles spasming, grinding bones and joints, and awakening sleeping, rarely used muscles; but also a mental flash of myself as Adrian Orlov, the bullet I had fired at the man slamming into his middle, folding him in half, sprawling him on the hard floor of his home.

I righted myself, grabbed the radio from the dashboard, and threw it into the passenger-side footwell, dragging Sneak's jacket over the top of it. I kicked open the door of the car and slid out. Marcus Lemon was on me immediately, his hands under my arms, guiding me back into the driver's seat.

"Whoa, whoa, whoa," he said. "Try to take it easy, ma'am."

I burst into loud, hysterical tears.

"Oh my god! Oh my god!" I wailed. "I hit something. I hit someone! Someone call nine-one-one!" I folded my arms and leaned on the horn, buried my face in my arms.

"It's okay." Lemon laughed, easing me off the horn. "I'm a police officer. You've barely dented your front bumper. Sit there and take a load off while I call this in to dispatch. How's your neck?" There were people gathering behind him, staring worriedly at me. "You're fine, ma'am. There's no need to cry."

The scene I had caused was working, apparently. Cars were slowing on the other side of the street to take in both accident sites. People were exiting shops and gathering on corners of the intersection. As Lemon radioed his station for backup, I watched a baby-blue Porsche Cayenne cruise by, the elbow of a leather jacket hanging from the driver's window.

Fred and Mike. Ada's men. They stared impassively at me as they rolled by. I shook my head. What were the chances? I told myself the shock of the crash, and my nerves at making it happen, were playing with my mind.

I sat back and looked in the rearview mirror. Sneak was nowhere to be seen.

JESSICA

The car sat facing down the slope of the ravine north of Glendora, sunken on melted tires, the empty, glassless windows like dark eyes absorbing nothing of the daylight. Molten metal had made a shiny skirt for the front of the scorched vehicle, silver rivulets dried into tendrils in the sand. Jessica ducked under the police tape surrounding the car and held it up for Diggy. Her friend was surprisingly unsteady on the loose ground for a big man with wide, flat feet. He stumbled over a rock and had to right himself against the car, brushing cactus needles from the hem of his jeans.

"Do we know this is the car?" Diggy asked.

"It's a Honda, so that's a start," Jessica said, checking the notes on her phone. "Some rangers reported it just four days ago, so the timing's good. Urgh, the smell."

The air tasted of burned rubber, gasoline, and leather. She looked out over the San Gabriel Mountain range around them, rolling, scrubby slopes. Cactus and mesquite on some of the mountainsides was chest high and so tangled it was impenetrable. Though she could see no movement, Jessica knew the sheer hillsides would come alive at night with howls and screams and squawks, mountain cats and coyotes digging rodents and rabbits out of tunnels, owls waiting for those brave little souls that escaped the paws and claws to venture out onto the rocky flats. This was a place of danger, of hunting, of feet scrabbling in sand and thorns hooking into flesh and blood spilling on stone. Whatever stage this had been in Dayly's downfall, Jessica sensed that the girl had been chased here, up against the rocks and cliffs, cornered by some predatory thing.

Diggy was sweating as he jimmied open the back door of the car with a crowbar. The trunk was ajar and empty. That was how burned-out cars were treated by the LAPD. After the initial report, the vehicle was searched for bodies, drugs, or weapons, then taped off and left to bake.

While Diggy checked the car, Jessica looked at the sand around the vehicle. There were the telltale footprints of rangers, police officers, and perhaps a couple of looky-loos. But there were two trails that led off between the creosote bushes away from the car, away from the road, into the hills.

Stepping carefully, Jessica followed the trail to its conclusion, knelt, and looked at the marks in the sand and gravel. There were scrapings she recognized from similar crime scenes she had seen in the past. The soft, wide indentations of a pair of buttocks and shoulders. Below them, maybe two or three feet down, sharp, curved crescent moons: the heels of shoes digging in, trying to find traction. Someone on their back, struggling. There was no blood here, but the moons in the sand made the hairs on the back of her neck stand on end.

"This doesn't look good," Diggy said when she arrived back at the car.

"I was about to say those exact words," she said. "I've got signs of a struggle over here."

"I've got this." He tossed her a tiny shred of metal. Jessica looked at the blackened, L-shaped piece in the light.

"What is it?"

"It's part of a SIM tray from an iPhone," Diggy said. "It pops out the side so you can put your SIM card in the device. There's a little door with a hole in it you have to open with a key. When I was in college I worked in a phone repair shop. I'd know that shape anywhere."

"So where's the rest of the phone?"

"Exactly," Diggy said. "That minuscule shred of the phone is all that I can find. The rest was probably consumed in the fire. We also have this." He placed a flat shard of burned metal on the hood of the car. Jessica had to peer closely at the object to discern what it was.

"A laptop?" she asked.

"Just the base," Diggy said. "The screen has melted away. The extreme heat scorched the outside to a crisp. This was the keyboard."

She watched him run his finger across a slash of burned black plastic melted to the top of the shard.

"Laptop and phone in a burned-out car," Jessica said. "This is bad news. Blair Harbour said Dayly didn't have anything on her when she robbed the gas station. Just a gun. No laptop. And if she'd had the phone with her, why would she have called Sneak from a pay phone? Doesn't make any sense that both should be here right now, with the car we know she was in."

"So, what . . ." Diggy thought out loud. "She's stolen Blair's car, gone back to her apartment, and retrieved her phone and laptop?"

"Possible," Jessica said. "Unlikely. Would she go back to the place where she was attacked just to retrieve these items? Or is it more likely she was attacked again here, and whoever had her phone and laptop brought them along and disposed of them in the car fire?"

"The latter sounds more likely." Diggy gave a rueful sigh. "Will you tell the mother or keep it to yourself for now?"

"I don't know. Not much point. We won't learn anything solid from this. The phone's gone, and if this was Dayly's laptop, any chances we have of searching it for clues are well and truly fried."

"Don't lose heart." Diggy gave a shifty smile. "I've actually seen a laptop come back from a worse state than this."

"Come back?"

"Yes, come back, return from the other side, be resurrected," he said. "Become the undead. Zombie tech."

"You think you could still get something readable off this?" Jessica picked up the shard of laptop and watched chips of ash fall from it to the hood of the car. "It looks like burned tree bark."

"Stranger things have happened." Diggy took the remains of the laptop from her carefully. "All we have to do is figure out if it was a hard disk drive or a solid state drive and work with what we find. If it's the hard disk, it'll be more difficult, certainly. We'll have to realign the drive and the controller card. Like putting a broken turntable back together, matching up the needle and the record. If it's a solid state drive we're just looking for a microchip, which might still be intact. The drive is protected by an industrial strength rubber gasket which can withstand temperatures of 620 degrees Fahrenheit."

"What temperature do cars burn at?"

"About 1500 degrees."

"Oh."

"You never know. There are variables."

"You seem excited," Jessica commented.

"Oh, I am." He smiled. "I've never done this before. There's something almost archaeological and redemptive about it. As if we're reassembling the artifacts destroyed by ISIL in Palmyra. All those shattered and burned and busted treasures meticulously put back together. If I hadn't gone into forensics, I certainly would have pursued a career like that."

Jessica nodded encouragingly and looked for a license plate on the car. There was none. She lifted the hood to check the VIN number, took her phone from her back pocket to check it against the stolen car report Harbour had entered at the West LA station. As soon as she looked at the screen, it went dark. Unidentified number calling.

"Hello?"

"Is this Jessica Sanchez?"

"It is."

"Listen up, bitch," the heavy, male voice said. "You need to stay away from Kristi Zea. She doesn't want to talk to you, and she doesn't want anything to do with the old case if it's being reopened. If Kristi—"

"Who is this?" Jessica leaned back on the warm car and watched the horizon.

"Just listen," the voice said. "Kristi will get a lawyer if she has to. She'll come after you for harassment and emotional trauma. Psychological, uh, you know. Stress. Point is, you got no right to chase her around, and if she has to, she'll sue your ass off for doing it."

"Oh, really?" Jessica said.

"Yeah, really, bitch." The man was pacing. Jessica could hear boots on a wooden floor. "But we won't start out that way. The legal route is the nice way. That comes second. First, we start the not-so-nice way."

"What are you going to do?" Jessica asked. "Come around my apartment and beat me up? Throw my shit around? Break my thumbs?"

"If it gets to that," the man said.

"Okay. Understood. Now how about you take a minute to listen, pal," Jessica said. "Kristi, you listen too."

"She's not—"

"I know she's there. You've got her on speaker phone because you're trying to make her feel better. You were hoping she could listen in while I whimper that I'm terrified by your threats and I'll stay away. I'm guessing you're a brother or a close friend, maybe someone she met drinking her guilt away at a piece of shit dive bar."

There was silence on the line.

"She called you up this morning, right?" Jessica continued. "She spent the night crying and drinking and freaking out about my phone call last night. You said you'd set things straight. Show this bitch cop that Kristi is not alone, that she has people looking out for her. She said it was a bad idea. You demanded the number. Am I close to the truth here?"

Jessica heard an intake of breath but carried on before the man could speak.

"You're not going to come to my apartment and heavy me into leaving Kristi alone. Kristi's not going to get a lawyer to make me go away. Both those options exist in a fantasyland where you, whoever you are, are willing to risk an assault charge for helping your friend, and Kristi is willing to stand in a courtroom in front of a judge while I explain to him why I'm so interested in talking to her. No; in reality, where we live, Kristi is going to sit down with me and answer my questions."

"Why would she do that?"

"Because the kind of harassment you're threatening to sue me for hasn't even begun yet," Jessica said. "I've made *one phone call* so far. From here, I begin turning up unexpectedly in Kristi's life. Maybe I pop into the bar she frequents and start talking to the local dropouts, poking around, demanding answers. I swing by her workplace and ask to speak to her boss. I knock on her mother's door and invite myself in for tea. I find out who *you* are, and I pay a visit to you in the middle of the night, maybe with five SWAT guys and a search warrant. All the while, as I'm touring Kristi's inner circle, I'm staying eagle-eyed for bullshit charges I can drop on the people in her life. After I've got Kristi's friends in my hand, I start messing with her. I speak to her landlord. I flag her with the tax department. I report her to the ASPCA for kicking her dog."

There was a scraping noise, and Jessica thought she heard hurried, muffled voices in the background of the call.

"Tell her she needs to speak to me," Jessica insisted. "She needs to put things straight."

The line went dead. Diggy gave an appreciative whistle.

"You'd really do all that stuff to get Zea to talk?" he asked.

"I wouldn't need to." Jessica tapped out a message. "I've done this a few times. You start with the mother's house. As soon as you get to the mother, the kid folds."

Jessica tried to focus. The Harbour case could wait. What she was seeing before her now had sent tingles of nervousness up her spine. Wherever Dayly Lawlor was, she needed help. Jessica sent a message to her forensic technology contact. She had been forced to go two states over to find an investigator who would help her track down the anonymous payer that had sent $800 to Dayly's bank account. All the police resources she tried in California were either busy, annoyed by the Brentwood house situation, or too amused by the video of her at Goren's house to offer anything but clever quips. It had taken an hour and a half to find the current whereabouts of a woman named Mariana who had shared Jessica's dorm room at the academy, who was now bunkered down in a basement lab in New Mexico.

You got anything on that anonymous account yet? Jessica asked. Her phone blipped almost instantly with a response.

I've got the guy, Mariana said. *Sending address. But if you're going to visit him, I'd suggest you take backup.*

BLAIR

I'd sent Sneak into a gas station to get me an ice pack for my sore head, but she returned with a bag of Popsicles that was difficult to mold around my brow, even more so when she extracted one and started sucking on it. I stood in the desert sun with condensation dripping down my face while she read text messages between Officer Lemon and a contact named only "D," which we took to be our missing girl.

> LEMON: R we really gonna do this?
> D: We give it a try. Y not? Worst case scenario someone finds out and beats us to it.
> LEMON: Worst case scenario I end up fired and u end up with ur ass in jail. I said it to u last nite and I'll say it again now. I WILL turn on u if I have to.

"What the hell are they talking about?" I asked.

"They're going to commit some kind of crime, clearly." Sneak frowned at the phone, sucking her ice pop now and then, which was staining her lips green. "We just have to figure out what it is. Bank heist? Murder?"

"*Someone beats us to it*," I repeated.

"Here's a thought," Sneak said. "Might be crazy. But maybe ten years ago I knew this guy who worked in a station in San Bernardino. A cop. Johnny Reselt. He figured out that every time there was an earthquake, the cameras in the evidence lockup blinked out. Not for long, maybe twenty seconds. So he gets himself assigned down there. The only way you can get put in the evidence lockup is by getting in trouble. Bringing the police force into ill repute, for example. So he paid me a grand to get caught with him doing coke in a public toilet. I got a drug charge and he got assigned to the evidence dungeon."

"Where is this story going?" I asked, massaging my stiff neck.

"Give me a minute. So Johnny's working in the evidence room. He starts quietly looking around at what they got down there. He figures out that the most high-profile case on the shelves is this rape charge against a local celebrity chef. Pretty famous guy. Does some TV shows, lives in a big house in the mountains. Apparently the chef guy cornered a teenage apprentice and locked her in the freezer room, and wouldn't let her out unless she gave him a blow job. So Johnny works in the evidence room, waiting patiently for an earthquake. Months go by, but then it comes. When the cameras blink out, he goes into the evidence box for the chef case, nabs the key piece of evidence against the chef, and stuffs it in his backpack. It was a shirt, in case you're wondering. The apprentice's shirt. Had the chef's jizz on it."

"How does all this relate to Dayly?" I asked.

"Johnny sold the evidence bag to the chef for, like, fifty grand." Sneak sucked the remnants of her Popsicle from the wrapper. "Maybe there's something similar going on here. Dayly and Officer Lemon are teaming up to rob the evidence room."

"And they're worried someone in the station is going to beat them to it?" I asked. "Before the case goes to trial? What are the chances of two crooked cops having the same crazy idea?"

"I don't know. Whatever this is, it has to have something to do with cops. Dayly's not making friends with Crips on one hand and cops on the other."

"Or it might just have to do with Lemon himself. The fact that he's a cop is a coincidence."

"I'm just spitballing here." Sneak hefted her handbag onto her lap and took a bump of cocaine.

"Keep reading the messages," I said.

"There's not much else. Looks like Dayly and Lemon were meeting regularly." Sneak scrolled through the phone. "They meet . . . four times over the space of three weeks."

"How can you tell that?"

"The messages just say stuff like *I'm here* and *Three minutes. I'm out back. Caught in traffic.*"

"Okay."

"There's a conversation two weeks ago that's interesting," she said. "Let me read it to you."

D: *What do you think?*
LEMON: *He knows his shit.*
D: *But can we trust him?*
LEMON: *I've looked at jacket. He's good for this sort of thing. If u want, I can try to get something on him but I don't think we need to do that. If we piss him off he's gone and so is whole deal.*

"*I've looked at jacket*?" I said.

"His jacket," Sneak said. "His rap sheet. Lemon

has run a check on a guy, whoever it is they're trying to decide if they can trust."

The radio in the passenger-side footwell crackled to life. Sneak and I looked at each other as we listened through the open windows.

"*Dispatch, this is L81, can you start me the paperwork on a stolen phone? Some asshole nabbed my cell while I was attending to that 11–82, over.*"

"*Oh, man, Marcus, are you serious? Over.*"

"*Yeah. Right out of my cruiser. I've checked the surrounding CCTV but I was parked in a blind spot. Witnesses saw a fat blonde woman.*"

"*Tough ride.*"

"*You said it.*"

"*Marcus, while I've got you, go show your face at the Mesa, would you? Ronnie's over there trying to steal bottles from the dumpsters again. In progress.*"

"*Be there in five. Over.*"

I drove with Sneak to the Mesa Inn, a tiny dive bar nestled in a strip mall between an insurance salesman's storefront and a pawn shop. The lettering on the front of the building looked reused from a cinema; green block letters on white racks. I parked a good distance from Lemon's cruiser, knowing that he would recognize the Gangstermobile from the earlier crash if he spotted me in the street. We sat watching as he negotiated the release of a burlap sack full of beer bottles from a man standing in the street behind the bar. Lemon's manner was gentle. His hands were out, open, appealing. I thought about his voice, warm and encouraging, as he guided my car back onto the road after issuing me a reckless driving caution with much professed reluctance. Sneak was leaning wide out her window, squinting in the sun.

"We need binoculars," she said.

"Police radio. Binoculars. Some GPS trackers. You could get yourself fully set up as a private investigator. Get a license and start charging for this stuff."

"I don't think so," she said.

"Why not? You're good at it."

"I'm never gonna leave the life," she confessed. "The street. I was made for it. For falling down over and over. That's my destiny."

"What bullshit."

Sneak laughed and looked at me.

"I'm serious," I said. "You could change your destiny right now. Change it back to what it was originally, before the accident that wiped you out of the Olympics. You were on track for great things."

"So was Dayly." She shrugged. "And now look. Something's turned her down the dark path. Maybe it's genetic. A family curse. I knew a guy once who was cursed. Ex-girlfriend put it on him. He was killed by a pelican."

"We don't know what's happened to Dayly." I put a hand on her shoulder. "Sure, it doesn't look good, but she might come out of this okay."

"They say all that stuff in rehab, you know," Sneak said. "'You can change your destiny right now,' that kind of thing. They're all about their quotes. Affirmations. They've got them painted all over the walls in pretty colors. Sometimes they put them on bracelets and T-shirts, wear them around. *Believe in yourself. Be grateful for every moment. Make a plan and stick to it. Trust the process.* Problem is, they're not from anybody, those quotes. They're not tried and tested in real life."

"Have you got a quote you live by that's tried and tested, then?" I asked.

"Yeah. Mike Tyson," she said, watching Lemon

return to his vehicle. "'Everybody's got a plan until they get punched in the mouth.'"

I thought about that. About how many wonderful plans I'd had for Jamie and myself before a set of handcuffs snapped shut on my wrists for the first time. Until life itself punched me in the mouth. Sneak righted herself in her seat and flicked a hand in Lemon's direction.

"Let's follow him for a while," she said.

JESSICA

Jessica didn't take backup to the neat little house on Hill Street in Walnut Park. She parked under a street sign that read, ominously, *Bumps ahead* and watched the house, waiting for the object of Mariana's warning to reveal itself, but it did not. The business address of Scream Inc. was a pretty stucco place with arched windows and low palm trees in the front yard, a red hummingbird feeder hanging from a rail near a door inlaid with stained glass. She went and knocked, waited, listening to the sound of footsteps on stairs. The woman who opened the door was younger than Jessica expected, squat and round, her hair dyed a blue-black that was stark against her pale and ginger-speckled skin.

"Jessica Sanchez?"

"That's me."

"I'm Tania Austen," the woman said, and smiled. A strong southern accent. "Come on in."

The house was as classically tidy and ordinary inside as it was on the outside. Persian rugs on hardwood floors, a rack on the wall for coats or bags that was emblazoned with the word *Family*. Jessica guessed the young woman lived with her parents. A stirring feeling had begun in her stomach as soon as she passed the threshold, a feeling at odds with her pretty surrounds. She followed Tania to a door off the kitchen and watched the woman fish for the right key from a bundle she extracted from her hoodie pocket.

"So you didn't say on the phone which item you were interested in," Tania said, slipping the key into a heavy padlock on the door. Jessica hadn't said much on the phone at all, only that she wanted to speak to Tania about a purchase she had made the previous month. Sometimes Jessica found cases unraveled themselves much more easily when she just showed up, not announcing her presence as a cop, not trying to dig too deeply into the situation in which she was about to find herself. Too many questions would make doors start blowing shut. As she followed Tania down a set of narrow basement stairs, the woman ahead of her didn't know Jessica was armed, that she technically required a warrant to enter the premises.

"I'm here to talk to you about Dayly Lawlor," Jessica said vaguely.

"Ah, right," Tania said with a smirk. "I'm not surprised. I haven't even put those letters up on the site yet. But word gets around, doesn't it?"

A rigidly organized basement. Jessica stood before a wide rosewood desk and looked at the shelves around her, custom-built display cabinets that were packed with labeled items. There were shelves of unframed sketches and bright acrylic paintings of ghosts and beautiful women next to items that seemed to have no category: a handbag with a torn zipper, and a pink teddy bear that appeared burned on one side, the cotton candy–like fur curled and blackened. Jessica turned and looked at a rack full of hundreds of tiny jars, each labeled with a name: *Schaefer, G. J.—Jones,*

J.—Gacy, J. W.—Norris, R.—Pike, C. She stepped closer and saw that some of the tiny jars were filled with what looked like hair. Gray, black, brown bundles. Others contained sharp, yellowish fibers in the shape of crescent moons. Tania was searching in a huge filing cabinet. Jessica spied files labeled with the words *Transcripts, Psych reports, Auth certs, Scene/autopsy pics.* The feeling in her stomach was deepening, a sick tightening just above her pelvis.

"It's in here somewhere, don't worry," Tania said, thumbing through the files. "Go ahead and admire the shop while you're waiting, but I've got to let you know, you're on three different cameras right now. Last year I had a guy come down here and try to steal a jar of Berkowitz's fingernails. I got the only jar in the country that's for sale and has an attached certificate of authenticity. That's one of the premium jars, top shelf. If you buy Dayly's letters, I can give you a good deal on a couple of non-premium jars."

"Are you talking about . . . David Berkowitz?" Jessica asked. "The serial killer?"

"Son of Sam," Tania said. "I've also got a pair of his prison shoes, too, if you're into that guy."

Jessica looked back at the shelves. At the little jars of hair and fingernails labeled with the names of famous killers. In the corner of the room by the door was an old fridge, humming, bolted and padlocked at the door. Jessica went to the opposite wall and examined a frame hanging high on the wall. In the frame was a slice of cream carpet partly soaked in a reddish-brown substance. She noticed the back of the frame was screwed to the wall.

"What's that?"

"Oh, that's not for sale." Tania came to Jessica's side. "That one's mine. That right there, missy, is a square of carpet one of the forensic investigators cut from the floor of the Columbine High School library two days after the shooting. I've got a certificate of authenticity for that one, too. It's worth more than everything else in here." She put her hands on her hips proudly. "Someone wanted to trade me a pair of Jeffrey Dahmer's glasses for it a couple of weeks ago. I thought about it, I tell ya. I really thought about it."

"So this is all . . ." Jessica wheezed.

"Murderabilia," Tania said, nodding. "You must have thought this was prison letters only?"

"I didn't . . ." Jessica lost her words.

"Here at Scream Inc. we deal in all aspects of murder. We've got confession tapes, psych reports, cranial scans, and medical waste. This here is one of Casey Anthony's handbags." Tania tapped the glass of the cabinet at Jessica's side. "Nabbed it from a yard sale the parents held a couple of years after the kid's death. You wouldn't believe what it would go for now. Are you an O.J. fan? I've got stones from the garden where Brown and Goldman were stabbed to death, but no certificates, unfortunately. I've got a line on one of the outdoor lamps from that scene. Guy says it has blood spatter on it, but they always say that. Should close that deal in the next few days. I can put you on the mailing list if you want to get an alert when the item goes up for sale. Unless you'd like to make an offer now?"

"I'm . . ." Jessica took a deep breath. "I'm just here for the Dayly Lawlor letters."

Tania went back to the filing cabinet. Jessica stared fixedly at a pair of scuffed high heels on a low shelf, tried not to think about what might be in the refrigerator by the door. In time, she heard the flutter of papers and went to the desk, where Tania stood carefully spreading out three pieces of paper on the desktop.

"Please don't touch," Tania said. "And no photos. That's all I ask."

Jessica looked at the papers. They were letters, typed on an electric typewriter.

Dear Dayly,

In your last letter, you were talking about my reasons for killing all those people . . .

A chill splintered her chest.

"So what am I looking at here?" she asked.

"What? You don't know?"

"I've come on behalf of a friend." Jessica smiled weakly.

"These are letters to a woman named Dayly Lawlor from John Fishwick, the Inglewood Bank killer. Fishwick was a famous bank robber. He's in San Quentin now, death row. The guy was really prolific, but he went nuts and blasted a bunch of people away in his last bank heist. Six adults and a kid." Tania moved behind the desk. "Some people, yours truly included, believe that one of these days Fishwick is going to reveal the location of some of his hidden caches of stolen money in one of these letters."

Jessica stared at the letters, reading snippets, her heart hammering in her chest.

"Now," Tania said, "Fishwick letters usually go for about five hundred a pop but in these ones, Dayly appears to be asking the man if he's her father. That's different. Special. There are new personal details about Fishwick that haven't been released to the public, including a murder confession from his childhood. And with the news story last week on the decision made about money of Fishwick's that has already been found, there'll be renewed interest in these letters. I'll be fighting off buyers with a bat. So my earlybird price is fifteen hundred apiece. I take Amex. I assume you've got authority from your friend to negotiate on their behalf?"

Jessica stepped back from the desk. The room felt very small and hot.

"How old are you?" Jessica asked.

"Excuse me?" Tania frowned.

"You heard me, Tania."

"I'm twenty-five."

"And this is what you do for a living? You gather up the remnants of people's pain and suffering and you sell it to creeps online?"

Tania balked, stunned. She looked up at the square of carpet from the Columbine massacre.

"Listen, lady," Tania said carefully. "What I do is no different from the work of any person who trades in historical artifacts. People buy and sell war memorabilia on the internet all day long. You go into the game room of any rich guy in the state and you'll find a gun that was used in the Civil War or stack of letters from someone in the trenches or a . . . a Roman spear. A flag torn down in some foreign battle. This is history." She gestured to the walls. "You can tour whole museums full of this shit. Only difference is that those pieces are from government-endorsed murders. These are the history of individual murders."

"This teddy bear." Jessica pointed to the burned pink bear in the cabinet beside her. "Whose bear was this? What happened to that kid?"

"Look, are you going to buy the letters or not?" Tania snapped. Her eyes were wide. "I didn't let you down here so you could judge me."

"I'm not buying the letters," Jessica said. She drew her gun out of the back of her jeans, her badge from her front pocket. "I'm confiscating them. I'm a cop.

These letters are pertinent in an ongoing missing person investigation."

"You got a warrant?" Tania asked.

"No, but—"

Tania brought her hands up from where they had hung by her sides, out of sight below the desk. In them was an enormous 12-gauge shotgun. Jessica looked down the barrel of the gun as the aim swung around at her, her own pistol useless, pointed at the floor by her side. She let her gun slip onto the carpet at her feet with a gentle thud.

"No warrant, no letters," Tania said.

Jessica jolted as Tania pumped the action of the shotgun. The sound was loud in the small space, like the crunch of truck gears. She felt the roof of her mouth turn dry with terror. When she spoke, her voice was gravel.

"How much did you say they were?" Jessica asked.

"Six grand for the lot," Tania said, the aim of the gun lingering on Jessica's stomach. "But for six and a half I'll throw in two jars of toenails. Non-premium killer of your choosing."

"Just the letters," Jessica said. She carefully extracted her wallet from her back pocket.

BLAIR

We watched Lemon's cruiser stop outside a house on Redduck Avenue. The house sat behind a tangle of wild vines that had almost consumed the low brick fence at the front of the yard. Sneak was on her phone, tapping the screen as she zoomed out on our location on GPS.

"Is it Redduck?" Sneak wondered aloud. "Or Red Duck?"

"I don't know."

"We're, like, two blocks from the police station," she noted.

"He's not calling it in, whatever he's doing," I said. We waited in silence. "What do you think? Dropping in on family? Maybe he thought he'd swing by and see what Grandma wanted."

"Maybe this is his place," Sneak mused. "We're not going to see anything from here. Do a drive-by."

I took the car around the block, slowing and looking carefully at the house with the vines as we went by. Number 17. The long driveway was packed full of items: buckets and gas canisters, chairs and folded tables, wooden boxes stacked high, rusted bicycles leaning against them, a tarp haplessly flopped over some of it, trying to protect the jumble of objects from the sun. I saw boarded-up windows at the front of the house, others taped with newspaper. Sneak unbuckled her seat belt and turned in her seat to get the longest view she could as we went by.

"Grandma's a bit of a pack rat," Sneak said.

"Weird," I agreed. We returned to the spot a block down from the house where we had pulled in to watch Officer Lemon disappear. The car ticked as it cooled after I turned off the engine.

"I'm going in," I said.

"You can't," Sneak scoffed. "He'll recognize you."

"I'm not going to waltz up and knock on the door," I said. "I'll just see what I can see and get out of there."

"Let me go." She opened her door. "He doesn't know me."

"He's on the lookout for a fa—" I swallowed. "A woman fitting the description witnesses gave him of the person who stole his phone. Blonde curls."

"What are you going to do if you get caught?"

"I'll handle it," I said.

Walking with a deliberately casual air is more difficult than it seems. I kicked my sneaker twice on uneven edges of the sidewalk on the way to the house. A truck parked on the road diagonally opposite read *Ramirez Commercial Plumbing*. A logo of a smiling plumber brandishing a wrench high above his head like a sword was painted on the side. I turned sharply down the driveway, watching the blocked-out windows for any sign of Lemon, and ducked behind the pile of trash at the side of the house. The backyard was packed with old, rusted cars that had probably once been vintage specials patiently awaiting restoration. A tortoiseshell cat was dozing on the hood of one, the grass so high inside the car body that I could see it through the windshield. The cat lifted its head at the sight of me. It was a large beast with a boxy skull, its face slashed through with scars.

I went to the nearest window and peered through a small rip in the newspaper covering the glass, but all I could see in the darkened room was a bookshelf crammed with sun-yellowed volumes. The next window was blocked completely, but the room after that was revealed through a crack between two wooden panels. I saw rolls of carpet or rugs numbering in the dozens stacked from floor to ceiling.

"Hey!"

A gasp escaped my throat before I could silence it. A wide-shouldered Latino man was standing in the driveway, wiping grease from his hands onto a filthy towel.

"Oh, hi." I smiled.

"Can I help you?"

"No, I'm fine. I'm sorry. I was just looking for my cat." I jerked my thumb at the cat on the hood of the car at the end of the driveway. "I'll get out of your way."

I walked toward the cat. It lifted its head again and gave a low, evil moan that made my scalp prickle with fear. I visualized it launching at my face, latching on to my skull with claws like razor wire. The day had already seen me suffer a minor car accident. I stopped, turned around, and kept my head down as I walked back up the driveway.

"You know what? He's fine. He'll come home when he's hungry." I flashed a warm smile at the man with the towel. I pointed at some wildflowers growing between the old, rotting wooden chairs stacked against the wall. "Nice place you got here. Eccentric. Cute flowers."

"It's not my place," the man said. "I'm the plumber. It's a hoarder house in there."

I stopped in my tracks. "Oh?"

"Yeah. Place is crazy. Stuff stacked up to the ceiling." The plumber wouldn't meet my eyes. "I've just come to clear out the toilet. You see that a lot with places like this. The water goes and they just keep using the toilet anyways."

"Oh, jeez."

"Guy's got a lot of dolls in there, too," he said. "And they're all naked."

We stood awkwardly, staring at our feet.

"I'll be gone in a couple of days," he said.

"Well." I started backing away. "I hope you . . . uh. Get it all cleared up."

"I will."

I walked quickly to the street, turned a sharp left and broke into a jog when I was safely out of sight. Sneak listened to my story as I pulled out the car, turned, and drove the way we'd come so I wouldn't have to pass by the house again.

"Who's the hoarder?" Sneak asked. "Officer Lemon?"

"I don't know," I said. "That's not what's weird to me. It's the plumber. I was walking out and he seemed almost determined to explain why he was there. Made sure I knew he'd be gone soon."

"I've been reading the rest of the messages," Sneak said. She had Lemon's phone in her hand. "I can't tell if they're lovers or not. There's a lot of strange talk from him in the beginning."

"Strange talk?"

"Yeah, like . . ." She scrolled the phone. "*This is going to change everything. A new life. Far away. I'm so glad you chose me.*"

"Sounds kind of romantic."

"Maybe." Sneak shrugged. "But that's the thing, right? If it's *You chose me* like *You chose me to be your partner* or *your lover*, why aren't there any messages before that time? I mean, the *You chose me* message is only the third message they ever share. So they met and a week later started talking like that?"

"She chose him for something else," I said. "The criminal enterprise, whatever it is."

"So why'd she choose him, of all people?" Sneak asked.

"Because he's a cop?"

"Why not some other cop?" Sneak said.

"I don't know."

"Later he says *Trust is everything.* And she says *It's the most important thing we have.*"

Sneak and I sat in silence.

"There's one from Dayly to Lemon that says *Are we on track?*" Sneak read. "He answers with *A week left, maybe less.*"

"When was that one sent?" I asked.

"A week ago tomorrow," Sneak said. "After that, the messages are all repeated."

"What do you mean, repeated?"

"It just says *Where are you?* over and over again," she said.

JESSICA

The line at the ticket counter at LAX was ten people deep. A large Greek family was spread out along the length of the counter, little kids playing on ride-on suitcases. Jessica stood tapping out messages on her phone as announcements sounded above her. Midday. She regretted not grabbing something to eat before she parked her car in the short-term lot, not excited about touring the sprawling food courts inside the airport.

In time she called a number on her phone listed as "Beans."

"What's the story?" she asked when the call connected. "You getting organized?"

"I'm always organized," Beans yawned. She heard him groan as he stretched, the rumple of sheets and blankets down the line. "Cool it, chicky. This is going to be great."

"You have to be there after eight." Jessica moved a step forward in the line. "He's got night shift. If you go earlier it'll all fall in a heap."

"No problem. We got this," Beans said. "So no one will be there when we arrive?"

"No one."

"I like it. I like it. I like it," Beans said. "You know, I looked at the key you gave me. It's a soap-bar copy, right? I haven't seen one of these in years. That's melted plastic, girl."

"So what? It'll work."

"So that's some old-school jailhouse shit." Beans laughed. "I admire your, like, cunning. I mean, who are you? MacGyver?"

"You're not old enough to know who MacGyver is," Jessica sighed.

"You don't have to do that no more, you know. You can copy a key from a photo if you've got something to show the scale."

"Never mind. It'll work."

"I gotta know," Beans said. "Is this whole thing a prank?"

"I'm not sure 'prank' is a serious enough word for what this is," Jessica said.

"Cool-cool-cool-cool. So it's, like, revenge, is it?"

"Now you're getting closer."

"Dude." Beans snickered. "This is epic. We got to go all-out here. Big guns blazing. Cut loose, John Wick–style."

"You have clearance to launch, Beansie," Jessica said. She had reached the counter, so she ended the call. She put her badge and wallet on the desk and smiled. "San Francisco. Next available flight."

BLAIR

I was procrastinating. Pushing aside the next step, the only logical step, in our search for Dayly. I'd dropped Sneak off, as she requested, on the corner of Hollywood and Highland, just down from the Madame Tussauds, where fans were waiting in a huddle to take pictures with a grimacing Beyoncé figure on the sidewalk. I watched Sneak disappear into the early evening crowds of tourists with shopping bags and huge colorful go-cups, knowing only what she told me—that she needed to run some errands, take care of her shattered life. It was clear she was going to score drugs, get a supply that would keep her stable through the next few days of searching for her child.

I parked on Sunset in the lot belonging to a Ralphs supermarket. I walked with my ice cream container to a little shop set in a strip mall between a nail salon and a UPS store. A bell rang above the glass door as I entered. The floors were sticky. A wall of dusty dog toys stood to the left of me and a row of leather chairs to the right. A gray pit bull leaped from the ground as I entered, eager to check me out, causing its owner to be yanked forward in her chair, out of what looked like a dream-filled sleep. I got the feeling the woman with the dog was just a prop for the charade that the veterinary office really stayed open twenty-four hours to deal with the needs of Hollywood's pampered pets. She had no handbag, and the groove she'd made in the chair looked old. There was a striking resemblance between her and the woman behind the counter, who looked up lazily from her computer screen as I entered, rubbing her long, pointed nose on a raggedy tissue.

"I was just hoping for a quick check-up appointment." I smiled, putting the ice cream container on the counter.

"Oh, yeah, right." The woman yawned into her tissue. "We can do that. It's a hundred bucks, flat fee, and then if we find anything that needs doing you'll be charged on top of that. How old is your dog?" She leaned to look over the counter.

"It's not a dog, it's a gopher." I peeled the lid off the container. The woman stood and glanced in at Hugh Jackman. He was standing on his hind legs, sniffing the air, little paws wringing pensively at his chest.

"Very funny." The woman sat back down.

"I'm not joking."

"We can't do a check-up on a gopher." She gave me a pitying look.

"Why not?"

"Because it's . . ." She gestured hopelessly at the container, waited for me to catch on. I just stared at her. "Look, lady, if you brought a mosquito in here we wouldn't run a check-up on that, either."

"You guys provide care for hamsters?" I asked.

"Ah, yes, but—"

"So what's the difference?"

She slumped in her chair, looking up at me. I waited. In time, the receptionist hauled herself out of her chair and walked through a door beside a rack of worming tablets, closing it behind her. The pit bull was whimpering, its tail thumping on the floor. I lifted Hugh Jackman out of the ice cream tub and ran him through my hands a bit. He crawled up to my shoulder and I let him sit there a while fiddling with a strand of my hair. When the door beside the rack of tablets opened again I put him back in the box.

The veterinarian was a man in his forties with high, bushy hair. He had just washed his face, water clinging to his dark stubble. He came and leaned on the counter beside me.

"This is real cute," he said. "Who sent you? Stevie Leaf?"

"No one sent me."

"What do you want?" he asked. There was a mustard stain on the collar of his white coat. "I got Kit Kat and Cristy, fifty a bag."

"I don't want any drugs. I didn't come here as a joke. I want my gopher examined."

He snorted. I folded my arms. In a few seconds, his wide grin drooped slowly. "Examined for what?"

"I don't know. Parasites, fleas, intestinal worms?" I shrugged. "Whatever you'd examine any other pet that came in here for. I want a full checkup. I've got money. Cash."

"You know, there's a golf course behind my house," the vet said. "They poison these things by the hundreds. Shovel them dead into bags. Using actual *shovels*, honey. You ever heard of gopher fishing? Hillbillies do it. It's a national pastime. Why you'd want to keep one as a pet is one thing, but why you'd spend good money having one checked by a vet is another."

"Why don't you just let me spend my money how I want to," I said.

"You're crazy." He stood, looked to the woman

with the pit bull for confirmation. "She's crazy. What do I care? I'll examine the damn gopher. I got nothing better to do."

"One more thing. On the door you say you do pet grooming."

"That's for dogs, honey. Dogs and cats, not lawn rats."

"Okay." I nodded as he took the container toward the door near the pill rack. "I'll wait here."

I sat by the woman with the pit bull, who had just about fallen asleep again in her chair. I patted the dog and watched the afternoon activity through the dirty windows to the street.

BLAIR

Sasha opened the door and stared through the gopher mansion at me, her face distorted through the warped and bubbled plastic. I shifted the house against my hip and smiled, but didn't get one in return.

"What are you doing here?" she said. "You didn't call."

"I came to show you my gopher," I said. "My very healthy, active, biologically sound lawn rat."

Sasha turned and walked into the house. I followed awkwardly behind her. I was about to put the gopher mansion on the kitchen counter when she barked from the other side of the marble surface, "Don't put that there!"

I walked toward the dining room table.

"Not there, either. No eating surfaces."

"Well, I can't stand here holding it the whole time, Sasha."

She opened the door and led me out into the back-yard, wincing as I placed the house on the glass out-door table. With the huge enclosure removed from my vision, I could see her eyes and nose were red and puffy from tears. I have learned over the years that it's better to let Sasha bring a problem to you. Pursuing it makes her retreat into a corner with denials that everything in her world isn't perfectly peachy and under her tight control. So I opened the top of the enclosure and brought the gopher out into my hands.

"Hugh Jackman," I said. "This is Sasha. I believe you two have met before. Sasha, this creature has been checked extensively by a vet. It is disease-, virus-, and parasite-free, and has been vaccinated against pinworms."

"Pinworms?" She grimaced.

"I've conducted my own behavioral analysis over a period of days and have determined that the bite risk is low," I said. "These observations are supported by the—"

"Just shut up, Blair." She pinched her brow. Her lip trembled. I stood there, waiting, while she attempted to shove her emotions back into whatever black hole she usually kept them tucked, a task as difficult as putting toothpaste back into a tube. Eventually she sat down at the outdoor table and I joined her. I put Hugh Jackman in the chest pocket of my polo shirt, and the little creature turned in a circle a few times and then balled up to sleep.

"Henry's leaving me," she said suddenly.

The afternoon garden was full of crickets and pretty gold lights. I stared out at it, trying to decide what to say. I knew exactly what I *should* say. All women do. I had been consoling friends about breakups since I was in high school, crammed into a toilet stall with four other girls, listening to the wailing of a member of our crew over a two-week *Romeo and Juliet*–type tryst broken up by a senior with huge breasts. I needed to tell Sasha that I was here. That I was listening. That she would be okay. That men sucked, were pigs sometimes. But I couldn't do anything in that moment but sit rigidly and stare at the beautiful garden, because terror had seized my limbs, a cold snap gripping at every fiber of my being.

Sasha and Henry were my son's parents. If they didn't stay together as one unit, they would become separate teams both playing for my son. For his time. His love. His attention.

His custody.

"I found a pair of women's sunglasses in Henry's car," Sasha said. She took a worn tissue from her pocket and balled it against her nose. "He met her on a bus, can you believe that? A fucking bus! What was he even doing, riding a bus? I haven't ridden a *bus* in decades."

I held my head in my hands.

"They're moving to Wyoming, apparently. To open a bed-and-breakfast."

"They're what?" I stood, the chair kicking out from behind me. "So Jamie—"

"Jamie doesn't know." Sasha sniffed, pushing back her frizzy hair. "Don't tell him."

"Sasha, this is awful," I said. "I can't believe this."

"I can see exactly what'll happen," she said, hardly listening to me. "This new woman will be super interesting to Jamie. He'll want to hang out with her all the time. His world is full of such *interesting* people, and here I am baking cookies he doesn't even like and nagging him to clean his room and brush his teeth. There's a woman back there, a cop, he says." She jutted her chin toward the house at the end of the yard. "Just moved in. He's been ducking over there and she's been teaching him to swim. I noticed her over there and went to say hello. She seems like a hard-ass. Busy. Always on the phone. I was planning on asking her what the fuck she was thinking, deciding all on her own that she'd teach my kid to swim without even meeting me, but you know what? I was too intimidated. What an interesting person, this police officer with her big empty mansion, chain-smoking and taking important calls and intimidating the fuck out of the neighbors. So very, very interesting. And then there's you with all your . . ." She glanced at me. Seemed to reconsider her words.

"My history," I said.

Sasha nodded. "You're interesting, too. All these interesting women in my son's life."

"Sasha, you are interesting," I said. "You're a great mother, and—"

"Spare me." She held up a hand.

"I'm serious," I said. "You're not only interesting but you're good. You're incredibly good at heart. A friend came to you and said, 'I've been arrested for murder. Will you raise my infant son?' And you said yes. Jesus Christ! Who does that? Who just takes on someone else's kid like that, without question, without judgment? You let me be a part of his life. When I'd been charged with *murder*."

"You didn't murder that guy." Sasha rolled her eyes. "It was to help the girlfriend, like you said. You're too holier-than-thou to murder anyone."

"I'm going to take that as a compliment," I said.

Sasha sighed. She looked beaten down. I wasn't getting through. I knew it might take weeks, months, to remind her of the great woman she was.

"What will Henry want in terms of custody?" I asked.

Sasha thought for a moment. Her shoulders were hunched. She lifted them, let them fall again. "I don't know. We haven't talked about it. I suppose he'll want fifty percent."

"But what about me?" I cried.

"What . . . ?" Sasha looked up at me. "What about *you*?"

"I know." I dragged my chair back into place. "I know. I'm sorry. I just said 'What about me' right in the middle of your breakup. I'm so sorry. That was a stupid thing to say."

But if Henry wants fifty percent custody of Jamie, that leaves Sasha fifty percent, and me zero percent, I thought. *Or it leaves Sasha and me twenty-five percent each.* It was getting hard to breathe. A door at the front of the house slammed. I heard footsteps thumping on the tiles, fast, then Jamie appeared with his school backpack on and threw open the door to the yard like a magician revealing himself safe and unharmed after being loaded into a box of rattlesnakes, wearing a straitjacket.

"I'm here!" he declared. He pointed at me. "Blair! You're here too!"

"Yeah, buddy. I just dropped by to—"

"Whoa! Look at this thing!" He shoved his nose against the side of the gopher mansion. "What is it? Is it . . . is it a mouse house? It's a mouse house! Oh, man! Oh, man! Have you got Hugh Jackman? Is he here?"

"Jamie, just settle down a bit, will you?" Sasha sighed.

"Have you got the gopher?"

"He's here." I scooped Hugh Jackman out of my pocket and handed him to my child. "Take him."

Jamie bundled the tiny gopher into his hands and ran to the edge of the porch, sitting down on the step. Sasha and I watched him giggling and snickering as the creature ran up his wrist to his shoulder. The boy took the gopher and rested it carefully on the crown of his head, laughing as it began digging and sifting through his hair.

"I know he's your child," Sasha said gently. I turned and looked at her. Her eyes were filled with tears. "I know you want more time with him. But I just can't think about how to work out a custody arrangement with you right now. I'm looking at having to put my kid on a plane to Wyoming every second week."

"I know," I said. My heart actually felt heavy in my chest, like a warm, dull weight sitting painfully on my ribs. "It was unfair to ask you to do so."

"I don't want to share him with anyone," Sasha said. We watched the boy together. "He's mine."

No, he's mine, I thought. I bit my lip to stop it from trembling. Jamie was rubbing the gopher against his cheek, smiling, his eyes closed. He held the creature to his face and the animal gripped his nose in both hands, sniffed the tip, child and pet connected as its tiny whiskers tickled Jamie's perfect skin.

The moment was eternal, yet suddenly gone forever. Jamie turned toward us, two women hiding their tears in the shade of the porch.

"I'm hungry," the boy said. "Where's Dad?"

JESSICA

The last time Jessica had been to San Quentin she had been visiting Jake Trelles, the Silver Lake Killer. The case that had begun it all. She'd had little hope of the man speaking to the cop who had put him away for the unsolved disappearances of women going back a decade, women like Bernice Beauvoir. Young, pretty, full of plans and ambitions, women walking to their cars in darkened parking lots or taking shortcuts between backstreets, the kind of women who had been fodder for serial killers seemingly forever. As she'd predicted, Trelles had stonewalled her on questions she still had about the case.

Now she put her gun, wallet, phone, and rental-car keys in the same coin-operated locker in the visitors' center and took her badge and ID to the bored yet skeptical women running the processing center. It was outside of visiting hours, and staff had been specially called in from the prison to see Jessica through. Routines broken. Rules bent. They didn't like it. Jessica stood with her arms outstretched as a guard ran the body scanner wand up and down her more times than was really necessary.

Jessica had been to San Quentin to talk to inmates

maybe five times in her career. The prison was an hour and a half's drive from the airport. Three hours of driving, one hour for a standard visit, and two hours' worth of delays across arrival and departure—waiting on the tarmac, getting coffee at the airport, getting through security, hiring and then returning the car. She asked herself why she hadn't recognized the pattern as soon as she saw the times attached to Dayly's airline tickets. Jessica consoled herself that without the letters from John Fishwick, Dayly's trip to San Quentin had been impossible to guess.

She followed a yellow painted stripe on the sidewalk toward death row. To her left, San Francisco Bay sprawled beyond the fences and watchtowers, glittering and thrumming with life under a hard blue sky. Ferries leaving Alcatraz, crab boats bringing in their loads, followed by enormous black seals. She showed her ID again at the heavy double doors to the row. The long room she entered was empty. The two lines of steel cages where full-contact visits were held were silent and still, their folding chairs stacked neatly against the inner walls of bulletproof glass and steel mesh. Vending machines hummed against one wall. The last time she had come here, she'd stood aside to make room while a little old woman carried a massive tray of snacks toward a cage where a man in his forties, presumably her son, sat waiting in his prison denims in the farthest cage, a pink party hat strapped on his head.

Jessica took a stool that was bolted to the ground near one of the glass visitation windows, as directed by a guard. When John Fishwick arrived he was not cuffed, and his pale denim shirt was rumpled. He was taller than Jessica expected, broad shoulders pulling the front of the shirt tight, a head of silver hair slicked back against the sides of his head. Jessica had only seen pictures of Dayly Lawlor, but she thought she recognized the girl's long, thin nose and deep, thoughtful brown eyes in the man's weathered visage.

"Well, this is a novelty," John said when he picked up the intercom handset. He took a pack of cigarettes from his back pocket, lit one, and blew smoke against the glass as he looked over what he could see of Jessica's body. "Visiting outside of hours. Cop or fed?"

"Cop," Jessica said. "West LAPD. I'm here to talk about Dayly."

"That's a long way for a cop to come to investigate an assault charge," John said. "So I assume it's not that."

"What?"

"She came here and visited. I assaulted her. That's why I'm in here and not out there, where I usually am." He pointed through the glass to the cages over Jessica's shoulder. "I lost my contact privileges. Won't get them back for a couple of years now, I suspect."

"Why did you assault her?" Jessica asked stiffly.

"She wrote to me asking if I'm her daddy, telling me she's all messed up about her life and this and that." He shrugged. "I didn't care. I kept her on the line after I saw her picture. She was a little honey. Most girls who write to death-row inmates are real warthogs. I wanted to see if I could get a piece of that ass."

"You didn't stop to think that she might actually *be* your daughter?" Jessica scoffed.

"No. I guess I didn't think too much about it." John rubbed his nose on the back of his tattooed hand. "A man takes what presents itself." Jessica noticed a deep, jagged scar on the inside of his wrist, no doubt a suicide attempt on the inside. She understood they were frequent on the row.

"So what are you here for, if not the assault?" he

asked. Jessica saw a flash of something in his eyes. Genuine interest poking through the false bravado, the practiced boredom, like a thorn hiding in a knitted sweater. "I haven't heard from her in a couple of weeks. What's going on?"

"She's missing," Jessica said.

"Oh," John said. Jessica watched carefully, but the wall had come down again. The corner of his mouth twitched, and nothing more. "Missing how?"

Jessica described the circumstances of the crime scene at Dayly's apartment, Al Tasik's bust on a car full of Crips with Dayly riding in the back. John listened, smoking, staring at his tar-stained fingernails.

"Maybe these Crip fellows found out about me," John said. "Knew she was coming to see me. Maybe they bought in to all the bullshit about the hidden money and threatened her."

"So there is no further hidden money?" Jessica asked. "I've read your letters to Dayly. You hint at it pretty strongly."

"Yeah. See, that's what you've got to do to get them here." John smirked. "The women. Chicks want to come here and visit, but they don't want to look like sickos. They don't want to tell their friends they're in love with a death-row inmate they've never even met yet, so they need a reason to visit, at least initially. They need a story. It's called a Pull. The serial killers—they're the most popular. Women write to them from all over the world. So their Pull is that they've got extra victims they want to confess about. Then the girls have a respectable reason to come here, you know, so they can solve a crime. Help the victims' families. You pull them in, and then you get your grabby-grabby."

"Grabby-grabby?" Jessica said.

"Yeah." John flashed his full set of teeth, at least

half of them gold. "There's a guy in here. The Silver Lake Killer. You heard of him?"

"I might have." She didn't know if Fishwick knew she'd arrested Trelles, but she wasn't going to take the bait if he did.

"He told this woman lawyer from San Jose that he has a partner out there somewhere to this day, a guy still killing girls. The lawyer started visiting on the regular, and within a few weeks she'd forgotten all about the whole partner story. She visits once a month now and pays a guard a hundred bucks for that end cage there, the one behind the pylon. Two years she's been coming here to give him a blow job and stock up his commissary account. They're getting married, end of the year."

"Awesome," Jessica said. "That's really wonderful. I'm so pleased you told me that." She gave him a big, sarcastic smile.

"I had my fun with Dayly while she was here. Shame I won't be seeing her again," John sighed. "Maybe I forced her a little, but I was sure she'd be thinking about it some, later on, maybe when she went to bed that night. She'd be back."

Jessica took a moment to swallow her revulsion. "Was it really worth it?"

He shrugged. "I could die tomorrow. I'm a highly desirable target in here. I killed a kid. All the other inmates have got a hard-on for me. So I've got to get what I can get, while I can get it."

"You're a real loony tune, aren't you?"

"Your face is classic." John thumped the steel table-top in front of him with his fist in hilarity. "You're so horrified. You know, I didn't even catch your name."

"It's Jessica."

"Jessica. Pretty. You're Latina?"

"Dayly is gone, and her activities in the past few

weeks have been strange," Jessica said. "We know that she was trying to hire a plane. You said in your letters that she wanted to 'fly away' into a new life. Those things together suggest to me that you had her pretty convinced that the money was real. Did she leave here knowing it was all a Pull?"

"I don't know," he yawned. "I don't really remember. I was pretty distracted during the visit."

Jessica sighed.

"The first one was real enough. Burying the cash in Pasadena, that was a mistake," John continued. He leaned back on his stool, cupped his hands at the back of his head and stretched. "I didn't think about who might get access to it. You've seen the reports. You know a bunch of construction workers found it."

"I do," Jessica said.

"Yeah, well, those guys should have just split it. Instead they handed it in. Can you believe that? Now the government's got it. It'll go to paying these idiots' wages." He nodded through the glass at two guards walking by behind Jessica. "Maybe I ought to send in some requests for how it's spent. I mean, it's my money. I got one pillow in my cell and it's storm gray. It's six years old."

"Uh-huh." Jessica nodded. "Almost as old as your youngest victim."

"Ooh." John smiled. "A smart-ass. I like smart-asses."

"If there's nothing else you can tell me about Dayly's disappearance, I've got to go." Jessica stood and smoothed down her shirt.

"I'm sure if I'd thought about it more at the time, I'd have realized hiding the money like that where just anybody could come find it was a mistake," John said. "But I was pressed for time."

"Uh-huh," Jessica said again.

"Maybe if I'd needed to hide a second stash, I'd have found a way to make sure I could control who got the money, if it couldn't be me."

"Really?"

"Yeah." He smiled. "I'd make sure I could choose my beneficiary."

"You know what I think"—Jessica leaned on the table—"I think you're trying to pull me in now. Trying to make me believe there really is more money. Or maybe you're trying to goad me into thinking Trelles had a partner who's still out there, and that I have unfinished business. Let me guess: he'll only talk to me through you. You want to give me a reason to visit you. To keep visiting. Eventually you'll have me pressing my tits up against the glass for a few years until we can get into the cage together and you can have your grabby-grabby."

John laughed, a hard, unexpected laugh that broke into coughs. "Now there's a great idea!"

"A good plan," she said. "I guess all you've got to do in there all day is plan things. But, like your career as a thief, it's doomed to fail. I'm pretty revolted by you, as I am by most of the men I've met in your position. And if there is money, and you did try to pass it on to Dayly, that plan hasn't worked either. In fact, it might just be the thing that's got her killed."

John sat quietly, a little of the bluster and bravado gone from his posture. Jessica waved and walked away, turning toward the guard station at the end of the room.

BLAIR

The night air carried smells up the side of the canyon: Mexican food trucks, fresh paint from the studios, downtown traffic. Ventura was searing with red and yellow lights, and the silver tips of the mountains sliced through the orange sky, an eternal lightning strike dividing land and air. I sat on the hood of my car at a lookout on Mulholland, playing with my phone, biding time to indulge my addiction while a night tour bus was reloaded with tourists who had been taking shots of Universal. There were red lights and puffing smoke now and then from the Harry Potter castle. Voldemort's birthday or something, maybe. I wondered if Sasha had read my son those books, how many hours it had taken at his bedside, Jamie fighting sleep against the pillow. I wondered if she'd done the voices. I would have. As the tour bus roared away I closed my eyes and dialed.

"Station Twenty-Two," a man answered. "Burke here."

"Oh, hi. My name's Blair. I'm just calling to speak to someone."

"Someone who?"

"Just anyone. You know. I just need a minute with someone."

"Ma'am, are you suicidal right now?"

"I . . . No. No! Sorry, what kind of station is this?" I asked.

"This is Station Twenty-Two of the Los Angeles County Fire Department. Montebello."

"Oh. I'm sorry. I don't want to tie up the line. I'll go."

"You're not tying up the line. You've called the mess room on the accommodation floor. But I can't understand what you want."

"Well, I—"

"She sounds hot!" came a muffled voice. "Put her on speaker!"

"Yeah, put her on speaker, Burkey."

"How many people are there?" I asked, smiling.

"We've got me, Betts, Carlisle, Jonesy, and Fitz," Burke said. "And we're trying to play a poker game here, so if you wouldn't mi—"

"I'll talk to her." A new voice, a rattle as the receiver was snatched. "This is Johnny Carlisle. I'm six five, blond, big hands, nice square jaw. Stubble. I can bench one-twenty. Think Daniel Craig, only taller and not fucking British. What's your name, girl?"

"If you're six five, I've got a baseball bat for a dick," someone said.

"Six five my ass."

"It's Blair," I laughed.

"Blair, sweetheart, that's a good name. I like that name. You know, most people call here looking for someone to come put out a fire," Carlisle said. "But I got a feeling you want someone to start one for you. I can hear it in your voice."

A low moan of appreciation from the crowd.

"Smooth, Carlisle."

"Where you at, baby?"

"Can we get back to the game, please? Jesus Christ. I got a good hand here!"

Lights fell over me. I hung up, tossed the phone into the front seat of the Gangstermobile. As the enormous Escalade pulled to the side of the road, I realized how lonely I had been as I drove from Brentwood to the Hills after my visit with Sasha and Jamie. Living on the outside meant times of loneliness. It meant uncertainty, trouble, unexpected events, people breaking up and getting together, people moving to Wyoming. I'd known as I turned off Cahuenga that I was going to do something dangerous. The time between dangerous acts was shortening. Alejandro stepped from the car and adjusted the cuffs of his black shirt, a strangely embarrassed downward glance. This was not a man who started casual liaisons with ex-cons who worked in gas stations. This was a man who had models and aspiring actresses dripping all over him in expensive nightclubs downtown. I'd been surprised that he answered my call, even more surprised when he said he'd come to the lookout.

"I did not expect to hear from you again," he said, mirroring my thoughts.

"You left your number." I shrugged.

"I'm strangely optimistic sometimes." He pushed me against the Gangstermobile and kissed me hard, grabbed my ass in both hands and dragged me against his hips. With every car that came around the bend, I expected an eruption of blue lights, the blip of a police siren. I was dancing on the edge again, tempting life to take me away from the hurt and panic over Jamie's custody, Sneak's grief, the endless years of ordinary life ahead filled with unpredictability and danger. I held Alejandro's shoulders and looked out over Los Angeles and thought about my prison bed, and how close it really was.

JESSICA

Jessica had taken a quick, half-hearted tour around the Bluestone Lane house and was standing in the living room, just locking the back door before she left for the night, when she saw the boy's head pop up over the gate like a blond, grinning Whac-A-Mole. She still held the key in the lock. A baby had cried on the flight back from San Francisco that evening, two seats away, kicking its legs and thrashing in its carrier, splintery, squealy noises making mincemeat of her brain, of any attempt to make sense of what John Fishwick had told her or not told her in the prison. She wasn't sure she could do another minute's interaction with a child, but before she could turn away from the door the boy hefted himself over the gate and landed on the grass.

"I've had a long, long day," she said, opening the door a crack. "I'm going to go home and sit on the floor of my shower with a cold beer."

"Have a swim instead," the boy suggested brightly. He was heading for the pool, tearing his shirt off. Jessica sighed and trudged out to greet him.

On the bottom of the pool, their legs crossed and their cheeks full of air, the two stared at each other,

mentally counting. After thirty seconds the boy released his lungfuls in a huge laugh and rose to the
surface in an explosion of electric-blue bubbles.

"No fair!" he cried when Jessica rose up with him.
"You made me laugh. Cheater!"

"I was literally staring at you without a single
emotion on my face. How is that cheating?"

"Your hair was going everywhere, like a mermaid."
The boy giggled. "Like Mendosa."

"Medusa?" she asked, grabbing him and nudging
him into the floating position.

"That one."

They floated side by side. Jessica calculated that
Beansie would be entering Wallert's house around
that very moment. Terror and excitement roiled in
her stomach.

"Why was your day so long?" the boy asked. She
could barely hear him through the water gushing in
and out of her ears.

"I went to San Francisco."

"Why?"

"To see a guy in prison."

"Whoa! Why?"

"Because I thought he had some information I
needed. He didn't."

"Why not?"

"Look," Jessica said, "I can't talk a lot about this.
The president asked me to go, and just you knowing
that I went could be kind of risky. Both for me and
for you."

"Really?" The boy dropped his feet. Jessica did the
same and stood before him in the pool.

"Yeah, really. The White House called me this
morning. Well, they tried to call, but I was still asleep,
so instead they sent a couple of guys in suits round
my apartment. They gave me the mission files to read

on the helicopter. I got out of the prison alive. Only barely though. The guy I went to see, he's pretty dangerous. He has a whole wing of the facility to himself. Guards round the clock. Laser-maze technology."

"Oh my god," the boy said.

"He has to wear this special helmet made from graphite," Jessica continued. "So that he can't read your mind."

Jessica and the boy stared at each other. A moment passed.

"Aw, you're such a jerk." Jamie splashed her.

She laughed for what felt like the first time in months. The kid was too easy. She dunked his head under the water for good measure and went to the edge of the pool, where her phone sat with the screen lit, a message tone dinging for the second time.

It's Kristi. I want to talk.

"Gotta fly, kid." Jessica climbed out of the pool. "It's the prez. He's thrown up the bat signal."

She watched the child climb out of the pool, shake off like a dog, and head back toward his house.

I'll be right there, she typed into her phone.

Grunions Bar was difficult to find from Sepulveda Boulevard: a cream building that could have been offices or a medical clinic, surrounded by car dealerships at Manhattan Beach. Jessica circled the block twice then parked behind the bar, trudging through gravel to the side door. She found an enormous space dominated by a U-shaped bar, television sets visible from every angle, a section with diner-style booths and sports memorabilia. In the semi-darkness, men and women on stools at the bar turned and watched her arrive. Every panel in the ceiling had been bought in some fundraiser or another by locals, and was scrawled with artwork from the simplistic to the complex—single names hastily written, airbrushed space-scapes, hand-drawn Dodgers and LA Kings logos. The wizened Irishman behind the bar asked her what she wanted, and she ordered a bourbon. At the front windows, Kristi Zea was sitting at a high stool and table, lazily tapping her phone.

Jessica thought that, just like Blair Harbour, the woman had aged far more than the eleven years that had passed since she had seen her. Kristi Zea had been a battered and bruised mess when Jessica interviewed her after her boyfriend's murder, but she had lightened and tightened into a pale, freckled, waifish girl with spunky blonde hair and lots of ear piercings as she dealt with her throughout the trial. The woman Jessica sat down before now had lines around her mouth that were too deep, giving her a sullen expression, and her piercings were gone, leaving little stitch-like indentations in her ears. The sports jacket she was wearing floated around her as she picked up her beer glass.

"Well, look at you." Kristi nodded. "You haven't aged a day."

"I bathe in the blood of my enemies." Jessica put her phone on the table beside her glass. "What made you change your mind about talking?"

"It was just like you said." Kristi shrugged. "The sleepless nights. The guilt."

The two women sat in silence for a long time. At the bar, a group of locals started shouting at the Dodgers game.

"I want immunity," Kristi said.

"Yeah. I thought you'd ask for that. You've been watching too much television," Jessica said. "The case isn't officially reopened. If it was, another officer would probably be assigned to it, not me. They might be in the position to offer you immunity on a perjury charge, but that would only be if you admitted in court, on the record, that what you said about what happened on the night of the murder wasn't exactly correct."

"So why the hell am I talking to you if the case isn't being reopened?"

"Because I asked you to."

"Why'd you do that?"

"Because I care," Jessica said. "I know the woman, Harbour. I know her son."

"The kid." Kristi nodded. "It's all about the kid for you. It has been for me, too, the past ten years. I think about that kid being born in prison. I read a thing in the *LA Times* about it. About how they give you an hour with the baby before they take it away."

A bartender came by and wiped their table. Kristi grabbed his arm. "Can I order another beer?"

"Afraid you'll have to go to the counter, ma'am."

"Oh, come on, just—"

The young man wandered away. Jessica went to the counter, keeping her profile to Zea so she would see if the young woman decided to run off. She brought a beer and a bourbon chaser back to the table.

"The woman was pregnant." Kristi gulped the bourbon, didn't wince. "I mean, fuck. Who does that? Who goes running into the middle of—"

"Kristi—"

"Of something that's not even—"

"What happened?" Jessica dared to put her hand on Kristi's, to grab the fingers firmly. "Just tell me. Forget about who's to blame. It's time to let it all out and tell the truth."

"If I can't get immunity, I want cash." Kristi blinked a little too slowly. Jessica wondered how long she had been in the bar. "Ten grand for my confession now. Twenty to say it in court."

Jessica slipped off her stool and took out her wallet, fished for a couple of bucks. She lifted her empty glass and slipped the notes underneath, then turned to leave.

"Okay." Kristi made a swipe for her arm, knocked the table stem with her knee, rattling the glasses on the table. "Okay. Okay. Okay."

Jessica sat back down. Kristi drank half her beer and rubbed her face, hard, as if she was trying to remove a stain from her cheeks. In time she lifted her eyes from the tabletop, and Jessica realized it was the first time the girl had made eye contact since their meeting began. Kristi took a deep breath.

"There was eight hundred grand's worth of coke in the house," she said.

BLAIR

At the Pump'n'Jump, my mind was full. Alejandro's breath in my ear and his hands shoving my jeans down. Dayly's frightened eyes behind the gun that wavered in front of my face. The crunching, shuddering halting of the car against the traffic light pole. I absently served customers and let these things cycle through my brain, anything but Jamie and Henry and Sasha, the breaking up of my son's family, the plunge into icy, turbulent waters. I thought about the plumber, Ramirez, at the hoarder house in San Jasinte. What had Officer Lemon been doing inside the house while the plumber came out to speak to me? Why hadn't he heard us talking? Was it his house, or the house of a relative or friend? I hadn't had any experience with hoarding during my time as a doctor. I'd heard horror stories from other pediatricians of children from such places coming in with rat bites, malnourishment, bedsores from sleeping on filthy, bare mattresses for months on end. Lemon had seemed like a regular, stand-up cop. He'd looked and smelled good as he leaned over me in the dented Gangstermobile.

At ten o'clock I started cleaning the drinks fridges,

restless and bored. Plenty of questions, no answers. I thought about Lemon's messages to Dayly.

Are we on track?

A week left, maybe less.

Where are you?

Where are you?

Where are you?

A pair of long-haired, guffawing teenage boys used the distraction that the drinks fridge was providing me to pour themselves a mega blue slushie and slip one of their own hairs into it. They feigned horror and disgust, threatened to post a picture of the contaminated drink to Instagram. I let them have the slushie, as I had three months earlier, and a few months before that. They were obviously too stoned to realize they had played the gag on me before, or perhaps they did it so often they couldn't keep track of their hits.

At eleven, my phone dinged. It was Ada.

You're not at your house. Are you at that shitbox gas station where you work?

I texted back. *Yes, I'm here. Is everything okay?*

I'm coming by.

I knew there was no point in asking Ada to explain herself. I exhaled and texted Sneak.

Can you come to the Pump'n'Jump now? Ada's on her way here and I don't want to be alone with her.

Sneak was a couple of minutes in answering.

Why?

WHY? I shook my head, bewildered. *Because Macaroni, that's why!*

I had been sharing a dorm room with Sneak, Ada, and thirty other women when the Happy Valley Macaroni Incident occurred. An inmate named Nelly Raddlett, new to the prison, had been loudly professing how thoroughly she had enjoyed the evening's macaroni dinner to a group of girls in front of the television set where Ada was trying to watch a rerun of *The Sopranos*. Raddlett pronounced the word mac-uh-*ron*-nee, not mac-uh-*row*-nee. The mispronunciation had so irritated Ada that by the fourth or fifth repetition, Ada had stood up, walked to the front of the room, and told Raddlett that if she mispronounced macaroni one more time, she was going to take a belt from the nearest guard and beat her with it.

I'd watched on from my bunk, curious to see if Raddlett was stupid or bold enough to mispronounce the word again, or if indeed Ada had the kind of clout in the prison to obtain a belt from a guard for the purposes of beating another inmate with it.

Both happened.

Thirty-one women and two guards stood idly by that night while Ada Maverick beat Nelly Raddlett for two solid minutes with a doubled-up leather belt over the mispronunciation of a type of pasta.

No, I mean why is she coming? Sneak asked.

Just get your ass here, I texted.

JESSICA

The noise around them had become nothing. Jessica gripped her drink and waited, like a rider on a roller coaster slowly ticking its way up the biggest hill. The plunge was coming. There was nothing she could do to stop it.

"Adrian and his brother, Brosh, were part of this . . . organization." Zea opened her hands. "The mob, I guess. I don't know. I'd seen other Armenian men at the house, and I'd overheard phone calls. But I don't know if it was like you see in the movies, with the meetings and the structure and all that stuff. I think they were just edging their way in, relying on their family connections to get work. Adrian came home really happy one night. He said they'd been given an amazing job by their cousins. He put this big duffel bag full of coke on the bed in front of me. When it hit the bed it was so heavy it made the whole mattress sink in the middle."

"When was this?" Jessica asked.

"A week before the murder. Adrian said we were going to sell the coke, distribute it and make a lot of money, and then his cousins were going to make it a regular thing. I was just so excited that he was telling me all this, you know? He'd always been so cagey about what he did, about his brother. I felt as though I was being let in. It was a new step for us in our relationship."

"How romantic." Jessica caught the eye of the bartender who had wiped their table earlier. The crowd was thinning. He seemed to have decided the no-table-service rule was up and nodded to indicate that he'd fetch Jessica another drink.

"I thought when Adrian said 'we' that he meant, like, *we*," Kristi said, pointing to Jessica, then herself. "So I wanted to help. Adrian wouldn't let me work. I was stuck in the house all day. I had no friends. But I knew these guys who could move junk like that real quick, so I took one of the bricks from the bag while Adrian was out and gave it to them. They were supposed to get the money back that afternoon. It was going to be a surprise, you know? It was supposed to show Adrian how useful I could be. I mean, it was New Year's Eve. Who has trouble moving drugs on New Year's Eve?"

"Your guys, evidently," Jessica said, feeling the roller coaster crest the hill.

"When I told Adrian, he was livid," Kristi said. "He started shouting, so we put on the music, but after a while he started beating on me. He'd smacked me a few times before, but nothing close to this. He said the drugs weren't supposed to be sold off like that. There were already buyers. Now they were down a whole brick, and my guys weren't coming through. I tried to hide in the laundry but he came through the door, and I guess that's when Harbour saw us through the window."

"Did she go right for the gun?" Jessica asked.

"No, she . . ." Kristi stared at the table, remembering. She gave a small, sad laugh. "She tried talking to us first. But I couldn't hear her. I was getting my ass wailed on. And he didn't even know she was there. When he got into those rages he would just zero in on you and nothing could stop him."

The two women sat together, one remembering, one visualizing. They held their drinks, staring into them. Jessica could see the house in Brentwood. Blair Harbour walking through the door, stopping dead in the foyer at the sight of small, lean Kristi Zea flopping around in Adrian Orlov's hands. Blood on the floor. The smack of flesh on flesh. It was something totally outside Harbour's world, her circle of existence filled with beautiful rooms in beautiful houses, stark, white, clean surgery rooms, the occasional upmarket restaurant with friends. People didn't fight in Harbour's world. They didn't put their hands on each other except to caress, comfort, embrace, heal. All blood was expected. Jessica imagined her shouting and pleading and not being listened to, trying to get into the fray, coming up against the hard muscles of a rage-filled man and never having felt something so impossibly immoveable before.

Jessica could see Orlov turning at the sound of the hammer on the gun. Outrage, panic, both he and Harbour moving, two steps in a dance that was over before the music began—him coming at her, her blasting him away.

"She picked up the gun as a warning, I think," Kristi said. "He went for her, got within a few feet and *bang*. She shot him. Just like that. I could see he was dead before he hit the ground, even from where I was. She was right to do it. He was going to kill me. There's never been any doubt in my mind about that."

Jessica held the table with both hands. The second drink came, and she didn't move. She knew what happened next, but needed to hear it. Needed to feel it rushing by her. Moments she could never recover, never correct.

"You called nine-one-one," Jessica said.

"Not right away," Kristi said. "I told Harbour that I would. I told her to go wait outside. There was no helping Adrian. She wanted to stay, help me, but I shouted at her. I told her to flag down the ambulance when it came, because our house number was real hard to see with all the palms out front. I knew the police would look at my phone, so I took one of Adrian's burners and called his brother. The bag of coke was still upstairs in the fucking bedroom, sitting out there in plain sight, and I didn't have time to hide it. I don't think I could even have lifted it."

"Was it his idea to lie?" Jessica asked.

"Yeah," Kristi said. "He said I was going to tell the cops that Harbour shot Adrian for some bullshit reason. That would get them focused on her. On her house. On her life. We didn't want them walking around our house, trying to come up with reasons why Adrian would want to hurt me like that, trying to, like, find out if the shooting was justified. I was going to be really upset, stricken with grief, you know? That way I'd get them out of the house as soon as I could. It was me who came up with the crazy stuff."

"What crazy stuff?"

"The weird stuff I said Harbour did. Like with the cheese sandwich," Kristi explained. "And the, uh, the poisoning of the orange juice. See, I had an uncle with schizophrenia. He thought he was being followed around. That people were poisoning him. That Jesus was talking to him all the time. He went crazy in a Walmart and the cops shot him. Nobody asked any questions. He was crazy, right?"

"So you never went into Harbour's house?" Jessica said. "You never tampered with her food?"

"No," Kristi said. "Oh, I mean, we did scratch her car, accidentally, but she was fine about it. She knew we didn't mean it. And she would complain to us about the noise, but she was never crazy. Not like I made her sound in my statement. I just followed the patrol officer around the house and pointed to things and said, 'Oh, yeah, she came in here and made a sandwich. She said the clock was talking to her, telling her to burn the house down. She stood here at the sink staring at nothing.' Half that stuff was from my uncle. When they shot him in Walmart he was trying to make a cheese sandwich behind the deli counter. I figured if I made Harbour sound crazy enough she might get off. You know, like, not guilty by reason of insanity?"

"Ingenious," Jessica said.

"The plan worked," Kristi said. "The cops stayed on the main floor. They took photos of the crime scene, took Adrian away, sat me in a corner where I could see what everybody was doing, gave me a drink of water, and listened to what I had to say. Nobody went upstairs for very long—they did a quick sweep to make sure no one was there. When Brosh turned up they let him walk right in. He said he'd go upstairs and get my laptop, get my contacts list, start calling people to tell them the news. No one stopped him. He took the bag with the coke and walked right out the back door with it. By the time the cops did a proper search later, the coke was gone."

Jessica could see Brosh Orlov, another big, broad man, exiting the house, skirting the boundary of the property, walking out into the street with the bag, unnoticed, like someone walking to the gym in the early hours with his bag of sweats and towels. Jessica knew exactly where she had been when this happened eleven years earlier. She'd been asking questions of

Harbour on her doorstep while officers searched her house. She'd been telling Harbour to turn around. She'd been reciting the Miranda warnings and unhooking the cuffs from her belt while Harbour stood there stiffly, shell-shocked, trying to understand what was happening while her world closed in around her.

Jessica took her phone from the tabletop and slid it into her pocket, drained the last of her bourbon.

"Where are you going? We're not done here."

"We're done enough," Jessica said. "For now. I'm going to tell Harbour that her time as a known coldblooded killer is over."

"What, right now?" Kristi Zea stood with Jessica. "But you said the case isn't being reopened. I mean, what's the point? Aren't you just going to upset her?"

"Upset her? No, I don't think so." Jessica put more money on the table. "I'm sure she'll be fucking elated. She's trying for increased custody of her son. The case isn't reopened yet, but this will reopen it. That's for damned sure."

"Okay, hold on, whoa." Kristi grabbed Jessica's shoulders. "You've got to think about me for a second here. Brosh and his guys, they've been relying on me to keep quiet all these years. If this gets out, they'll come looking for me. This was all meant to be for you. You made it sound like it was just for you."

"It wasn't," Jessica said. She turned to go. People were beginning to stare at them.

"I'll deny everything," Kristi said. She was shaking all over, her mouth twitching with rage. "You put me on a stand and I'll say exactly what I did the first time. That she shot him. That she's crazy. That she beat me, and-and-and for weeks she'd been threat—"

Jessica crossed the room, went out into the gravel parking lot, took her phone from her pocket and stopped the recording app. The scrolling numbers froze, sealing the end of her interview with Kristi Zea. She emailed the file to herself and unlocked her car. As she slipped into the driver's seat, an email from Diggy landed in her inbox.

It's aliiiiiive! the subject header read. *Interesting bits recovered from Lawlor laptop.*

BLAIR

Ada arrived in a Mercedes S-Class, matte black with gold rims. The teenagers who had scammed me for the slushie were across the street, pacing and chatting and planning their next ingenious caper, and they stopped at the sight of the car, staring. I was surprised to see Fred and Mike slip from the back seat of the long, wide vehicle. More still when Sneak climbed out of the front passenger seat.

"I found this dummy trying to hitch a ride on Virgil." Ada jerked her thumb backward toward Sneak as the group walked in. "I half expected her to give Fred a hand job when she got in."

"I made it," Sneak muttered to me, coming to my side. "Let the record show I got into a car with Ada Maverick and got out again, alive. You sell lottery tickets?"

"I'm here to talk to you about this," Ada said to me. She put a hand out and Mike passed her a large folded sheet of paper. She swept an arm across my counter, knocking cardboard displays of Twix and Baby Ruths onto the floor to make room for herself. Without asking, Fred took a Snickers from the shelf under the window, peeled open the top, and started eating it. Ada weighed down the piece of paper at the corners. Sneak and I leaned in. It was a United States Geological Survey map of downtown San Jasinte. I took a moment to examine the different levels of lines, sailing blue topographical isolines slashed through with the thin black outlines of properties and streets, red marks that could have been power lines or gas.

"Where'd you get this?" I asked Ada, glancing at the parking lot to check for any incoming customers.

"These guys found it at Officer Marcus Lemon's apartment," Ada said, smoothing out the map.

"I'm sorry." I blinked. "*Where?*"

"I had them break into his apartment," Ada said. "You told me he was an interesting person for us. Turns out he was."

"Oh, Jesus." I looked at Sneak. "Lemon's had his phone stolen and his apartment robbed right after. He'll know something's up."

"Forget about it," Ada said. "They trashed the place and hit three other apartments on the same floor. It will take him a while to notice the maps are gone in the mess. My guys don't do things half-assed. Now why don't you tell me what these are all about?" She gestured to the map. "There are others."

She clicked her fingers and Mike extracted more papers from his jacket pockets. Some were printed screenshots from the internet. I picked up one from a website called the Los Angeles Open Data portal, one from the San Jasinte County website. San Jasinte township was featured again on the Data portal page, crossed with lines, these ones heavier than those on the survey map and joined with little red bubbles. A key gave me the "data layers." Sewer easements. Sewer flow direction. Sewer pipes.

The buzzer above the door sang and I looked up

to see Jessica Sanchez walking into the crowded store with a laptop under her arm.

"Jeez, the whole team's here," Sneak said, unwrapping an Almond Joy.

"I need to talk to you." Jessica strode forward and pointed at me. "It's important." She grabbed a bottle of water from a rack near the counter and opened it, guzzled a quarter of it. Her face and neck were reddened with some emotion I couldn't decipher.

"Take a number and get in line, bitch," Ada snapped at Jessica. "I was here first."

"What is all this?" Jessica looked at the maps. She set her laptop slowly on the counter, thoughts obviously whirling through her, slowing her limbs. "Where . . . Where did these . . ."

"Marcus Lemon had these," Sneak said. "We don't know why."

"I know why," Jessica said. Ada came around the counter to give her space. She threw open her laptop and opened her email account. I heard crackling and noticed Fred opening a Hot Pocket.

"Could everybody please stop eating things?" I yelled. "I have to pay for this stuff, you know."

"Look here." Jessica pointed. There was a document open on the screen, plain text, a list of words. Under a heading that read *Websites last visited* I noticed *Los Angeles Open Data portal*.

"These are bits and pieces recovered from Dayly's burned laptop," Jessica said. "Looks like she and Lemon were both researching the sewer system under San Jasinte, sharing the information."

"Burned?" Sneak said. "You found her laptop burned? Where?"

"Oh, um." Jessica looked at me for help that I could not offer. "I didn't tell you. I—"

"Never mind." Ada slapped the countertop for attention. "What else was on her computer? Anything that says what they were looking at the sewer system for?"

"No, but there are these." Jessica pointed to a list on the page. We all leaned in again. "This list comes from a document on the laptop named 'L's Recon.' L must be Lemon, so I'm guessing this is reconnaissance that Officer Lemon was doing on some houses in San Jasinte." She read directly from the file. "*Number eleven Redduck. Two men. No—Number thirteen Redduck. Family of four. No—Number fifteen Redduck. Woman lives alone. Possible. Check?—Number seventeen Redduck. Hoarder house. Old man. Looks good. Check?*"

Ada snatched the smaller maps away and traced Redduck Avenue on the largest map with her finger. The hairs on my arms were standing on end.

"We were out there yesterday," Sneak said. "At number seventeen. It was a hoarder house, just like it says here. So number eleven must have two men living in it. Number thirteen must be a family of four. Sixteen has a woman that lives alone. We saw Officer Lemon go into the hoarder house, and there was a plumber there, too. These houses follow the sewer line . . ." She shook her head. "But . . . I can't work it out."

"I think I can," Jessica said. "Watch this."

She opened a video file from the email inbox. I saw CDCR in the address of the sender: California Department of Corrections and Rehabilitation. A black-and-white image filled the screen. Two people in what looked like a steel cage, shot from above. A muscular old man was sitting on a plastic fold-out chair. Almost knee-to-knee with him in the small space was a young woman I recognized immediately.

"Dayly," I said.

"John!" Sneak gasped, pointed.

"Who?" Ada asked.

"John Fishwick." Sneak tapped the screen. "That's . . . He's a guy I had a thing with once."

"It's not a small club," Ada said. "What makes *him* so special?"

"Where was this taken?" Sneak asked Jessica.

"It's at San Quentin State Prison. Death row. These are the full-contact visiting cages. This is from two months ago. I went and saw John and asked him about the visit, but I knew I couldn't trust what he said, so I had the guards send me the security footage as well." She hit the button on the video. The figures started moving, talking. We all listened as Fishwick told Dayly about a river near the house where he grew up in Utah. Jessica paused the video and told us about John Fishwick's bank robberies, the massacre in Inglewood, the buried cash found by construction workers and turned over to the government. "I've watched the video. He doesn't tell her anything about anything during the visit, or in his letters to her," Jessica said. "In the cage they discuss the possibility of him being her father, briefly, but he's not willing to submit to a DNA test. They chat about his upbringing, her studies. And then this happens."

We watched as John Fishwick suddenly leaped from his chair. Dayly didn't seem to realize the contact was coming. He grabbed her and slammed her body into the side of the cage with his, forcing his mouth onto hers, his hands on her cheeks. I watched as guards rushed the cage, dragging Fishwick off the distressed girl, who slumped into the corner, crying and rubbing her face.

"Oh my god!" Sneak covered her mouth with her hands.

"He attacks her. He kisses her," Jessica said. "At first I thought that was all he was doing, but now—"

"Now you know." Ada smiled. "He passed her something."

"What do you mean?" I asked.

"Right there." Jessica rolled the video back, played the kiss again. "See how his hand comes up, covers their mouths? That's in case the package slips out."

"What package?"

"He's got something in his mouth," Ada said. "I've seen it in prison a hundred times. It's a kiss pass. You tongue a pill or a secret message or a paper clip or something. You go kiss another inmate, pass it to her in the kiss. You grab her face, just like that, so you can make sure the package gets across, make sure nobody sees the pass. Watch Dayly when she falls to the floor. She makes a motion as if she's wiping her mouth in disgust. She's taking the package out and pocketing it."

We watched the kiss again three times. I searched my memory.

"I saw something at the apartment," I said. "A little shred of tape on Dayly's desk. It was sort of folded weirdly, doubled over on itself, making a tube. Maybe it was the seal. He wrote something on a piece of paper and rolled it up tight, covered it in tape to stop it getting wet in his mouth, maybe. Does that sound right?"

"He would have had to do that." Ada nodded. "If we're talking about a secret this big, he couldn't put it in the letters. Or tell her on the phone. Or tell her in the cage. One of the guards would have heard it."

"So did she know it was coming?" Sneak asked. "The message?"

"She must have," Ada reasoned. "The exchange is pretty swift. Seamless."

"But how did he alert her that he'd be passing her something if the guards are watching his letters and calls?"

"Oh, there are ways," Ada said. "You get the message out through another inmate who tells their visitor, who calls her up and tells her. Or you just show her the package during the visit. Let it poke out between your teeth. She'd have understood what he wanted to do."

"So, wait a minute," Mike broke in. His lip was curled in horror. "This chick willingly kissed a guy who's probably her *own dad*?"

Everyone looked at Mike. I was as shocked that Mike had spoken at all as I was at what he said. I was used to the almost complete silence of Ada's goons.

"*He* kissed *her*," Sneak said. "She didn't really do any kissing. She *was kissed*."

"Will you idiots try to focus on the issue at hand here?" Ada snapped.

"I thought it was weird, him attacking his own daughter like that," Jessica said. "I asked him about it. He was very convincing. He told me the whole buried cash thing is bullshit. It was just a story to lure her in so he could . . . you know. But then he told me that if he was going to do it again after he buried the first lot, he'd have devised a way to make sure that only the person he chose got the money. It sounded specific. Like he'd thought about it before. He said he'd want to choose his beneficiary."

"How?" I asked.

"I don't know," Jessica said.

"All that doesn't matter," Ada said. "What matters is putting all this together and finding out where the cash is. Because that's where Dayly is. Whether she's the *chosen beneficiary* or whatever the fuck, that note that he passed to her tells her where the money is. It's probably coordinates. Longitude and latitude. And that tells *us* where *she's* going to be."

We looked at the maps before us. At 17 Redduck Avenue, where Ada's finger was pressed against the small rectangle indicating the hoarder house into which I'd seen Officer Lemon disappear.

"So what's with the sewers?" I asked. "If the cash is in the hoarder house?"

"Maybe it's under the house," Sneak said.

"Or maybe it's nearby," Ada said. "These houses, eleven through seventeen, they're not far from the sewer line." She traced a line from the hoarder house to a blue line with red bubbles on it that streaked across San Jasinte. "Maybe thirty, forty yards. Explains the presence of the plumber. He'd have experience working underground. Accessing the tunnels. I think they're using the house as a way to get underground unnoticed, get into the sewer lines. That's why they reconned the other houses."

"Why?" I asked.

"To see which one would best hide their activities," Ada said. "Not the house with the family of four. Not the house with two guys living in it. The hoarder house with the old man."

"So where does the sewer line go?" Sneak asked. "Once they get into it?"

"Well, this way heads for downtown," I said, tracing the sewer line on the map. "But look. If you follow it in this direction, it goes right under the police station where Lemon works."

"Who buries a wad of cash under a police station?" Sneak asked.

"No one move," a new voice said. I looked up, and over Ada's shoulder I saw Al Tasik standing in the automatic doorway of the Pump'n'Jump. He took a step forward, made the buzzer sound, and came more fully into my view. He was holding his gun out from his hip. It was pointed at Sneak.

"You," he said to her. "You're coming with me."

JESSICA

Everyone had frozen. Ada's goons had their hands in their jackets, ready to draw, but the beautiful Black woman stood there giving them no instructions. In the fragmented seconds of stillness, Jessica thought about doing what she really came here to do. Now that everything she knew about Dayly and John Fishwick was out on the table, she wanted to complete her next task. A task she dreaded with all of her being. She looked at Blair and thought about just saying it, here, now, in front of everyone.

I'm sorry. I was wrong. I know the truth about you.

Instead she turned to her colleague. "Tasik, what the fuck is this?" she snapped.

"Emily Lawlor," Tasik said, taking Sneak's arm. "I'm arresting you on suspicion of the murder of your daughter, Dayly Lawlor. You have the right to remain silent."

"Tasik." Jessica grabbed his sleeve.

"Back off, Sanchez." He shoved Sneak into the counter and cuffed her. "Or I'll be back after I've processed this one to arrest your friends Maverick and Harbour for parole violations."

"Y-you have no evidence to arrest Sneak," Blair stammered. Ada was gathering up the maps on the counter, folding them, giving them to her men. "You can't do this. She didn't . . . Jessica, do something!"

Jessica followed Tasik to his car. Sneak trudged beside him, staring at the ground, lost.

"What are you working with here, Tasik?" Jessica said. "Talk to me."

"I've got a couple of Crips snitches who say Lawlor and her daughter had a fight on the night she disappeared." Tasik shoved Sneak into his vehicle. "I've got some suspicious texts. Meetings. Harbour and Maverick might be involved. I don't know. I'll have it out with this one in the interrogation room first, then I'll connect the dots."

"Bullshit," Jessica snarled. "I'm working with these women, okay? We're close to a solution here. This arrest is a time-waster. It's painfully obvious."

"You can have her after I've sweated her out a little," Tasik said. "She knows more than she says she does. She's a lifelong scumbag, Sanchez. Maybe you're having trouble telling the difference. You haven't been around as long as I have."

"Oh, fuck you." Jessica shook her head. "You're not going to get this woman into the interrogation room. I promise you that. I'll have you explaining yourself to Whitton at the fucking station fifteen minutes from now while I uncuff Sneak and let her walk."

"Sneak?" Tasik snorted. He slammed the door of the cruiser behind his captive, opened the driver's door. "Fair enough, Sanchez. You want to tussle over this heap of shit? Get in."

Jessica ran to the passenger side and leaped into the vehicle.

BLAIR

Ada grabbed a Coke for herself from the fridges on the wall and made a sweeping motion at me with her hand.

"All right, let's shut this circus down. Fred, get the back door."

"I can't just shut the shop." I winced as she picked up my keys from the counter and threw them a little too hard at me. "I've still got three hours on my shift."

"Forget your fucking shift, Neighbor." She started walking out. "We know where Dayly is. Let's go get her."

In the parking lot I tried to get into the front passenger seat, assuming Ada would want me riding up front with her so we could talk through what we'd just discovered. But Mike muscled in beside me, nodding to the back door.

"You ride with Fred," he said.

I sat coldly in the back seat, trying not to look at Fred, who perched stiffly in the seat like a G.I. Joe doll in the rear of a plastic Jeep. His big, tattooed hands were on his thighs, flat, tense. From what I could see, Mike was sitting exactly the same way in front of me, looking at me now and then in his side mirror.

I started getting a queasy sensation: the notion that, had I really protested about shutting the Pump'n'Jump or getting into the car with Ada and her crew, I would have been made to go against my will. At every stoplight I imagined myself trying to open the door and finding it locked. Feeling Fred's hand on my shoulder, maybe his arm sweeping around my body, dragging me back into the car. Sneak's words rang in my ears.

I got into a car with Ada Maverick and got out again, alive.

I chewed my nails as the city became the long, dark, sweeping freeway. Ada lit a cigarette and I watched its red burning tip rock back and forth on the steering wheel. Lit billboards appeared through the windshield, gathering speed, whizzing by us. The road to San Jasinte was becoming so familiar now it was as if I was heading home. Ada turned on the radio as we breezed past signs for Joshua Tree National Park. A talk show was playing.

" . . . *apparently refer to them as 'swarm parties,' George.*"

"*Swarm parties?*"

"*Yes. Similar to flash mobs, which rose in popularity in the mid-2000s, swarm parties involve a large group of strangers suddenly assembling at a designated place to engage in a celebration.*"

"*Right, so what we're seeing here, Erica, is a swarm party in full effect right now at a residence in Woodland Hills. The news desk is saying that upward of a thousand people have descended on Esperance Drive, where a house seems to be at the center of one of these so-called swarm parties. Residents are reporting loud music, motorbikes both in the house itself and in the street, and some kind of . . . drag rally happening out front. I'm told most of the house's windows have been smashed and there are some belongings out on the lawn. Part of the garage has been burned down. No word of any arrests yet. This doesn't sound like any party I've ever been to, Erica, I can tell you that much."*

"Well, it's not the party that matters, George, it's the attendance. The aim is to get as many people to come along as possible so that the figures can be shared on social media. The damage, the mayhem, is a kind of scorecard. You don't organize one of these things at your own house, that's for sure."

Long patches of black mountains looming over bare earth. I watched the city become farmland, the temperature in the car seeming to dip the farther we drove from the city. I thought about Ada's smile in the Pump'n'Jump. The rare sight of it, and the weird, satisfied quality it had.

Another voice sounded in my head. It was Jessica Sanchez this time.

She can smell money. That's why she's here.

"We need to talk," I said eventually.

"About what?" Ada said.

"About our plan," I told her. Fred was looking at me, his face unreadable in the dark. "Our priority is finding Dayly. Making sure she's okay."

"Of course it is."

"We don't know what else we're walking into here," I said. "If the plumber, Ramirez, and Lemon and Dayly have set up what we think they've set up, then it's possible she won't even be there. When I saw her, she was running. She was scared. Something had gone wrong, and—"

"I've got a plan, Neighbor," Ada said. "You don't need to worry about it."

I wrung my fingers. One of Fred's hands had moved from his lap to the pocket of his jacket. I thought about my phone in my backpack, which was at my feet.

"My plan is to find Dayly," I said. "And if there's anything else going on . . . I mean. I don't want anyone to get hurt. Or for us to, you know, to get involved in something that's, uh . . ."

My words drained away. Fred was watching me from across the bench seat. Ada was watching me in the rearview mirror. Mike was watching me in his side mirror. A vision flashed through my mind, of a cat in a car full of Dobermans. I eased breath through my teeth and tried to focus on the road ahead.

JESSICA

Jessica sat quietly in the front passenger seat of the police cruiser, listening to Tasik's breathing beside her, refusing to look his way, to let him sense that she was scared. She was indeed scared. The tension in the car reminded her of the night in Lonscote Place, when she'd lost grip of every aspect of her police training, every expectation she had been given since joining the force. Your partner will back you. Your cries for assistance will be answered. You'll always have some notion of what the appropriate action is—rarely will something be so bizarre, so left-field, that you won't have a trained response in your back pocket. But that night she'd dealt with a flesh-eating being and her partner had abandoned her. Her world had been turned upside down, the rules shattered, her trust dissolved. Now she was back there. She should have been on the side of the man next to her, but she found herself constantly checking on Sneak in her side mirror. The plump, downtrodden prostitute and drug addict looked at home in the back of the cruiser. But there was a calm on her face that defied her situation. It was almost as though she expected what happened next.

On Wilshire, Tasik breezed through the intersection, past a Jamba Juice full of people, instead of turning left toward the West LA police station. Sneak didn't react. Jessica felt a cold bolt of energy hit her veins. Tasik glanced at her, and she knew.

"It was you, wasn't it?" Sneak said, giving voice to Jessica's thoughts.

Tasik glanced at her in the rearview mirror. They were heading north toward the mountains. Signs for Glendale. He switched on the radio.

" . . . *having difficulty containing the situation due to strained police resources and the sheer number of people descending on Esperance Drive. Police say at least two cars are on fire in the street, and that the owner of the residence in question is a male LAPD officer who is not, at this time, present on the scene. Police choppers have . . .*"

Tasik switched off the radio.

"Okay," he said. "I'll bite. What do you think you know?"

"I know you killed her," Sneak said. Jessica could see Sneak wiggling subtly against the back seat. She could tell the other woman was working her handcuff chain under her buttocks, stretching her shoulder joints to the limits to let the bindings slide down the backs of her thighs to her knees. She'd seen it a thousand times, and Tasik would have noticed it, too.

"I did, did I?" Tasik said.

"You got that bad cop stink about you," Sneak said. "I've known a lot of cops in my time. Some of them are good people. Some are wimps with badges who got picked on in high school and want revenge. And every now and then there's a real predator, and I can see that in you."

"Give yourself some credit," Tasik said. "You've got a bit of the old hunter blood in you, too. You're a scavenger. A liar and a cheater and a thief. But, push comes to shove, you've got claws and teeth. I can see that in *you*. And I saw it in your daughter."

Jessica put her hand on her gun, but she didn't draw it. She couldn't believe what she was hearing. Needed to wait. To know for sure. To see some physical sign of the danger. Tasik was too comfortable. He eased back in his seat, rolled his window down, and put an elbow out. Jessica could feel the rise of the mountain roads under them. He knew these roads, took the corners lazily, the headlights now and then picking out luminescent eyes in the shrubby undergrowth, shining on sheer cliff faces. He was fully relaxed now. Mr. Coyote going home to his den on the rocky ridge, where the poison creosote guarded his secret, safe place.

"It was just like I told Sanchez." Tasik gestured to her. "I picked Dayly up by chance in a car full of idiot Crips. She hasn't been living the life like you, Emily. I could see that. She was still a little fresh. High on cheap crack and scared out of her mind. She didn't know the bag with the guns was there. I pulled her away from the crowd and asked her what the hell she thought she was doing. I was really giving it to her. Maybe I trumped it up a bit, her situation. I told her she was facing jail time, that was a certainty. I told her the type of guns they had in the trunk had been classified as weapons of terrorism, so she was facing thirty years on the inside, minimum. She was crying her eyes out. Panicked. Like a shaky little puppy."

Sneak now held the wire mesh screen between them, the cuffs stretched between her wrists.

"I was hoping for a blow job at best," Tasik laughed. "And then suddenly Dayly started pouring out all this stuff about hidden money and a killer on death row and her junkie mother. I couldn't follow it at first. It was so crazy. I was shocked, you know? She had to calm down some before she could give it to me straight. She said she knew where millions of dollars was buried. If I helped her out on the gun charges, she would let me in on this thing she had going to dig up the hidden money. I didn't believe it, but I cut her loose anyway, just to see. Just in case she was onto something, you know? It was worth the gamble. If I came back and it was all just some story, I was going to get my blow job, one way or another."

"Was she right?" Sneak asked. "Was the money there?"

"I sure hope so." Tasik smiled. "There's no way she can check this thing out. You know why? Because this Fishwick guy, he says he buried the cash in the late eighties. Back then the place was a big open field with a fence on it and nothing else. Now it's got— wait for this, this is just classic—a fucking *police station* on it. Can you believe that? The only way she can find out if he's lying or not is to dig to the spot, *under* the station."

"And she wanted your help?" Jessica piped up.

"Nope," Tasik said. "Luckily for me, Dayly already had everything set up. She'd sourced a young cop from inside the station to make sure nobody who worked there got wind that someone was tunneling under the building. Then the two of them got together and recruited this plumber with a rap sheet for digging holes under jewelry stores and casinos, a guy who knows how to make a tunnel and get under a place on the quiet. I'm hearing this and I'm thinking, what the fuck? This girl looks like she's barely old enough to hold a job, and when I go check out the cop he's the same. A baby. But that's it, you see? That's what I was trying to tell you, Sanchez. These people are born like this. They have criminal minds.

Scavenger instincts. They're built in." He tapped his temple.

"So the two other guys don't know about you?" Sneak asked.

"No," Tasik said. "It was her fuck-up. My cut was supposed to come out of her end. Dayly tells me that all I have to do is wait for pay day, when the two boys break through to the spot where the cash is supposed to be. Could be tonight, if everything's still on track."

"So what went wrong?" Sneak asked. "It sounds to me as though everything was running like clockwork."

"Your greedy-ass daughter went wrong," Tasik said. "That's what."

BLAIR

Everything was blue. The white moon cast the side of Ramirez's truck a pale, icy blue. The dark blue mountains rising beyond us, reaching into a blue-black sky. Ada switched off the engine, parking right outside 17 Redduck Avenue, behind the truck, only feet from the driveway. She was not a woman who parked discreetly, who crept through back gardens, who scaled fences and ducked under windows. Fred screwed a silencer onto the barrel of his gun. I listened to the metal-on-metal grinding sound of the device in the silence.

Ada and Mike got out. I reached toward my backpack.

"Leave it," Fred said, shuffling toward me across the seat. I popped the door and got out. The air was cold and thin. I thought about running, until Fred's hand landed on my shoulder. The hand stayed there all the way up the driveway to the front door. Ada and Mike had their own guns out, held close to their chests, pointed upward. I stood off to the side with Fred while Ada slowly turned the knob. The door came unstuck from its jamb with a crack sound that was almost wet, sticky. Ada and Mike disappeared inside and Fred shoved me forward.

"Look"—I half turned to him—"I don't want to be a part of this."

"The time to make that decision came and went a while ago," he said.

"Just let me walk away."

"Shut up."

A narrow passageway. In the darkness, things were brushing against my arms—the gentle slicing of magazine and newspaper pages from volumes stacked as high as the ceiling. There was a light on in one of the back rooms, illuminating a wild forest of items crowding in from every corner. An undergrowth of paint buckets, bicycle parts, rubber tubing, stuffed toys. A waist-high maze of plastic tubs filled with Tupperware, silverware, picture frames, clothes, cans of food. Against the walls, rolled-up rugs and strips of carpet leading to a canopy of broom and mop heads, ladders, kites and clocks of every conceivable shape and size haphazardly hanging, some working, some not. I smelled rotten meat and curdled milk as I passed the kitchen, which was covered in knee-deep debris. I spied three fridges, a table turned on its side. A fly or moth batted weakly against my cheek as I walked into a second hallway, the insect drunk on the endless spoils around it or exhausted from trying to find a way out through the blocked windows.

The lit room was crowded with a sea of books, clothes, shoes numbering in their hundreds, twisted and dry models that made me think of collections I had seen in photographs of concentration camps. In a filthy bed in one corner lay an ancient man, buried under blankets so that he was almost invisible. I pushed past Ada and Mike and rushed to him.

"Oh god." I reeled at the smell, brushed damp hair from the man's forehead. "Sir, are you okay? Oh, Jesus. Jesus."

I peeled the duct tape from his mouth. His eyes were huge and wet.

"Help me," he rasped. There were no teeth in his mouth. "Help. He-elp."

"It's okay. We're here now. I'm going to lift you—"

"Put the tape back on," Ada commanded. She pulled my arm back and made me face her. "Leave him."

"I can't leave him like this," I pleaded. "He's severely dehydrated. Look at the whites of his eyes. Look at the color of his skin. At any moment he could go into cardiac arrest."

"I said put the tape back on." Ada's eyes were burning in the light of the lamp on the floor beside the man's bed: two distant gold flames. "He'll still be here when we get back. He makes a fuss now and he'll blow our cover."

"There are . . . t-two m-men," the old man wheezed. The blankets sank and rose as he drew ragged breaths. "And a wo-o-oman. They c-came and . . . I've been h-here, trap-ped, and . . . I don't know h-how many days . . ."

"The woman," I said. "Young blonde? Curly hair?"

The man nodded.

"Where is she? Is she alive?"

"She stop-ped c-coming," the man said.

Fred appeared in the doorway, murmured to Ada. "Tunnel's in the kitchen. No sign of anyone."

I turned and saw Mike raising his gun toward the old man's face. I slapped it away without thinking, an electric pulse of terror hitting my heart like a punch. The big man grabbed a hank of my hair and I felt the sharp edge of the square gun barrel in my throat.

"That was a stupid thing to do," Ada said, stepping close to me. Her face was expressionless, like a wax mask, only the eyes alert and following mine closely, curiously. "Swiping at a man's gun like that."

"He was going to—"

"Yeah." Ada nodded. "He was going to waste the old guy. Are you catching on now, Blair? We're not here for Dayly. We're not here to rescue filthy old coots from their reeking beds. We're. Here. For. The. *Money*."

Mike's gun was crushing my windpipe. It was impossible to swallow. I looked at Ada and eased out pained words. "Jessica warned me about this," I said.

"And you should have listened." Ada tapped my nose with the end of her pistol. "You're too trusting. Smart, yeah. Capable, of course. But way too trusting. And for god's sake, you eat up a bleeding heart story like no one I've ever known."

"Just leave me with the old man," I said. "Do what you've got to do. I'll stay here. I won't make a sound."

"You're as bad as Dayly, trying to save your dying, dirty animals." Ada knocked a naked Barbie doll off a cluttered shelf. It cascaded down a mountain of trash, dislodging magazines and paper cups, wooden toys. "This man is a pig."

"Please let me go."

"I don't know if I'll need you down there or not," Ada said, nodding her head the way we had come, toward the kitchen. "So for now you're coming with me. But as a favor to you, because you're a good person, I'll leave the old man alive. How about that? See. I can be good, too. Mike?"

Mike moved the gun away from my throat and pushed me aside. He took a roll of duct tape sitting on the dusty carpet by the bed and grabbed a handful of the old man's lank, greasy white hair, lifted, rolled the tape around his head twice as if he were binding up a leaking pipe. I watched Mike drop the man's head back on the pillow and brush his hands off.

Ada pushed me toward the kitchen. Shielded from view by a pile of debris, a hole in the linoleum floor gaped four feet wide, leading to blackness as pure and impenetrable as ink. Fred climbed backward into the hole ahead of me, and I heard his feet hit the rungs of a ladder.

"Get down there," Ada said, prodding me in the back with her gun.

JESSICA

"I saw it coming from pretty far off," Tasik said. They were rolling slowly now along the cresting road, looking for something. "If there's one thing a practiced liar like you would know, it's that you find a story and you stick to it. Dayly's story started wavering. Suddenly she couldn't tell me how much money was supposed to be under the police station. Was it ten million or fifteen? Then, what do you know? She's suggesting it might only be two. She wouldn't answer her phone. Wouldn't let me speak to the old man, Fishwick. I wanted to talk to Lemon and Ramirez, become a full partner in this thing, but she's telling me if they find out about me they'll flip. I've only got her word on everything that's happening, and I'm starting to discover that she's lying. She would tell me she was alone, when there I am sitting outside her apartment, looking at her inside with Lemon, the cop. She became unreliable, and that's when I knew she was going to double-cross us."

"How?" Sneak asked.

"The money." Tasik nodded. "She was going to use Lemon and Ramirez, the plumber, to get the cash out of the hole. She was going to have me sitting nearby like an idiot waiting for my cut, keeping her safe from jail, and them expecting her to share the cash when she goes and swipes it out from underneath them. She was going to run off with all of it by herself. I could feel it. It's what I would do."

Tasik seemed to find what he was looking for, pulled the car off the road onto an unmarked fire trail. Jessica's grip tightened on her gun. She knew she had to take control. Disarm Tasik, cuff him. But her yearning to hear the rest of the story, to know what happened to Dayly, had her frozen in her seat. She knew that if she moved, if she broke Tasik from his spell, she might never get a full confession out of him. He liked the sound of his own voice. Wanted them to know how clever he'd been. But all of that could dry up in a second. A part of her wanted to believe this was his surrender. That he wasn't leading them out here, into the dark of the mountain ranges, to kill them both. She couldn't accept that another cop would do that. Didn't want to accept it. Because that would be the final nail—that would show her once and for all that not only was she not a part of this family, but she didn't know the members of it. Not at all.

The headlights illuminated a horizontal white boom gate. Tasik nudged it open gently with the bumper of the car.

"Greedy little girl," he said, almost to himself.

Jessica watched the wide dirt road ahead of them, dust swirling in the lights, desert bugs flickering and flapping gold in the beams. She wondered if Dayly had been alive when she was driven out here. If she'd sat in the dark as her mother was sitting now, knowing this was the last road she would ever travel down, her final destination.

"I confronted her in her apartment," Tasik said.

"I'd had enough. She was telling me they'd hit a snag. There was a rock the size of a Volkswagen Beetle in the tunnel and they'd have to blast through it. She'd tell me when they were through, but she didn't know how long the delay was going to be. I called bullshit on that. She was buying time to make her escape, I knew. I figured I knew where the guys were, I could tap their phones and find out when they hit pay dirt. I didn't need Dayly anymore. But she fought me at her apartment, got my gun and got away. I know from pursuing girls like her my whole career that the best thing you can do is let them think they're in the safe zone. Let them calm down. So I grabbed her laptop and phone from the apartment and followed her on the quiet. She hitched a ride to Koreatown, hit a gas station for some cash and a car and was headed out west, probably to see Lemon and Ramirez. That's when I took her down. I chased her up into the mountains here and ran her car off the road."

Jessica watched Tasik's eyes as he switched off the engine. A coyote yowled somewhere near in the dark, a high, anxious sound.

"You killed her," Jessica said. She could feel how wide her own eyes were in the dark. Disbelieving, but also tensed, ready. "You torched the car with the laptop and phone inside. And you brought her here and dumped her." Jessica looked out the window beside him.

Tasik said nothing. His eyes were hard, challenging her in the dark, both his hands on the steering wheel. Jessica thought for a moment of quick-draw cowboys on dusty streets, tumbleweeds blowing by, a comic image thrown up by her brain to try to quell the terror in her heart. She drew her weapon, and her veins flooded warm when Tasik didn't draw his.

"Don't you *fucking* move," she snapped.

She was twisted sideways awkwardly in her seat, the gun close to her chest, her elbows splayed in the small space. A smile was playing on Tasik's lips. Her training and experience over the two decades she had been in the job hadn't prepared her for disarming a man sitting in the same car as her. She'd never been stupid enough to get herself into this kind of fix.

"Keep your hands right where they are," she said. She had two options. Have Tasik reach down and pull the gun from his own hip, or lean over and do it herself. Neither was good. She was trapped and he knew it. Seconds were ticking by in which Jessica knew he would be formulating a plan, so she'd better put her own into action. She took a hand off of her gun and reached forward.

She grabbed the gun, lifted it from the holster on his hip, leaned back. She relaxed. He was waiting for that. For the fraction of a second that her muscles loosened. His fist came up, outside of her range of vision, smashed her jaw in a brutal uppercut that pounded her head into the window.

Darkness. Only seconds' worth. Her hearing sucked back before she could control her body. She was flopped sideways in the seat. Her brain wouldn't issue commands to her limbs. She sagged helplessly as Tasik disarmed her.

"Get out," he said to Sneak.

"You're not going to kill me," Sneak said from the back seat. "You're not going to kill a fellow cop. Four people from the Pump'n'Jump will be able to testify that Sanchez and I got into your car. There'll be CCTV at the gas station."

"I'm not going to deny I arrested you, or that Jessica came with me," Tasik said. "I've been playing this game a long time, Emily. You know that. All I have to tell them is that you slipped your cuffs to the front, as I knew you would do, and you waited until we were in a quiet backstreet in Koreatown so you could fake a seizure in the back of the car. Sanchez and I stopped to assist you, you attacked her. Took her gun and killed Sanchez, then made me put her in the car. You forced me to drive up here into the mountains, where you confessed to killing Dayly. You told me you'd dump me and Sanchez in the same spot you did her."

Jessica tried to keep her breathing even, stopped trying to move. She knew she had to regain complete control before she launched her attack on Tasik. She couldn't groan, couldn't struggle. While he thought she was unconscious, he might delay finishing her.

"She's down there?" Jessica heard Sneak ask. "You threw her down there?"

There was silence. Jessica didn't need to hear an answer.

"I'll tell them I was lucky enough to overpower you," Tasik said. "But you put up a good effort."

Jessica felt blood running from her mouth, down her limp arm, onto the seat. She opened her eyes a crack. She wondered if Tasik kept a backup weapon in the car's glove box, only a couple of feet away from her. Most cops she knew did.

"You know that Ada and Blair are onto the money," Sneak said. Her voice was lower, thinner than it had been. She was losing hope. "You've got to, right? You know we've been asking questions. You saw us there at the gas station with the maps. You know Ada and Blair will be heading there right now, to San Jasinte. They might get there and get the money before you, while you're wasting time here with us. Let me go. Leave me here so I can find my child. Go get the money and run."

"I've got time," Tasik said. "I've been monitoring

Ramirez's texts. He thinks he's got another three hours until he breaks through. Best case scenario for me is the two parties run into each other and there's a shoot-out, and I walk in to find the cash sitting by a neat pile of bodies, waiting for me. Lemon and Ramirez won't be expecting Maverick and her goons and Harbour. But no one at all will be expecting me."

"What if Ramirez's wrong?" Sneak said. "What if they break through early and you turn up and no one's there?"

"Fine. I know where everyone will be tomorrow. Lemon and Ramirez will be loading a plane they've booked to get to Mexico at an airfield near there. Maverick will be at her club. She's not leaving. Not with her business interests in the area. And Harbour will be at her apartment. She's got a kid. She's not going anywhere. I've been in her apartment before, and I know she can fight, so this time I won't be messing around."

"You," Sneak said. "It was you who broke in."

"I was trying to scare her off," Tasik said. "Scare both of you. It didn't work. If you could put up less of a fight tonight than she did, I'd be really grateful. But this has to look authentic, so we'll need to play around for a little while, at least."

He pushed open his door, walked behind the car and opened the door beside her. Jessica heard Sneak yelp as the man grabbed her.

"Enough talking," Tasik said. "Let's start."

BLAIR

I turned awkwardly and started moving down the ladder, and spied in the mess of items near the edge of the hole a long barbecue fork with a wooden handle. I pretended to trip, grabbed at the mess, swept the fork and some other items into the hole with me.

"Watch it, Neighbor."

"Sorry," I said. In the darkness at the bottom of the ladder, Fred had a flashlight pressed into his palm, giving off a soft glow. I pretended to examine my ankle for scratches caused by the near fall and slipped the handle of the barbecue fork into my shoe, pulled my jeans down over the top of it. Mike and Ada climbed down the ladder and stood quietly in the dark. Fetid air, heavy with a metallic taste, the unmistakable reek of human waste and stagnant water. I could hear the breaths of the people around me. They were shallow, fast, measured: the breathing of people who had done this before, people who had sat in cars outside banks in balaclavas, waiting for the doors to open. People who had waited in the bushes near the guarded entries to stash houses. Thieves. Hunters. Some silent consensus was reached, and I was grabbed and guided along a gloomy dirt tunnel braced with untreated wood. Ada was beside me, Fred ahead and Mike behind us. The dirt tunnel ended in a smashed concrete curve of wall. I climbed through, was shoved to the right on a path. I could see nothing beyond the edge of the path, but some primal awareness told me we were walking in a narrow tube with one horizontal surface on the right meant for traversing the passage on foot. My arm brushed pipes and ridges in the wall in the dark, and I reached up experimentally at one point and touched the concrete ceiling, felt rubber tubing, spokes, more pipes.

"Keep moving," Ada whispered, poking me in the ribs with her gun.

We moved at a painful pace in the dark. Now and then Fred slid his palm slightly off the flashlight, illuminated the next few empty yards of sewer. I couldn't bear the silence.

"No one has been who they say they are in this," I said quietly.

"What?" Ada said.

"You," I said. "I thought you were genuinely helping us find a missing girl. I thought you were paying your debt to me."

"Well, you're an idiot. That's not my fault."

"And Dayly," I said. "You saw that man up there. The old man. He's been suffering. How long has he been there? Weeks? Dayly was a part of that. I thought she was different. But Dayly and Lemon and Ramirez did that to him so they could get down here."

"So Dayly's a heartless piece of trash, like her mother," Ada said. "You're a whole lot more surprised than you should be, Blair, if you want my opinion. I don't know how you've maintained your faith in people all this time. You've been locked up longer than I ever was. You should have learned in the can that deep down inside, everybody's just out to get their cut."

Fred stopped suddenly ahead of us. Ada dragged me against the wall. There was a pause, and then a voice rippled down the tunnel toward us from up ahead.

"Dayly?" the voice called. I recognized it as belonging to Officer Lemon.

Fred dropped to one knee, let the flashlight fall by his side, and started firing in the direction of the voice.

JESSICA

The pale moon was hanging low. Jessica glimpsed it through the windshield as she sat up, threw open the glove box, and searched for Tasik's personal weapon. Nothing. The car's service manual. Her bloody hands danced over the interior of the car, looking for her own weapon. She glimpsed Tasik outside the car, struggling with Sneak, his big fist raining down on her. One gun in his holster. The other nowhere to be found. Jessica didn't risk opening her door. She slid across the car and onto the dirt road, but the sudden rush of blood to her head after the blow to the face made her stagger, roll her ankle on a rock. Tasik heard her and turned.

He left Sneak and launched himself at her, slammed her into the side of the car. Jessica hit the ground. His boots on either side of her, blows hammering downward. She turned under him, struck upward and kicked out, got his knee and sent him sideways. Sneak was there, bashing him in the head with her fists, clubbing downward while he pot-shotted her in the ribs.

Jessica pulled herself into a half crouch beside the car, prepared to straighten, to fight again. The gun had fallen from Tasik's jeans but it was lost in the dark, and a shot would be impossible anyway. Sneak and Tasik had tangled together, Sneak an obvious prison fighter, gouging the man's face, clawing with her nails. Jessica backed into the car again, started it up, and slammed it into reverse. Then she waited, her hands gripping the wheel, until the inevitable happened. Tasik overpowered Sneak. Got her good in the temple with a long, straight blow. Sneak rolled away on her side, gripping desperately at the dirt while her world spun. Jessica slammed her foot down on the accelerator.

A wet crunch. That's how she would think about it later. The kind of sound a bag of bones and water would make if someone dropped it from on high. The car ground to a halt in a cloud of dust only a couple of yards from where Tasik had stood. The man himself had been shunted backward, thrown into the dirt maybe twenty feet away. She hadn't hit him hard. But what she'd done had been effective. Jessica got out, went to Sneak and helped her to her feet. Sneak wandered forward in a daze, stepping toward Tasik, hardly looking at Jessica. The officer went to the man on the ground.

"Tasik"—Jessica's teeth were locked, her voice a low growl—"you're under arrest."

Jessica bent over the groaning, coughing, writhing mess that was Detective Al Tasik on the dirt, the two of them illuminated by the car's headlights. Jessica turned the cop on his side to let him recover. His ribs were surely broken, and he was drifting in and out of consciousness, but he would survive. Jessica was so relieved as she clipped the cuffs onto Tasik that she didn't even hear the car door slam shut behind her. It was the beep of the horn that startled her, brought her back to reality. Sneak was sitting in the driver's seat of Tasik's car. She assumed Sneak must be about to bring the car closer to assist Jessica in hauling the man into the back seat. But Jessica stood and watched, dumbfounded, as Sneak reversed the car back a good ten yards and beeped again.

Jessica looked blindly into the headlights.

"Sneak?" she called.

Sneak revved the engine. Beeped again.

"Sneak." Jessica put a hand out, begging, her fingers spread. "Don't do it. Don't! Don't! Don't!"

The cruiser burst to life. Jessica threw herself out of the way, and heard that hard, wet sound again as the car crunched over Tasik's body. Jessica held her head and watched helplessly as Sneak reversed over the man and then ran forward over him again. On the second reverse, Jessica uncurled her rigid body and dragged herself to her feet. Trying not to look at the mess on the ground before the car, she staggered in shock toward the driver's-side door.

Sneak rolled the window down slowly, watching Jessica from the corner of her eye. Her hand appeared with Jessica's phone in it. She dropped the phone out of the side of the vehicle and rolled the window up again.

"Sneak," Jessica warned. "Don't you dare. Don't you leave me h—"

Jessica watched the car jerk into a hard three-quarter turn, the red brake lights burning dusty clouds as Sneak sped away.

She looked at Tasik. The man's body lay in a twisted heap on the road nearby. Jessica picked up her phone and looked at the screen. The reception bar was empty.

"Fuck my life," she said.

BLAIR

Ada shoved past me, her gun blasting, bullets from her and Fred hitting the walls of the tunnel ahead, making white sparks. I turned to run and Mike grabbed my arm. I made a swipe for the barbecue fork riding against my ankle but lost my balance and was dragged along with the big man toward the firefight.

"Come on, bitch! Let's go."

A sound like a harsh whisper against my ear. I realized with horrifying clarity that a bullet had just whizzed mere inches past my head. Lemon was firing back. The tunnel kinked slightly, a gentle corner, the only thing that had stopped Lemon from seeing our weak little light before he heard us. I listened to the firing ahead as it slowed to a stop.

We waited, grouped together. My ears were ringing. Fred let his hand slide from the flashlight for just a second, illuminating the tunnel ahead. There was no one there. Lemon had been alone, heading back toward the ladder we had come down. I caught a glimpse of him flopped on his side on the ground a few yards away. I ran to him and crouched down, put my hands on his chest. Though I couldn't see well enough, I felt blood running so fast and wet and hot it had to be fatal. My hands were soaked with it immediately, my shoes squelching in it on the muddy floor. Lemon coughed blood. I remembered the kind young man who had helped me after my faked car accident and forgot the cruelty the same man had apparently displayed against the old fellow in the hoarder house.

"It's all right," I lied to the dying man. "It's all right."

"Dayly?" Lemon gasped. He scanned the faces above me. "Is she—"

"She's not with us," I said. "We thought she was with you." I knew he was dying fast. The breaths were becoming shallower. "Do you know where she is? Is she safe?"

He died under my hands. It was a sound I recognized, even in the blackness.

A humming, uneven and distant, pushed gently through the chaos in my mind.

"What is that?" I asked. No one answered. I was pulled away from Lemon. We walked. In time the humming became a grinding sound. A jackhammer. In a hundred yards, a glow began to form. I realized it was coming from another smashed hole in the side of the sewer tunnel. Fred stopped by the edge of the hole and pocketed his flashlight, gently leaned forward to see what was ahead.

The grinding sound was deafening now. He held up a finger in the dim light. *One guy.*

He waved us forward. *We go now.*

Mike gripped my arm. I followed Ada and Fred into the second dirt tunnel. Ahead of us, the wide body of Ramirez stood with his legs braced, grinding downward at the end of the tunnel into a piece of rock the size of a basketball. He was wearing ear muffs, trying to split the rock with the machine. As we approached, Ramirez set down the jackhammer and bent to pick up the broken stone. The sound of the device was still echoing around us as Fred and Ada raised their weapons.

"Watch out!" I screamed. Ramirez turned at the last second, a bullet slamming into the dirt wall ahead of him, tagging the hem of his jeans harmlessly. In a single movement he twisted, grabbed a gun from his waistband, and fired at us. There was no cover. Mike and I fell together against the dirt wall. He shoved against me, fired over my head. I rolled away and grabbed the barbecue fork from my ankle, rolled back and stabbed Mike's chest as hard as I could.

I hit pay dirt. The fork popped through the fabric, sank hard into the flesh of his right pectoral, only an inch or so deep. I thought it was enough, the shock of it, the sudden pain that made him drop his gun. I turned and scrambled to my feet, tripped, gained traction and ran the way we had come.

I fell against the side of the tunnel when bullets started shunting into the concrete wall of the sewer pipe ahead of me. They weren't firing at Ramirez anymore. They were firing at me.

I froze, the barbecue fork still in my hand, and turned to look at them.

Ramirez was on the ground, clutching his belly. Fred dragged the man to the side of the tunnel and dumped him in a heap. Ada beckoned me, the black eye of her gun locked on my face. Panting with exhaustion and terror, I walked back toward my enemies. I couldn't meet Mike's eyes. He rubbed the double holes under the wet fabric of his shirt as though he was soothing a bruise.

Ada took a shovel from a collection on the ground and threw it at my feet.

"Dig," she said.

JESSICA

Her knees hurt. Policing was a killer for bad knees, hips, shoulders—all those pieces of equipment that needed to be strapped on. Heavy belts and flak jackets. Jessica thought she must have scraped her knee on a rock on the road when she rolled away as the car rocketed toward Tasik. There was blood on her shins, her elbows, her hands, dirt on her clothes. Jessica knew that if she stopped a car coming up the mountain before she got within range of a cell tower, she would have some explaining to do.

She rounded a bend and the canyon opened up before her. Los Angeles dazzled far below, a scattering of gold lights.

She was higher up the mountain than she realized. Below her, the road snaked between the canyons, empty. She sighed and marched on.

BLAIR

The earth was hard. Pale, crumbling rock, the occasional pocket of blessed sand that sopped to the ground at our feet. I worked shoulder to shoulder with Fred, Mike jamming his shovel in low to clear the dirt from around our feet while preserving the injury I had given him. Fred and I cleared the split basketball-sized rock together, our hands touching as we shifted it upward, the absurd intimacy of foes forced together.

Now and then I turned to look at Ada, who had the gun trained on Ramirez. The man lay panting and clutching his stomach, drenched in sweat, his body slumped awkwardly against the curved side of the tunnel.

"Just through here," Ada was saying to him, pointing at the wall where Fred and I were digging. "A couple of feet at most. That's what you're saying? You better not be fucking with me, Ramirez."

"It can't be far," the man heaved. His eyes wandered to me. It was clear he recognized me from the driveway outside the house. I wanted to tell him it wasn't me who had brought this on him. That I hadn't been responsible for whatever happened to Dayly, that I was as much a slave to the people around us as he was. But there didn't seem to be time.

"You can let him go," I told Ada. She looked at me. "He'll survive if he gets medical attention soon."

Ada raised her gun and shot Ramirez in the head without taking her eyes off me. I turned to the wall before me, dug madly, relishing in the simple act of throwing, lifting, twisting, dumping the soil, trying to escape this moment. An hour passed. Maybe more. The final moments of my life. There was no phone to distract myself with this time. No Alejandro. I was going to die down here in the earth, directly below a police station, exactly how deep I didn't know. Sasha was going to have to explain all of this to Jamie. She could barely account for what I had done to Adrian Orlov a decade earlier. I had no idea how she would deal with this. A strange thought occurred to me in the blackness, that my best hopes of Jamie ever knowing that I hadn't meant to get myself involved in the horror in which my body would be found was Jessica Sanchez. Jessica, the woman who had arrested me all those years ago—she knew that all I'd wanted was to help my friend, to find and save Dayly. Jamie would never know that I'd tried to save Lemon, to save Ramirez, and that I'd wanted to help the man in the house at the beginning of the tunnel, who would surely die as Ada, Mike, and Fred made their retreat. I could only hope Jessica would tell my son I was a good person. I almost laughed. Hours earlier I had been standing on Mulholland Drive with Alejandro, flirting with the idea of leaving my life behind again, and now all I wanted in the world was to be able to go back to it again.

My shovel hit what I thought was a rock, but Fred snapped to, grabbed my shovel off me and pushed me away. He hit the spot I'd hit again, made sand fall, and I heard what he had heard: a hollowness.

I stood back with Mike and Ada while Fred dug. The dirt around the suitcases was loose, disturbed decades earlier by John Fishwick's hand. Mike dragged down an enormous suitcase wrapped in a plasticky film not unlike what Sasha covered Jamie's school books in. The first case was covered in a once-white film that was now filthy, patterned with toucans that were aged and pale. The second case was wrapped in plastic wrap covered in pictures of yellow tigers. The third suitcase, from the bottom of the stack, was indiscernible.

There were no words exchanged. Mike stepped forward, took a knife from his belt and flicked it open. I stood watching as he slashed open the wrapping around the toucan case and unlocked it, shoving it open.

Stacks of hundreds. Messy, faded, used bills bound with elastic bands and stacked neatly. The suitcase was jammed so full of cash that stacks got caught in the lid when it opened and flopped out onto the floor.

We all stood and stared at the money.

"What do you think?" Ada asked.

Mike cocked his head. He counted the stacks on the top briefly, reached out and pressed down on the piles, tried to gauge the way they sprang back against his hand.

"Seven at least," he said. "Three cases. Twenty-one million all up. Probably more."

I looked at Ada. She was smiling at me. The smile never wavered as she lifted her gun and shot me in the leg.

A white-hot pain, too sudden and shocking to give voice to. I hit the floor, grabbed my limb, felt the blood bubble up for the first time, seeping into my jeans. Nausea came and went. I braced for darkness, but it didn't come. I looked up and realized Ada was turned away from me. She was looking at the sewer end of the tunnel, at Sneak, who was bloody and filthy and holding a police-issue Glock pointed right at Ada's face.

Ada was stunned at first, but she recovered quickly, a snake rearing and then turning liquid, coiling on itself, reconfiguring for another strike.

"I wasn't going to kill her," Ada said.

Sneak cocked the weapon.

"I wasn't," Ada laughed. "Come on. Why would I have shot her in the leg if I was going to kill her?"

"Get out," Sneak said. "All of you. Get out."

Mike and Fred and Ada grabbed the handle of a case each, lifted them, and walked out. As Ada passed me, I realized the wrapping on the last case was covered in crows, their wings spread and beaks open.

When the crew had been gone a few seconds, and the sound of their footfalls had faded from the tunnel, Sneak bent down to help me up. She was covered in blood. I thought of the man in my apartment in the night, the feel of his hands on me. Those same big, calloused hands having already grabbed me in the West LA police station and shoved me into a wall. The work of those hands on my friend, now. It seemed stupid to have not made the connection before.

"Tasik," I said. It was all I could manage.

"Yeah." Sneak nodded.

"Did Jessica get away?" I asked.

"Yeah," Sneak said again. "But Dayly didn't."

She helped me hobble to the sewer tunnel.

"I'm sorry," I told her. I squeezed my friend's shoulder as we made our way into the blackness before us.

She didn't answer me. We walked steadily but slowly along.

Ada and her guys must have had trouble getting the cases up the ladder, because when Sneak and I reached the street they were only just loading them into the Mercedes. Under the streetlight I saw Fred dump two of the cases—the toucan and crow cases—into the trunk, filling the space entirely. Mike hefted the tiger case onto the back seat and both men got in beside it. Ada looked back at us as she opened the driver's-side door. For a moment I thought she would wave, but she didn't, and I realized how foolish the idea had been. We weren't friends. We had never been friends.

Twenty-one million dollars. I thought about John Fishwick in his cell, about the kiss with Dayly, the secret note. It had all been for nothing, both his efforts and hers. Dayly was dead and John's money was now in the hands of one of the baddest women I had ever known. Ada got into her car and started the engine. As she drove away I wondered what John would think of her, what she planned to do with his money.

His *un*chosen beneficiary.

"Birds only." I breathed the words at the same time as they flickered through my mind.

"What?"

"His chosen beneficiary." I was suddenly almost screaming, gripping my head. "Birds only. BIRDS ONLY!"

Ada's car exploded in a hot, white flash followed by a burst of yellow and red light. The vehicle came to a stop, the windows blasted out, doors thrown ajar, the roof bowed and partially peeled back from the rear pillars like the lid of a tuna can.

I ran. Sneak ran beside me, both our bodies forgetting our injuries completely, shot through with adrenaline and fear. The back of the car was a mess of blood and carnage, Fred's and Mike's bodies slumped in their seats, the frame of the car on fire around them. Ada was slithering from the front seat as I reached her. I hooked my arms under hers and dragged her away from the burning vehicle.

She had all her limbs. I silently counted them, like I had once been in the habit of doing when a child appeared on my surgery table just pulled from a car wreck or a house fire. Two arms. Two legs. Ten fingers, ten toes. She rasped a deep, labored breath and fell into coughs. I dragged her onto the wet lawn of a nearby house and batted away the small flames licking at her clothes.

Birds only. John Fishwick's means of making sure he could choose who got his money. He told Dayly, and only Dayly, that she should open the cases wrapped in patterns of birds and not the one patterned with tigers or any other animals. I guessed it was a hand grenade that had gone off in the tiger suitcase, maybe two of them, but I didn't know. I held Ada while she struggled to breathe, her lungs filled with debris and smoke. Eventually she rolled on her back and looked at me.

"I wasn't going to kill you," she wheezed. "I'm too nice."

"Shut up, Ada," I told her.

The sound of a car trunk popping drew my attention away from Ada. People were coming out of their houses all around us. I followed the sound I had heard and saw Sneak across the street, loading the battered and singed but still mostly intact toucan suitcase into the trunk of Al Tasik's car, where the crow case already lay. The precious contents had survived the blast. I looked back and saw that the trunk of Ada's burning Mercedes was open and empty.

There was nothing I could do to stop my friend. I was exhausted, wounded, and Ada lay across my lap, drifting in and out of consciousness. Like Ada had done, Sneak looked back at me as she slammed the trunk shut on the suitcases full of cash and went to the driver's door of her vehicle. But unlike Ada, she did wave. And she mouthed the words "Thank you."

I watched her drive away as sirens began to sound in the distance.

JESSICA

It was five o'clock in the morning by the time Jessica unlocked the front door of the Bluestone house. Something had brought her here instead of home, when all she longed for was her shower, her bed, the cold caress of her pillow against her cheek. Perhaps it was the decision she had made about the house as she walked down the mountain after witnessing Tasik's death. She had walked until her feet hurt, until her shoes had rubbed blisters into her heels, her phone only relenting to the influence of reception as she hit the silent city of Glendora. From there she had called her station, asked someone to rouse Whitton and get him to call her. He hadn't been at the crime scene on the mountain when she was driven back up there to show crews where Tasik's body lay, the general area in which he had indicated he had thrown Dayly's corpse to its final resting place. When Whitton called her now she answered the phone standing on the back porch of the Brentwood mansion, stepping quietly through the early marine mist toward the pool gate.

"Where are you?" he asked.

"I just got back," she said. "They sent me away.

Didn't want me contaminating the scene. I'm at the Brentwood house."

"Well, get your ass here," Whitton said. "I want a full explanation of what happened on that goddamn mountain."

"No," she said, slipping off her shoes and bloody socks. "Not yet. I'm checking the house here, then I'm going to go home and sleep. This afternoon sometime I'll come in, and I'll be bringing a stack of affidavits for IAG with me. One on the Lonscote Place shooting. One on my arrest at Goren Donnovich's house. One explaining my position on the Brentwood house, and one about what happened last night on the mountain."

"While you're at it, you can write one about what the hell you did to Wallert's place," Whitton snapped. "I've got three teams of boots still over there, cleaning up. You know what a couple of thousand people on a rampage does to a person's property? They're saying there isn't a shred of glass intact in the entire place. The garage burned to the ground."

"I don't know what you're talking about," Jessica said. She rolled up her dirty jeans and slipped her sore feet into the cool water. "I'll see you later."

She hung up and opened her news app. The swarm party at Wallert's house was the lead story. There was a short video of police storming the premises in riot gear, firefighters blasting the flaming garage with hoses. Teens and young people running everywhere, ducking under the coiling paths of tear gas canisters. Jessica scrolled for photographs of the interior of the house, the graffitied walls and smashed furniture, an artistic shot of a pink plastic cocktail glass shaped like a naked woman lying on the trashed kitchen floor. Young Beansie, a man she had arrested a year earlier for organizing a similar sort of party on a golf course, had outdone himself this time. The article was saying five thousand people had been on the scene.

For a second, to Jessica, it seemed as though thinking about Wallert had suddenly summoned his ghost. She smelled bourbon, sweat, his familiar stale reek. But then she felt his hand on the back of her neck and knew he was real. He yanked her upward and Jessica almost fell into the pool.

"You fucked with the wrong guy," Wallert snarled.

His fist hit her like a hammer blow, exactly on point, crunching against her temple and cheekbone at once. She saw blackness, begged it not to envelop her completely. The deck of the pool area was against her mouth suddenly, tasting of chlorine. He was on her back, punching downward. She managed to roll and slap the gun away as it came up toward her face. It clattered loudly on the deck. She could hear her own desperate cries but not control them. It didn't matter. What mattered now was fighting back. She doubled up, grabbed his shoulders, rolled with him, got some blows in. But he was in a fury so dark it gave him strength beyond anything she had ever felt. In seconds he had her pinned again, his big hands closed around her throat.

In the terrifyingly calm place between losing the ability to breathe and blacking out, she spied Jamie standing ten feet behind Wallert. She knew the boy was screaming, pleading, but couldn't hear him. Her face and neck felt hot with trapped blood, her legs spasming. Jamie had the gun pointed at the back of Wallert's head. Jessica could see the boy's mother in him then. She could see Blair Harbour standing over Kristi Zea and Adrian Orlov in their house eleven years earlier, begging, pleading, trying to save a life.

Jessica felt a sadness rush through her. Not for her own life, which was sliding away from her in great, heavy chunks, like ice melting into the sea. The sadness was for him. He knew he had no choice. It was her or Wallert.

Jessica watched as the boy balked in desperation, turned the gun in his hands and hurled it by its barrel at the back of Wallert's head.

The aim was true. The butt of the pistol glanced off Wallert's thick skull, hard enough to shock him, to break the chain of fingers around Jessica's throat. She rolled and grabbed the gun as it landed, smacked Wallert hard against the side of his head.

The man collapsed beside her. Jessica coughed and held the ground with both hands as her brain tried to deal with the sudden rush of oxygen. Jamie was standing there with his hands by his side, sobbing madly. It occurred to Jessica how young he looked then. How terror had instantly stripped him of the strength and power and heart she had seen in his face seconds earlier. She rolled over beside Wallert's body, dragged his arms behind him, cuffed his wrists.

She beckoned the boy and he came, and she held him at the edge of the pool while he cried against her chest.

"Great job, kid," she said. She gave him a few encouraging thumps on the back. "Great job."

BLAIR

She was in the gas station for about five minutes before I noticed she was there. She was that quiet. That patient. The man I was serving, who completely blocked her from view, had to be six and a half feet tall, a gentle giant counting out his gas and sandwich money in quarters, making little stacks of coins on the countertop beside my crossword.

To merit: *Deserve*.

I tidied the bowl of peaches by the register while I waited, checking the clock on the wall to calculate how long until the end of my shift. It was a Sunday. A Jamie visiting day. I'd taken the early shift with the hopes of getting him down to the pier for lunch, but at the rate my customer was going, I was starting to lose hope.

When the big man turned away, I saw Jessica Sanchez standing in the middle of the Pump'n'Jump, reading a magazine from the rack. She was still bruised and battered from her ordeal a week earlier, when my son had saved her from an attack by a colleague of hers at her house in Brentwood.

Sasha had told me about the attack on Jessica Sanchez while I lay low for a week in my apartment, recovering from my gunshot wound. I'd spent my days twitching at the sound of every car door slammed in the street, wincing when the phone rang. It was easy to convince myself that the police knew of my involvement in the events at San Jasinte, though I'd done my best to disappear from the scene without leaving a trace of myself. After Sneak had driven away I'd abandoned Ada on the lawn I'd dragged her to, knowing she'd be fine, and gone back to the old man in the hoarder house. I'd unbound him, given him water, and dragged him out to his own front lawn, where emergency personnel responding to the car explosion would find him. Then I ran as best I could. Like a prison escapee fleeing into the growing dawn, I'd run as hard as my leg would allow, stopping two suburbs over when it seemed safe to hail a cab. I'd gone home and removed the bullet myself. For days I'd stayed home, peering out the curtains, waiting to be arrested after a witness identified me, or my prints were found on the shovel in the tunnel, or Jessica Sanchez connected me to the murders, the heist.

But the arrest never came. And now she was here.

She saw that I was free, put her magazine down, and came to the counter. I looked out at the lot, half expecting to see squad cars screaming in. There were none.

"I didn't think I'd see you again," I said. I tried to collect my thoughts. "What . . . ah. What are you doing here?"

"I just came to say hello," Jessica said, leaning on the counter. "And to see if you'd heard from Sneak."

"No," I said, truthfully. "I haven't. If I had to guess I'd say she's in Jamaica by now. We had a Jamaican chef in the kitchen at Happy Valley for a while, and she always liked the food. I heard they found Tasik's car at the airport, so . . ." I shrugged.

"She'll come back for Dayly's funeral," Jessica said. "Surely."

"I don't know." Dayly's body had been found flung down an embankment off a fire trail in the Glendora mountains, the same road where Al Tasik had been killed attempting to take Sneak's and Jessica's lives. Los Angeles news outlets had had a hell of a time trying to account for the dead cop's actions, how they were connected to the body on the mountain, whether they were connected to the bodies in the tunnel, the bodies in Ada's car. I assumed Jessica herself was trying to straighten the police out on the whole case.

"I'll tell you one thing," I said to Jessica. "If I do see Sneak, whether she comes back for her daughter's funeral, or she comes back because she's a drug addict and a thief and those kinds of people are creatures of habit, I won't be telling you. No offense."

"None taken," she said. "I'm not trying to pursue Sneak."

"Why not?" I asked. "From what you told me on the phone, it sounds as though Sneak murdered Tasik right in front of you. She drove over him multiple times."

"That's what I told you on the phone, yes," Jessica said. "But that was only twenty-four hours after the event. I was still shocked. Traumatized."

She shrugged helplessly.

"I'm not sure I remember clearly exactly what happened on the mountain," she said, avoiding my eyes. I saw a small smile flash on her lips and then disappear. "All I know is that Sneak and I defended ourselves. Perhaps Sneak used the car to try to incapacitate Tasik, and then ran over him multiple times by accident. It wasn't her car. She wouldn't have been familiar with the controls. I wasn't in the vehicle with her, so I don't think I can assess her intention."

"Right." I smiled. "But what about her theft of John Fishwick's millions from the tunnels?"

"What am I going to charge her with there?" Jessica asked. "I can't prove the cash from the tunnel ever existed. I don't even know if that was Sneak. All I've got from the witness accounts is a bruised and battered blonde woman at the San Jasinte scene putting two suitcases into a car. The suitcase in Ada's car was full of shredded paper and explosives. It might be that wherever Sneak is, she's flat broke."

I bit my tongue. Then I couldn't help myself.

"I think it was about fourteen million," I blurted.

Jessica laughed. "I hope she doesn't spend it all on blow."

"What about Ada?" I asked. "Are you going to go after her?"

"I'd like to see Ada behind bars again," Jessica said. "I'm not going to lie. She's a dangerous person. But from what I hear, that's going to be a losing battle for whoever takes on the case. She's already out on bail. She has the best lawyer money can buy, of course, and she's blaming the whole thing on her dead goons. They forced her to go there. They killed Lemon and Ramirez and made her watch."

"Slick," I said.

"The slickest," Jessica agreed.

Jessica seemed to be examining my face, wanting to say more, wanting to promise, perhaps, that she also wasn't coming after me. But that seemed obvious. There were no squad cars on the lot. No cuffs on her belt. I fiddled with the crossword pages.

"How's your face?" I said eventually.

"It's all right." She touched the stitches in her cheek tentatively. "In fact, it's better than all right. You come that close to death, leaving the fray with a punch in the face and a bruised throat feels like a win. Look, truth is, I wanted to come here today to see if you've got a minute to discuss me giving your kid a reward for his efforts. He saved my life. He deserves it."

"Oh, well." I smiled. "I don't know. I guess I can get behind that. What were you thinking? He likes Nintendo games."

"I was thinking more along the lines of giving him his mother back," Jessica said.

A splinter of pain in my chest. I stood watching Jessica's eyes as she recounted her recorded conversation with Kristi Zea to me. She told me about the bush outside the laundry window of the Orlov house. The forensic analysis of the bite mark in the cheese sandwich. Adrian's brother and the cocaine in the bedroom on the night of the murder. I listened silently, my hands on the counter, hardly able to breathe. Jessica finished talking and wiped a tear from her eye discreetly.

"It's my fault, what happened to you," Jessica said. "I want to put it right."

She gave me a chance to speak, but I couldn't say anything. The words wouldn't come, so she continued instead.

"I'm going to accept the bequest of the Brentwood house on Bluestone Lane," she said. "That'll exclude me from the LAPD forever, but I have a feeling coming back was going to be difficult anyway." She gave a laugh that was tinged by sadness. "I've been a bad girl lately. Really bad. And our relationship, me and the force, it's been strained for a while."

"Okay," I said. It was all I could muster.

"I want you to go and live in the house," Jessica said. "If you can afford a dollar a month, that's what I'll charge you in rent. You'll be close to Jamie."

"Jessica," I said. My hands were shaking. Tears

were falling from my own eyes. I wiped at them unsteadily. "Why would you . . . Why would . . ."

"I'm going to do everything I can to get your exoneration up and running," Jessica said. Her gaze was fixed on the floor, thinking through it all. "It'll be a long process. There'll be an official review. A lawyer will take you pro bono for a civil case. I'll testify, and so will a colleague of mine who's been helping me, a very kind man. A scientist. I think we've got a good shot. More than a good shot. And after your conviction is vacated, you'll be in a much better position to negotiate more custody of Jamie. Maybe even get your medical license back."

"This will ruin you," I said. "This will ruin your reputation."

She turned to me and grinned. "My reputation? Oh, honey. That was dead and buried a long time ago. There are weeds growing on its grave."

I went around the counter, grabbed Jessica, and held her close. The hug came naturally, spurred by excitement, shock, but in a second it evolved into something else. A fierceness rippled through me. An ache in my bones, the memory of handing my baby over, of every cold, hard night I slept inside the walls and gates of a prison. In a flash I saw Sasha visiting me, sitting on the other side of a glass panel. I saw myself hunched on my bed, poring over photographs of my child. I gripped Jessica while fury and gratitude raged against each other inside me. Without knowing the depth of my confusion, without possibly being able to know, she laughed awkwardly, uncomfortably. A woman who was hurting, who didn't like to be hugged. When I let her go she stepped away from me, brushed herself off, like she'd come here and said what she needed to say and now didn't know what to do. She went to the door and stood there, and we stared at each other, the two of us looking across an impossible divide, both on the edge of something new.

"What the hell are you going to do, then?" I said. "If you can't be a cop."

"I was thinking of starting something of my own," she said. "A friend suggested it. Something small. A place where I get to pick the cases. Where I get to follow my interests." She tapped the burrito stand with her hand, thinking. "I might call you up, if you don't mind. I'll need help."

"You'll know where to find me," I said. She smiled, and I smiled back, because I didn't yet know what would win in my heart, the anger at this woman or the appreciation. All I knew was that I was bound to her now. The woman who had damned me, and the woman who had saved me. The key to getting my son back, and the very thing that had taken him away in the first place. Jessica was at once my old enemy and my new friend. A little warmth was stirring in me as I stood there. Forgiveness, maybe. What Ada would have called my bleeding heart.

The automatic door buzzer sounded as Jessica walked out into the sunshine.

ACKNOWLEDGMENTS

I'm indebted to everyone who helped me along during the writing of this book, including my wonderful husband, Tim, my parents, Ocean and Richard, in-laws, Lyn and Dick, and my friends and family. Gaby Naher and Bev Cousins saw me through my classic mid-book crisis as they always do, and Kristin Sevick and Lisa Gallagher offered invaluable feedback on early drafts. The irreplaceable Kathryn Knight is my main editor. I am represented the world over by wonderful teams of publishers and editors, and without my studies at the universities I have mentioned in previous acknowledgments pages I would not be where I am today in my career.

Dr. Liz Morton at the Drummoyne Veterinary Hospital was kind enough to answer some quirky questions on rodent care for me, and fans Alex Maguire and Marcel Thompson helped with research questions. There's a crime in this novel inspired by an episode of the podcast *Sword and Scale*, by Mike Boudet. Mike also consulted helpfully on ice cream container types.

A certain serial killer currently residing on death

row in San Quentin, whom I will not name, provided some background material on life on the row and the killer mind.

This was one of the hardest books I have ever written. I wrote draft one while pregnant with my beautiful, clever, and funny daughter, Violet. Subsequent drafts came along while I held her, nursed her, or watched over her after she was born. Violet, in your tiny life so far you've taught me precious lessons about daring, persistence, patience, and love, and I'm so thankful to you for them.

Read on for a preview of

THE CHASE

CANDICE FOX

Available in March 2022 from
Tom Doherty Associates

A Forge Hardcover

CHAPTER 1

From where she sat at the back of the bus, the driver's death was a confusing spectacle to Emily Jackson.

She had a good view down the length of the vehicle from her position, leaning against a window smeared with the fingerprints of happy children. Her seat was elevated over the rear wheel axle, so as she rode she could see youngsters jumping and crashing about the interior, playing games and teasing each other across the aisle, occasionally throwing a ball or smacking a catcher's mitt into a rival's head. Half of the other parents on the bus were ignoring their children's activity, gazing out the windows at the Nevada desert, some with AirPods in their ears and wistful looks on their faces. Others were making valiant attempts to dampen the chaos and noise: confiscating water bottles, phones, and toys being used as weapons, or dragging wandering toddlers back to their seats. Forty minutes of featureless sand and scrub beyond the garish structures and swirling colors of Vegas was a lot for kids to endure. When the bus bumped over a loose rock on the narrow road to the prison, Emily saw all the other passengers bump with it, the bus and its riders synchronized parts of a unified machine.

She didn't have to nudge her son, Tyler, as they approached the point at which Pronghorn Correctional would come into view. Tyler had been coming to the annual pre-Christmas softball game at the facility since he was a kindergartner, and had only missed one year, when his father strained his back fixing the garage door and couldn't play second pitcher against the minimum-security inmates as he usually did. Tyler's familiarity with the journey seemed to give him a sixth sense, and she watched as he flipped his paperback closed, shifting upward in his seat. No landmark out there in the vastness told mother and son they were approaching the last gentle curve in the road. Hard, cracked land reached plainly toward the distant mountain range. Then the pair watched through the bus's huge windshield as the collection of wide, low concrete buildings rose seemingly out of the sand.

"Who's your money on this time?" Emily asked the teen. A five-year-old in the seat in front of them started pointing and squealing at the sight of the prison up ahead. Tyler considered his mother's question, watching the boy in front of him with quiet distaste, as if he hadn't once been just the same, so excited to see Daddy at work.

"I'm betting inmates," Tyler decided, giving his mother a wry smile. "Dad says they've been practicing during yard time for months."

"Traitor." Emily smirked.

"How 'bout you?"

"Officers," she said. "If you're going for the cons, I've got to go for the correctional officers or your father won't sp—"

A thump cut off Emily's words.

It was a heavy, sonic pulse, not unlike a firework exploding; a sound Emily both heard and felt in the center of her chest. Her brain offered up a handful of ordinary explanations for the noise even as her eyes took in the visual information that accompanied it. *A blown tire,* she thought. Or a rock crunching under the bus's wheels. Some kind of spontaneous combustion in the vehicle's old, rickety engine, a piston or cylinder giving out due to the rugged terrain and the desert's usually blinding heat.

But none of those explanations aligned with what Emily saw.

The driver slumped sideways out of his seat, caught and prevented from falling into the stairwell only by the seatbelt over his shoulder. A fine pink mist seemed to shimmer in the air before dissipating as quickly as it had appeared. Emily grabbed the seat in front of her and held on as the bus swung off the road and slowed to a stop in the shrubbery.

Her eyes wandered over the scene at the front of the bus. The passengers in the first two rows were examining their hands or touching their faces as though they were damp. Hundreds of tiny cubes of glass lay over the driver, the dash, and the aisle, the side window having neatly collapsed and sprayed everywhere, exactly as it was designed to do. Emily recognized Sarah Gravelle up there, rising unsteadily from her seat and walking to the driver's side. Emily could see, even from her distant position, that half of the driver's head was gone. Sarah looked at the driver, and everybody watched her do it, as if they were waiting for her to confirm what they already knew.

Sarah stumbled back to her seat and sat down. Emily's tongue stuck to the roof of her mouth, her body suddenly covered in a thin film of sweat.

Sarah Gravelle started screaming.

And then everyone was screaming.

* * *

Grace Slanter put down her pen and pressed the speakerphone button to answer the phone that was ringing on her wide desk. Few calls came to the warden's office without first being channeled through her assistant's office in the room down the hall, so she was expecting someone familiar on the line: her husband, Joe, or the director of Nevada corrections, Sally Wakefield, a woman she spoke to almost daily. When the line connected, there was a second click she'd never heard before, and her own voice gave a ringing echo, as if it was being played back somewhere. *Robocaller,* she thought. But that was impossible. This was an unlisted line, not the kind that could appear on a database in some sweaty underground scam-mill.

"Hello, Grace Slanter."

"Pay attention," a voice commanded.

Grace felt a chill enter her spine, high, between her shoulders, as though she'd been touched by an icy finger. She looked down at the phone on the desk as though it held a malevolent presence, something she could see glowing evilly between the seams in the plastic.

"Excuse me?"

"There's a bus stopped in the desert half a mile from the prison walls," the voice said. It was a male voice. Soft, clipped. Confident. "If you go to the window behind you and look out, you'll see it sitting on the road."

Grace stood. She did not go to the window. The warden had been trained to respond to calls like this one, and though she'd never before had to put that training into action, the first thing she remembered was not to start following the directions of the caller until she had a grasp on the situation. She went to the door of her office instead, the furthest point from the window, and looked down the hall. There was not a soul to be seen.

"Are you looking at it?" the voice asked.

Grace stepped up onto the couch against the wall, to the left of the desk. She could see the bus out there, a distant white brick in the expanse of land beyond the concrete walls and razor wire of the prison. It had one wheel off the road, the vehicle tilted slightly, leaning, as though drunk.

"Okay," Grace said. "I see it. What's your name? I want to know who I'm talking to."

"On that bus are twelve women, eight men, and fourteen children," the voice said, ignoring her questions. "They're the families of guards inside the prison. Your employees. Your people."

"Jesus Christ," Grace said. The annual softball game. Inmates versus officers. The families always came to watch. It was an event designed to appease the prison staff stuck minding vicious criminals during the holiday season while their families gathered at home. The peacemaking gesture usually lifted the dismay after the rosters for Christmas Eve, Christmas Day, and New Year's were drawn up, so that officers went into those shifts with at least half a smile on their faces. After the game there was lunch and drinks for the unlucky families in the conference building outside the prison walls.

Grace staggered down from the couch and gripped the edge of the desk. Her training was forgotten, her senses blurred. She went to her chair and fell into it, relieved by the familiar feeling of her own warmth on the seat, something comforting in the chilling seconds that passed.

"The driver of the bus is dead," the voice on the phone said.

Grace tried to remember the location of the panic

button on her desk, the one that would send an alarm to her colleagues inside the building, and an automatic "assistance needed" call to the nearest law enforcement agencies. All she had to do was remember where that single button was. But her mind was spinning, reeling, and for a long moment it was a struggle just to breathe.

"Are you listening, Grace?"

"I'm . . . I'm listening," she said. Grace drew in a deep breath and then let it out. She found the button under the desk by her knee and pushed it. A red light came on above the door to her office, but no sound issued. In seconds, her assistant, Derek, was there, huffing from the run up the hall, two guards right behind him. It only took one look from Grace to send them sprinting away again.

"What do you want?" she asked.

"I want you to let them out."

Grace had known the words were coming long before they were spoken. She drew in another deep breath. Across the two decades she had been in senior management at Pronghorn, she'd run over this scenario in her mind a hundred times. She knew what to do now. She was regaining control. There was a procedure for this. She grabbed her pen again and started jotting down notes about the voice and the time of the call, keeping an eye on the window as she sat twisted sideways in her chair.

"Which inmates are we talking about?" Grace asked. "Who do you want me to release?"

"All of them," the voice said.